I0545294

# PAROXYSM

## by Matt Hughes

*Paroxysm*

Copyright Matthew Hughes 2013

Published by Matthew Hughes, July 2013

ISBN: 978-1-927880-02-9

Cover illustration by Ben Baldwin; interior and cover design by Bradley W. Schenck

# Contents

# 1

A casual visitor would never have suspected that the low-rise, blond-brick structure on the outskirts of a small town in one of the fly-over states would be the source of so many deaths. But the place had never had any casual visitors.

Officially, it was a repository for outdated military records, and that description tallied with the utilitarian, floor-to-ceiling shelving that filled its windowless interior. Each shelf was crammed with alphabetically ordered file folders that bore authentic, color-coded labels.

A closer inspection would have revealed that the electronic security around the building was much more sophisticated than its purported contents warranted. The armed military police might have seemed too many and too vigilant to be safeguarding nothing more than a collection of manpower reports and convoy manifests that dated back to the Korean War.

But there had been very few close inspections during the more than two decades since the facility had been constructed, equipped and staffed. The inspectors had ignore the camouflaging paper stored above ground. Instead, the focus was on the work taking place in the three stories built beneath its government-issue surface. The first inspection had come in 1973, just before the installation's commissioning; a team of specialist engineers had fine-toothed the intricate matrix of gaskets, traps, filters and vacuum pumps that hermetically sealed the lower floors from the rest of the world. The pumps and fans had started up, and had run continuously ever since.

The last inspection, undertaken in mid-2007, had been much more casual. A major general and his aide wandered around the labs and data processing center for fifteen minutes, idly fingered the equipment, stared at the staff, then announced that the facility was to be permanently moth-balled. The visitors did not go down to the ultra-secure lowest floor – referred to by the scientists who worked there as "the well" – because there was not much to see, except for steel containers stored behind triple-sealed safety glass. And no matter how many stars the major general had on his collar, if he went down the well, he would not be let out again before enduring a tedious half hour of decontamination.

Between the first and last inspections, the installation had been of interest only to the small group of carefully chosen people who worked in it, and to the fewer than ten very senior people in the military and the government whose need-to-know status encompassed its existence. Not even the soldiers who guarded the place knew what went on underground. But they knew that any inquiries in that direction would mean a quick transfer and a damaging paragraph in the permanent record.

Six months after the major general brought the order to shut down, with most of the salvageable equipment already stripped and shipped, and with most of the staff pensioned off or reassigned, the brigadier who had commanded the unit for almost all of its existence arrived for his last day on the post.

The MP at the front gate came out of the guardhouse as the car pulled up, and bent to look in the windows. He recognized three of the men in the car: the brigadier, a lean, hard-faced career officer, coming to clean out his desk; his aide, a smooth and sly-eyed major, who would be following the general into retirement; and the plump, balding man who had been chief of civilian scientific personnel. The guard noted that the scientist looked nervous and unhappy; but then that was nothing unusual. Each man held up a plastic laminated security pass worn on a chain around his neck.

The driver was new, a middle-aged man in a cheap suit fresh off the rack. To the military policeman's observant eye, the man's style said *former soldier*; the puffy flesh under the eyes said *active service boozehound*.

The general leaned forward from the back seat. "This is Raifort, my new driver," he said.

The guard leaned over to the car window. "I'll need to see his pass, General."

"Of course. Show him your pass, Raifort."

Everybody on the post knew that the long-service noncom who had been the general's driver for several years was away on emergency compassionate leave. His wife had been severely injured in a hit-and-run the week before. The general had declined a replacement from the unit's dwindling complement, saying he would instead hire a civilian for his final days, someone who could continue to work for him after he retired.

2

Raifort proffered a plastic-laminated blue card. The MP studied it. It was a temporary pass, allowing the man onto the post as long as he was escorted. It had been signed by the general.

The guard opened the gates and waved the car through. It rolled to the end of the driveway, turned and passed down the side of the building to where a ramp sloped down to a roll-up steel door.

The door opened, and Raifort wheeled the car carefully into the underground parking garage, putting it in the general's marked space next to the glassed-in guard post beside the elevator. Here the four men left the vehicle and went through the same procedure of showing their passes.

The MP in the booth pushed a button and the elevator door opened. The four men entered and the aide used his key to unlock the control panel and press the bottom-most button. The elevator descended silently for thirty seconds.

When the door opened again, they exited into a concrete world. Floor, ceiling and walls were a uniform hard gray. They came into a space ten feet square, containing a steel desk, chair and lockable filing cabinet, the key to which was on the belt of an MP master sergeant. The belt also carried a holstered pistol. The noncom saluted, then inspected their passes.

"Last day, Ted," said the general to the sergeant. "Sorry to see it end. Been good duty."

"Yes sir," said the noncom. "Good duty."

A steel door was set into the wall opposite the elevator, an electronic key pad beside it. The sergeant tapped in the day's code and stepped back.

The moment the door swung open, a draft of air was sucked from the lobby. All of the space that lay beyond the door was negatively pressurized, so that air blew into it from the outside. For thirty-four years, air had only moved from out to in. Had it ever moved the other way, alarms would have screamed, automatic doors would have slammed shut, and anyone on the wrong side of those doors would have stayed there a long time. Perhaps forever.

But that was back when the facility was active, back before the convoy of specially fitted trucks had come to carry away a small sample of each carefully engineered micro-organism and precisely constructed molecule that had been made down the well. The samples had been put in storage in a vault whose security apparatus made Fort Knox look like a five-and-dime store. The rest of the material – enough to make life thoroughly miserable if not impossible for a billion people – was boiled, irradiated, scorched by ultraviolet light, chemically disassembled and neutralized, then finally flash-incinerated

3

at steel-melting temperatures until nothing much remained. The nothing much was nonetheless sealed in lead lined concrete forms and buried in a disused salt mine in Utah.

Now the labs were empty, the personnel reassigned or retired, the equipment stripped away. The guards continued to carry out the security procedures because no one had told them not to. So the four men followed the wafts of cool air through the steel door and into a room where they disrobed and hung their clothes in green lockers. Rings, watches, even the security passes, were stored away.

An MP watched from a glassed-in enclosure, and did not press the button that opened the door to the next room until he saw that all four men were completely naked. He noticed that Raifort's left thigh ended just below the hip, where it met a government-issue artificial leg.

The next room contained benches and shelves of clothing, loose fitting shirts and pants, underwear and slippers. The four men dressed, then the major opened the door – this one an ordinary wooden panel – and they stepped into another concrete corridor. It led them to a suite of offices.

The brigadier and the major had adjoining rooms, their dimensions and contents conforming to the specifications laid down in a Pentagon manual. The junior officer followed the senior into the larger office, but the brigadier waved him away. The major then went instead to his own cubicle, while the brigadier instructed Raifort to assist the scientist.

The general's office contained a desk, three chairs, a filing cabinet and a credenza – all supplied by the military and all to remain where they were. The only non-issue items in the room were in frames on the walls: a citation for efficiency, a certificate attesting to the brigadier's mid-class standing at his graduation from West Point, and a few photographs.

The general quickly took them down and stacked them on the desk. A moment later, the major came in with a similar pile of memorabilia: his had fewer photographs, and the citation was for marksmanship. The major piled his stuff on top of the brigadier's and picked up the pile.

The general did not give the office where he had spent most of the past twenty-three years so much as a parting glance. He strode out into the hall, followed by the laden major.

The scientist and Raifort came out of the former's office down the hall. The balding man carried a plastic box filled with the kind of paraphernalia that accumulates on some people's desks: balanced steel sculptures that rotate when touched; ball bearings hung by wires from a metal frame, so that they clacked together in syncopated rhythm; colored liquid gels trapped between

4

panes of plexiglass that imitated wave action when tilted. The driver held a second box that contained more of the same.

They reentered the corridor, but went past the door by which they had entered from the dressing room. They stopped at a steel portal next to a glassed-in booth, where yet another armed MP pressed a control that made the heavy door slide open.

Beyond was a tiled room with benches where they undressed and deposited their "inside clothes" in bins. At the far end of the room was another guard in a booth, a steel exit and a hatchway with a hinged panel set into the wall. After disrobing, the major passed the pile of framed documents and photos through the opening. Raifort and the scientist did the same with the boxes of bric a brac.

Naked, they walked to the exit door next to the hatchway. The door did not open. The brigadier looked at the MP corporal in the guard booth. The man was clearly trying to make up his mind.

"Sorry, general," the noncom said after a moment, "but I have to ask your man to..., well, to put his leg through the hatch, sir."

The brigadier looked at Raifort. The driver went and sat down on a bench. "What the hell," he said, and began unstrapping the prosthesis. When it was loose he handed it to the major, who carried it to the hatchway and passed it through.

The one-legged man stood up on his remaining limb.

"Could you help me, sir?" he asked the major. The officer allowed the driver to put his left arm over his shoulder, and supported Raifort as he hopped to the doorway. The guard opened the door and they went into the decontamination suite.

The procedure here was thorough, but much less comprehensive than if they had been returning from the well. They showered in chemically treated water using specially formulated granular liquid soaps – long showers that involved particular attention to the parts of the body covered in hair, and to folds, wrinkles and indentations. They dried themselves under hot air vents, then stood with eyes closed for five minutes in a room lined with intense ultraviolet lights. The major helped support Raifort.

While they were so occupied, the items they had passed through the hatchway were carried by a conveyor belt to a small sealed chamber. Here the officer's documents, the scientist's knick-knacks and the driver's leg were subjected to similar procedures. The goods were sprayed, doused and scrubbed by technicians who used remote manipulator arms to reach through the chamber's glass wall.

5

At the end of the process, the objects were delivered by conveyor belt to two security officers, who carefully inspected each item, even to the point of removing the cushioned pad that capped the artificial leg. The officer tapped the end of the hexagonal steel rod that descended through the plastic body of the leg from its top to the knee joint. Its top was flush with the plastic surface. It was solid.

The items the four men had brought from their offices were compared one by one against detailed descriptions on a list. Nothing that was not pre-approved as personal property and authorized to be removed would be allowed to leave the premises.

The security personnel delivered the goods to the locker room where the brigadier's party had left their clothing. But the four men had one more procedure to endure before they were reunited with their possessions.

They entered a small room whose exit was controlled by another guard in a booth. An MP lieutenant rose from a desk. He saluted, then carefully maintained a poker face as, beginning with the brigadier, he ran his fingers through the hair of each man and asked each to open his mouth. Then he put on a disposable plastic glove, and went back to the general.

"Sir," he said.

The brigadier about faced and bent over. The lieutenant made sure that the general had nothing to conceal. The MP discarded the glove in a bin, got another from the stack, and approached the major.

The scientist, when it was his turn, said, "Here's something I won't miss."

"Yes, sir," said the MP.

When Raifort had been checked, leaving him red faced, the lieutenant nodded to the MP in the guard booth, and the door to the locker room swung open. Raifort hopped to the bench where his artificial leg lay and strapped it on. They dressed and picked up the items they had brought from the offices. The general opened the door to the lobby, and they left.

The master sergeant with the pistol and MP brassard stood to attention and saluted. The brigadier took the salute, and said, "Goodbye, sergeant."

The man moved the control that opened the elevator doors. "Goodbye, sir," he said.

Two minutes later, the brigadier's car was through the front gate and heading toward the interstate highway. It traveled north for twenty-five minutes at the speed limit, being passed by every other vehicle going in the same direction.

"I don't think we're being followed," said the major.

"I agree," said the brigadier. The scientist let out a trembling breath. Raifort said nothing.

"Take the next exit going east," the major said.

The driver nodded. A mile further on, he eased the car off the interstate and onto a two-lane blacktop. For the next half hour, the major occasionally issued terse instructions, and Raifort followed them until the car pulled into a played out gravel pit, next to an abandoned farm that was scheduled to be bulldozed for a miniature golf course.

At the center of the place was a roughly circular, water-filled hole twenty yards across and more than ten yards deep. The gravel excavators had long ago struck an underground spring; when there was still gravel to be taken, a pump had kept the hole from filling up. Now the pump had been hauled away, and the pit had filled with opaque green water, on which floated a mat of algae.

Raifort stopped the car near the slimy pool and switched off the engine. He opened his door and swung around in the driver's seat so that his feet touched the ground. Grunting, he pulled up his pants leg and unstrapped the prosthesis. Meanwhile, the major got out the other side and walked around the car. Raifort handed him the leg.

The scientist was in the front passenger seat, with a box of his desk toys on his lap. He reached into the box and brought out one of the devices. It was a three-dimensional lattice-work of stainless steel rods, with a cap and base of dark, polished wood; when it was tilted, a polished brass ball rolled from level to level.

The balding man wiped his sweating hands on his shirt, then gave the toy's top a clockwise twist. The wood separated from the metal with a *click*, and the lattice-work of bars collapsed in on itself, the ball rolling free. Most of the rods remained connected, but two separated and came loose. The scientist handed these two past Raifort to the major.

One of the rods ended in a hexagonal socket; the second had a hole through its middle that exactly fitted the squared off other end of the socketed piece: put together, they made a T-shaped socket wrench.

The major put them together. Then he removed the pad at the top of the leg and applied the socket to the end of the steel rod that passed through the plastic thigh. He pressed the socket down onto the plastic that surrounded the rod, and maintained the pressure steadily for almost a minute.

The pressure caused heat. The plastic had the particular quality of contracting when its temperature was sufficiently raised. As the major pressed down on the material surrounding the top of the six-sided rod in the center of the false limb, the plastic shrank and allowed the socket to slide snugly down over the steel. The major turned the T-wrench.

7

The rod did not run all the way from the cushion pad to the knee. Instead, it was a lock-nut that held the top of the artificial leg to the rest of the prosthesis. Now the top came off, revealing a cylindrical compartment six inches deep and an inch-and-a-half in diameter.

The major carefully upended the leg, and held his hand beneath the hole in its middle. An object slid silently out of the cavity. It was made of dull black metal, of a size and shape to fit precisely the space in which it had been hidden. Rounded on the ends, it resembled a giant version of the gelatin capsules the pharmaceutical industry uses to package individual doses of antibiotics.

The major hefted it gently in his hand. "Well, now," he said, and looked at the brigadier.

"Very well, indeed," said the general, and smiled.

The scientist looked away. He did not like to think about how he had carried the capsule from down the well up to the washroom beside his office. He had concealed it in his colon, knowing that body cavity searches took place only at the very last security check.

Before that, he had spent weeks watching and waiting for brief opportunities. He'd loitered, sweating, until his subordinates would leave the deep lab; or he'd send them on manufactured errands, to give himself time to steal, little by little, the substance that was now in the capsule.

The lab's storage facility had contained ten flasks of the stuff, each holding five hundred centiliters of the agent. The agent was not part of any active research program. Field tests were over. The material was now in secure storage, kept against the day when someone in authority ordered its use.

To the ten flasks, he had contrived to add an eleventh. Who would notice an extra container at the back of the storage locker? Then, over a period of weeks, he had surreptitiously transferred fifty cc's from each legitimate flask to his extra one. At the end it was easier, because most of the staff were gone, but sometimes it was hard to come up with a plausible reason for going down the well.

"Just checking a couple of things," became his regular refrain. His colleagues, especially those who were lucky enough to be reassigned instead of forcibly retired, told each other he was in denial. *Making work for himself,* they said. *Poor asshole.*

Then, came the last-but-one day, the day before the trucks would come to haul away the ten flasks. He had gone into work, with the specially made capsule in its rectal hiding place, feeling like he was going to lose it – literally – any second. *They never check you going in, never on the way in,* he kept telling himself as he passed through the layers of security.

8

And then down the well, the capsule pressing on his anal sphincter like an enema with a mind of its own. Then getting it out – *what a mess* – and filling it from the bootlegged storage flask, which he then had to rinse clean in the lab sink and toss into the disposal bin.

Then reinserting the capsule into his rectum, thinking *Christ, what if there's a droplet of the agent on the casing?*, knowing all too well what the stuff would do to him. Thinking about it all the way up to the washroom that was down the hall from his office. Then more distasteful mess, until finally the capsule was hidden in his desk, behind some papers.

The next day, the trucks came, took away all the chemicals, all the microbes. He'd supervised the loading and signed off on the ten flasks. Then he'd waited, and waited, and waited: for the knock on the door in the middle of the night, for the MPs filling his office doorway, for the handcuffs and the barred windows and the rest of his life in a federal penitentiary.

But none of that ever came. Instead, here he was on a fine, crisp morning in a beat-up old gravel pit, with the major holding up the capsule and the brigadier smiling from the back seat of the car.

And Raifort clearing his throat, in a meaningful way.

Raifort didn't know what the capsule contained, and didn't care. "Can I have the leg back?" he said. "And I think I got something else coming."

"You do indeed," said the brigadier. "Well done, sergeant." He turned to his aide. "Major?"

The general handed the major a briefcase through the car window. The major gently placed the capsule on the ground, received the briefcase and opened it. Inside it was filled with foam padding, into which a space for the capsule had been cut. The major fitted the capsule into the cavity, closed the briefcase, and handed it back to the general.

Then, using the T-wrench again, the major quickly reassembled the artificial leg and passed it back to Raifort. The driver strapped on the prosthesis and got out of the car to make it fit properly by walking a few steps on it.

"This is a damn good leg," he said. "Better than that piece a crap the VA give me."

The major also disassembled the steel tool and handed it to the scientist. "Put it back together," he said.

The balding man stared. "What for?"

The brigadier leaned over the front seat. "Because details count," he said. "You do the details right, the big things tend to stay on track."

The scientist shrugged and put the toy back together. It was easy; he'd practiced doing it so many times that he could fit the components together

9

and snap the thing into shape in under fifteen seconds. The brigadier and the major had made him practice.

Raifort was clearing his throat again. The brigadier made a motion with his head, and the major went to the back of the car and opened the trunk. He came back to the front of the car with a zipper-top canvas bag, placed it on the hood and opened it.

Raifort looked into the bag and made a sound in the back of his throat. He pulled out one of the bundles of twenty dollar bills and riffled it.

"Whatever we just did, general, it was worth it," he said, rummaging around in the bag.

The general got out of the car and produced a chased silver flask from his breast pocket. "And that was only the beginning," he said, handing Raifort the container.

The one-legged man uncapped the flask, sniffed its neck delicately, then put it to his mouth and up-ended it. His Adam's apple bobbed once, then twice, and was heading back for a third time when the major put a small-caliber automatic to the back of Raifort's head and pulled the trigger twice.

With the muzzle pressed tight against the victim's skull, the shots sounded no louder than a couple of vigorous hand claps. Liquor spewed from the driver's mouth, but he was already dead before the first drops touched the ground.

The brigadier's flask tinkled musically on the stones. He bent and picked it up, wiped its mouth and took a swallow as major went back to the car's trunk and pulled out a length of heavy chain.

The brigadier called the scientist to assist the major. The civilian worked unhappily but efficiently to help wrap Raifort tightly. Then the scientist grabbed the corpse's ankles – one flesh, one steel – and prepared to lift, but the major said, "Wait a second."

He went back to the trunk and brought out a long-bladed chef's knife. The scientist looked away as the major slit the dead man's belly. "Stop him from floating when he gasses up," he said. "Okay, let's put him to bed."

He grabbed the shoulders of Raifort's jacket and the scientist took the legs. They carried the body to the edge of the green pool, swung it together twice, and on the third time they tossed it so it arced out and down, broke the green surface and disappeared from view. The major threw the pistol and knife after it while the greasy ripples were still slurping at the rim of the pit.

The major drove them away from the gravel pit, the scientist beside him. The brigadier sat in the back, with both the briefcase and the bag of money.

They drove to the airport; the general had chartered a private jet. It flew them to Portland, Oregon, where a bank deposit box yielded three false passports. They put the capsule where the passports had been.

They bought a used car for cash, and crossed the border into Canada before dark, in plenty of time to catch their Air Canada flight to Hong Kong.

A week later, they were comfortably housed in a small commercial hotel on the outskirts of Kuala Lumpur, conducting exploratory meetings with the clients.

## 2

Lou Meecham's grip tightened on the Toyota's steering wheel, and he kept his eyes on the winding, two-lane blacktop that was pulling him deeper into central Oregon's Prescott Valley. With the windows rolled up, the only sound was the hum of the little white car's dinky-toy wheels on the asphalt, and right now that was all he wanted to hear.

Then the soothing hum was broken by a sigh. Adele was not going to let it slide. He'd once told her she'd have made a great shortstop: she never let anything drop. So now Lou ducked his head a fraction lower, like a turtle trying to pull back into its shell, and waited for the inevitable.

"All I'm saying, Lou, is you don't have to take that kind of thing from people."

Her voice still had that same warm, honeyed sound that he remembered from thirty-five years ago, back when he'd been a raw buck sergeant waiting to ship out, and she'd been his new bride. He'd been flat bellied with a full head of hair, she'd been soft and rounded, and together they'd been heaven. He'd never got mad at her, not then, not now. How could he? She was his one true bearing on the world's map, the single fixed point that let him navigate his way out and back again.

He kept his eyes on the road and his tone mild. "Can we drop it, Adele?"

She sighed again. "They had plenty of tables. If you'd just said, 'Let me see the manager...'"

"Can we *drop* it?"

She turned and looked out the passenger window. Oregon's low, folded hills eased by them. "Sure, we can drop it. Like we've been doing all these twenty years."

He made a noise in his throat like a tired old circus bear being prodded to do tricks. She wanted to let it go, but habit set a hard rule. "Well," she said, "you don't have to let people push you around. Waiters and cab drivers and customers..."

He looked at her. "Adele, please. We took this vacation to get away from the hassles. So let's leave it, okay? We'll get lunch back at the hotel, it'll be fine."

His eyes hadn't changed, still looked at her as if she was some kind of wondrous, technicolor vision that might suddenly fade and leave him back in sepia-tinted mundanity. She put a hand on his arm. "Ah, Lou," she said.

He smiled. "It'll be fine."

"If only, just one time, you'd push back, let yourself get mad, you'd see that most people are just as scared as you are."

He snapped back to the road again. "Whattaya sayin, scared? I'm not scared. I just don't want any trouble. I just wanna be left..."

A roaring shadow fell over the little car, and a buffet of air rocked it on its suspension. A highway bus swept past them, the tops of its thrumming wheels level with Lou's eyes. He gripped the steering wheel harder, as the Toyota was jostled by the larger vehicle's slipstream. "What the hell?" he shouted.

A five-ton yellow rental truck zoomed past, riding the bus's bumper, then a black panel van. Lou looked up as it passed him. The windows were closed and tinted black. He could see vague shapes behind the glass.

Four more identical vans followed, then came a carry-all with the markings of the state highways department. As it passed him, Lou looked across at the two men in the front seats. The nearer of the two, a lean jawed, crew-cut blond in his thirties, glanced down at Lou with disinterest, then turned to say something to his driver. The highways truck sped up, passing the other vehicles and disappearing around a curve ahead.

Lou eased up on the gas, putting room between himself and the vans. "Must be a convention or something, at the hotel," he said.

"This road doesn't go anywhere else," she agreed. "I hope they're not going to make a lot of noise tonight."

A mile farther on, the road curved around a hill and continued across a low-rise concrete bridge that spanned the Prescott River. The highways department truck stopped on the gravel shoulder just short of the abutment. A few moments later, the bus swished by, rattling a loosely mounted road sign that informed travelers that the lakeside resort town of Prescott Springs lay beyond the river.

13

Not long after, the Meechams' car followed the vans across the bridge, heading for the cluster of frame houses grouped in a few blocks south of Prescott Lake, and the town's centerpiece, the granite pile that was the Prescott Springs Hotel. Halfway between the river crossing and the lake the Toyota passed a weather-beaten old brick structure, its front partially built of opaque glass blocks, behind a sagging chain-link fence. A sheet-metal sign dangling from rusty chains above the padlocked gate advertised the place as the bottling plant of the "Prescott Springs Mineral Water Company, Established 1892." A smaller placard at eye level conveyed the additional information that the plant was closed.

Back at the bridge, the sound of the Toyota diminished into the distance, and the highways truck's doors flew open. Six men got out, dressed alike in coveralls and orange vests with fluorescent stripes. Except for Wexler, the blond from the shotgun seat, all of them were in their twenties, hard-looking, easy moving men with flat eyes. They worked quickly and purposefully, not needing to be told what to do, arranging plastic cones and wooden sawhorse barriers to block the road at both ends of the bridge.

When the barricades were in place, two of the men lifted handheld traffic control signs from the carry-all, and went out on the road at either end of the span. The rest of the crew ranged themselves along the bridge's parapet, and began a desultory tapping at the concrete with hammers and cold chisels, like geologists taking samples. Wexler unclipped a walkie-talkie from his belt and rapidly tapped the "send" button three times. The radio squawked twice in reply.

For two or three minutes, there was no sound or movement other than what the young men were doing to the parapet. Then a beat-up blue pick-up came around a bend in the road and pulled up at the barrier. The truck bed was piled high with bales of alfalfa, the driver a stringy old woman in overalls and a straw hat.

The blond man approached the driver's window. "You live in Prescott Springs?"

The old woman nodded. "I run sheep on a place the other end of the lake. What's the trouble here?"

"No trouble," said Wexler, nodding to the sign holder to open the barrier. "Maybe some cracks in the pilings. We're just checking it now. You can go through."

14

The pick-up ground forward with a clash of gears, and the barrier closed behind it. Two minutes later, a Dodge minivan came around the curve, driven by a soft faced man wearing a designer shirt and a Cartier watch. His carefully coordinated wife looked alertly at the activity on the bridge, while the two kids in the back seat kept their eyes and fingers on their hand-held video games.

Wexler smiled at the driver. "Hi. You folks live in Prescott Springs?"

"No," was the reply. "We're just going to picnic by the lake."

The blond man shook his head. "Sorry. May have to close this bridge soon. Since it's the only way in or out of town, you could be stuck here a couple days." He pointed with his chin back the way the minivan had come. "Saw a pretty nice spot back down the road, you want to try it."

The driver spoke over his shoulder to the kids in the back. "Sorry, guys."

The wife frowned, but the kids paid no attention. The man shrugged, said "thanks," put the vehicle through a three-point turn, and headed back down the road out of the Prescott Valley.

Minutes passed and nothing more came down the road. The only sounds were the men's aimless tapping at the parapet and the chuckle of the river washing past the bridge supports. One of the men picked up a pebble from the deck and dropped it into the water, listening to the "floop" it made as it broke the surface and watching the ripples rapidly break up on the moving flow. The man reached for another pebble; as he did so, he found Wexler's gaze on him, and a shiver went up his back as he read the message in that furious stare. Then he saw something that instantly made him drop the stone, reach for his hammer and get looking *busy*. A black limousine with tinted windows eased into view around the hill and approached the barrier.

The squad leader turned to follow the other man's gaze, then snapped to attention as the car came to a stop and the rear passenger window rolled halfway down. The face framed by the glass and chrome was of a man in his late fifties. The lean cheeks and thin lips bespoke an ascetic temperament, to which the dark, sunken eyes added more than a tinge of cruelty. Before his retirement from the military, Parker DeVoin had never been the kind of general soldiers would gladly follow into hell; he was instead the kind of martinet who would consign to perdition any man who failed to meet his exacting standards.

His eyes swept over the activity on the bridge, then came back to the squad leader. "Your report, Mr. Wexler," he said.

"Phase one on track and on time, General."

DeVoin nodded. "Carry on, Lieutenant."

"Sir!"

The man almost threw a salute, but checked the reflex in time. The limo window rolled up and the car moved across the bridge toward town. The lieutenant turned to the man who had dropped the pebble.

"Hagen!" he barked. "Relieve Medford here." He indicated the man with the slow/stop sign. "I want you where I can see you."

Hagen left his hammer and vaulted over the barrier in time to catch the sign the Medford tossed to him. Another car was coming, and he walked out into the middle of the road. The squad leader came up behind him, put his lips close to the younger man's ear and said, "This ain't Bragg, asshole. There's no company punishment, no confined to barracks. You fuck up, the general's gonna tell me to put one through your useless, empty head, and you know I'll do it."

Hagen swallowed hard. "Yes, sir."

"Now stop the car and be polite."

"Yes, sir."

Bridge Road ended by curving into the town's principal thoroughfare, which ran from west to east along the south shore of the lake. On the maps it was identified as Prescott Avenue, but the locals called it Main Street. It was three short blocks of small stores, taverns and restaurants that did eighty per cent of their annual business during the four months that Prescott Springs was filled with tourists.

The east end of Prescott Avenue was anchored by the town's baseball diamond, beyond which it connected with Mill Road, still named for the long defunct sawmill that had provided the lumber for most of the town's buildings. The west end was dominated by the chest-high stone wall that surrounded the Prescott Springs Resort Hotel.

The hotel had been built to ride the wave of health faddism that had enlivened some levels of American society in the late nineteenth century, producing cure-all "tonics" like Coca Cola and breakfast foods like Kellogg's corn flakes, the latter being first touted as a cure for masturbation. Prescott Spring's contribution to the mania had been its mineral waters, piped into the hotel from a naturally occurring source beneath an outcropping of limestone a hundred yards west along the lakeshore. When the hotel became a popular destination, its owners added a bottling plant and profited by shipping Prescott Springs water as far south as San Francisco and east to Chicago, until the "wellness" craze evaporated at the turn of the century.

After the initial enthusiasm passed, bottled mineral water never became as popular a soft drink in America as it was in Europe. Prescott Springs continued to supply a few specialty stores, and its outpourings enjoyed a mild resurgence with the post-World War II controversy over fluoridation of municipal water systems. By the 1990s, when the national taste again veered toward bottled mineral water, something more might have been done with what Prescott Springs had to offer. But by then the inheritors of the hotel and bottling plant had long since sold out to a chain based in the east, and the distant decision-makers had no interest.

In late 2007, with tourism slumping along with the rest of the economy, the chain downsized and put both assets on the market. It was more than two years before they sold. The new owner, an anonymous numbered company, immediately instituted cost-saving measures that resulted in severe cutbacks among the hotel staff and a flat-out closure of the bottling plant.

The damage done to the economy of Prescott Springs showed in the empty streets and boarded up houses. The PriceRite clothing store was bare, a "FOR LEASE" sign propped in the display window. At Sarah's Gift Shop, above the display of flint arrowheads, folk art carvings and ceramic ashtrays, the sign read "CLOSING SALE – 50% OFF." In front of Fung's Groceries,a straggle of men had nothing better to do in mid-afternoon than pitch pennies. Outside Bob's Tavern, two angry drunks in work clothes were pushing each other toward a fight, while a ring of beer drinkers had come outside to egg them on.

As the Meechams' Toyota rounded the curve from Bridge Road and headed for the hotel gate directly across from the tavern, Lou knew that Adele's eye was not on the street scene; he caught her trying to sneak a peek at her watch. The coffee shop closed at three, and they'd had nothing to eat since breakfast. She'd be wanting to nudge him husband, but would restrain herself because there was already tension between them. But because he had seen the surreptitious time check he considered himself nudged anyway.

The fight outside the tavern was escalating. The pushing had now become grappling, and soon both men were rolling on the sidewalk, flailing at each other ineffectually with blows that would have been haymakers if the combatants had been sober.

Lou indicated the brawl with a flick of his balding head. "There, you see?"

Adele looked vaguely toward the disturbance, now falling behind them. "See what?"

He shook his head. "Never mind."

He steered the car into the hotel grounds and parked in the lot on the west side of the building. As they walked toward the front door of the hotel, Adele urged him to hurry, but Lou stopped, his attention caught by the scene in the parking area.

"Wait a minute," he said, and went to look.

The bus was parked against the hotel's side wall, its baggage compartment beneath the passenger cabin propped open, so that a chain of men could pass duffel bags from the bus to the hotel's rear doors. The five-ton rental truck was nearby, its back door open; men with dollies were manhandling heavy crates and spools of cable out of it and wheeling them into the building.

All of the men were young, none past their early thirties, Lou noted, except for a handful of older guys who were directing the work. They were casually dressed in denim and sweats, but there was nothing casual about the way they emptied the bus and stacked the bags just inside the hotel's metal-covered service door. They worked quietly and briskly, with no banter.

"What is this?" Lou said, mostly to himself.

Adele took her husband's arm. "I want lunch," she said. "It's almost three."

He allowed himself to be pulled away.

# 3

Jeff Cameron could see right away that his boss was having an even worse day than usual. Jeff stepped lightly down the service stairs that spiraled down from the kitchens, looking good in his red, white and black waiter's outfit the way he'd looked good in his high school baseball colors, thirteen years before when his pitching had almost made him all state, and the prospect of a try-out for the majors didn't seem out of the question. But that was before Sharon found out she was pregnant, and suddenly it was marriage and little Trevor and the need to land a job – any job – to pay those bills that kept coming in, month after month.

It could have happened for him. He had the arm and he had the eye. He could pitch a respectable fastball and a reliable curve. And he had that indefinable something else: there were times when he would stand on the mound, and his whole being would seem to expand, as if he could project his spirit beyond the limits of flesh. It would reach out, until the ball and the strike zone and all the air between was one indivisible whole. Then he would throw, and time would cease. The ball would be where it was going to be – where it *had* to be – even before it left his outstretched fingers.

He never told anyone about those times, those moments when he lost himself in the purity of perfect action. He held them to himself. They were something outside the rest of his life, a gift that he cherished each time it was bestowed upon him.

But that was the past. The present was a wife and a kid and bills and a town that was wasting away.

So now he came down the back stairs of the hotel, still coordinated, the residue of that carrot-haired, small-town high-school hero still resident behind his green eyes, toting a bag of trash for the dumpster, to find the hotel's perpetually agitated general manager getting in the way of a gang of tough-looking young guys who were methodically filling the freight elevator with stacked duffel bags.

Plump and always slightly moist, Herb Trainor did not so much manage the staff as constantly *fuss* at them while they did his bidding. Now he was going through his full repertoire of imperious noises and gestures, his ring of keys jangling on his Gucci belt, but the hard-bodied young men were paying him no more heed than they gave to the chipped green paint on the walls.

Two years back, when he had been promoted to general manager, after old man Gladhew broke his hip in a spectacular tumble down the main staircase, the hotel's new head man had tried to get the staff to call him Mr. Trainor. But not even the youngest chambermaid could bring herself to do it, and so he remained just plain Herb – or sometimes "that sorry asshole Herb," when he wasn't around – to every member of the dwindling number of Prescott Springs citizens who earned their livings keeping the rooms tidy and the guests fed.

"What's up, Herb?" Jeff asked. "We being invaded?"

Trainor spun around. "Out of here, now!" His voice squeaked a little when he was really cranked up. "This area is off limits to all staff!"

"Okay, Herb," said Jeff, and handed him the trash bag that Zack Weaver, the catering manager, had told him to dump.

Trainor took the plastic sack without thinking, then thrust it back into the waiter's hands. "Outside," he said, his eyes bulging slightly more than usual, "then get back upstairs."

Jeff worked his way to the open back doors, dodged a duffel bag being tossed from one link to the next in the human chain, and threw the trash into the dumpster. He ducked his way back through the doors, just as Trainor was urging caution on a man who was trying to corner a large crate on a two-wheel dolly. The man did not moderate his speed, but tossed off a "Yes, sir!" as he went by.

"The hell is all this, Herb?" Jeff said. "Who are these guys?"

"Guests!" the manager snapped. "Guests of the new owner, and he wants absolute security! Now, you get back to the coffee shop – no wait!" He looked at his watch; lunch was almost over. "I want you to round up all the management personnel and tell them to be in my office, fifteen minutes, no exceptions!"

Jeff shrugged. "You got it, Herb," he said, and remounted the stairs. *Some kinda shit is coming down on old Herb this time,* he thought.

It had been coming down on Herb Trainor for a week now, beginning with a hand-delivered letter that had curtly ordered him to cancel all reservations from Friday, August 4 through the following Monday. The hotel, the letter said, had been block-booked by an unnamed organization. Trainor was to contact anyone who had a reservation and tell them not to come. Those who complained or threatened reprisals were to be offered a free weekend in a first-class suite with unlimited room service.

The letter had been signed by one Parker DeVoin, whom Trainor had never met, but who had been identified to him by the regional manager of the chain that used to own the property as the new proprietor of the Prescott Springs resort hotel, mineral springs and all. The missive had sent Herb Trainor into a three-day fluster of phone calls, e-mails, registered letters and faxes, until he was sure he had fulfilled its instructions.

Today, he had hovered about the lobby since noon, seeing that the last of the guests were checked out, fussing at every staff member who could not avoid him in time, and waiting for Mr. DeVoin to arrive. A brusque phone call early in the morning, from someone who had not bothered to give his name, had said that the new owner would come this afternoon.

Ten minutes ago, a long black limo had wheeled up to the main entrance, and out had stepped a spare man in his fifties, in a Brooks Brothers pinstripe, his lean face as forbidding as that of a sixteenth century Jesuit. He was flanked by three aides or associates. Trainor hurried to fling open the heavy front portal, with its leaded stained glass renderings of figures from pioneer days, while the aged doorman was still reaching for the handle.

The manager assumed his most obsequious expression. "Mr. DeVoin, Herb Trainor. I trust you will find everything is as you, er, wanted it to be." He extended a perspiring hand, which DeVoin did not deign to notice.

The general took in the lobby, then his hooded eyes locked onto Trainor. "My guests are arriving downstairs at the rear," he said. "You will make sure that they are undisturbed. Complete security."

Trainor wiped his palms on his pant legs. "I thought you'd like to look the hotel over... take a tour of..."

But DeVoin was already walking toward the elevators, followed by two of his party: swarthy, mustachioed men in expensive suits with a European cut – they had already dismissed Trainor with a glance. The fourth man lingered long enough to lay a grip on the manager's soft bicep, hard enough that

Trainor winced. He was in his late fifties, the blue eyes and bristle cut graying hair giving him the look of a Prussian staff officer in mufti, but the accent was pure American heartland.

"My name is Macklin," he said, and cocked his head toward the trio who were now entering one of the elevators. "You'll find that he prefers to be obeyed."

He let Trainor's arm drop and crossed to the elevator. The door slid closed after him, and the manager saw the needle of the old fashioned floor indicator rotate to the top floor. The letter had given instructions to prepare the Roosevelt suite – named not for FDR but for Teddy; he had once booked it, but then had to cancel the visit when some crisis in North Africa had ruled out an Oregon hunting spree.

Trainor wiped his hands on his pants again, hoped the champagne was chilled to the right degree, then headed downstairs to make sure the new owner's guests were undisturbed.

The hotel coffee shop was almost empty. A few guests lingered over refills. Zack Weaver, the catering manager, was at a table near the lobby door, totaling receipts. A heavy middle-aged man with deep lines delineating his developing jowls and a bald spot the size of a saucer, he looked up as Lou and Adele entered from the lobby, then came out from behind the table to block their entrance.

"I'm sorry," he said and checked his watch. "The luncheon serving is over. You can ask room service to send something up to your room."

Lou wanted to look anywhere but in Adele's direction. "Look," he said, "we don't need anything fancy..."

Weaver cut him off. "I'm sorry. The coffee shop closes at three, and..."

Adele spoke up. "And it's not three. It's five-to, and we are here. We are staying at this hotel, and we want lunch."

Lou Meecham turned to his wife, with his hands raised and making gentle patting motions, like a man trying to push fog out of a room. "Honey, let's not make a big deal."

But Zack Weaver had more on his mind than two late and hungry coffee shop patrons. He had already received Herb's summons, via Jeff Cameron, to be in the general manager's office in a few minutes. He didn't know what was going on – DeVoin's letter had instructed Trainor to say nothing, and he had followed orders – but clearly something had kept the boss swimming in

22

a pool of his own grease all week. Weaver hoped it didn't mean what most of the staff assumed: a final shut-down and everybody out of work. Without the job's medical benefits, he couldn't afford to care for his chronically ill wife.

"Fine," he said, and motioned the Meechams to a booth, handing them a pair of menus from the stack at the front counter. "I'll get you a waiter."

He stepped into the kitchen. Doris Auberon, the grandmotherly short-order cook, was wiping down the grill while Jeff Cameron sluiced plates and cups in the double sink.

Weaver said, "Two late-comers out here. Can you get them what they want and then out of the way?"

Doris voiced a short and not very grandmotherly comment, but Jeff dried his hands on a dish towel, said "Sure, Zack," and followed the kitchen boss out to the coffee shop. He picked up two place settings and a carafe of iced mineral water from the server station beside the kitchen door and crossed to where the Meechams were sitting. He laid out the cutlery and napkins, put two tumbler glasses on their table, and filled both with the cold, sparkling water.

"There you go," he said, "pure Prescott Springs mineral water. Best there is."

Lou Meecham, took a sip, then a gulp. "This is good stuff," he said to Adele, who shrugged. To Jeff he said, "You ought to bottle this."

"They used to. I worked in the bottling plant maybe eight, nine years. My dad was there right up until he died. They ran it more than ninety years. Pretty well built this town."

Adele was interested now. She took a sip of the water, liked it. "So, what happened?"

"Don't know. Last year, some new people bought the hotel, closed down the bottling plant. Put half the town out of work. I lucked into this job when a buddy moved to Portland, but a lot of people didn't do so well."

"That's a shame," Adele said.

"At least you'll all be healthy, drinking this stuff," Lou said.

"No, sir. Only the hotel gets it, piped right in from the springs. Folks in town drink lake water." He looked at his watch. "Anyway, I'd better take your order. Cook's going to want to set up for dinner, soon. Got some nice smoked salmon."

"Sounds good," Lou said.

"Me, too," Adele added.

It was not a happy group that met in the general manager's office at three o'clock. The entire management staff ranged around Trainor's antique desk on institutional furniture that looked better than it sat. Weaver was the last to arrive, and found chain-smoking Thel Parmentier, the housekeeper, in the only comfortable chair. Next to her was Ignatz Morens, the head chef, a thin and fractious man who looked as if at any moment he might start screaming, though he never raised his voice above a sour mutter. Tom Peebles, the morose chief groundskeeper, leaned against a wall, arms folded, staring out the window at the south lawn. Herb's two assistant managers, a pair of interchangeable young men named Wallace and Stowe, perched on the edge of the love seat, leaning forward with identical postures, even to the way each laced his fingers together and clasped them over one knee.

Weaver settled himself on a side chair and waited for Trainor to speak. The general manager took a linen handkerchief from his desk drawer – the second of the day, he realized – and wiped his clammy palms. "Well," he said, and was immediately interrupted by a buzz from the phone at his elbow.

The conversation was brief, and the other staff heard only Trainor's side of it, which was limited to one "hello," two "yes, sirs," an "I will, sir," and a "goodbye." When he hung up, he had to reach for the hanky again, this time to wipe away the beads that had erupted on his forehead and upper lip.

"What the hell's going on here, Herb?" said Thel Parmentier around a half-smoked unfiltered cigarette, her left eye squinted shut against the smoke curling up to her henna-dyed curls. "That some kinda army bunking down in the west wing?"

Trainor wiped his hands again. "I don't know. It's the new owner. I wasn't allowed to say anything, but he's up in the Roosevelt, and he's personally block-booked the whole place for the week-end. I don't know who the hell the guests are. All I know is the owner – his name's DeVoin – wants the whole staff assembled in the grand ballroom at five tonight."

Weaver hadn't seen the busload of young men yet. "What've we got going here, Herb?" he asked. "This new guy bring in a bunch of Mexicans or Filipinos to take our jobs? Come five o'clock, do we get told it's so long amigo and haul it outta here?"

Peebles pushed himself off from the wall. "Those ain't no Hispanics. They're Americans, and serious folks. Looked like Mormons or something."

"Jesus," said the housekeeper, removing the butt long enough to spit a shred of tobacco onto Herb's maroon carpet. "They're not making this place some kinda cult compound, are they? We got enough trouble in Prescott Springs without turning it into another Waco."

24

"I don't think so, but... I don't know," said Herb. "They're not saying anything except 'do this, do that' and keep your mouth shut. And that's what I'm telling you. Get everybody back here for five, and for god's sake don't start any rumors or feed any you hear. I don't know what the hell's going on, but right now we've all got jobs and with any luck we'll still have them tomorrow."

Jeff brought Lou and Adele a last refill of coffee and laid the check down. Lou took a sip. "Is that spring water in the coffee?" he asked.

"Yes, sir. All the water in the hotel comes from the spring. Folks, I hope you don't mind me asking you to settle this now. You see, I'm on swing shift, got to leave now and be back for five o'clock."

Lou got up, opened his wallet, handed Jeff a bill and told him to keep the change. "Wish we could take a few bottles of this water home."

"Thank you, sir. So do I."

Adele watched Jeff head for the kitchen. She stood up. "Nice kid."

"Yeah," said Lou. "Too bad he's stuck in this nowhere town."

She took his arm. "He reminds me of somebody."

"Oh yeah, who's that?" said Lou, and softly stroked her knuckles with his palm.

"You, when I met you."

He leaned into her. "Feel like a nap?"

She put more honey in her voice. "Just a nap?"

"Well, maybe not at first."

She chuckled and made the first move toward the lobby door.

Jeff left by the front door, walked down the driveway and headed along Prescott Avenue. There was almost no traffic, just a black panel truck with tinted windows that came out of the hotel grounds, drove down Prescott and parked by the baseball diamond.

As Jeff passed Bob's Tavern, the street door opened, letting out a waft of cool, beer-flavored air, a mournful country song and two middle-aged men in old work clothes. Frank Tedesco and Joe Brzuskniewicz – Joe B. to everyone who knew him – had loaded the bottle trucks Jeff drove when he'd followed his dad into the Prescott Springs plant. For almost a year now, they'd been eking by on unemployment benefits and occasional odd jobs done for under-the-table payment. Their prospects did not look good, and they knew it.

25

"Hey, Jeff," said Frank.

Jeff stopped. "Frank, Joe B., whatta you say?"

Frank shrugged. "Not much."

"Whattaya hear at the hotel?" Joe B. wanted to know. "There was talk they might be taking on some more groundskeepers."

Jeff shook his head. "Nah. Word is the new owner's thinking of cutting back. Let the place run wild over the winter, clean it up in the spring."

Joe B. spat. "Shit, ain't that the way?"

"I heard you guys were up for one of them government tree-planting projects," Jeff said.

Frank looked down at his cracked shoes. "Uh-uh. They don't say it, but they're saving those jobs for kids."

"Bad times," Jeff said.

"Least you're working," said Joe B.

"Oh, yeah, and I'm clearing about ten bucks a week more than I'd get on unemployment. And that's *with* tips."

Frank gave Joe B. the elbow. "Whyncha let the man be? He didn't shut down the goddamn bottling plant."

His buddy ducked his head. "Yeah, well, sorry, Jeff. It's just, guys like us, we never figured to end up pushing fifty and on the bum, you know."

Jeff laid a light punch on the older man's bicep. "No sweat, Joe B. What the hell, it's gotta get better, right?"

Frank sniffed. "Could it get worse?"

"Yeah. Hey, Sharon's waiting for me. See you guys."

"Come on," said Frank, "let's go feed the goddamn ducks." He pulled a half-eaten peanut butter sandwich from his pocket and crossed the street to the shoreline park.

"Fuck all else to do," said Joe B., and followed.

Jeff continued down Prescott Avenue to Arnie Fung's grocery store. The bell mounted on a spring atop the half-glassed door tinkled as he entered. The place was empty except for Arnie, a lean and quiet man in his mid-thirties, and Alexander Macreedy, who had been Prescott Springs' sole medical practitioner since he took over the practice, still located in a storefront two doors down from Fung's, back in the late 1960s. The doctor was small, with delicate hands, and seemed to wear the same combination of tweed and flannels year-round. A shapeless old trilby confined an always unruly shock of white hair.

"Hey, Jeff," said Arnie. The doctor just nodded.

"Arnie, Doc." Jeff got milk from the cooler and bread from its shelf, and brought them back to the counter. A rack of comic books caught his eye and he picked out one that featured a spandexed superhero rising out of an erupting volcano.

The storekeeper totted up the doctor's order, took the money and started putting the groceries in paper sacks. Macreedy looked at the printed cash register receipt, then pointed to two large bottles of Canadian water. "These have gone up five cents again," he said.

"It's what the distributor charges me," said Arnie.

"It's a hell of a thing when a man's got to pay through the nose for a necessity like pure water," Macreedy said.

There was a rack of rental DVDs near the comics. Jeff selected one and put it on the counter with the comic book.

"These are tough times," said Arnie. "Things don't get better by spring, I may even have to sell up and go into partnership with my cousins in Astoria." His expression said the prospect was not a pleasant one.

"I'd hate to see you go," said Jeff. "We go back a long way." They'd grown up together, been more like brothers than friends. Arnie had been their school team's catcher when Jeff had been the star of the mound.

"*You'd* hate it? You don't know my cousins." He finished the doctor's packing, and handed him the sack. "How about you, Doc? You feeling the pinch?"

The doctor rested the sack on his slim hip. "Ironically, no. Doctors generally do better in hard times."

"That right?" said Jeff.

"'Fraid so. Depressed people tend to hurt themselves more. Or each other. Then they end up at my place needing stitches or a stomach pump." He reached into the sack, broke open a package of peppermints and put one in his mouth. "Tell you something, though, I've never seen it this bad."

"We've had tough times before. I remember my dad being out of work in the early eighties," said Jeff.

The old man moved the candy around in his cheek. "Well, maybe it's just cause I'm older and crankier now, but I don't think it's the same. Seems like these days so many people are always getting mad – no, I'll tell you what it is, it's like a lot of people *want* to be teed-off all the time. Like it was some kind of civic virtue to be all puffed up with righteous anger about the government, or welfare or the French."

"You don't think people have a right to get mad, Doc?" Arnie asked.

"Sure they do," said the old man. "You got a right to want to get rich, too. But you shouldn't pump up your appetite for material comfort and pretend its a mark of moral purity. Greed is still one of the seven deadly sins. So is anger.

"So what I'm saying is get mad, sure, when you see things you can't stomach. But don't try to make being mad some kind of holy state of being. An-

27

ger ought to be something you fall into when you've got no other choice. It shouldn't be a whatchamacallit, a choice of lifestyle."

He clamped his battered old hat down on his head. "Hell, listen to me," he said. "Occupational handicap of old men – we like to lecture. G'night." He headed for the door.

"See you, Doc," said Arnie. He rang up Jeff's order. "That's three thirty-eight and a buck for the DVD." He took Jeff's proffered five and made change. "*The Alamo*," he said, as he put the disk in the sack. "You still a John Wayne freak?"

"Yeah. Why not?"

"Tell you, I always thought Fess Parker made a better Davy Crockett."

Jeff picked up the sack. "Was that bottled water the doc was buying?"

Arnie nodded. "Always has. Told me once he opened his practice here cause of the water. Since they shut down the bottling plant, he has me order it in from Vancouver Island."

"The things you can learn about people you think you already know. That man delivered me, and I never knew he was a health nut."

"A doctor can't be a health nut, who can?"

"I guess," said Jeff. "Hey, gotta get home. Hope you don't have to go to the cousins."

"Tell me about it," said Arnie. "I'd have to live with them, eat my auntie's sticky rice three times a day." He shuddered.

Jeff made a face. "I'm outta here."

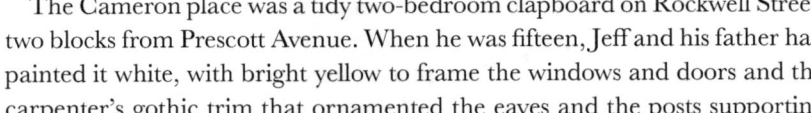

The Cameron place was a tidy two-bedroom clapboard on Rockwell Street, two blocks from Prescott Avenue. When he was fifteen, Jeff and his father had painted it white, with bright yellow to frame the windows and doors and the carpenter's gothic trim that ornamented the eaves and the posts supporting the front porch. *Like a plate of badly scrambled eggs*, was how his mother had described the result, but the old man had thought it cheerful and liked how it stood out from the other homes on the street.

Jeff had lived there all of his life, except for a few years in the converted garage he and Sharon had rented after they married and Trevor came along. Then his dad died of a stroke, right in the middle of a sentence at the lunch table in the bottling plant, and he was gone by the time Jeff got the message and brought the truck back. The will left the house to Jeff's mother, but she had no taste for widowhood in a place where memories crowded in from every corner. After the funeral, she deeded the house over to Jeff and went to live in Portland with her sister, whose own husband had passed away years before.

Jeff and Sharon had been surprised at how quickly the house became theirs, how it wasn't strange to make love in the same bed he'd been conceived in, nor to see his old room decked out in Terminator and Matrix posters that the video distributors supplied to Arnie, and which he let Trevor have when the promotions had run their course.

The walls were thin and the picket fence wouldn't have kept out an over-weight sheep, but the house was somehow their safe place. Whatever the world might throw at them, it would bounce off the clapboard as if from a castle's stone walls. It was home. It was where things were all right.

Jeff came up the walk toting the sack of groceries, made the porch in two big steps, went through the front door, down the short hall past the closed living room door, and into the comfy old kitchen with the oversized formica-topped table. Sharon was at the stove. Lunch was going to be wieners and beans again. She turned to him those same soft gray eyes that had pulled him trembling across the gym at a grade eight sock hop, when he'd been sure he'd rather be eaten alive by Jaws than walk all that way through all of those stares, to ask a girl he didn't know if she would care to dance with him.

It was ten years now, and maybe there were a couple of pounds more on her hips, and a line or two at the corners of her mouth. But she was still an extension of the most compelling moment of his life, and nothing – not a sur-prise pregnancy nor sudden parenthood nor any of the thousand other things that can go wonky in a teen-age marriage – had taken away the little flip that his innards performed whenever he first caught sight of her again after being away for a hour or two.

He put the sack on the counter by the sink, came up behind her and put his arms around her still small waist, then slid his hands down so that his palms cupped her mound through her worn and faded jeans. He nuzzled aside her shoulder length auburn hair that smelled of sweet, cheap shampoo, and kissed her nape. She let out a little exhalation of air and circled her ass against him, just once.

"Where's Trevor?" he breathed into her ear.

"He just got home from school. Listen," she said. He did, and heard the muted sounds of a X-Box streetfighting game emanating from the living room.

"That ought to keep him busy," he said. He squeezed her though the denim with one hand, while the other came up to cup the underside of her right breast. "What do you say, lady?"

She slid a hand back between them and gripped him. "Okay, but quickly. He's probably hungry."

They stole upstairs, stepping over the stair that creaked, locked the bedroom door and made love quickly and almost fiercely, in the hot slats of sunlight falling through the half drawn Venetian blinds. It was good, the way it was always good, from the beginning to the middle to the last moment of helpless completion and the soft kiss he left on her sweat-beaded belly as he took his weight off her and snuggled her into his arms.

But she pulled away. "Come on," she said, reaching for her jeans. "Can't let little kids starve while you take advantage of innocent women."

"You weren't so innocent a couple minutes ago." He stretched. "Thank god for swing shifts."

She looked down at him, and he noticed that the lines around her mouth seemed a little deeper. Then she unlocked the door without saying what she was thinking and went back downstairs.

He lay back and went blank for a while, just lazing through the after-love mellowness, the sweat drying on his chest. Then he got up and took a quick shower, and changed into jeans and a tee-shirt. When he came down to the kitchen, Sharon had his lunch warm in the oven. Trevor's smeared, empty plate and filmed milk glass were on the counter by the sink. The boy had gone back to his video game.

Her plate was on the rack below his; she'd waited for him to come down. She put the plates on the table and filled two more glasses with milk. They sat down together and began to eat.

"It would help with the budget if you ate lunch at the hotel," she said.

"Better atmosphere here," he said.

"When Uncle Mike worked there, all the staff got their meals for free."

"When your Uncle Mike worked there, it was different. This new owner, he squeezes a penny till it drips."

She raised a forkful of beans halfway to her mouth, then put it back down on the plate. "Jeff, what are we going to do?"

He kept eating. "About what?"

"About everything. We're just barely scraping by, and Trevor's going to need a new winter coat."

He said nothing.

"And what happens if you get laid off?"

"Why don't we worry about that when it happens? Or *if* it happens. Come on, let's eat."

30

"I'm not hungry," she said, and took her half-filled plate to the sink. She was going to scrape the uneaten food into the trash container, then thought better of it and put it in the refrigerator. She shut the fridge door and stared at a picture Trevor had done in school that was stuck to the avocado green enamel by a mushroom-shaped magnet. It showed F-14s strafing a tank column. She remembered he'd called the missiles *Rockeyes*.

"I talked to my dad today," she said. "He called from Seattle."

Jeff let out a long sigh. "I don't want to go into this now."

"We've got to talk about it sometime, Jeff."

He picked up the glass of milk and drank some of it. It tasted sour, even though he knew it was fresh. "Sharon, don't," he said.

She leaned her head against the cold green surface. "Well, we can't hold out much longer, can we? And dad says he can get you a job at Wagner's."

He drank the milk down. "Sure, what kind of job? Stacking boxes on a loading dock for the minimum wage. I might as well stay right here. This is our home."

"Dad felt the same way. But when it got bad, he moved to the city."

Jeff pushed back from the table, but didn't get up. Instead, he rested his forearms on his thighs and looked at his worn Nikes. Where his little toes made the fabric bulge, the cloth was beginning to split.

"He doesn't have to worry about kids any more, does he?" he said. "I don't want Trevor growing up in a city. You got dope, you got violence, you got hookers hanging around the school yard."

She turned and put her hand on his shoulder. "And what's he going to have here? A town full of out-of-work men, and maybe any day now an out-of-work dad? You know, most of his friends have moved on. He's spending more and more time alone."

The best part of him wanted to let her warm hand stay there, but pride said he had to shrug it off. He did it gently, ducking out from under her touch.

"I don't want to fight, babe." He stood up, turned away. "I brought him a comic book. Where is it?"

"He already took it back to the living room. Jeff, honey, don't run away. We've got to talk."

But he was heading for the living room now. "Later," he said, over his shoulder. "I promise."

The living room furniture was old stuff, some of it from his childhood, some bought at the goodwill store when they'd first been married. He used to sit on that same rug watching G.I. Joe cartoons after school. His parents' wedding photo was on the mantelpiece, in black and white, with his and Sharon's in color beside it. Both couples looked young and hopeful, with just a hint of fear beneath the smiles.

At twelve, Trevor was a small-sized version of his father, sitting cross-legged on the rug, his fingers tap-tap-tapping the game control. On the screen, a ninja-clad figure swung a fighting staff at a muscled punk in a blue mohawk – one, two, three – and the punk lay down, flickered and disappeared. Two more hoods moved in from the ninja's rear, and Trevor made the character leap into the air, change direction and come down swinging.

"Hey, tiger," Jeff said.

The boy didn't look up. "Hey, dad."

"I bought you a comic." It was spread open on the rug, face down.

"Yeah, thanks." The eyes never left the screen. "I'm gonna finish it later."

Jeff watched the mayhem. Now some fat sumo wrestler with a Japanese sword was after the ninja. "The good guys winning?"

Trevor looked up and gave his father a brief smile, then went back to work. "They always do," he said.

Jeff reached down and smoothed his son's copper colored hair. "Hey," he said, "I rented us a movie."

The boy grunted.

"John Wayne. *The Alamo*."

"I'm kinda into this game," Trevor said, without looking up again.

Jeff went back to the kitchen. Sharon was doing the dishes. She didn't turn around. "We got to talk," she said.

"Later, okay?"

"Can't be much later, Jeff."

He sighed, but wanted to swear. "I know, babe. Look, I might as well head back. We'll talk about it when I get home."

She turned to look him in the eye. He could see she'd been crying again. "For sure?" she said.

"Promise." He moved to her, put his hands on her waist and kissed her cheek, tasting salt. She laid her head against his shoulder. "It'll be all right," he said.

# 4

In the main ball room of the Prescott Springs hotel, the thick crimson curtains had been drawn across the french windows along the north side of the room, creating an echoing gloom. Only the east end of the vast oblong shaped space was bright, with track-mounted spotlights lighting the dais where jazz bands and string quartets had entertained generations of resort guests. Moving back and forth across the barrier between light and shadow, a squad of specialists was connecting the elements of a surveillance and communications command center. At the back of the stage, a framework of collapsible metal shelving held a bank of video screens that flickered on and off, one by one, as a technician tested slide switches on a central control board. At a nearby table, another tech checked the connections on a high-frequency radio transceiver. The young men worked with quiet voices and practiced proficiency, their fingers clicking over the buttons and switches.

On the ballroom floor below the dais, another pair of specialists had already uncrated a tower computer deck. Now they plugged in its high-resolution monitor, keyboard and mouse, and booted the system. The computer hummed and muttered to itself while it zipped through preliminary checks.

The moment the system was up, Dr. Phillip Sandrini stepped out of the darkness. A soft-bodied, balding man approaching his fortieth year, with glistening watery eyes and embryonic jowls, he clasped to his well developed paunch a monogrammed calf-skin briefcase, from which he extracted a compact disk. The disk flashed rainbow colors from a polished upper surface that bore no commercial label, just a hand-printed notation: *Model 3-A, Project Paroxysm.*

Sandrini's pale, fluttering hands waved the technicians aside, slipped the disk into the drive, and tapped the keyboard twice. As he sat down, the drive began to whir, and a graphic appeared on the screen. It read: *THE IN-FORMATION ON THIS DISK IS CLASSIFIED. UNAUTHORIZED ACCESS IS PROHIBITED AND SUBJECT TO SEVERE PENALTIES, INCLUDING IMPRISONMENT IN A FEDERAL PENITENTIARY.* He paid no attention, tapping a thumbnail against his prominent front teeth while he waited for the disk to cycle through its warning program. Then the screen cleared to another Windows™ menu, and he grasped the mouse and used it to click on an icon.

A new graphic came up, just red letters on a black background, the same words that were on the hand-noted label. Sandrini turned and beckoned to the junior officer who was supervising the technicians. When the man came over, Sandrini and said, "Keep your people away from me. I'm going to do some parameter tests on the model and I don't want to be disturbed."

"Yes, Doctor," the squad leader said. The man's face and voice were neutral yet Sandrini could sense the professional soldier's distaste at having to take orders from some civilian science-weenie. After all the years he had spent among career soldiers Sandrini could read the signs. He felt like reminding the officer that without this particular weenie's work, he and the other mercenaries wouldn't be getting paid – and well paid – to do their jobs.

Sandrini's own motivations went far beyond the money – although the money was good, *very* good. But Paroxysm had been the goal posts of his career as a researcher into new ways of turning human beings into meat. And after years of heuristic slogging, punctuated by a few brief and dazzling insights, he had scored big-time; he had developed a weapon so elegant, so purely clever, that it could revolutionize warfare.

Paroxysm was no rough hewn approximation of a weapon, no working model needing further development. Sandrini had perfected his killing system, tailoring it to the Pentagon's detailed checklist of qualities and attributes. It was cheap to manufacture. It was easy to deliver, and a little went a long way. It could be used against military formations or civilian populations. It activated in seconds, and the effects lasted for hours – long enough to reduce a full battalion to a handful of shaking survivors surrounded by heaps of their comrades' corpses.

Sandrini had blazed the trail on this one. It had started out as pure research into the toxic properties of organophosphates, the family of chemicals from which commercial pesticides were made. But while wading through the existing literature on organophosphate poisonings, he had chanced upon an obscure reference that indicated the substances might have potential psychoactive effects.

He had followed that faint lead through years of twists and turns that had brought him to a professional triumph. Paroxysm was the culmination of all Sandrini's hopes, and it should have made him a leader among the small and insular community of his kind. But instead of the accolades he had earned, he got a short visit from a major general, who informed him that the project had been wound up. Budget cutbacks, the general's smoothly polished aide had said, while the two-star wandered among the retorts and centrifuges, smoking a cigar.

It was something to do with red states and blue states, DeVoin told him later. Their facility was in a state whose electorate had backed the wrong party. They competed for funds against a similar research outfit that had the good fortune to be in a state and district represented by the dogs that were currently on top in the congressional pit fight. So all stockpiles of Paroxysm were to be transferred, along with all files and notes. His research team was being scattered to other units, and Sandrini's own contract as a civilian consultant to the military would not be renewed.

"Eight years of undergrad and post grad schooling, twelve years of painstaking and sometimes brilliant work, and then you toss me out like so much trash?" Sandrini had said to Colonel Megrim, the career military bureaucrat who was chief of the research staff. But the colonel had just shrugged and gone to lunch. Sandrini was not the kind of man to elicit sympathy.

Sandrini faced coming onto a job market that had few openings for sophisticated weapons developers. His skills might have been adaptable to other ends, but it was hard to pitch his abilities to potential employers when he was prohibited by federal law from discussing how he had used those skills over the past dozen years. He was serving out the last few weeks of his contract in a state of mingled outrage and desperate apprehension when Major Tag Macklin had invited him to join General DeVoin for a round of golf.

"I don't play golf," Sandrini said.

"Don't worry about it," Macklin replied.

So he had trudged the fairways of the private club where DeVoin played, hacking ineffectually with borrowed clubs, and wondering what the hell this was all about. The general had been his superior since he arrived at the establishment, and Macklin had been a continual part of the environment. But the two had never passed more than a few words with the scientific personnel. They dealt through Megrim.

The offer that DeVoin made on the fifth green, far from any potential eavesdroppers, was a complete surprise: Sandrini could have well paid work in his own profession, serving the needs of certain "private clients" whose identities were only sketchily alluded to. It was the best opportunity Sandrini was liable to attract, better by far than a temporary assistant professorship at a third-rate college, or – worse yet – teaching high school science in some midwest burgh. He took the offer.

Now, while Sandrini prepared the computer model for a test run, he heard Macklin enter the hotel ballroom and cross the parquet dance floor, boot heels thudding on the polished wood, to where the scientist sat staring into the monitor.

"Sandrini, the general wants to see you."

"It's *Doctor* Sandrini, and I'm busy here." His right hand slid the mouse across its foam pad, moving the cursor around the screen.

Macklin put his hand over Sandrini's and leaned his weight upon it, immobilizing the mouse. "Put it this way, *doctor*," he said, "the man who bought you all your toys wants you to final-brief the people who are paying for them."

He let up the pressure. The scientist shook his cramped hand and looked up at Macklin with the same look he'd given schoolyard bullies thirty years before. And then he used the same technique that little Phillip had relied upon to one-up them and regain his sense of superiority: show them something really neat that he could do, and which they were too dumb to do themselves.

"You haven't seen this," he said, indicating the monitor. "Test runs on Taliban prisoners in Kandahar in 02, using the original formula."

Macklin bent down and looked impassively at the screen. He saw a dozen olive-skinned men in baggy shirts and trousers fighting bare-handed in a prison camp compound. The violence was vicious and unrestrained. They were killing each other with hands, feet, even teeth.

"These were hard-core jihadists, true believers," Sandrini said. "Five minutes before this was shot, they were at their mid-day prayers." He watched a bull-like Pashtun tribesman seize a smaller man and rotate his head until the neck snapped. "Incredible."

Macklin kept his face unreadable, but Sandrini knew he was enjoying the spectacle. "Let's get upstairs," he said.

Sandrini reluctantly killed the playback. He rapidly clicked the mouse through a succession of menus, then left the system idling. He rose and turned to the man who was supervising the technical crew. "I'll be back in a half-hour," he said. "Have everything ready for a dry run."

"Yes, sir," said the non-com – the accent was Northern Ireland – and looked to Macklin. Only when the major confirmed the order with a nod did the man turn on his heel and head for the men on the dais, snapping out commands.

The ballroom's carved oak doors opened onto the hotel's main lobby. As Macklin and Sandrini emerged from the operations center, a guard reached to close the doors, then took up a position in front of them. He wore a suit and tie, and had a rectangular plastic name tag pinned to his left lapel. It read, "Hi, my name is Arthur."

Macklin reached into his pocket and took out two similar tags. He handed one to Sandrini and affixed the other to the breast pocket of his suit as they strode toward the elevators. "Try and look like a salesman or something," he said.

Sandrini jabbed the pin through his tie, then turned it so he could read the inscription. "This says my name is Ehor," he complained.

"Live with it," Macklin advised. He pushed the elevator button and they waited. "How's it going?" he asked.

Sandrini watched the floor indicator needle cycle downwards. "We're on track."

"You'd better be," Macklin said.

Sandrini pushed the elevator button, too, even though he knew the car was descending. The door slid back, and a balding slump shouldered man brushed past them. "Excuse me," he said and walked across the lobby toward the news stand.

Macklin and Sandrini entered the elevator, the doors closed and they went up to the top floor.

Lou Meecham was halfway across the lobby before Macklin's face registered. He stopped. A cold shiver blossomed at the base of his spine and rushed up to make the muscles at the back of his neck tighten and ache. It was as if a hole had suddenly opened in the world and he had dropped through it into someplace cold and dangerous. "Macklin," he whispered, and his hands trembled.

Herb Trainor looked up from the front desk, saw Meecham and reached to pluck a slip of paper from the rack of pigeon holes behind him. "Mr. Meecham?," he called.

Lou Meecham did not respond. His consciousness was turned inwards.

"Mr. Meecham?" Trainor repeated, coming out from behind the desk and crossing the lobby. "Just a moment, sir."

Lou still did not hear him. Trainor stepped in front of him and held up the slip of paper. "Mr. Meecham? Sir? It's past check-out time."

Lou came back from far away. "There's a man...," he said, a tremor in his voice, his hand half-raised to indicate the elevators. "I just saw a man..."

Trainor waved the paper. "Mr. Meecham, please. It's past check-out time. I've written up your account. I was just about to come up and see if there was any trouble."

Lou returned to the here and now. He saw the bill in the manager's hand, focused on his damp, pink face.

"Trouble?" he said. "What trouble? What are you talking about?" He took the paper and looked at it. "What is this?"

"It's your bill," Trainor said. "You're supposed to have checked out by now. The entire hotel is booked for a conference."

"What? No. No, we've got reservations for another two days. Here." He took a letter from his jacket pocket. "Look."

Trainor took the letter. It was on hotel stationery, dated two months previously, and signed by one of his assistants. It said the Meechams were booked for another two days.

He handed the letter back to the guest. "There's been some kind of mistake. Our computer has you scheduled to leave this afternoon."

"Your computer got it wrong," Lou said. "Excuse me."

"But, Mr. Meecham..," Trainor began, and was cut off when Lou simply turned and walked back toward the elevators, the errand that had brought him down to the lobby wiped from his mind at the sight of Macklin.

The elevator door slid closed, confining Lou Meecham in its small space. It was an old-fashioned lift, lined with some kind of plush velour and with a heavy door cover of worked brass. Lou did not push the button for his floor, but leaned his forehead against the cool yellow metal.

Something he had long ago put away, pushed it deep down where it ought to have stayed buried, was now coming up in all its fly-blown, stinking horror. It was the sounds that came first, the whir of Huey blades, the squawk and static rush over the radio, the quiet *thump* that the mortar round made as it slid down the tube and locked with the firing mechanism. The weapon was not rigged to fire as soon as the specially marked round was in place; it waited for a finger to press the manual trigger.

The finger was Lou's. He could remember now the smooth feel of it in his hand, warm from the Central American sun, slick from his own sweat.

And he could see again the dark round hole of Macklin's service .45, the muzzle inches from Lou's eyes, scarcely wavering, as hard and deadly as Macklin himself. And the voice behind the weapon, steady and calm, saying, "Do it, sergeant. Fire. That's an order."

And his own voice, younger, scared, saying, "Captain, there's no bad guys in that village. We were in there yesterday. They're friendlies, just a buncha Miskito Indian farmers, for Christ's sake!"

Macklin's thumb snicked back the hammer on the .45. "I order you to fire, sergeant," he said, in a conversational tone. "Now do it or I'll blow your fucking head off."

The brass door slid open, the grooves and swirls of its art-deco design scraping across Lou Meecham's forehead. He stepped back, as two of De-Voin's men entered the elevator from the lobby. Their nondescript slacks and short-sleeved cotton shirts, with the square plastic name tags over the pockets, were supposed to make them look like a couple of young salesmen at a weekend convention. But the eyes they swept over Lou had the flat dismissive disdain that he'd seen before, in bars and briefing rooms, whenever elite fighting troops had to share air and space with civilians or rear-echelon personnel.

One of the men pushed the button for a floor above the Meechams' room, then both stepped to the back of the car. Lou pressed the button for his floor, and ran a quick glance over them. The sleeve of one man's shirt rode up a little as he folded his arms, revealing the bottom half of a tattoo. Lou saw the point of a sword or dagger, and the word "*blut*" which he thought was German for *blood*. The man murmured something to his companion, and they both laughed. The words had not been in English, but the tattooed man's name tag identified its wearer as Terry Johnston, from Akron.

The elevator reached Lou's floor and he exited, his legs shaky and a breathless quivering in his chest. Before the door slid closed behind him, he heard "Terry Johnston" say something else to his companion, and the barking laugh that followed was not a good sound.

He walked down the corridor to the room, feeling in his pants pocket for the big skeleton key that the old-style door locks required. Just before reaching the door, he dropped the thing, and it bounced away on the threadbare old carpet. He bent to retrieve it, but his legs were shaking so badly now that he had to get down on his knees to keep his balance.

Still on his knees, he tried to fit the key into the lock, but his hand trembled so that the key rattled against the lockplate. Finally, he held his right hand in the left and tried to insert the key into the hole, only to see the keyhole swing away from him as Adele opened the door.

"Lou," she said, reaching down to take his arms and draw him to his feet. "What is it? Are you sick? Come and sit down."

She led him to a chair, then ran to the bathroom for a glass of water. He took it from her, spilling a fair amount of it because his hands were still trembling, but gulping the rest of it down.

Adele hovered over him. "Honey, what's the matter? Are you having pains? Talk to me!"

Lou put down the glass, and looked up at her. He wanted to tell her everything was fine, he wasn't having a heart attack. He wanted to put his arms around her, reassure this woman who loved him that nothing was really wrong.

But he couldn't. Because something *was* wrong. Somehow, the past he had thought was all done, all left somewhere behind him, where it could never find its way to the peaceful, sane life he lived today, somehow that past had leaped over all the barriers he'd erected, crashed through the walls he'd raised to shelter him and Adele, and now it was right here with him, in this hotel, in this room, in his head.

He stood up. Adrenaline was flowing. He went to the closet, got their suitcases, flung them onto the bed and began pulling open drawers.

"We've got to get out of here," he said. "Something's wrong, really wrong... I knew it... all those men... and I saw Macklin! Christ, Macklin!" He bundled his shirts and Adele's blouses into the bags. "We gotta go! We gotta go now!"

He knew his agitation must be frightening Adele even more than his appearance. A heart attack she probably could have dealt with. It was a possibility that a wife had to accept when her husband was past middle-age with a growing paunch and a well developed stress level.

She took a bundle of socks and underwear out of his hands and turned him round to face her. "Lou, you're scaring me," she said, gently but with iron. "Stop it! Stop it now! I don't know what you're... What men? Who's Macklin?"

Lou reached for the clothing, tossed it into a corner of the biggest suitcase. He shivered. "I can't tell you. I don't know! It's like something from the war – something's going on, and you don't know what and nobody will tell you... and then you find out a little, and a little more, and then suddenly you're right in the middle of it, and it's right inside you... *lousy, ugly shit!* and you just can't deal with it!" He shivered again. "We gotta get out of here!"

He slammed the suitcase closed, made to lift it from the bed, but she leaned her weight on it.

"Wait a minute," she said. "What are you talking about, the war?"

All he wanted now was to get them out of there, fast, before he stepped deeper into the whatever-it-was, the quicksand, that he could *smell* around them, as if it were an odor that trailed behind Macklin wherever he went.

"I'll tell you later." He put a hand on her arm. "Please, let's just get packed and get out of here. I'm asking you, Adele."

40

In the presidential suite, the phone rang. Macklin answered. It was Trainor. He asked to speak to DeVoin and Macklin knew there was trouble just from the slight treble overtones in the manager's voice. He handed the phone to the general.

"I'm sorry to bother you, Mr. DeVoin," the manager's voice came over the line, "but there's been some kind of mix-up."

DeVoin listened, giving the matter only half his attention, while he continued to take in Sandrini's briefing. The scientist was standing before a wall-sized map of Prescott Springs, using a pointer to note the town's key buildings and geographical features. The main audience was the two swarthy men who sat in plush armchairs before the map, following Sandrini's exposition. The younger man was giving the older a running translation of what the scientist was saying; occasionally, the older man asked a question which his aide relayed in English to Sandrini. An expert in Arabic dialects would have identified their accent as originating in Yemen. Another Yemeni might have been able to tell that they came from the same clan in which the bin Laden family claimed membership.

DeVoin heard Trainor out, then said, "No, don't you do anything. What room are they in?" He listened and wrote down a number. "All right, leave it to me."

He hung up and turned to Macklin. "Trainor's screwed the pooch. There's a couple in 411 with two days more to go on their reservation. Be very sorry, tell 'em their entire stay is on the house, whatever it takes, but get them out before Wexler closes the bridge." As Macklin turned to leave, DeVoin added, "And take somebody to help with the bags – no hotel staff."

In their room, Lou and Adele were ready to leave. Lou called the front desk. "Have our bill ready, we'll be right down." He listened, shook his head. "I don't want to talk to anybody. Just have that bill ready."

He hung up and grabbed the suitcases. Adele opened the door and they hurried into the corridor. The elevator chime sounded just as Lou reached for the call button.

The door opened. Macklin was there, flanked by the German with the tattoo. Lou froze, then tried to bluff it out, stepping onto the elevator and beckoning Adele after him. He did not look at Macklin.

Macklin had long ago forgotten Sergeant Lou Meecham, but he was too much of a natural predator not to recognize fear when it was right beside him, and too smart not to wonder why this man was deathly afraid of him. It took less than ten seconds for his memory, once activated, to put an identity to Lou Meecham's features.

Macklin's next act was practically instinctive: he reached to his belt at the small of his back and efficiently produced the Czech-made 7.2-millimeter automatic he had taken from a captured Sandinista political cadre whose hands could never have worked the weapon's sweet slide again anyway, once Macklin's interrogation techniques had been applied to them.

He put the pistol to Adele's right ear. She froze, and said, "Lou."

Her husband looked up, first at the gun, then at Macklin's smile.

"Sergeant Meecham. Or should I make that Mousey Meecham?" He nodded to the German, who pressed the top floor button. The elevator door closed. Lou looked away, but he could see the reflections of the four of them in the polished brass, distorted like a tableau seen through yellowy vapors in hell.

# 5

Jeff Cameron hustled across the almost empty hotel parking lot toward the hotel's side door. He glanced at his watch, knowing it was going to tell him he was late, but still wincing when it gave him the news. At the rear of the lot, men were doing something to half a dozen black panel trucks whose window glass was too tinted to let Jeff see inside. The men were loading what looked like video cameras and electronic gear into the vans, and ordinarily that would have been interesting enough to have brought Jeff over for a look-see, but there was no time now.

Once, through the swinging back doors, Jeff hurried down the service corridor to the staircase, glad he had not changed out of his uniform before going home – it saved time now when he was late getting on station.

He took the stairs two at a time, came up in the kitchens and prepared to receive a salvo of invective from testy Zack Weaver, probably with support from Ignatz Morens: the chef de cuisine routinely referred to waiters as cattle with shit for brains.

But the kitchen was empty, the pots and plates stacked where they had been left shining after the lunch-time clean-up, the grills and ovens cold, the counters bare of *mise-en-place* set-ups and ready-made salads. It was eerily still, the way Jeff had never seen it. Ignatz Morens had always been first to arrive and last to leave – early arriving staff sometimes wondered if the skinny little Swiss slept in one of the cupboards.

There was a subdued murmuring of voices from beyond the double doors that led to the main dining room. Jeff followed the sound, and found the entire staff – not just kitchen workers but maids and laundry crew, ground-skeepers, bellhops and managers – some sitting, but most standing, among the sixty cloth covered tables that filled the spacious room. Jeff didn't have to listen to any of the conversations to know what the subject of discussion was:

the fear could be heard in the melange of clipped phrases, querulous whines and repressed grumbles that hung over the people like an audible fog.

He saw Weaver at the edge of the crowd, one foot up on a chair, smoking a cigarette too fast to be enjoying it. Jeff went over to the catering manager.

"What's going on, Zack?"

Weaver blew a thin stream of smoke from a tiny opening between his tight lips. "Wish I knew. Herb Trainor called the meeting, but I don't think he knows what it's all about. Orders from the Roosevelt."

"New owner?"

Weaver nodded and took another drag. "Yeah."

Jeff looked around. Only one or two faces showed no strain, and those were the youngest, the ones with no kids or mortgages to feed. "You think this is it, the big lay off? They shutting down?"

Weaver shrugged. "I don't know." He thought of his wife and the medical bills. "God, I hope not."

The doors from the lobby burst open and Tag Macklin walked in, trailed by Herb Trainor. The manager looked a little dazed as he followed Macklin to the raised platform opposite the kitchen doors, where they put the head table at formal dinners.

Macklin stood at military at ease, looking out over the heads of the assembled staff. Trainor fidgeted and cleared his throat a couple of times, then wiped his hands on his back pockets.

"People," Trainor said, then cleared his throat yet again, "if I can have your attention, please. This is Mr. Macklin, representing the owners. He, er, has an announcement."

A sound went through the crowd, the collective grunt made by scores of people bracing themselves for bad news. Thel Parmentier, the housekeeper, elbowed one of her maids aside and stepped to the front, lighting a fresh cigarette.

"Hold it, Herb," she said. "If we're getting the ax, I think we oughta hear it from you, not some suit who just got here."

The crowd made another noise, an audible signal that Parmentier had just voiced its collective sentiment.

Trainor was flustered. He wiped his palms again, and coughed. But Macklin stepped forward and gestured the manager into the background with a flick of his hand that did nothing to conceal his contempt.

44

"Ma'am, I appreciate your point of view, I really do," he said in a voice that told them he wouldn't have tossed them a toothpick if they'd all been drowning right before his eyes. Then he paused, just to let them sweat a little, before he said, "No need to be upset. The hotel has been block-booked for a few days by the company I work for. We're having a sales meeting about a new computer product. For security reasons, we want the place to ourselves. We'd like you to go home, take a few days off. This is not a lay-off. You'll all be paid. That is all."

The crowd erupted in a flutter of questions and cross-talk, but Macklin was already halfway to the lobby door, leaving Herb Trainor to carry the load the rest of the way. The manager edged after him, but the employees moved forward to block his path.

"What about it, Herb?" said Thel Parmentier. "That the truth or are they bringing in people to take our jobs, or what?"

Trainor wiped sweat from his upper lip with a handkerchief he took from a jacket pocket. "I don't know. They don't tell me shit."

"We don't like this, Herb," said a voice from somewhere in the crowd and that was followed by a half dozen others, all speaking at once.

"*You* don't like it?" Trainor squeaked. He'd had enough stress, enough sweating blood every time the phone rang with another message from the presidential suite. Everybody here was junior to him, and he could afford to let off a little temper.

He almost stamped his foot, but turned it instead into a step forward. "*I'm* supposed to be running this place, I don't know any more than you do!" He wiped his brow. "Tell you one thing, that's some funny corporation booked in today."

"Whatta you mean?" asked Thel Parmentier from behind a veil of cigarette smoke. "What kinda funny?"

"Nearly fifty people, all men, all look like football players?" Herb's voice was rising in pitch now. "No old guys, no young kids, no women? What kind of computer sales force has no nerds and geeks?"

"So?" said the housekeeper.

"So? So, I dunno. But it's not right. Somebody's not telling us something, and I don't like it."

"Well, whatta you think we should do?"

And there was the problem for Herb Trainor. He could fuss with the best of them, but when it came time to grapple with a problem they hadn't taught in his hotel management course, he blew himself out pretty fast.

"How the hell do I know?" he said. "Just go home and see what happens next."

Jeff left by the back doors, part of a stream of hotel employees heading for their cars in the side lot or proceeding on foot onto Main Street. It felt funny to be out like this; it reminded him of nights after a late game, when players and spectators alike would walk home through the summer evening air. It didn't matter whether they'd won or lost on nights like this one, because their feet always seemed to float just a hair or two above the sidewalk, and the shimmer of streetlights reflecting off the rippling lake water was like heaven glimpsed from the corner of your eye.

"No way on earth I'm leaving this," he said to himself. "No way."

As he crossed the main street toward Bob's Tavern, he heard running footsteps behind him, then felt a hand on his shoulder.

Jerry Steves had been a chunky, blond kid when they'd played ball together. Now he was an even chunkier young man who worked the same waiter's shift as Jeff. His younger brother, Ray, who was getting some part-time hours as a groundskeeper, was right behind Jerry.

"Whattaya say, Jeff? A beer?"

Jeff shook his head. He'd never liked Jerry all that much. "Nother time," he said. "For once I'm gonna tuck my kid into bed."

At a window on the top floor of the west wing, DeVoin and Macklin watched from the presidential suite as the staff departed. Last to go was Herb Trainor's two-year-old Accord, which pulled out from its parking spot next to the back door and left through the gates.

Then Macklin held a portable transceiver to his ear and clicked its send button twice. Almost instantly, the radio squawked three times in reply.

"We're clear," he said.

DeVoin took a deep breath. "Phase two," he ordered.

Macklin depressed the send button again and spoke into the mike. "Two," he said, then repeated the syllable once more.

The phone rang. Macklin picked it up, spoke a couple of words, listened, then hung up. "The hotel's empty," he told the general.

DeVoin crossed the sitting room to where Sandrini sat with the two men in European suits. The scientist had a sheaf of papers in his lap and was indicat-

46

ing a table of figures to the one who spoke English. He, in turn, was speaking in quick bursts of Arabic.

"Gentlemen," DeVoin said, "Phase two is now underway, and the operations center is all set up in the ballroom. Dr. Sandrini, would you take our guests down there and show them the lay-out?"

"Certainly," Sandrini said, rising and shuffling the papers back into his briefcase. "If you'll follow me."

"Major Macklin and I will join you directly," DeVoin said, and waited for the Yemenis to go. Then he and Macklin crossed to the bedroom door that opened off the sitting room, turned a key in the lock, opened the door and stepped through.

The bedroom was plush and deliberately old fashioned, with a four-poster bed and a large French armoire, both in black walnut. The heavy velour drapes blocked both light and sound from entering or leaving. The brass lamps on the mahogany night tables were capped by Tiffany shades with beaded fringes hanging from their stained glass domes. They threw a gentle, civilized light onto the frightened faces of Lou and Adele Meecham, who sat bound and gagged in a pair of straight-backed chairs against one wall, guarded by a thin-nosed mercenary. The man pushed his shoulders away from the wall and came to attention as DeVoin and Macklin entered.

"All secure here?" DeVoin asked.

"Yes, sir." The man looked straight ahead. DeVoin remembered him from a field test he'd overseen in Guatemala in the early eighties. Ex-Foreign Legion. A good all-rounder with better than average weapons skills, although with a liking for pain – other people's pain. Belgian, but not a French-speaking Walloon. A Flemish-speaker. "It's Van Deming, right?"

"Yes, sir."

"What's your assignment?"

"Perimeter security chief, main entrance, sir."

"Well, get to it."

"Yes, sir." The mercenary saluted, but before he left, he gave the Meechams' bonds one last check.

DeVoin positioned himself in front of the bound couple, looked down on them and let out a long sigh. "Well, well," he said, "Mousey Meecham. This is a surprise, Sergeant."

Lou grunted something through the gag. DeVoin motioned to Macklin, who came over and unknotted the cloth. "Hers too," the general said, and Macklin ungagged her.

47

"I'd prefer it if you didn't shout for help," DeVoin said. "There's no one to hear you anyway."

Lou worked his jaw to get the stiffness out. He was afraid – anybody who was helpless in Macklin's hands had every reason to be afraid – but it didn't do to show weakness in front of these men.

"What is this?" he said.

"Just a little operation."

"This is no army operation. That man who just left is not an American soldier."

DeVoin shrugged. "Well, things change."

"Looks like you never did," Lou said.

Macklin drew back his hand as if to strike Lou, but DeVoin stayed him with a gesture, and said, "Not necessary."

He weighed Lou up. "I'm surprised you remember. It was only that one afternoon, such a long time ago."

Lou managed to look him straight in the eyes. "I never forgot you."

"I'm touched."

"Or what you did at Rio Coco."

DeVoin bent down until his lips were level with Lou's ear. "What *we* did, sergeant. I seem to recall you fired the mortar."

"It was *you*. *Your orders*. And your trained weasel here to back you up."

DeVoin stepped back. This time, he let Macklin strike, a backhanded blow that rocked Lou's head sideways. Adele screamed.

But it was no time to show fear. Lou raised his voice. "You wasted a whole village, a friendly village! Old people, little kids!"

"Had to be that way, Lou. If we'd come down on a hostile target, there would have been a firefight, and anything could've happened. We couldn't let classified materiel be exposed to the risk of capture. You can see that, can't you?"

"All I can see are those people dying, choking on that stuff we dropped on 'em. What was it, DeVoin? Some kind of mustard gas?"

The general laughed softly, an old man remembering the simpler enthusiasms of youth. "Something almost as primitive, sergeant. Something stone age." He clapped his hands together and rubbed them. "But now, Major Macklin and I have things to do. We'll see you and your charming wife in the morning."

Adele spoke up. "What are you going to do to us?"

DeVoin smiled. "*We* will do nothing to you, madam, I assure you. It's not convenient to have you running around loose right now, but in the morning

48

you'll be released unharmed. Here...," he positioned a television set so that they could see it, and turned it on, "...just relax."

The channel setting brought in a Eugene station that was airing a rerun of a show in which cameras followed real police into arrests of drunk drivers, wife beaters and other low-impact criminals. The theme song was playing: something about bad boys and what they were going to do when the law came for them.

DeVoin and Macklin left, locking the door behind them. They walked to the elevators, the major shaking his head.

"Problem?" asked DeVoin.

"I think we should just shoot them now."

"Corpses with bullet holes don't fit the scenario. I'm sure they'll find some way to die, once we turn them loose."

The elevator arrived, and the two men went down.

In the main ballroom, the operations center was up and running. The video screens were live, and technicians were seated at the control panels, running checks. Their supervisor, a bullet-headed ex-SAS sergeant major named Leith, who spoke with the harsh throaty vowels of back-street Belfast, stood behind them directing the run-throughs.

There were three rows of screens, with four to a row. Leith pointed to the last one on the third row – labeled C-6 – and said, "Try that one again."

The tech keyed a mike that snaked up from the panel of switches before him and said, "Unit Four, Unit Four, run your last sequence again."

The video screen showed a perimeter security man in the hotel's side parking lot. The image was blurry at first, then got clearer when the camera pulled back for a long shot; now it zoomed in for a tight close-up on the man's face.

"That's all right then," said the supervisor. "Tell him to line up on the street."

The technician spoke into the mike, and the camera image swung left in a tracking blur, then zeroed in on Bob's Tavern. The operator adjusted the lens slightly, and the bar's window filled the screen. Leith could see right into the room, to the tables where some of the hotel staff were drinking beer.

"Good," he said. "Now the sound."

The tech spoke into the mike. "Video checks, Unit Four. Give me a sound test."

Outside, on the black van with tinted windows that supported Unit Four's camera, the concave dish of a parabolic microphone rotated on its gimbals until it pointed at the tavern. In the hotel ballroom, the sound of country music and a hubbub of chatter came through the speakers, the vibrations picked up from the barroom window.

"Tell him he's five by five," said the supervisor.

The technician did so, and saw the image on the screen tremble then shift as the black van started up and headed for its predetermined position. The tech moved a switch on his console. "Unit Five, Unit Five," he said. "Video check now."

Nearby at the table that held Sandrini's computer system, the scientist continued his briefing of the two Yemenis. He had already explained how Paroxysm worked on four areas of the human brain. Three were the hypothalamus, the septum and the amygdala, all located low in the central brain. These were the "old-brain" structures which, when properly stimulated, could provoke any animal to unrestrained rage and aggression. Humans, however, had a kind of "fail-safe" neural mechanism: the frontal lobes, part of the highly developed "new brain" that imposed a damping effect on surges of rage, allowing them to be channeled and focused. Paroxysm spurred the rage-generating structures of the lower brain into overdrive, while it isolated the frontal lobes that could have controlled or moderated the resulting aggression. As Sandrini explained it, it was as if the subject's consciousness became a helpless Dr. Jekyll who could only watch as Mr. Hyde did his worst. Hafiz's aide had to make a lengthy explanation of the literary reference.

Now Sandrini was moving on to a discussion of how Prescott Springs had been "prepared" for the demonstration. He touched a key and the computer monitor displayed a bar graph that looked like a row of skinny office towers rising from left to right, each succeeding rectangle a few stories higher than the one before.

"The aim," the scientist said, "was to create stress levels similar to those affecting troops preparing for battle. First, we closed the town's other major source of employment – a spring water bottling plant – then we cut back here at the hotel. Next we put the remaining employees on part-time and swing-shift schedules, and floated rumors about a total shutdown, so that even those who still had jobs were afraid they could be thrown out of work at any moment."

He tapped the last bar on the graph. "The result is as you see: most people in Prescott Springs are worried sick about their future. The general stress level in a town like this ought to be in the twentieth percentile; Prescott Springs is reading well above the eightieth and would probably keep on climbing, if we let it."

DeVoin and Macklin entered and crossed the ballroom floor to join the group around Sandrini's computer. The older Yemeni was saying something to his aide, and the younger man now turned and addressed his question to the general. "Mr. Hafiz reminds you that these are not trained soldiers. They are civilians caught unawares."

DeVoin smiled. "Not to worry, Mr. Hafiz. We'll give you a good show, and you can judge from what you see."

DeVoin had a salesman's instincts – without them, he'd never have carved a career for himself in the world of "black" programs that the Pentagon kept away from the prying eyes in Congress. Sometimes you bullshitted the decision-makers; sometimes you let results speak for themselves. Now was a time for the latter strategy.

But Sandrini was no salesman; he just loved to lecture. "Well, yeah, it would be better to test under actual battlefield conditions," he said, jumping in after DeVoin's last word, "but then we'd be looking at an aerosol application. That would take a considerably greater quantity of the chemical than we were able to... abstract from the research facility. The results, however, would have a greater confidence level."

DeVoin coughed. "I don't think we need to go into all the technicalities at this stage, Doctor," he said, and even Sandrini heard the undertone that said *shut up*. The general gestured the Yemenis toward the bank of video screens. "Gentlemen, if you'd care to inspect the surveillance system."

But Hafiz shot his aide a glance. The young man said, "Mr. Hafiz would like to hear more about the confidence levels."

DeVoin could have torn Sandrini's head from his body, but his smile was suave. "Of course," he said. "Please continue, doctor."

The scientist knew he had screwed up. But having opened the door, he now had no choice but to enter the room DeVoin would have preferred the Yemenis to pass by. Because, if there was one area in this operation that might go a little hinky, where events might get out of control, it was the matter of the delivery system. The chief salesman knew it, and now the customers were about to find out too.

"Paroxysm," Sandrini said, "was designed to be delivered as an aerosol. You could either spray it from an aircraft, like crop-dusting, or shoot it at the enemy in modified artillery shells. But it would take a large quantity to affect a population spread out over the area of Prescott Springs. Because of the limited supply available to us for this test, it was thought best to expose the subjects to the agent by means of the water supply."

He looked at the general, but DeVoin's attention was apparently captivated by the video screens. Hafiz nudged his aide.

"And so...?" the young man coaxed.

Sandrini shrugged. "So, we're dealing with a mucho delicate organophosphate molecule, designed to break down quickly. It has to be short-lived, because you would want friendly troops to be able to occupy the ground soon after an application, mop up, and control the battlefield."

When the younger Yemeni had translated all this, the older man made a curt hand gesture to Sandrini. "Continue," said the aide.

"Well, there are things in the lake water – contaminants, minerals – and chlorine in the distribution system, so there's a risk – a *very slight* risk – of chemical mutation. It's just possible that what the test subjects receive may not be exactly, one hundred per cent, the same chemical we put into the water."

This time, Hafiz did not wait for the translation. In a heavily accented English, he said, "Doctor, my organization has paid several million dollars for this demonstration. Now you are telling me it *may not work?*"

DeVoin summoned up his smoothest tone. "There's no chance of that, Mr. Hafiz. No question of it. Dr. Sandrini is just splitting hairs. You know what these scientists are like." He put his hand on Sandrini's shoulder. "Isn't that right, doctor?"

The promise behind DeVoin's eyes made Sandrini's testicles creep up, searching for safety in his body cavity. "Oh, of course, General." He nodded very fast, the several long strands of hair that he liked to comb over his bald spot coming loose and falling to his shoulder. To the Yemenis, he said, "I'm sure there won't be time for the material to break down to the point of its becoming ineffective. It's just that it may take a little longer to reach the trigger centers in the central nervous system, depending on body weight." He nodded some more. "But it will definitely work. I stake my reputation on that."

"You certainly have," DeVoin said. "And now, gentlemen, let me show you our surveillance system." He led them toward the video screens. At the general's approach, the Belfast man brought his heels together smartly and said, "*Shun!*" The technicians came to attention.

DeVoin scarcely appeared to notice. "As you were," he said.

Hafiz murmured something to his aide. The young man said, "Mr. Hafiz commends you on the quality of your troops."

DeVoin inclined his head and smiled. "Thank you, sir. They are the finest soldiers money can buy."

Hafiz smiled back. "*Our* money," he said.

"Yes, sir." He turned to the supervisor. "I believe we're ready for Phase Three?"

"We are, sir."

DeVoin looked at Macklin. "Let's get on with it."

Macklin stepped to the communications center, keyed a switch, and put his mouth to the microphone. "Homestead to Pinochle," he said.

A speaker on the console hissed and then the reply came, "Pinochle."

Macklin gave the order. "Pinochle, you are go, repeat, you are go."

"Roger, Homestead," said the voice from the speaker. "Out."

There was silence. Macklin switched off the mike and turned to DeVoin. "Phase Three, General."

# 6

The black van had been parked since mid-afternoon in the tumbled-down ruin of a hay barn five miles from the bridge into Prescott Springs. The three men DeVoin had assigned to this part of the operation had not passed the day lounging around or playing cards. Two had kept watch at either end of the old building, one scanning the road that ran by the front of the barn at a distance of about two hundred feet, the other keeping an eye on the open crop land behind. Neither had seen anything worth reporting. The third man had stayed close to the van's radio.

Now the two watchers opened wide the barn's doors on creaking hinges, while the third man climbed behind the wheel and started the engine. The two men on foot walked out to the road and scanned it for traffic. There was nothing, and one signaled the driver to come out.

The van bumped along the short rutted track to the road, and the two sentries climbed in. The vehicle nosed onto the blacktop and turned toward Prescott Springs. The driver brought the speed indicator up to a point a few miles per hour below the speed limit and drove sedately toward town.

The van's passage was without incident until it was two miles out from bridge. Then the driver saw a distant pair of headlights appear in his sideview mirror. "Company," he said.

The others craned to look through the van's heavily tinted rear windows. "Coming up fast," said one of them, with the flattened vowels and slight nasal tone of central Canada.

The third man opened a locker bolted to the floor of the van and extracted an unloaded M-16 assault rifle.

"Here you go," he said in an accent that was pure back-road South Carolina. He handed the weapon to the Canadian and brought out another for himself, then reached back in for two full magazines of ammunition.

The driver heard the snicks and clicks of the weapons being readied, but kept his eyes moving between the road and the vehicle that was closing the distance between them. He calculated that he was now a little more than a mile from the bridge – say a minute-and-a-half – and relaxed. Whoever was on his tail would be Wexler's problem.

"Put 'em away," he told the men in the back. "We're covered."

When the van reached the flashing lights and road flares that marked the blocked bridge, the driver slowed long enough to let the bridge squad leader identify him, then wove through the barriers and followed the road into town. Before the van cleared the bridge, Wexler had already turned his attention toward the vehicle coming up behind.

The car was a late model Range Rover, with all the options, driven by a sharp faced man who didn't balk at paying three figures for a pair of shoes and four for a suit. His name was Tresider. He made an easy $300,000 a year selling moderately valuable tax planning advice to people who'd recently made more money than they'd ever known what to do with – lottery winners, heirs of recently dead doting aunts, and the like. He was not used to having low-echelon civil servants block his smooth and enjoyable ride through life.

"Do you live in Prescott Springs?" asked the blond man in the highways department reflector vest.

"What business is that of yours?" Tresider responded.

The man patiently repeated the question.

"I'm visiting," the tax planner snapped back. "A friend has a cabin on the lake and he's letting me use it for a few days."

Then the man offered some nonsense about cracks in pylons, and being stuck in town. Tresider simply began talking over the squad leader's words, a technique he'd learned in dealing with bureaucrats. "That's not my concern," he said. "I intend to be here all weekend anyway. Now move that barrier and let me through."

"Can't do that, sir," was the response. "My orders are to let only local residents cross, all others to be turned back.

Tresider couldn't believe it. "You let that car ahead of me go across," he said.

The highways man said nothing.

It had been a long time since the tax planner had not got something he wanted, and he did not feel like breaking the pattern now. "We'll see about this," he said, and opened a briefcase that lay on the passenger seat. Out of it he took a satellite phone, and fixed the blond man with a meaningful look. "What's your name?" he said.

Without waiting for an answer he began to punch in the private number of a senior state official who confidentially – and quite illegally – passed Tresider the names and phone numbers of lottery winners.

Satellite phones had their own separate heading in Wexler's orders. No one with such a phone was to be allowed to cross the bridge under any circumstances, and he could extrapolate from that fact that if he let the man in the Range Rover complete his call there was a definite potential for compromising the mission.

The lieutenant reached into the car and wrested the phone from the man's hand while he was still dialing.

"How dare..." Tresider began, but stopped abruptly when Wexler's other hand entered the vehicle holding a small black automatic pistol.

"Get out of the car, sir," Wexler said.

Tresider did. Wexler gestured toward the carry-all with highways department marking. "This way, sir."

It was the politeness that did it, Wexler knew; it kept them off-balance and docile, didn't panic them the way shouted orders and insults might have.

They walked toward the carry-all. "Look, whatever this is, there's no need..." Tresider said.

"Stop here, please, sir." They had reached the open doors at the rear of the vehicle. Wexler looked up and down the road, saw nothing. "Place your hands on the top of the vehicle and put your head back," he said.

Tresider did as he was told. "Look," he started again, but never finished, because Wexler had already returned the automatic to its holster under his shirt, and had drawn from his back pocket a loop of thin wire strung between two pieces of polished hardwood. He dropped the wire over the tax planner's head, crossed his wrists to tighten it around the man's neck, and simultaneously brought up his knee into the small of the victim's back. He yanked back smartly and broke Tresider's spine even as the sudden shut-off of oxygen to the brain brought unconsciousness.

The body slumped to its knees, the arms and head coming to rest on the floor of the truck. Wexler told two men to put the corpse in the back of the Land Rover and cover it with a plastic sheet from the carry-all. They would

56

drive it toward town and park it off the road near the bottling plant. As the vehicle pulled away, he took out his walkie-talkie and said, "Homestead, this is Blueberry."

The radio crackled, and Macklin's voice came back. "Homestead. What's your report, Blueberry?"

"Confirm Pinochle," Wexler said. "Also, we've had a flat."

"Copy that, Blueberry," Macklin radioed back. "Is the flat fixed?"

"All fixed," the lieutenant said.

"Copy fixed. Homestead out."

The black van with the three men in it eased around the curve where Bridge Road turned into Prescott Avenue and entered the hotel grounds. Across the street, in Bob's Tavern, Frank Tedesco and Joe B. sat by a window seat, each nursing a draft beer. Frank saw the van go through the hotel gates.

"There's that black van again," he said.

"So what?" Joe B. said.

"Yeah," Frank agreed. "So what?"

In the operations center, Macklin and DeVoin watched two of the video screens that showed the van entering the hotel grounds.

Outside, perimeter security men, discreetly scattered around the grounds, tracked its progress across the main parking lot on the west side of the hotel. It went out by the rear gate onto a narrow service road that ran along the lakeshore to a small cinder-block building behind a chain-link fence. The van's headlights illuminated a sign on the gate. It read: *RESERVOIR INTAKE – NO SWIMMING – NO BOATING – NO DUMPING – NO TRESPASSING – BY ORDER.*

The van pulled up and the driver cut its lights, sending the sign into darkness, but he kept its engine idling. The vehicle's side door opened and the Canadian and the South Carolinian got out. The former reached back into the vehicle and dragged a bulky bundle out of the van. He pulled hard on a ripcord, and the bundle began to hiss and move, transforming itself quickly into a small rubber boat.

While the Canadian readied the inflatable, the South Carolinian took out a compact electric pump and a hose, which he connected together. He handed

57

a power cord through the window to the driver, who plugged it into the van's dashboard cigarette lighter. The South Carolinian then brought a second hose, which he ran into the lake.

The driver, after plugging in the pump's power cord, slid from his seat into the rear of the vehicle, opened a locker, and removed a one-piece anti-chemical-warfare suit. He climbed out of the van and put the suit on, then fitted the attached hood, with its plastic face mask and self-contained breathing apparatus, over his head. The South Carolinian came over and checked the suit's seals, making sure the driver was fully insulated from the world.

When they had run through all the checks and the driver was sure he could breathe, he reached again into the back of the van and brought out a locked metal container.

The South Carolinian knelt by the box, then reached into his shirt and fished out a key suspended from a chain around his neck. He pulled the chain over his head and used the key to open the box. Inside, nestled in a custom-fitted womb of plastic foam, was a black metal object, cylindrical in shape and rounded on both ends.

The South Carolinian stepped back, and the man in the airtight suit reached down and took up the canister. He held it gingerly, with both hands, as he walked the few steps to where the lake rippled against the stony shore.

The Canadian had the inflatable in the water, and had assembled the two plastic oars. He stood knee-deep in the wavelets, holding the little craft steady while the driver placed the canister in the stern, then carefully followed it into the boat. The Canadian fitted the oars into the plastic tholes that were glued to the gunwales, and the driver took them and began rowing away from shore. One end of a nylon rope was tied to a plastic cleat set into the boat's stern, and the Canadian held the rest of it looped in his hand; he played out line as the boat pulled away.

Still holding the rope, the Canadian moved to a particular point on the beach, down near the water's edge. The South Carolinian moved inland thirty feet or so, almost up to the driftwood tossed on shore by winter storms. Both men looked for and found the stones marked with splotches of paint that would have passed for bird droppings if anyone had even thought to look at them. They had been precisely placed by the "survey crew" DeVoin had sent in three days previously, causing Herb Trainor yet another panic because it was accompanied by rumors that the hotel was to be torn down and replaced with time-sharing condos for Japanese tourists.

The man in the boat continued to row offshore, angling over until the Canadian and the South Carolinian were in a straight line astern, and he could only see the former who was playing out the line, which floated on the water. He continued to row until the line was fully extended and the man at the water's edge raised a hand.

The man in the boat shipped oars and rechecked his orientation once more: with the two men on shore lined up and the measured rope at its full extension, he was now directly over the mesh-protected intake pipe for Prescott Spring's municipal water supply. He reached for the canister, held it upright and firmly twisted one end.

The black metal turned in his hand and came free, revealing a rubber stopper that sealed the bottle's neck.

The man held the canister over the side, still upright and as far away from the boat as he could, and gently removed the stopper. Even though he knew his air came from a self-contained supply, he now stopped breathing. He dipped the plug in the lake water to rinse it; then, holding the bottle's mouth as close to the water's surface as he could, he allowed the thick, glutinous liquid inside to pour into the lake. It came achingly slowly, like molasses, and when it was all out, the man dipped the container into the water and emptied it again several times to wash the bottle clean. Only now did he resume breathing. Then he put the stopper back in, replaced the screw-on cap, and leaned over the side, first washing the canister, which he stowed away in the boat, then scrubbing his gloved hands thoroughly. At last, he signaled the men on shore to pull him in.

As soon as the boatman had begun pouring the chemical into the lake, the South Carolinian had left his position and returned to the van. There he put on a military issue gas mask, and brought another to the Canadian. He took the line and continued to haul in the little boat while the Canadian snugged the rubber and plastic form over his face and checked that he could breathe. Then he handed back the line and went to switch on the pump he had assembled earlier.

The machine hummed, making no more noise than a microwave oven, sucking in lake water and sending it rushing out across the stony shore. The boat now reached shore and the man in the ACW suit stepped out into the shallows and stood there while the South Carolinian lifted the gushing hose and systematically sprayed him from head to waterline, paying particular attention to his chest, belly, arms and hands.

When the man was thoroughly hosed, the South Carolinian turned his attention to the boat itself, sluicing out all its inner surfaces and washing down the oars while the boatman held it lengthwise above the water. Satisfied that they had washed away any contamination from the bottle's contents, the men now prepared to leave.

59

The Canadian brought an oversize trash bag into which went the ACW suit, the boat – they had slashed it with a knife for quick deflation – the rope and the bottle and its box. The pump and hoses were stowed in a locker inside the van, and the bag was thrown on top. The men climbed back into the still running vehicle.

As he spun the wheel to turn the van back toward the hotel, the driver picked up the portable radio, pressed the button and said, "Homestead, Pinochle."

Macklin's voice crackled from the speaker. "Homestead."

"Bucket's in the well," the driver said. "Repeat, the bucket's in the well."

"Copy your bucket," Macklin said. "Out."

In the operations center, Macklin checked his watch. It was just under twelve minutes since he had signaled the van to leave its hiding place in the ruined barn. "That's thirty seconds under nominal," he said.

The driver brought van slowly back to the hotel and parked in the rear lot. The three men got out, entered the building through its back doors, and reported to their secondary assignments.

Herb Trainor knew a lot of things that the new owner didn't. Like the fact that the solenoid switch on the hotel's oil-fired heating system had a tendency to act up in damp weather. Or that the circuit breaker for the south-side second floor outlets would trip if anybody plugged in a vacuum cleaner while the guests had all the lamps and televisions on.

Trainor also knew that there was an unobtrusive way to get into the hotel even when an overbearing owner thought it was shut up tight as a turtle's asshole. And ten minutes after he drove away in his Accord, the manager was making his way back in.

The original heating system at the Prescott Springs Hotel had been a steam boiler that piped hot vapor to radiators in the guest and common rooms. Before the age of cheap oil, the boiler had been fueled by coal.

Even high-grade anthracite is a messy commodity that generates black dust at every stage of its extraction, transportation and storage. The builders of the hotel had not wanted their guests to be inconvenienced by the necessary movement of fuel into the building. Horse-drawn drays laden with hundredweight sacks of coal would never clatter into their resort's yard.

Instead, they constructed a two hundred yard long tunnel from the hotel to a siding of the rail spur that used to lead into the valley from Evans. In the tunnel they installed a set of tracks similar to those found in the diggings where the coal originated. Fuel was off-loaded from a gondola car and shoveled into mine carts, which were pushed and pulled directly to the hotel's basement coal bins by men's muscles.

In the 1950s, when the industrialized world abruptly ended two centuries of coal dependence and switched innocently to the enticements of diesel and bunker oil, the tunnel was closed at both ends. In the 1990s, it was reopened by Herb Trainor, who sometimes found it useful to be able to return to the hotel and observe his underlings surreptitiously, after they had all seen him drive away.

Now the manager trudged along the century-old tracks, following the cone of light made by the flashlight in his hand. He kept to the center, because the walls were still thick with coal dust. At the hotel end of the tunnel, he came to a pair of wooden double doors and unlocked them with a big old skeleton key.

The wooden frames of the coal bins had been long since removed, and the big underground room had become a storeroom for items that had gone completely out of fashion and never come back in. It was now mainly filled with the cast-iron lawn furniture and animal statuary that had been the height of good taste in the late nineteenth century.

Herb Trainor locked the tunnel doors behind him, and lit his way by flashlight along a corridor between heaps of black metal. At the end he unlocked another door that admitted him to the narrow staircase that connected with every floor of the hotel. He began to climb.

At the first level up, he paused. At this point, the staircase was interrupted by a landing in an alcove which opened onto the service corridor near the side door of the hotel. There were no doors on the alcove, and anyone passing through it to mount further up the staircase would be in full view of anyone in the corridor.

The manager remained still for several seconds, listening for a voice or footstep that would tell him the corridor was occupied. But he heard only the voices of men in the parking lot outside, and decided it was safe. He quickly ascended to the first-floor kitchen.

Here there was a door between him and anyone who might see him. Using his master key, he quietly locked it, then did the same on the second floor, and the third. On the fourth floor, Trainor stopped to catch his breath before opening the door that led into the west wing of the hotel. When his heart had settled to its usual fluttery rhythm, he inched the door open a crack and peeked through.

The corridor was empty. The manager stepped out, locked the door to the service stairs behind him, and tiptoed to the nearest room. He had made sure this room was not assigned to any of the new owner's guests, reserving it for his own use.

He let himself in, then silently locked the door. He made sure the curtains were drawn before he lit a small table lamp. The sandwiches, fruit and wine he had brought up earlier were where he had left them.

Herb Trainor sat in the room's most comfortable chair and ate his supper. When he was finished, he opened the curtains a finger's breadth and watched the activity in the parking lot.

What he saw made no particular sense. It was just a lot of men scurrying around some vans. He closed the curtains tightly again and stretched out on the soft bed. He had brought a paperback, the latest in a series about a post-apocalyptic America. It was a tale of a desperate, violent land, where only the fastest and deadliest could survive.

He enjoyed the book, and finished it before he turned out the lamp. He undressed and got into bed, pulling the fresh sheets up to his softly rounded chin. Tomorrow, he would haunt the service stairs, keeping his eyes and ears open for the inevitable moment when something would go wrong – then he would appear as if from nowhere, solve the problem, and show his new employers just what kind of man they had in Herb Trainor.

The last bars of *The Green Leaves of Summer* swelled to a crescendo as the woman on the mule rode out of the Alamo, a swaddled baby held tightly in her arms. Jeff depressed buttons on the DVD player's clicker and the disk popped out of the machine.

"Good flick," he said.

"They all died," said Sharon. "Stupid waste."

"It's just a movie, mom," said Trevor.

"But it's based on real life," his father said. "You'll learn about it in school." He turned to Sharon. "Sure they died, but they died for something."

"And they left women to bring up kids without fathers; what's the good in that?"

Trevor saw his dad look up at the ceiling and shake his head. He knew the gesture always got under his mom's skin, and he heard the sharper tone in her voice when she said, "And all this about that movie being based on real life is pretty iffy. I read somewhere about what really happened at the Alamo. They didn't all die heroically on the ramparts or whatever you call them."

"What are you talking about? How do you know how they died when there were no survivors?"

"There were *lots* of survivors," she said. "Thousands of Mexican soldiers. And they told about how Davy Crockett and some of the others tried to get away by running into the reeds down by the river. But they got captured and that general ordered his men to shoot them and stab them with bayonets."

Trevor saw a look of scornful disbelief on his dad's face. "Oh, where'd you hear all this?"

Mom said, "I don't know, a magazine or somewhere."

Dad sneered. "That's bull. I don't believe it. We would've heard about it in school."

The boy was watching his parents building up to a fight over nothing. They were doing it more and more lately, starting with any little thing and making it get bigger and bigger, until they were yelling at each other about stuff that had happened years ago, even before he was born.

"You guys," he said, "it's only a movie."

Sharon looked at her son, sitting between them on the sagging couch in his camouflage-pattern pajamas, the ones she'd got him when he'd asked for the real thing. She had been about to say something that would have notched the squabble up another degree, but when she saw the expression on Trevor's face – like a brave little kid trying to stop a conflagration by tossing a toy bucket full of sand on it – she bit back the hard words. "You're right," she said. "It's only a movie."

She raised her eyes to Jeff's, and made that little mouth move that said, *I don't want to fight.* He looked sheepish in return, and changed the subject.

"Whatever happened to that coonskin cap I got you?" he asked the boy. He'd found it in a second-hand store in Evans, a little relic of the Crockett craze of the 1950s.

"I dunno. It's somewhere."

"I was thinking, I got tomorrow off, maybe we should go out in the woods. I could borrow Arnie's rifle, we could look for a deer. A little venison in the freezer wouldn't hurt."

Trevor's eyes danced. "I bet I could find a deer," he said. "Bet I could get real close."

"Well, first I'd have to teach you how to shoot." He turned to Sharon. "Twelve's plenty old enough for that."

She made a mom face, but said nothing.

"All right!" said the boy. Then a change came into his eyes. "Does it hurt a lot, for the deer?"

"It's gotta hurt," said his father. "But if you're a good hunter, you hit 'em in the right place, the deer's dead almost before it feels the pain. The shock kills them – *wham!* – just like that. It's not nice, but sometimes you have to do it."

Trevor thought about it. "Okay," he said.

"Okay," said Jeff. "So now you better get some sleep, early day tomorrow. Give your mom a hug."

The boy put his arms around Sharon's neck, and it was as sweet a moment as a mother gets between the time they get on their feet and the day they walk out the front door to make their own place in the world. She kissed his cheek. "G'night," she said.

"Night, mom."

He went upstairs and brushed his teeth, leaving his parents on the couch. Jeff slid over to Sharon, laid his head against hers. "Sorry," he said.

"Yeah," she answered.

"I don't know what it is. Anything sets us off."

"It's this town. Everybody's scared, and that makes them mad, but there's nobody to really blame, so we take it out on each other."

"It's lousy," he said, and kissed her above the eyebrow.

She snuggled into him, and he put his arm around her shoulders. "This swing shift business, you're not here when the news is on. Sometimes I watch it while Jeff's eating dinner. It's like this all over the country – people looking to work out their fears by blaming some other guy, some other group. When did we get like this?"

"I don't know," he said, and slipped his hand from her shoulder to her breast. "But let's don't let it get into us, whattaya say?"

She rubbed against him. The mad had not gone that far away, but she could let it fade into the distance if she concentrated on what his fingers were doing through her sweater and bra. She decided to concentrate.

She felt her nipple stiffen under the layers of fabric. "We haven't done it twice in one day for quite a while," he said.

"Well, maybe some of us are getting old," she said and ran her hand up his inner thigh. "Whoops, not that old, I guess," she amended, and gently squeezed the part that was rapidly hardening.

64

"Maybe you'd better tuck Trevor in," he said. "Don't want him developing any complexes."

She laughed and got up, and crossed to the door, where she framed herself deliberately, shoulder and hip languidly rubbing against the old wood. "Stay right there," she said. "I'll be back."

"The old couch?" he laughed.

"Sure. We'll pretend we're teenagers again."

"Okay, but I'm not taking time to show you how everything works."

"Hey, taking time was never your problem," she said and went upstairs.

Five minutes later, he heard her descend again, but instead of entering the living room she went down the hall to the kitchen. He heard her voice in a brief conversation, then she came into the living room and shut the door.

"Now where were we?" she said. She grasped the hem of her sweater, pulled it over her head.

"Did you call somebody?"

"The doctor. I think Trevor's coming down with a bug or something."

"He sounds okay to me. He really wants to go out in the woods tomorrow."

"I want the doctor to look at him first," she said. "He sounds kind of chesty."

"Speaking of chesty," he said, as she unhooked her bra and slid the straps down her arms. She smiled and unzipped her jeans, giving her hips a little flip.

"Dr. Macreedy said he'd come over in the morning," she said, sliding the jeans down her thighs.

He knew it was the wrong thing to say even as it came out of his mouth, a perfectly dumb thing to say when he was sitting there with his penis hard as old-growth wood and his pretty young wife practically naked in front of him, her breasts swinging full and soft, only inches from his face. "Huh, try get some city doctor on a house call," he said.

She stopped, the waistband of her jeans down to her knees, about to raise one leg and free it from the denim. She looked at him through a falling wave of shining auburn.

"You want to fight or fuck?" she asked, sweetly.

There was no question about it. He reached up and ran a finger down the slope of her breast to the nipple. "Good call," she said.

# 7

Frank and Joe B. still sat at their window table at Bob's Tavern, looking out across the empty main street to where the lake rippled at the shore. Each had again managed to make four beers last all the way through an evening and into midnight. The unexpected rush of released staff from the hotel had suddenly filled the place just after five, then one by one the cooks and waiters and bartenders had faded to homes and families. The regulars had come and gone, and now the two jobless men twirled the last swallows of lukewarm beer in the bottom of their glasses, and watched Bob Preiss, the bar's morose owner, as he worked his way around the tables with a room service cart that had long ago been permanently borrowed from the hotel.

Preiss collected empty glassware and bottles, lining them up in a shallow plastic basket on the cart's top, which also held a plastic pail into which he dumped the contents of ashtrays. The gray ash was just about the same color as the tavern keeper's hair, face and apron. He picked up a half-filled bowl of nuts in which some drunk had stubbed out a cigar, then put it back down on the table.

"Screw this," he said. "I'll do it in the morning." He turned to the two at the window. "Time you guys went home."

Frank and Joe B. drained their glasses and rose slowly. Joe B. gestured at the mess on the tables. "Need any help with this, Bob?"

Preiss looked around the room. Whatever fun there may once have been in owning a neighborhood tavern was long gone, Joe B. thought. Cleaning up wouldn't be any more enjoyable just for being left until morning, and the hotel staff had made it a good night.

"Okay," he said. "You wanna come in early, maybe I can give you a couple hours."

"What time you figure?" Frank asked.

"Say eight?"

"That case," said Joe B., "how bout you let us sack out in the back? Make sure we're not late."

Preiss made a noncommittal grunt, the kind of all purpose noise any good bartender learns early on. "You a little worried about the reception at home?"

Joe B. tugged his shapeless nose. "My Marie, she's got a temper sometimes."

"Mine too," said Frank.

The tavern owner shrugged. "What the hell. I keep a cot back there, some blankets. You won't touch the stock?"

Joe B. said, "Bob, how long you known us?"

"Yeah, okay. But get on back there now. I got to kill the lights and get outta here. You guys aren't the only ones get your asses ripped, you're late making it home."

In the bedroom of the presidential suite, Lou Meecham tugged again at his bonds, but the knots had been tied by an expert. His legs and shoulders ached from forced immobility, but he would have accepted double the pain if it could have bought him release from the sensation of being helpless when the woman he loved was in danger.

Impotent rage flashed through him for the umpteenth time since Macklin had led them captive into this room, but again he fought it down, because he knew it made it worse on his wife, having to see him powerless to aid her. He turned to her, but she had let her chin slump to her chest. Her eyes were closed, her breathing slow and regular.

Adele was wide awake. She had seen how hard it was on her husband to be unable to save them from this nightmare, and had lowered her head and composed herself as if in sleep. She was terrified of what these men would do to them, regardless of the general's glib promise to release them in the morning. But what good would be served by letting her fear push her husband toward a stroke or a heart attack? She was not a particularly brave woman, and by no means a powerful one, but in an emergency she would do what she could – and if all she could do was sit still and pretend to sleep, then that's what she'd do.

The tv station had gone off-air. The screen showed only a tuning pattern of colored bars, with a white-on-black digital clock in the lower right corner. The hypnotic high-pitched whine of its audio signal filled the room. Adele concentrated on the in and out of her breathing.

Lou closed his eyes. The television's sound throbbed in his brain like a sonic excavating tool, digging into the strata of his life, revealing images of the past. There were things there he didn't want to look at again, things he had pushed down deep and covered up with layers of daily routines and habits, so that he would never again have to think about what he'd been, what he'd done, and what he *hadn't* done.

But now the layers peeled away, and he was back there again. He saw the huts along the Rio Coco, the way it was all those years ago. He was in the long grass on the hill above the village. He saw the farmers coming in from the bean fields, heard the voices of old women and kids among the huts. The faintest odor of smoke from cooking fires mingled with the smell of burro dung and his own nervous sweat as he'd done what DeVoin and Macklin ordered.

There had been no mission briefing. The thing had smelled bad from the start. Lou had sensed that this one was hinky from the moment the Old Man had called him to the command tent and told him he was going out on a special assignment. The major had indicated the two officers who had flown in from Tegucigalpa on the unmarked Chinook fifteen minutes before.

"You'll be out a couple hours," he said. "All you got to do is whatever they tell you, and keep your mouth shut."

He'd known the Old Man long enough to ask, "Why us?"

And the major had known the sergeant long enough to level with him. He indicated DeVoin, and said, "Because that officer has the power to fly in here, jerk me around and make me hand over my best men, and there's fuck all I can do about it." The Old Man spat. "Spooks."

"They didn't tell you what it's about?"

"They didn't tell me jack shit," the officer said. "If it's any help, they told me they wanted the sergeant with the best rep for leading back the same number of grunts he led out. That's you."

It was why they called him Mouse Meecham. Because he was small and quiet and careful, all traits that paid off in the jungle, for him and for the men who relied on his skills. Others might lead their men into Sandinista ambushes or down trails where the bad guys had rigged wires that would trip bouncing betty mines – not Sergeant Meecham. He looked after the kids the army gave him until he could hand them back to their moms and girlfriends, still in one piece.

Lou's eight-man squad had been stood down for a rest after a week of daily recons along the Rio Coco, on the Nicaraguan-Honduran border, looking for infiltration by Miskitos who'd sided with the Sandinistas. They'd turned up nothing. The villages up and down the sluggish brown river were out of the war for now, the farmers able to go about their ancient occupation without fear that someone would come out of the trees to turn their already hard lives into hell on earth.

But that was before DeVoin and Macklin pored over a map, searching for a quiet, out-of-the-way backwater, where they could go out in the field and not have to worry about being killed by Cuban-trained soldiers who had no love for gringos.

Lou Meecham rounded up his squad, made sure they were equipped for a short trip into relatively friendly country, and led them to the helicopter. DeVoin looked them over. "You're familiar with the 81-millimeter mortar?" he asked.

"Yes, sir," said Lou. It was a standard infantry weapon.

"Good enough. Get the men aboard."

The copter's blades began turning as the troops climbed in and took seats on the benches facing fore and aft. On the deck between them were a mortar and two cases of mortar bombs, each holding four rounds. The olive green lids had the word *SECRET* stenciled on them and were dogged down by bands of sheet metal, fastened by seals.

The chopper took them to a landing zone near the base of a grass-covered hill. DeVoin had Lou's men unload the mortar and ammo cases. The bird flew away the moment they were clear of the rotors.

The colonel ordered the squad to follow him and Macklin up the hill. He stopped them just short of the crest of the hill and told them to put down their burdens. Then DeVoin sent all the men but Lou to go halfway back down the hill and wait. He instructed the sergeant to set up the 81, and while Lou was doing that DeVoin and Macklin went uphill to scan the far side of the rise.

The sergeant could have told them what they'd see: on the other side of the hill was a village of some two dozen families, maybe a couple of hundred

Miskito peasants, plus an unknown number of ducks, geese and donkeys. The squad had been here less than thirty hours before. The people were friendly, especially the little kids, and there were no Sandinistas in the neighborhood.

DeVoin and Macklin came back from the look-see to find the squad gone and Lou waiting by the mortar. He had positioned it to fire at the open grassland back beyond the empty LZ where the chopper had dropped them.

The sergeant thought he had this one figured out. It would be a a test fire of somebody's – almost undoubtedly DeVoin's – pet project. The special rounds would contain plastic flechettes or coils of steel wire that had been half-snipped through every quarter inch or so, perhaps arranged in a new pattern that would give a better dispersal of flying death within the kill radius.

Every army had its inveterate tinkerers, people who liked to mess around with ordnance, trying to build a better mousetrap. DeVoin must be one of that fraternity, and he would want to try out his particular brainstorm somewhere out of the way, in case it fizzled and exposed his reputation to shame and ridicule.

The two officers came down the slope to where he had set up the mortar. Lou was waiting for the order to load and fire when he got his first surprise. While DeVoin used a pair of wire cutters to break the seals on the ammo cases, Macklin instructed the sergeant to turn the weapon one hundred and eighty degrees. But that meant they would be lobbing shells over the hill toward the river.

"Sir, there's a village over that way," Lou said.

Macklin smiled. "Don't worry about it, Sergeant."

"But sir, they're friendlies."

"I gave you an order, Sergeant," said Macklin, in a level voice.

Lou looked to DeVoin. The colonel was now personally carrying the bombs from their cases and stacking them next to the weapon. They looked like standard 81 millimeter rounds, except that the nose of each was painted yellow, and there were words – too small to read at this distance – stenciled on the side.

The sergeant turned back to the captain. "But sir, I'm trying to..."

The smile never left Macklin's face as he snapped open the flap of his holster and brought out a .45 service automatic. He stepped back, racked the slide and pointed the pistol at Lou's face. "Turn that weapon around, or I'll shoot you," he said, pleasantly.

The captain's hand was rock steady, and the muzzle of the .45 loomed in the sergeant's vision like a tunnel into eternity. He tore his eyes away and looked to the senior officer.

70

DeVoin was enjoying the confrontation. Lou had seen the expression on a certain kind of soldier, the rare kind for whom killing was not an unpleasant necessity of service, but an anticipated pleasure. No doubt the colonel would enjoy seeing his brains spattered out the back of his head.

"Yes, sir," Lou said. He seized the mortar by its tube, lifting until the base-plate's spikes came out of the spongy ground, then turned it around to point uphill. The spikes sank back into the soil and he shortened the bipod legs, readjusting the angle now that the 81 no longer faced downslope. When he had the weapon repositioned, he stood back.

Macklin gestured with his pistol toward the eight yellow nosed bombs that had now been neatly stacked beside the mortar.

"Set it for manual triggering, Sergeant, and load the first round."

Breathing hard, Lou squatted beside the mortar. He flicked the triggering switch away from automatic, and picked up one of the finned bombs.

The sergeant's hands shook so badly he couldn't read the warnings sten-ciled on the projectile's sides. The fins rattled as he brought it to the mouth of the tube and let it slide down. He heard the base of the bomb lock with the firing mechanism.

"Set the elevation at sixty degrees and prepare to fire," said Macklin behind him.

Lou adjusted the elevation screw until the needle indicated sixty, and put his hand on the manual trigger. It was warm and slick with his own sweat.

DeVoin produced a pair of field glasses from a case strapped to his belt, went up to the brow of the hill and focused on the village.

"Ready," he said.

"Open fire, Sergeant," Macklin said.

Lou's finger froze on the trigger. He was thinking of the villagers, the chil-dren – there was one little girl with a thumb in her mouth, and when she had pulled it free to accept a piece of Juicy-Fruit gum, the digit had been three shades lighter in color than the rest of her hand.

"Do it, Sergeant," Macklin said. "Fire. That's an order."

Lou turned to look up, his eyes were beginning to mist. "Captain, there's no bad guys in that village. We were in there yesterday. They're friendlies, just a buncha Miskito Indian farmers, for Christ's sake!"

Macklin smiled. His thumb snicked back the hammer on the .45. "I order you to fire, Sergeant," he said, in the same voice he would have used to order a burger and fries in the officer's club. "Now do it or I'll blow your fucking head off."

Lou thought about it. He had a pistol on his hip, and he'd killed men before. He could fire the mortar, then go for the sidearm while the officers were distracted. But he'd seen enough and heard enough to know what would happen. Sure, asshole lieutenants sometimes ended up dead in the chaos of firefights. But colonels were another matter; when colonels got killed, other colonels got interested.

Lou closed his eyes and squeezed the trigger. The 81 *whumped!* and he heard the round snuffle away through the humid air, on a deadly arc that would take it spiraling down to the brush fence that marked the outskirts of the village. Seconds later, he heard the oddly muffled *crump!* of the bomb's detonation, then a woman screamed.

"Five degrees up," said DeVoin from his vantage point near the brow of the hill.

With the muzzle of Macklin's pistol at his ear, Lou adjusted the elevation screw, dropped another round into the tube, and triggered its launch. The bomb disappeared over the hill, and again he heard the soft sound it made as it exploded, then a child's voice rising steadily in pitch to a shriek.

DeVoin called back, "That's on the money. Fire for effect!"

The sergeant set the firing mechanism on automatic and, one by one, dropped in the other six strangely marked rounds. He heard each one impact in the village, but before he fired the final round the screams had faded. He heard the last bomb explode in the midst of silence.

DeVoin had watched the whole thing. When the firing ceased, Macklin holstered his pistol and moved upslope beside the colonel. He took out his own field glasses and surveyed the results of the mortar attack.

Lou didn't want to see what was on the other side of the hill – but he had to. His shaking legs took him to the crest, until he could look down on the village. He had no glasses, but he didn't need them to know that nothing lived down below.

The mortar rounds had done no damage to the huts; whatever explosive charge they contained was just enough to disperse the trails of yellow vapor that lay between the small buildings. But the gas had killed every living thing: the grandmothers stirring the cooking pots, the old men smoking their fat rolled cigarettes, the boys and their fathers coming home from the fields, the mothers with babies on their hips.

The people of the nameless village, along with their livestock, lay in the dusty tracks that wound among their homes. From atop the hill, they looked like bundles of old clothing. The bodies were thickest near the village gates; they had died trying to run to the open fields, away from the clouds of choking death that had rained down out of a tranquil evening sky.

72

Lou Meecham turned away, staggered a little distance back down the slope, retching. Macklin lowered the field glasses and glanced his way. "None of this ever happened, Sergeant. We were never here," he said, in his quiet officer's club voice.

Lou was still hunched over, hands on his quivering knees. He spat bile. "You bastards," he whispered, "you heartless, murdering bastards."

DeVoin came down from the hill crest. He smiled. "If you say anything about this, to anyone," he said, "I will hear about it. And I will send somebody to 'collect' you. Then no one will ever hear anything from you again."

"I hope we're clear, Sergeant," Macklin said.

Lou said nothing, only wiped his mouth and looked into the captain's passionless green eyes. "Good," said Macklin. "Now get your squad up here to collect the mortar."

On the short flight back to the base camp, Lou stared out the open door of the Huey. He'd been planning to do another tour in country; now he just wanted out. He told the Old Man, and the major didn't argue.

"I don't know what happened out there, and God help me, I don't want to know." The next day he handed Lou a set of travel orders. "Go home, Sergeant. Go home and forget this shithole."

The whine of the tv filled the room, then cut to the meaningless hiss of static as the Eugene station went off the air. Lou Meecham stared into the electronic snow and saw images he thought he had left half a world and half a lifetime behind.

"Lou," said Adele. "Listen. I hear engines. Maybe they're leaving."

Lou took his eyes away from the pictures in his memory and listened. Over the noise from the television he heard three or four engines turning over in the parking lot below. Then several more cut in. He heard vehicle doors slamming, orders barked and acknowledged.

Down in the parking lot, two dozen mercenaries came out of the hotel's rear door and scattered to the vans, three to each vehicle. The civilian clothes were put away now, and they wore their combat fatigues. They had been issued kevlar helmets and electric stun guns. Each member of the three-man teams knew his job: one to drive, a second to operate the video cameras, the third to provide security for the other two.

They had all been briefed and had seen videos that showed the degree of opposition they could expect to encounter. They were adequately armed and

73

well trained to meet the anticipated threat level. They were also very well paid.

They loaded into the vans, slammed the doors, and pulled out, the vehicles taking divergent routes away from the hotel, driving to pre-assigned points throughout the sleeping town, where their video cameras would pick up what was about to happen in Prescott Springs. The video signals would be beamed directly to an array of dish antennae they had earlier mounted on the hotel roof, then cabled down to the bank of screens in the ballroom.

One of the vans rolled down Prescott Avenue, turned right onto Rockwell Street and continued past the Camerons' house. Two blocks further on, the blacktop ended at a diamond shaped checkerboard sign mounted on a steel crash barrier. Beyond was second-growth spruce and pine forest that ran south to the river and east all the way into the hills. The van stopped, made a three-point turn, and parked with its blacked out windshield pointed back the way it had come. A red LED came to blinking life on the mini-cam mounted above the passenger door, and the surveillance unit tracked from left to right and back again on a silent electric motor.

In the hotel ballroom, a screen showed the camera's view of Rockwell Street in a slow moving pan. Technicians checked each screen and murmured into throat mikes as the vans reached their observation points and checked in.

Sandrini paid no attention to the flickering images on the bank of video screens. His attention was completely focused on his computer monitor, which displayed a bell curve graph of data generated by yet another run-through of the mathematical model that predicted how Paroxysm would affect the population of Prescott Springs. The scientist tapped the keyboard, entering a string of numbers that changed a key parameter in the complex set of equations that powered the model. The curve of the graph flattened slightly. Sandrini nodded, and entered another sequence of digits, watching the curve change again.

DeVoin sat in a straight-backed chair slightly behind the scientist, his fingers interlaced together in his lap and his feet flat on the floor. He watched the bank of video screens impassively, and only a very careful student of human body languages would have detected the tension behind the control.

Mr. Hafiz was such a student. He had survived to become a senior member of an organization that operated in countries whose governments were often unfriendly to his group's aims. Sometimes that unfriendliness was expressed by men with rubber hoses and electric shock generators in basements where the walls echoed with the screams of Hafiz's colleagues.

He noted the general's nervousness and registered it as normal pre-operational anxiety. His own pulse did not climb above seventy-two beats per minute.

The supervisor made a final check on his clipboard, spun on his heel and crossed the floor to come to attention before DeVoin. "All in position, sir!" he barked, the Ulsterman accent torturing the final syllable into a harsh *Sorr*.

DeVoin glanced at his watch. "Good. Now we just wait for morning."

# 8

Dr. Macreedy's house was in the gentle hills above the lake and east of the town, a region of country lanes and small holdings. His kitchen faced south, and the early sun poured through the big window, flooding the room with warmth and light. The old man carried his breakfast dishes to the sink and rinsed them under the tap, then dried his hands on a cotton towel.

He picked up the jacket of his faded tweed suit from where it had spent the night draped over the back of a chair and shrugged his way into it. His medical bag, an antique black Gladstone, waited on the table next to a half-empty tumbler of mineral water. He closed his hand comfortably around the bag's worn leather handle and hefted the familiar weight. Then he picked up the glass and swallowed the liquid. The day's routine was begun.

His trilby hung on a peg by the back door. He reached for it and clapped it on, noting as he always did that it no longer fit as snugly as when it had been new – when there had been considerably more hair between his scalp and its sweatband. He left by the kitchen door, letting it lock behind him, and paused on the back porch to savor the sweet smell of an Oregon morning.

He carefully descended the stairs to his ancient Ford sedan, and got behind the wheel. The car's engine turned over reluctantly, sputtered and died. The doctor cranked it again, keeping his foot on the gas until whatever gremlin was living under the Ford's hood accepted that he wasn't going to give up.

He put the car into gear and eased onto the country road. He had two house calls to make: the Cameron boy and seventy-year-old Karen Wilmott, who would need the stitches removing from a gash in her leg that he'd sewn up two weeks ago. The wound had been inflicted by Karen's Border Leicester ram, which every now and then forgot who was the true boss of the Wilmott farm and took a run at her. Usually, the old woman reminded the animal by giving it a sharp rap across the snout with her cane, but this time she'd had her back turned when the impulse entered its dim sheep's brain. Luckily, Karen had heard its rush across the fold and managed to sideslip in time to avoid a broken hip, which at her age could have been the last injury she'd ever sustain. But a ridge on the ram's unpolled horns had ripped through her overalls and split her flesh.

She'd driven her pick-up one-handed to his office, the other hand pressing a handkerchief to the bleeding cut, and he had cleaned the wound and sewn her up, while she kept up a continuous excoriation of the ram and of herself for not recognizing the signs of an impending attack. As always, Doc Macreedy was impressed by the breadth of the old woman's scatological vocabulary, which enabled her to go on for minutes at a time without repeating herself.

"Why don't you get that thing's horns chopped off?" he'd asked, when she paused for breath.

"Ah," she'd scoffed, "the festering son of a hog would only bite me, wouldn't he?"

Now Macreedy slid his Ford onto the muddy track between second-growth pines that led to the Wilmott farm and drove into the yard. He parked behind Karen's old blue pick-up, cut the engine, and got out. He was halfway to the kitchen door when he heard a high-pitched yelping howl from the woods that climbed the slope behind the small frame house. *Coyote*, he thought, then *but what's a coyote doing out this time of day?* As the sound faded away, it left a deep silence, an unnatural quiet. The doctor stopped at the foot of the back stairs. The kitchen door was open.

"Karen," he called. His voice died on the morning air. He called again, climbing the stairs, but there was no answer.

The kitchen was deserted. A half-empty coffee cup sat on the sink counter, its contents still lukewarm to his touch when he picked it up. He called a last time, but there was no response. He quickly checked the other rooms, found Karen's unmade bed but no other sign of her.

The sheep fold was an open shed surrounded by a loosely arranged fence of scrap lumber. The gate, a homemade affair of wire fencing and wooden poles, sagged wide. Beyond was an enclosed meadow of a few acres, where Karen grazed her small flock. It was empty.

Macreedy could put together the sequence of events. Something, a coyote or a feral dog, had spooked the sheep. The old woman had come out to calm them, but when she'd opened the gate, the animals had broken out and gone into the woods. Now she was out there somewhere rounding them up, and probably tearing loose his carefully made stitches.

Something about the sheep fold caught his eye. In a corner by the back wall: a splash of blood. He bent and touched it; it was fresh.

Now he was sure. Something had got in at Karen Wilmott's sheep. Now they were scattered and she was gone out after them. He went a few steps into the pasture, listened, but heard nothing. He called again, but there was only that eerie yelp, further away now, and a sound that might have been the terrified bleating of a ewe. He considered going into the trees after Karen, but realized he'd most likely end up lost in the thickets that grew between the pines. *Besides*, he thought, *I'm a doctor, not a shepherd. I'll come back this afternoon.*

Trevor woke up with a sore throat and a stuffy nose. Still in his camouflage pattern pajamas, he went out into the upstairs hallway. Through the closed bathroom door he could hear his dad singing some goofy old song in the shower. The boy coughed, and it felt like a file rasping the back of his tongue. He needed a drink.

The warm smell of frying bacon and drip coffee wafted up the stairs. He followed it down to the kitchen, where his mother stood at the stove in a pink housecoat, turning the sizzling strips over with a fork. She smiled at Trevor as he came in the door, rubbing red-rimmed eyes. "Hey, sweetie, how you feeling?"

"Throat hurts," he croaked.

"Have some juice," she said. She got a plastic carafe and a packet of powdered juice mix from the cupboard over the sink. She rinsed the jug under the tap, then filled it with cold water and mixed in the brightly colored powder. She poured him a glass and watched as he gulped half of it then made a face. She felt his forehead; there was a slight fever.

"The doctor's coming to take a look at you."

"I'm okay."

"Sure. Drink some more juice. It'll help your throat."

He finished the glass and she poured him some more. "Can I eat in front of the tv? It's cartoons."

She moved a lock of hair back from his forehead. Ordinarily, he would have ducked the motherly caress, but today he was sick.

"Okay," she said. "I'll call you when it's ready."

"Thanks, mom," he said. He went into the living room, and moments later the usual Saturday morning babble and thump of animated entertainment began rocking the house.

Jeff came downstairs, his still wet hair darker than its usual carrot red. He stroked his hand up and down Sharon's back while he poured a cup of coffee.

"Pour one for me," she said, and he did while she drained the bacon on a paper towel and got out the plate of pancakes that had been warming in the oven. Then he sat at the table, sipping the hot brew while she apportioned breakfast onto three plates.

Jeff stretched. "Mmm. Day off. How long since I've had a Saturday?" He was looking forward to taking Trevor up into the woods to look for deer sign. He didn't get enough time with the boy any more.

Sharon put his plate in front of him and her own on the other side of the table. "He's got that cold." She took the third plate and went into the hall that led to the living room.

Trevor was kneeling in front of the set, his back to her, the empty tumbler on the floor beside him. She was about to speak, to say, "Here's breakfast," but then she noticed the movement of his bare feet that pointed back at her soles turned upward. The boy's feet were beset by a tremor so rapid that the toes appeared to be vibrating against the carpet. As she looked, she realized that her son's entire body was gripped by a continuous shiver. *Christ,* she thought, *he's having a fit!*

For the boy, it had begun as an indescribable feeling at the base of his spine, as if someone had switched on a warm light down there and it had immediately started to swell and glow more brightly. Within seconds, tendrils of sensation began to rush up his backbone, bursting at the base of his skull in small explosions of delight. Then the glow spread across his entire body, making his skin ripple and shiver. His breath came quick and panting.

But that was just the opening movement. Now the outside world began to change. He'd been watching one of his regular Saturday morning shows, one in which a crew of muscular, super-powered heroes took on villains of galactic-scale nastiness. They flew in spaceships that fired blasts of coruscating energy, but each episode's climactic encounter found one of the good guys pitted in hand-to-hand combat against a monstrous enemy.

79

The show had just reached its final battle when Trevor began to feel strange. As the chemical agent flooded the lower reaches of his brain, the images on the television slowed until they almost stopped moving altogether. The evil visage of the episode's villain, a purple-skinned demon with curling horns and clawed fingers, filled the screen, yellow eyes slitted and black lips curled in contempt.

Staring at the image, he could almost see a flicker as the television's electron gun fired its stream of particles at the glowing screen, pixel by pixel, from upper left of the screen to the lowest right-hand corner. *So slow*, he thought. *Why so slow?*

But that was the last rational thought. As if a floodgate had opened in the back of his mind, the boy felt a trickle, then a flow, then a roaring *torrent* of emotion sweep into his being. It lifted him up in one great surge, so suddenly, so commandingly, that he couldn't at first even recognize which feeling it was that had seized almost total control of his existence. His consciousness, the person he thought of as *me, Trevor*, was tossed to the farthest edge of his being, shrunken to an insignificant mote which clung to the back of the surging beast into which the rest of him had somehow been transformed.

That tiny fragment of self looked on from a great distance while some inner part of him swelled into a vast, raging monster. *Yes, raging*, he thought, because he recognized that the emotion carrying all before it was anger – a wonderful, roaring, cascading cataract of sheer fury. If the drug had left him enough presence of mind to have looked into memory, he might have recalled what it was like to be a little kid, out of control and throwing a tantrum, letting it all just bust loose. But now was no time for memory or thought of any kind. Now was *action*.

He'd been kneeling. Now he flowed to his feet with a smooth sureness, his gaze fixed on the purple-skinned demon. His body seemed to know exactly how to position itself, soles flat on the worn carpet, toes slightly arched to afford maximum grip, knees flexed. He'd seen it a thousand times in movies and tv shows: *arms like this, shoulders just so, set and balance and let fly!*

Sharon, frozen in the doorway, saw her son rise up in one fluid motion, so fast his limbs seemed to blur. He assumed a martial arts stance, poised and limber on half-bent legs, then his right foot came off the floor, he pivoted on his left, and slammed a roundhouse kick into the face of the purple demon. The tv screen shattered, its electronic innards throwing a shower of sparks into the room, along with a rising column of greasy black smoke.

Sharon screamed and dropped the plate of pancakes and bacon. The boy whirled so fast that she thought she heard a *whoosh* of displaced air. She had time to register the expression of sheer manic joy that animated his features, then he launched himself at her.

For Trevor, hovering on the furthest edge of perception, the kick directed at the tv monster had been pure pleasure. He'd felt the raging part of him gather all of its magnificent anger, shape it like a burning spear of force and hurl it straight into the face of the enemy. The shattering of the glass made him want to laugh; the fireworks that followed were so comically slow, the shooting sparks traveling in leisurely arcs like drifting motes of dust in afternoon sunlight.

*This is so great,* the distant Trevor thought. He wanted to attack something else, *right now!* and his eyes swept left and right, up and down. It was then that he heard the hoarse rumble of his mother's startled scream, slowed down like an old record played at the wrong speed. He leapt high into the air, spun around and landed facing the doorway. No sooner did his feet touch the floor than he his knees bent and he sprang at her, fingers tensed like talons. A high-pitched giggle bubbled out from behind his bared teeth.

Even before the tv set blew out, Jeff knew something strange was happening to him. He'd been sitting at the kitchen table, a forkful of pancake and bacon in his mouth, when his tongue had suddenly gone dry as ashes. As his left hand reached shakily for the half empty coffee cup, his right began to vibrate so fiercely that the fork he was holding struck against the rim of the plate like a fire bell's clapper. Then tremors like bolts of cold lightning began to flash from his coccyx to the top of his skull. It was the most terrifyingly wonderful sensation he had ever experienced.

He stood up. The muscles of his legs quivered and jerked like those of the electro-shocked frogs they used to experiment on in high school biology class. He took a deep, quavering breath. As he let it go, all the physical symptoms smoothed out. The tremors stopped, his diaphragm loosened so that the air flooded in and out of his lungs as if they were a giant bellows.

He stretched his back muscles, closed his hands into fists. He felt immensely powerful, totally *tuned-up*, and ready, *right now!* to – he didn't know what he was ready to do, but he knew he was powered up to maximum charge, just waiting for the target to present itself so he could lock on and...

...and sparks erupted from the living room into the hallway, followed by his wife hurtling backwards, slamming up against the banisters of the staircase with an impact that drove the air out of her, and with their son's hands locked around her throat.

Jeff did not think. The thinking part of his brain was a tiny point of light far off in infinite space. All the rest of him was filled with joyous, red rage, as he threw the kitchen table and chairs out his way with one sweep of his arm and charged into the hallway.

It took him less time to cover the distance than to think of doing it. His left hand seized his son by the hair and yanked the boy's head back, while his right drove forward in what should have been a bone-crushing blow to the jaw. But the teenager was as fast as his father. He let go of his mother's throat, and flung himself into a backwards somersault. The move tore his hair from his assailant's grip – some of it stayed behind – as the boy flew back, heels over head, into the living room.

There he landed on his feet, barely skidding on the worn carpet, and once again instantly set and launched himself forward, this time at his father. But the man was already rushing to make his own attack. They smashed together in the doorway, feet scrabbling and slipping as they sought purchase. Their fists jerked in and out in short, savage blows, then the boy jabbed up with spread fingers to tear out his father's eyes, while the man clubbed down with closed hands on the boy's neck.

Either could have delivered killing, maiming blows, but both were operating at speeds and with heightened reflexes that allowed them to slip and dodge, to duck and turn.

The fight lasted only seconds, but those seconds seemed to be hours. They battered and tore at each other. Each hardly felt the damage the other was doing, so intent were they on doing more harm.

Finally, the man broke through the boy's defense, and delivered a blow to the temple that caused Trevor's eyes to roll up into his head. He would have sunk to the floor, if his father had not closed his fingers around the young throat.

Jeff began to squeeze with pure power. There were no names now, no dad and son, no Jeff and Trevor Cameron. Their names and identities had been buried so deeply beneath the thick, red flood of wondrous rage that neither would have recognized the few syllables that differentiated them from any other homicidal beast.

For Jeff, it was a source of immense satisfaction that the enemy's eyes were popping from their sockets, that his face was turning purplish blue. The only thing that diminished his pleasure was the annoying sound in his ears. Someone was calling a name, shrieking it, while trying to pry his fingers out of the flesh in which they were buried.

When Sharon had slammed backwards into the staircase, the impact had driven the air from her lungs. She had slumped to the hall floor in shock as Jeff had torn Trevor's hands away and the two had battered each other in the doorway. But when her husband bore their son down to the floor and began strangling him, she pulled herself together and leapt onto Jeff's back.

He threw her off with one back-handed sweep of his arm and renewed his grip on the boy's throat. She flung herself onto him again, tried to yank his head back, screamed his name – "Jeff! Stop! You're killing him! You're killing our son!" – but he shrugged his shoulders and tossed her effortlessly aside.

Back she came, jumping on him from behind, like kids playing piggy-back. This time she went for his fingers, prying them up from Trevor's neck, bending them back until he must either let the boy go or let them break. And all the time she screamed his name into his ear.

The man felt his fingers hurting. He grunted, not from the pain but in the happy recognition that as one enemy faded, another had fortuitously appeared. He let go of the boy, tore his hand from the woman's grip and tossed his head back. The top of his skull struck Sharon's forehead. He heard her grunt. Her grip loosened and she slid from his back and slumped to the floor.

He whirled, eyes flickering from the unconscious boy to the dazed woman. Neither posed any immediate threat. He felt a slight disappointment that the best of it was now over. All that was left was the finish.

The woman was bigger than the boy, so he'd kill her first. It couldn't be called thinking in any human sense of the word. It was more the way lions decide which one of the zebra herd they'll single out and bring down, the way young bulls choose their opponents for springtime head-butting contests.

It was thought without words, without real consciousness. He focused on the woman's throat, mentally marking the spot where he would hit hard and fast, crushing the larynx. She would choke on her own internal bleeding and asphyxiate when the swollen, bruised tissues cut off her air. He could see a pulse throbbing right next to the target spot. He positioned himself to strike, grinning.

But back behind the wordless thoughts, there was a sound inside his head, a distant, persistent nattering. He wanted it to just go away – he was busy, he was having a good time – but it kept nagging at the edge of awareness, as if someone was waving to him from the periphery of his vision, or tugging on his sleeve.

It had been easy to ignore when he'd been fighting. Now, with the immediate threats dealt with, the signal had more force. Reluctantly, he turned part of his attention to the inner nuisance. It resolved itself into a small voice, calling from far away.

*Hey!* the voice was saying. *Hey! Whattaya doin? Jesus, get a grip!*

He focused more closely on the words. Less than a second had gone by. His body remained poised to tear into the woman. He was still locked on, still targeting where he would deliver the blow, even as the internal voice grew louder. *Stop, stop, stop!* it was saying. *No, no, no, no, no!*

The volume increased, as if someone were simultaneously speaking and walking toward to him. And then suddenly there was no longer a separation between speaker and listener; the voice flowed *into* him, and *was* him – always had been him, although he had been pushed off to the edge of nowhere by the explosion of rage. But now Jeff Cameron was back and in control.

He saw his wife slumped against the hall staircase, her face ashen and her eyes unfocused. Blood trickled from her nose, and there was a spreading bruise on her forehead.

*Oh my God,* he thought, *I did that.*

He looked at the boy. Trevor lay face down in the doorway to the living room.

*What the hell is happening here?* Jeff thought. He began to kneel beside the boy. But then his son moved, half raised himself from the floor and shook his head. The movement triggered the rage again. Suddenly the killer beast was back in the man's head, pushing the conscious Jeff Cameron aside, taking control, reflexively tracking and ready to attack whatever moved.

Jeff felt himself thrust aside and mentally grabbed for the dwindling control. In his mind's eye, he was gripping the mane of a great, flame-red tiger that sought to surge past him, bent on death and violence. He hauled back with all the inner strength he could exert.

He could barely hold it. The boy was struggling to rise, and his movement triggered a murderous impulse in the man, as when a dog sees a rabbit break from cover under its nose and run.

*Out!* he told himself. *Now!*

It was so much easier to move than to hold back. He leapt into the hall, tore open the front door, thrust aside the outer screen so hard it slapped the clapboards like a rifle shot. He was down the steps in one leap, on the sidewalk in three strides.

Action tipped the struggle for control back toward the beast in his head. It shoved Jeff Cameron down into a dark pocket at the back of its awareness and started looking for something to kill.

The camera atop the black van parked at the end of the street swiveled to track the man who had just burst out of the white and yellow house. The video signal beamed to a dish on the roof of the hotel and fed down to the command center, where Sandrini had been sitting before the bank of screens, waiting for the show to start.

"Somebody's going public," he said, as the image zoomed in and tightened on Jeff. DeVoin, Macklin and the Yemenis left their seats and crowded around behind the scientist.

"I would say this one's fully engaged," Sandrini commented, then spoke into a microphone, ordering the surveillance team to tighten the shot further for a facial close-up. The image blurred then jumped into tight focus on Jeff's face. Hafiz said something under his breath, one short barking syllable.

Sandrini didn't know any Arabic, but he understood well enough what the Yemeni meant. "Yeah," he said, looking at the rage that stamped Jeff Cameron's guy-next-door features, "I wouldn't want to see this guy this close for real."

"Be the last thing you ever would see," said DeVoin. He turned to Macklin. "I'd say it's time to let Mr. and Mrs. Mousey out to play."

Macklin smirked. "Yes, sir." He headed for the door.

On the screen, the camera pulled back for a longer shot. Jeff turned toward Prescott Avenue and began to lope along the sidewalk, his shoulders hunched and his head slung forward like a predatory beast sniffing for the first scent of blood. He came to a cross street and turned randomly left.

85

As his father disappeared from the camera's view, Trevor Cameron was coming almost fully back to consciousness. He got to his knees and focused on the sound that had drawn him back to awareness. It seemed to come from beyond the open front door, a wordless chant of rage, the deep ululating call of a monster.

His battered mother, slumped like a discarded doll in the hallway, he ignored. The sound was everything; it pulled him to the front door.

He stood on the porch, legs trembling, open-mouthed, gulping great drafts of air through his aching throat. The dizziness began to clear. He looked around: the street was empty.

Shakily, but with a growing recovery of strength and coordination, he descended the stairs. The voice was constant. He wanted to move toward it like a hound to a lure. He had gone a fair distance toward the center of town before his brain cleared enough for him to realize the sound was coming from inside his head.

But by then he knew what he wanted to do, and where he wanted to do it.

# 9

Dr. Macreedy drove into town from the east, along Mill Road to Greeley Street, then right on Custer Avenue and left onto Rockwell. He parked across from the white and yellow frame house.

The front door was wide open. He found Sharon Cameron in the hallway, barely conscious. He examined her quickly, ascertained that she had suffered a solid blow to the head. There might be concussion.

As he knelt over her, her eyes began to refocus.

"Can you tell me what happened?" he asked, continuing to examine her. There was no sign of any other injury, but there was every indication of shock.

She tried to get up, but he pressed her gently to remain sitting. "Take it easy," he said. "Tell me what happened."

Her voice was typical of the shock victim: deceptively calm, so that a casual listener might have assumed she was describing something that had happened to someone else, years ago. Except for the odd pauses and breaks in the telling.

"It was Jeff... no, first it was Trevor. Trevor kicked the tv... did you know those things explode? I was in the doorway, and he turned around and... he was hurting me," she touched the back of her neck, "and then Jeff came in. He was crazy, they both were. It was a big fight, hitting... then Jeff started strangling Trevor, so I pulled his hands... he was really strong... he hit me with his head..." she touched the bruise and winced. "Then he sort of stopped and looked at me funny, and ran out the door. Trevor got up and went after him."

She was silent for a moment, thinking of something. "We got to get out of here," she said, slowly and carefully. "They might come back."

"We've got to get you to a hospital. Wait here." He went into the kitchen and picked up the phone. An ambulance would be best. He got a dial tone and punched 911, but all he heard then was the faster-than-usual busy signal that means no circuits are available. He hung up and tried again, with the same result.

He went back to where Sharon was sitting. "Damn phone's out," he said.

She struggled to rise and he helped her. She looked at the front door. "We can't stay here," she said.

He took her into the kitchen, sat her down at the table. "I'll get you some clothes and we'll go in my car."

He went upstairs, found her a t-shirt, jeans and running shoes and brought them to her. She didn't seem to know what to do with them, so he gently dressed her.

He walked her to the hallway, his arm around her waist. "Come on. Time to go."

He escorted her out, down the stairs and along the walk, using careful pressure to keep her moving, across the street to the passenger side of the car. Once outside, her shoulders hunched and her eyes flicked back and forth, up and down the street.

As he opened the door for her, they heard a thin, keening sound, distant and faint. Sharon froze.

The old man looked around, but the street was empty except for them and a black van parked far down at the edge of the woods. "The hell was that?" he said.

The sound came again, the ascending shriek of an animal in pain, suddenly cut off before it reached a peak. In the silence, Sharon began to shiver heavily.

"Get in," Macreedy said and pressed her into the passenger seat. He got in on the driver's side and coaxed the reluctant engine into life.

His first concern was to get Sharon Cameron to a hospital. But as he reached for the gear shift, he paused. Being the only medical practitioner in Prescott Springs made him the *de facto* public health authority. "I've got to ask you something," he said.

She made no reply, just stared out at the street, eyes constantly moving.

"Did Jeff and Trevor eat anything out of the ordinary this morning, or last night? Maybe mushrooms?" He couldn't see the Camerons getting into drugs, far less giving some to the kid, but sometimes people would pick and eat the darndest things if they found them growing in the back yard.

Sharon spoke tonelessly. "I made pancakes and bacon. We all ate some. I took a few bites while I was standing at the stove cooking."

"Anything to drink?"

"Jeff had coffee. Trevor had juice."

"What about you?"

"I poured myself some coffee, but I didn't drink any."

Macreedy moved the old trilby back and scratched his head. "Was the juice from a can or the kind you mix with water?"

"A mix," Sharon said.

The doctor took his hand off the gear shift and opened his door.

"Where are you doing?" Sharon said.

"It'll only take a moment," he said, getting out of the car. "Just a hunch. Let me have your keys."

"I don't want to be here alone," she said.

"I'll be right back. You can lock the car door."

When she gave him the house keys, her hand shook. He wondered what it was like when your whole world suddenly went violently insane. He wondered if he would cope any better.

Seconds later, he was at the kitchen sink, the tap running. He rooted through the cupboards until he found an empty jar that Sharon had frugally rinsed out and saved. He filled it with water and closed the lid tightly, took it back to the car and got them moving toward Prescott Avenue.

He handed her the jar, and she sat it on her lap. "You think there's something in the water?" she said.

"Let's just say I wouldn't be surprised."

She looked at the jar's contents, so ordinary. "But what would it be?"

Macreedy shrugged. "Who knows? I've read about this kind of thing. Been happening all over. People get sick, there's no reason why. They do some tests and it turns out they're allergic to stuff that's seeped into the water table."

"You mean like fluoride?"

"Fluoride's nothing. No, it's farm run-off full of fertilizers from the fields and hormones that they put into livestock. You've got lead and smog chemicals from auto exhaust, heavy metals that somebody dumped in a ditch thirty years ago, acid rain that drifts in from halfway across the world. It all blends together in lakes and groundwater, a whole soup of contaminants and crud. It gives people symptoms that can look like anything from asthma to cerebral palsy."

"Trev did have the sniffles," Sharon said. "Do you really think..."

"Right now I don't know what to think," said Macreedy. "Medically, I'd say it sounds like Jeff and Trevor have both jumped straight into full-blown psychotic episodes from a standing start. But you're in the same environment, and you're unaffected. So, to me that says there's some kind of chemical triggering mechanism. And, since the only common factor I can see is that they both drank water, that's where I'd look first. The hospital lab in Evans will be able to tell us."

The main doors of the Prescott Springs Hotel faced the early sun, so that the stained glass figures of a lumberjack leaning on a double-bitted ax and a farmer walking behind a plow glowed like images of secular saints.

One of the mercenaries swung the door wide and let the morning light sting the eyes of Lou and Adele Meecham. His automatic in hand, Macklin prodded them out onto the old fashioned verandah. "Down the stairs, out the gates and into the street," he said. "From there, you're on your own."

"I don't get it," Lou said.

"You will. Now move out."

Adele took Lou's arm. He looked down at her hand, saw the angry stripes on her wrist where they had tied her. A sour taste of frustration and rage rose from his empty belly to his dry mouth. He wanted to turn and put one on Macklin, just the way the instructor had taught him in unarmed combat classes all those years ago: *heel of the hand straight to the base of the nose, drive it in fast – remember it's speed not weight that makes the difference. You splinter his nasal bone, shove it up into the brain, and your man is dead before he hits the ground.*

But Macklin had the little Czech pistol, and Lou knew he'd enjoy it, knew he'd be looking at Adele to see how she'd be taking it as he put a bullet into her husband. Besides, even if he could have given the major what he deserved, Lou Meecham knew he wouldn't do it – it would make him no better than the low creature Macklin was.

He swallowed dryly. "Come on, hon," he said, keeping it light. "Let's get out of this dump."

Macklin followed them down the granite steps, onto the driveway that led to Prescott Avenue. Half a dozen mercenaries, wearing fatigues and holding riot shields and police batons, were spaced in a line just inside the gateway, facing the town. In charge of the squad was the thin-nosed Belgian who had tied them up last night. Macklin gestured to him with his chin and the squad leader came to attention.

"See that these people leave the grounds," the major said.

The Belgian clicked his heels. "Sir. Degree of force, sir?"

Macklin smiled. "Use what's on your belt, if you need it." He looked at Lou. "Probably won't, though. Sergeant Mousey never did want to be a hero."

90

With that he turned his back and went back into the hotel.

The Belgian softly slapped the Taser clipped to his web-belt. "Know what this is?" he said.

Lou shook his head.

"Taser. Electric stun-gun. It shoots two little darts at you, they stick in your clothes. They have wires that go back to this battery pack. Soon as the darts touch something, that makes a circuit. Then you get fifty thousand volts in you. You wake up sore all over, pants full of crap, maybe bite your tongue off." He gestured toward Prescott Avenue. "So now out you go, take your chance. Or get put out there unconscious, let the lady look after you."

Adele squeezed Lou's arm a little tighter. He could feel her warmth through his shirt sleeve. It sent a sudden chill of desperate love for her through him. To the Belgian he said, "What's out there? What are we going into?"

The man unclipped the stun gun from his belt and leveled it at Lou. "Why don't you go see for yourself?"

They went. Down the walkway, through the gates, onto the sidewalk of the empty main street. It was a quiet morning in a small town. Adele looked back at the soldiers in front of the hotel. The Belgian gestured mockingly with the Taser, like a sadistic parent motioning a little girl to go stick her toe into the cold sea.

She looked up and down the deserted street. "Lou?" she said.

He patted the hand that held his arm. "Come on," he said. "Let's get away from these bastards."

They crossed the street toward Bob's Tavern. The Belgian watched them until they were on the far sidewalk, then he clipped the Taser back on his belt. He nudged the soldier next to him. "Of course, if any of these pigs makes real trouble..." He produced a small automatic pistol from a flap pocket on his fatigue pants.

Lou and Adele reached the sidewalk outside the tavern. Prescott Avenue was still deserted, the pavement and buildings charged with the peculiar still-ness of empty early morning streets. Lou felt as if he had been dropped into an old episode of *The Twilight Zone*, and any moment now a giant would loom monstrously over the buildings, reach down and scoop them screaming into its immense grip.

Or Rod Serling would step out from around the next corner to make cryptic observations through a plume of cigarette smoke, arching an eyebrow to underscore the irony.

But nothing came. No threats, no enlightenment. Lou Meecham was left to figure it out for himself, as he'd been trying to do through the whole sleepless night. But all he could deduce was that something awful was going to happen to Prescott Springs, the kind of awfulness that DeVoin and Macklin had built their careers on.

It would be chemicals, that was obvious. That was what they *did*. Some kind of nerve gas, he thought, like the stuff that destroyed the Miskito village. He'd come out of the hotel half expecting to see a helicopter quartering the town, spraying a deadly mist behind it like a high-tech crop-duster.

But there was no copter, and no member of DeVoin's rented army was wearing anti-chemical warfare gear. So now he scanned empty Prescott Avenue and wondered what the hell DeVoin was doing. He turned, and looked out across the lake and *of course!* he thought. *The water.*

The kid, the waiter, had said the hotel was fed from its own water supply. The town water supply was separate, so that's where they'd put it. Maybe right now, in kitchens all over Prescott Springs, unsuspecting townspeople were choking and gasping, the way the little Miskito girl with the light colored thumb always did in Lou Meecham's dreams, the dreams that he came out of shouting, clawing his way back to wakefulness, shaking and sucking in great lungfuls of air.

He never told his wife what those dreams were about, always said he couldn't remember. And now he was afraid that he had inadvertently propelled both of them into a waking nightmare. But if it was just the water, and if he and Adele didn't drink any, then they ought to be okay. So now the thing to do was to get under cover, away from DeVoin's men, find a basement or an empty house to hole up in, or hide out in the woods until the bastards left town.

Part of him knew it couldn't be that simple. The general would never have turned him loose if he was going to be the one guy who could walk out of this town and tell the authorities who filled it with corpses. He and Adele would never have seen today's sunrise if DeVoin thought they had any chance of making it to sunset.

There was a threat in this town, a deadly threat. He didn't know where it would come from or how he would handle it. But he remembered enough of the old habits, the old training. First thing: know where the enemy is, and what he's capable of.

That meant recon. He'd have to stash Adele somewhere safe and then start mousing around the area, see if there was anything dangerous up the block or around the next corner. He'd start by checking out the tavern; it ought to be empty this early in the day. He sidled over to the front window and peeked in.

92

With the morning light filling the street, it was hard to discern anything in the barroom's dark interior. At first it was all shadows and indistinct shapes, but then he realized that something was coming from the back of the room toward the window, something man-sized and moving fast.

Lou jumped sideways as the tavern window exploded from inside. A man had been hurled through the opening. He landed on his back and shoulders among shards of glass and splintered wood, but though he was middle-aged and beer-bellied, he bounced instantly to his feet as if he were a circus tumbler, and leapt back through the hole in the wall like a high school track star.

Crashing sounds and animal grunts came from inside the building now, and Lou crept up to where the wooden sill hung half askew and looked within. He saw three men, all his age or older, trying to kill each other bare-handed amidst a welter of broken tables and chairs. They were making thick, brutish sounds in the backs of their throats, baring their teeth like ferocious apes from a bad Hollywood movie, hammering each other with fists and feet.

It was a straight-out free-for-all, no two-against-one, Lou saw. As soon as one of the combatants would gain the upper hand over one of his opponents, the third would leap onto the winner and bear him down. Then the one who had been getting the worst of it would spring up and attack either his original adversary or his rescuer.

It was like a Three Stooges movie sped up to triple time. The three men rolled and bounded and flew at each other in speed-blurred motion. Lou could have laughed if it hadn't seen clearly that the only end to this melee was murder. These guys were doing their best to kill each other. Eventually one would go down and stay down, and soon after only one of the other two would remain standing.

Would he then come looking for fresh meat? And maybe find it in the persons of a man and a woman who had never moved that fast even twenty-five years ago?

Lou ducked down and edged away from the window, back to Adele. He looked back to the hotel. The Belgian smiled broadly and drew an index finger across his throat, then laughed. Lou took his wife's moist hand. "Come on," he said, "we'll try around back."

Furtively, eyes flicking back and forth to every window and doorway, he led her around the corner of the tavern, away from the hotel and Prescott Avenue, looking for a place where they could hide from whatever Parker De-Voin was doing to Prescott Springs.

Jeff Cameron loped along the sidewalk of Jackson Street, heading toward Prescott. Here the houses were a little larger, the fences a little more substantial than on his own street. He checked the windows of each place he passed, looking for motion, for signs of life, for targets.

He had slipped back into the rage now, done it knowingly, letting it wrap itself around him like a warm coat. Diminutive ripples of sensation flowed up his spine, and his face was set in a wolfish grin.

Something was moving on the sidewalk up ahead, something dark and small. As he closed the distance, he saw it was a crow, pecking at something in a crack between the slabs.

His eyes swept the ground before him. He was crossing a pot-holed gravel driveway. Without breaking stride, he bent and scooped up a rock that fit his palm. Then his gaze locked onto the bird. Still running, he cocked his arm to throw.

His rush had brought him within the crow's alarm radius, and it was already prepared to leap into flight when it registered the sudden motion of the man's arm. It took off fast, wings digging deep into the air to gain height and put distance between it and the approaching threat.

To Jeff, the bird moved treacle-slow, like a shot from a nature documentary. He could see how the articulated bones beneath the feathers bent and flexed, how the wings cupped volumes of air, compressing it them to create lift and forward movement.

He realized that he was once again in that transcendent state that he thought he had left behind forever, the last time he walked off the pitcher's mound. Everything was one perfectly connected whole: man, bird, rock, motion. The space between them was an illusion; all the factors that combined in the ballistics of what he was doing were irrelevant, a side issue to occupy a lesser consciousness.

He threw the rock. So fast did it travel that it thrummed the air.

The crow was ten feet off the ground, forty feet away and outward bound when the stone's flat trajectory vectored it inevitably onto the target. The wings were at maximum raise, just before the next descending stroke, but there would never be another downstroke for this bird. The missile flashed beneath the crow's right wing, impacted behind the skull and tore the head from the neck.

Both parts fell to the asphalt, the body continuing to flop for a moment before lying still. Jeff drew a breath that filled him like a first love, and ran on.

In the hotel ballroom, Sandrini froze. "That last sequence on three," he said. "Give me playback."

The live video feed was displaced by a recorded image. It showed Jeff Cameron running down the street, picking up the rock and hurling it at the crow. The high-definition camera had caught the spray of blood and feathers as the bird died.

"Run that again," the scientist said, biting on a fingernail. He watched it again. "Jesus," he said.

DeVoin had come up behind him. "What?" he said.

"Watch this." Sandrini had them run the sequence again, slowed down. The stone left the man's hand, flew straight and true to the bird and brought it down.

The general was not moved. "So?" he said.

"He threw a rock."

"So?"

"So, he *used a weapon*, General. They're not supposed to do that."

Mr. Hafiz and his aide moved closer. "Please go on, doctor," said the senior Yemeni.

DeVoin didn't like it, but Sandrini was temporarily out of control. Something had come along to seize his scientific curiosity and he had to follow it. His fingers were already at play on his computer keyboard.

"You can see it here." He indicated the data ranked on the monitor. "In every test, none of the subjects used weapons. Hands, feet, teeth, sure. No weapons."

The general snorted. "They were prisoners, for Christ's sake. They *had* no weapons."

Sandrini was nodding fast, waiting for DeVoin to finish so he could make his next point. "Sure, okay," he said. "But the coordination. I mean, how many people can knock a bird out of the air? His coordination is supposed to be impaired. Well, that doesn't look impaired to me; it looks enhanced."

It was time to remind the scientist who was in charge here. "With respect, doctor," said the general, in a tone that implied no respect at all, "you're making a mountain out of a pile of crap. It could have just been a lucky hit."

Sandrini heard the menace in DeVoin's voice, but his professional pride was in play now. "It doesn't fit the computer model, General."

"Computer models are not reality, doctor. I prefer to wait for more substantive data before we jump to conclusions." He turned his back on the indignant scientist and watched the monitors.

Mr. Hafiz watched them both, then moved his gaze once more to the image of Jeff Cameron, loping into the distance with the lithe assurance of a predator. The Yemeni stroked a knuckle along his jaw line, and entertained a new thought.

The doctor's old Ford moved along Rockwell at a good speed. A half a block from Prescott Avenue, it passed a late model Japanese import parked at the curb. Neither Macreedy nor Sharon saw the old woman until it was too late.

Thel Parmentier had been crouched behind the parked car's rear bumper for five minutes now. She'd been ready when Macreedy and Sharon Cameron had come out onto the street. She'd been furious when he'd gotten out of the car and gone back into the house.

She'd almost let herself go rattling after them, still wearing the damned ugly nightgown Ed had given her last Christmas. But she knew her spindly legs couldn't cover the distance fast enough, even though she felt better than she had for longer than she could remember.

Of course, she'd been plenty fast enough for Ed, when he'd come down to the kitchen, hacking around his morning cigarette, ready to start crabbing at her about whatever his rheumy old eyes lit upon. Ordinarily, she'd have ignored him through her first cup of coffee, then opened up with the usual counterattack as they ate the breakfast she made. He'd complain about the eggs, and she'd tell him just how high he stood on the all-time list of useless husbands.

But not today. Today, before he could say a word, Thel had put down her coffee, reached for the big cast-iron frying pan, and swung it in a whistling arc that was barely interrupted by its collision with his age-spotted bald spot. His knees had only begun to sag, and the cigarette butt was just launching from his lower lip when she backhanded the pan's edge into his forehead.

The second impact sounded like a dropped melon smacking a concrete floor. Ed's eyes bulged from their sockets. Blood gushed from his nostrils. His tongue lolled out of his open mouth, and he collapsed like a puppet with its strings cut.

A tiny, distant Thel felt a spark of pity for his crumpled form, felt a tinge of revulsion at the sight of the brains leaking from his shattered brow. But the big, happy, raging Thel shivered with pleasure and thought, *Okay, who's next?*

96

Now she raised herself up a little to see where Macreedy's car was, while she swung the frying pan lightly to and fro. It was almost close enough. She smiled toothlessly, waited another second, then sprang from cover.

Macreedy saw his patient Thel Parmentier come out from behind the parked car on his left and cross the distance to his car with astonishing speed. She leaned over the fender and swung something big and black at his windshield. The glass shattered into a web of rectangular shards, held together by the safety film. Macreedy's right foot went for the brake pedal, but the car's momentum kept it moving. The side view mirror caught Thel under the ribs. The blow knocked her off her feet and tore the pan from her grasp, leaving it embedded in the glass.

The Ford shuddered to a stop a few feet down the road. Macreedy only had time to say, "What the..." before the old woman was back. She ripped the frying pan clear of the windshield, sending sparkles of glass rattling across the car's black hood. Then she briefly peered in through the driver's side window, checking to see where he was, before she swung the weapon high for a second blow.

Macreedy couldn't budge. He looked up at Thel Parmentier's grin, saw the rictus of delighted rage, and sat frozen in horror.

"Move it!" Sharon screamed in his ear, as she jammed her left foot down hard on the gas pedal. The engine snarled a protest – the driver's foot was still on the brake – but the Ford juddered forward. The motion pushed Macreedy back in the seat, and his brake foot came up a little, so that the car shot forward, front wheels spinning and smoking.

Thel Parmentier swung. She missed the driver's window. The frying pan *spanged* a deep dent into the door frame. The impact sent a shock up her bony arm but she kept a grip on the handle and chased the car as it began to pick up speed.

The last time she'd moved that fast had been when she dove to catch the bouquet at her cousin Evie's wedding, fifty-two years back. She'd missed then and she missed now. The Ford screamed away up the street. She took a few steps after it, then stopped. She'd never catch it now.

97

*Damn and blast!* she thought. *Missed the cold-handed pill-pusher!* She drew back and hurled the frying pan at the fleeing car. Fast as the Ford was moving, the missile was faster. It smacked the rear window a satisfying *crack.*

Inside the car, Sharon screamed as the rear window starred from the pan's impact. But the pan bounced off, clattered on the rear bumper and fell into the street, where it spun and rattled against the asphalt like a tossed coin.

Thel Parmentier went and picked it up. After warming up with Ed and Doc Macreedy, she felt ready to do some real damage.

Macreedy's car careered up Rockwell toward Prescott, swerving from side to side. The doctor was frozen, gripping the steering wheel straight-armed, as if he were holding off a pit bull that wanted to tear out his throat. Sharon steered clumsily, one-handed from the passenger side, while her foot kept the throttle to the floor. The cracks in the windshield cut the view ahead into a chaotic jumble of fragmented images.

Sharon looked back over her shoulder, saw the old woman standing in the street. She eased up on the gas, moved her foot to the brake pedal, and stopped the car. Its engine faltered and stalled. She put the gear shift in neutral and turned the key, holding down the gas pedal. The starter whirred, but the engine wouldn't catch.

She tried it again, while her head turned to cover every direction. "Oh God, Oh God, Oh God," she whispered. "Come on, come on, come on!"

The engine stayed dead. And now the whirring of the starter was slowing as the battery drained. A smell of gas filled the passenger compartment. She stopped trying to start the car and turned to Macreedy. The doctor was staring straight ahead through the small hole in the glass, but she doubted he was seeing anything other than a mental replay of Thel Parmentier's murderous grin.

She shook him gently. "Are you all right?"

He swallowed, then took a deep, ragged breath. His hands unclenched from the wheel. He shook himself, and quickly turned to look back the way they had come.

"It's okay," Sharon said. "She's not following us."

"I've never..." He swallowed again, dryly. "I've never experienced anything like that before. I've treated that woman's arthritis for ten years and I'd never have thought she'd..." He shook his head, sucked in air and blew it out. "How about you? All right?"

Sharon nodded. "I guess so. I hope I'm not getting used to this," she said.

The doctor gripped his medical bag by one end and thrust it into the shattered glass of the windshield, breaking out a hole he could see through. Sharon hunched down in her seat and used her feet to kick more of the glass free, until there was only a fringe of rectangular shards clinging to the frame.

"Can you drive?" she asked.

He nodded. "Yeah."

"The car won't start."

He sniffed the gas. "She's a little temperamental. Let the fuel evaporate for a couple of minutes. I'll get her going."

Sharon's eyes continued to canvass all points of the compass. "We've got to get the hell out of here," she said. "God knows how many more of them have gone like Jeff and Mrs. Parmentier."

"We will. Just keep an eye out for anybody coming."

They waited a minute that passed like an hour. No one came down the street, but they heard screaming not far away. Then the doctor engaged the ignition. He let it whir gently for a few seconds, until it sounded as if the battery was just short of flat. At the last moment, he jiggled the key and the engine rumbled sluggishly back to life, then roared as he continued to give it gas.

Macreedy put the car in gear and they moved slowly up the street, veering occasionally to stay well clear of parked cars that might conceal another ambush.

Sharon opened the glove compartment. "You don't have a gun, do you?" she asked.

"Never felt the need," said the doctor.

"Well, I'm feeling it now."

# 10

In the hotel ballroom, Sandrini said, "That's Macreedy, the town doctor. Drinks bottled water, so he hasn't been affected."

Hafiz watched the car pull away from the camera. "He's trying to get out of town."

"Not much chance. If he makes it to the bridge, Wexler will stop him," said DeVoin.

Sandrini cleared his throat. "I've got to point out that that old lady also used a weapon. They're not supposed to be thinking that clearly."

The general was not impressed. "Doesn't mean anything. Frying pans, rocks, or this." He pointed to another screen where a stocky man squatted on his front porch, methodically using a kindling hatchet from the nearby wood-pile to chop a child's corpse into small pieces. "They just pick up whatever comes to hand and use it. Your POW test subjects probably would have done the same if they'd had the opportunity."

"I'm not convinced," said Sandrini. "I'm still having trouble with the coordination enhancement. I'd like to have some of these people in the lab."

Hafiz watched the monitors. "You might not like it so much," he said.

Space had not been a constraint when the founders had laid out the Prescott Springs townsite. Between the backyards of each street's row of houses, the town had put graveled service lanes. Now Jeff loped along one of them, eyes moving, checking over back fences and into garages and carports.

He felt good. The nagging little voice had faded back to the edge of things. He was at full charge, as if electricity were buzzing and sparking along every nerve channel. All he needed was a focus for the energy, a target, and he would flow toward it like a shark going after a wounded seal.

He'd seen that happen once, when he was a kid. His dad had taken him surf fishing near Bandon on the coast. They'd been casting into the swirl of water off some big rocks. The long gray shape had come up from below, so incredibly big. It hit the harbor seal and tossed it through the air in a spray of blood and foam. Then, as the torn and bleeding animal had struggled toward shore, bleating to its pack mates, the shark had circled and come at it again on the surface. While Jeff and his father watched from above, the killer caught its prey in the shallows.

It came in fast but easy, rolled over onto its side and tore open the seal's belly. The guts roped out, white and slimy, not twenty feet from where Jeff stood and watched with avid horror. The seal was still faintly alive when the fish came back for a final pass, its hinged jaws agape, black eyes rolled back. The rows of serrated triangles sank deep, the great tail swung with lazy power, and the shark carried the seal out to sea, and down into the depths.

The memory caused surges of electricity to ripple up Jeff's spine. He shivered and flexed the muscles of his back. *Give me a target!*

The little voice was saying something again. He knew he ought to listen, would have to eventually. But it was like being snuggled down under warm covers on a cold morning, clinging to the half-dream, resisting waking up just one more minute, one more breath.

The voice was getting louder now. He could feel he was going to have to yield. Goodbye to the shark. Goodbye to the energy crackling in his chest, the blood pounding in his belly. Back to that flat, tasteless world.

He was near the end of the lane, where it met Rockwell. In a moment he would circle back toward home. He could feel that other Jeff Cameron edging toward the driver's seat, reaching for the controls.

Then Jerry Steves stepped out of his garage, blood on his overalls and on the big kitchen knife in his hand. His heavy shoulders rolled as he loosened them. He smiled an awful smile, and Jeff recognized it as the same expression his own face was wearing.

Jerry had been a power hitter on Jeff's old high-school team. A big, blond, Nordic kid, not usually fast enough around the bases to stretch a solid double into a triple, but he could put the ball where he wanted. Today it was obvious where he wanted to put his knife.

He held it low, edge up for a ripping stroke, and moved to his left as he closed with Jeff. Today he was very fast.

But Jeff was faster. As Jerry moved in, Jeff stooped, snatched a handful of grit from the lane's potholed surface, and threw it into the man's eyes. No sooner had the spray of gravel left his hand, than he bent again, grabbed a fist-sized pebble and flung it at the other man's head.

Jerry ducked and the rock bounced off his shoulder. He came on again, but Jeff had already turned and raced for the fence into a yard he had just passed. He vaulted the cedar boards like a track star, and sped toward the shade tree that grew in the middle of the yard.

Against its trunk leaned an iron-headed rake with a long hardwood handle. Jeff would have preferred something a little more deliberately weaponlike, but the rake was the only thing he had seen that he could reach before Jerry Steves reached him.

He seized the tool in both hands and spun to face the way he had come. Jerry was just coming over the fence, the knife in his teeth. Jeff charged him, the rake thrust straight out like a spear. He aimed the metal head at his opponent's eyes, but the blond man parried easily and circled to his right.

They edged around each other, ducking and feinting, still smiling the same smiles. Jerry's eyebrows flicked up twice. His blue eyes twinkled. "Some kinda fun, huh?" he said. His voice was thick.

"Oh yeah," said Jeff. He jabbed at the other's throat. "Whose blood's that on you, Jerry?"

"Not mine," was the answer, and the knife flashed at Jeff's middle. He jumped clear and they circled again.

The nagging part of Jeff came back on the line then. He didn't want to be distracted just then, but the voice kept insisting that *Jerry Steves is a friend! Back off!*

Warily, the rake still up as Jerry tried to circle around him, Jeff said, "Jerry, you want to be doing this?"

The other man just snorted and kept crabbing sideways.

Jeff tried again. "I mean, you want to do this it's okay by me. But is there a part of you says this is nuts?"

Steves took a step back, but kept the knife poised between them. The smile got wider. "Damn straight, it's nuts. But who gives a red-rimmed fuck? Christ, man, we come a long way through a whole storm of shit since the last time we felt this good. Who knows how long it's gonna last? Who knows if we're ever going to feel so good, ever again?"

His eyes narrowed and he rolled his shoulders to loosen them. "Yeah, it's nuts. It's fuckin' crazy. But I'm goin' with it. And maybe I take you with me."

He rushed in, in a complete change of pace and style, swinging the heavy chef's knife like Errol Flynn flashing a sword. Jeff thrust the rake at his eyes, but Jerry ducked under and kept swinging.

102

Jeff backpedaled, trying to keep the distance between them as he beat on Jerry's skull with one end of the rake's iron head. Blood seeped from the blond hair and ran down the man's forehead. But he came on, the smile never leaving his face.

All Jeff could do now was parry. The knife rang of the rake's iron, bit into its hardwood. Sparks and wood chips flew.

Jeff was forced steadily back. The grass was slick with dew. Then he felt a wall press against his shoulders. Jerry had forced him all the way across the yard, backed him against the house.

And he was still coming on tirelessly.

The blond man held the knife in a two-handed grip now. He hacked at Jeff's defense like an Amazon Indian breaking trail through rain forest.

He cut down hard just behind the metal sleeve that held the rake head to the shaft. The wood had taken too many blows. Now it split, the head dropping away. Jeff was left with a five-foot length of ash, sharp where the knife had severed it.

"Not your game, Jeff," said Jerry Steves. He smiled again. Then he thrust the knife out the way he must have seen some duelist in a movie hold a sword – arm straight, back of the hand up – and bore in for Jeff's gut.

He came in straight and smiling, the fight all over but the bleeding, and Jeff stuck the sharp end of the rake handle into Jerry's throat.

The wood went in smoothly, passed through skin, muscle and cartilage, and lodged between the sixth and seventh vertebra, cutting Steves' spinal cord. He collapsed, his weight pulling his body off the wooden spear. A stream of blood spurted out, soaking the front of Jeff's shirt with sticky warmth.

Jerry Steves lay on his back and tried to say something to Jeff, but all that came out was a final gout of blood from his still-pumping heart, and a bubble of air from the severed windpipe.

Then he died, and a trace of the smile remained on his half open lips.

*My game after all,* thought Jeff. He loped across the yard and vaulted the fence into the lane. He kept the bloody rake handle.

In the hotel ballroom, DeVoin was better pleased. "Now we're getting some action," he told the two Yemenis.

Several of the screens showed the effects of Paroxysm on the citizens of Prescott Springs: a woman in a housecoat and a man in pajamas fought viciously on a front porch; a little boy cheerfully romped around a backyard chicken coop, twisting necks; an old man lay curled fetally on a sidewalk, hands clasped over his head, while a teenaged girl thoughtfully circled him, taking her time about planting solid kicks to his ribs.

Macklin touched the general's elbow and pointed to another screen. It showed Lou and Adele Meecham edging carefully past the front wall of Bob's Tavern, ducking under the broken window. They just made it past the saloon's entrance when the wooden door burst open. Bob, Frank and Joe B. tumbled into the street, still trading punches and kicks.

DeVoin chuckled. The Meechams had ducked inside the open door and now were peering from the glassless window at the three-way free-for-all in the street. "That was lucky," the general said.

"Not for much longer," said Macklin. "Here comes the guy with the spear."

Jeff stepped out from between two of the wood-frame stores on Prescott Avenue, drawn by the sounds of the brawl outside the tavern. He watched Bob, Frank and Joe B. flailing at each other, sized up the situation, then went forward, holding his primitive spear two-handed across his chest.

A part of his mind recognized the three combatants, knew them as neighbors if not friends. That part of him wished them no harm. But it was impotent to affect the major part of his new being, the part that was happily calculating which to strike first and where – Frank, he thought, a two handed blow across the back of the skull from behind – and what to do if Bob or Joe B. then came at him.

He had it pretty well plotted, he thought, when he was interrupted by a sound from behind him. Macreedy's old Ford rounded the corner from Rockwell onto Prescott at what must have been high speed, judging from the way its suspension rocked. But to Jeff's speeded up senses, it seemed to move sedately, and the screech of its tires was more like the squawk of an outraged cartoon chicken.

He stepped back onto the sidewalk and let the car go by. As it had made the corner, he had seen Sharon's horrified look of recognition through the empty space where the windshield should have been. He looked down at himself, saw Jerry Steve's blood on his shirt and hands, and on the stick in his hand. He shrugged.

Macreedy was already slowing the Ford to a halt as he passed Jeff. The street ahead was blocked by the continuing brawl among the three men from the tavern. He put the car in reverse and backed in a quarter circle; he'd find another route.

But the undependable car chose that moment to stall again, backed against the curb outside Fung's grocery store. Macreedy cranked the starter, but this time it wouldn't catch. The depleted battery had not had time to recharge, and after a few seconds the sounds from under the hood slurred to a mumble.

"That's it," said Macreedy. "We'll have to find another car." He opened the door.

"Oh God!" Sharon said. Through the window she saw her husband standing on the sidewalk not thirty feet away, fouled by blood, the rake handle still in his hands.

Their eyes met. He looked intensely excited, but under it he was faintly abashed. It was as if she'd caught him having a hell of a good time doing something he should have been too old for, like fooling around with toy soldiers or out in the back yard playing quick draw with a cap gun. He didn't move toward her, just looked at her with a mix of expressions, like some kind of homicidal sheep, she thought.

Then he moved, and he was coming *fast*. She flinched back into her seat. But he didn't go for her door or window; instead he went *over* the car – *thump!* left foot on the fender, *thump!* right foot on the roof, landing slap on both feet on the other side of the vehicle, just in time to lay out Frank Tedesco.

Frank had been temporarily thrown clear of the three-way fight with Bob Preiss and Joe B. Joe B. had head-butted him in the belly, and he'd gone down on his ass. Then, when Joe B. had moved in for a kick, Bob had slammed a fist into Joe B.'s ribs, and the two had traded a flurry of blows.

Frank picked himself up and was watching for an opening when Macreedy's car careered around the corner, slid to a stop, backed up and stalled. Tedesco smiled. The doctor made a more interesting target, he thought, the three-way battle with Bob and Joe B. having begun to go stale. His former opponents were now rolling on the ground trying for mutual headlocks. They were evenly matched; neither was doing the other much damage.

When Frank saw Macreedy open his door he went for him full speed, saw the doctor slowly look up, his expression all comical startlement as Frank drew back his fist. Then suddenly Jeff Cameron was in his face, dropping down out of nowhere and whacking him on the top of his head with a stick so hard his knees buckled.

As Frank sank unconscious to the pavement, Jeff reversed the rake handle to hold it point downward and prepared to thrust it into his opponent's belly. But before he could strike, he was knocked off balance.

Macreedy had stepped out of the car and shouldered Jeff out of the way. *Fine,* Jeff thought, and positioned himself to run the doctor through. *You first.*

But Macreedy neither fought nor fled. He was saying something and pointing at the Ford's interior. Jeff glanced in, saw Sharon clambering ever so slowly over the driver's seat, her eyes on him, her mouth working.

The little inner voice was getting louder again. He wished it would shut up and leave him alone, but he knew he had to listen. Like a child abandoning a favorite game to do a grown-up's bidding, he let that part of him he had kept distant flow back into the center of his consciousness.

He focused on what the doctor was saying. It was like trying to follow the slurred speech of someone who had suffered a debilitating brain injury and could speak only with painful slowness.

*Yoo-o-o-o-u-u-u-u-r-r-r wi-i-i-i-i-f-f-f-f-f-e-e-e. Ne-e-e-e-e-e-d-d-d-d-s-s-s-s he-e-e-e-l-l-lp-p-p,* he made out. Then Macreedy went on – it seemed to take him forever to complete a sentence – about getting Sharon to a hospital.

While he was talking, the doctor knelt down and examined Frank Tedesco's bruised face and limbs. "He's out cold," he said, but by then Jeff wasn't trying to listen.

Sharon was crawling out of the car. When Jeff turned to her, she flinched back. He realized he must be moving very fast, so fast he'd scared her again. He'd have to ratchet himself down, until he was functioning in what would feel to him like slow motion.

He smiled at her, slowly reached out a hand to her frightened face. "It's okay," he said, very slowly. "I think I can control it."

She froze at his touch, wary, then relaxed a little. "Are you sure?" she said.

He nodded and she moved back, her face slowly registering startlement. He tried the gesture again, more slowly, and saw her relax. "I would never hurt you," he said.

She put her arms out and he took her into his own – carefully, slowly – and patted her back. Her tears were wet and warm on his neck. The rage faded further. He watched it die down, like a fire starved of air.

The doctor was talking to him again. He released Sharon and listened attentively for a moment, then interrupted. "Try to talk a little quicker, Doc," he said. "It seems I'm running at a faster speed than you guys."

Macreedy understood. He'd in fact been talking extra slowly and carefully to Jeff, trying not to agitate someone who was clearly in a manic state. Now he spoke rapidly. "We've got to get to the hospital in Evans. Frank probably needs to be looked at, too." He peered into Jeff's face. "Can you handle whatever this is?"

"Guess so," said Jeff, then repeated it more slowly to make sure he was getting through. "You any idea what the hell's happening to everybody?"

"Something in the water's my guess," said Macreedy. "Don't drink any more of it."

Frank Tedesco started to come around. "Thick skull," said Macreedy. "But is he going to start in again?"

"Probably," said Jeff. "Help me hold him down."

With Jeff, Sharon and the doctor sitting on the man's chest, belly and legs, his thrashings didn't accomplish much. Jeff brought his face close to Frank's and spoke urgently.

"Frank, man, I know there's a part of you listening to me. You got to let that part of you take over."

Tedesco growled. "Fuck that noise! Get offa me!"

"Listen, I know how you feel. I'm the same. It's something in the water, makes us want to fight. You gotta hold it down. For Chrissake, look at the blood on me – that's Jerry Steves! I almost killed my own kid!"

He saw confusion enter the other man's expression, diluting the rage. Frank Tedesco was coming back from the edge of his own inner universe.

"Okay," he said. "I hear you. Keep talking to me."

They talked him down, then they let him up. The doctor and Sharon tensed when the middle-aged man sprang to his feet like a high school gymnast.

"Try to move a little slower," Jeff suggested. "Sharon and the doc, they're not powered up like us."

Frank said he got it. "Sorry," he said to the woman; he tried to make it slow, but it still came out like a samurai's bark.

Bob Preiss and Joe B. were still wrestling in the street, rolling around and trying to pummel each other like a pair of prizefighters in a horizontal clinch. "We better break that up before somebody gets hurt," Frank said.

"Something's wrong, General," Sandrini said. "They've stopped fighting."

"Could be just a dosage problem," DeVoin offered.

Sandrini watched Frank Tedesco come to his feet and talk to Jeff. "No. Paroxysm has definitely mutated in the water system. Different chemical, different reaction."

"But they *are* being affected," Hafiz said.

"Oh, they're affected, all right," the scientist said. "They're mad as hell, but they're not *out of control*. General, I recommend we abort."

"I'm not ready for that, doctor," said DeVoin.

Sandrini wiped his hand down his face. "Look, I ran some rough numbers through the model, based on what we've seen."

"And?"

Sandrini crossed to his computer and indicated the graph on the monitor. "There are going to be survivors. Those survivors will be asking questions. So I say we get out of here soonest, before anybody starts trying to figure out what's going on."

"Are we in any danger?" Hafiz asked.

DeVoin blew out his cheeks. "We are in a stone building, guarded by a platoon of professionals. If it will make you feel more secure, I will have Mr. Macklin break out the small arms."

The Yemeni had not survived in his shadow world by taking unnecessary chances. "It would make me feel more secure," he said.

The general turned to Macklin. "Arm the headquarters squad and station them on the front porch, ready to deploy as necessary. Then I want you and a couple of men to get us a sample of what these people have been drinking."

Macklin paled a little. "Wouldn't it be better for me to take charge of the HQ squad and stay here? In case there's trouble?"

DeVoin regarded his aide coolly for a long moment. "It might be better for you, Major," he said. "But it would be better for the mission if you made sure we get what we need."

Macklin swallowed. "Yes, sir," he said and went out.

To Sandrini, the message of the computer model was self-evident. "General, with respect, the demonstration is a bust. The chemical has mutated."

DeVoin glanced at the data, then looked back at the video screens. "With equal respect, Dr. Sandrini, the mutation may be offering us an even greater opportunity." He turned to Hafiz. "Are we of one mind on this?" he said, quietly.

The Yemeni nodded. "Continue your monitoring, doctor," he said. He motioned with his head to DeVoin. The two men walked a little way out onto the empty ballroom floor, put their heads together and conferred in whispers.

Joe B. and Bob Preiss had been going at each other full bore without a break for more than nine minutes. That was long enough to tire a couple of professionals in good condition; it was more than enough to use up the reserves of men who were in sight of their fiftieth birthdays. Paroxysm had fired up their adrenal glands and convinced their livers to release emergency blood sugar supplies – it had even triggered release of endorphins that masked the pain of injuries – but it didn't confer superhuman stamina.

Macreedy and Frank Tedesco tackled the tavern owner, dragged him clear of the tussle and talked him back into his right mind in less than a minute. It took Jeff and Sharon a little longer to get their man back on earth; Joe B. had years of accumulated anger to work off.

But finally the two were sitting in the middle of Prescott Avenue, heads down and breathing hard, sneaking peeks at each other from under their lowered brows. Bob felt a tender spot on his jaw, reached into his mouth and wiggled a loose tooth. "What you hit me with?" he asked Joe B.

Joe B. looked at the blood seeping from split knuckles. "Everything I got," he said.

Lou Meecham observed the action in the street from behind a row of trash cans in the space between Bob's Tavern and Fung's grocery store. He recognized Jeff Cameron as the red-haired young man they'd talked to in the hotel coffee shop yesterday. He saw him move from a towering rage into some kind of post-combat edginess, and watched him bring the other men out of the madness that had gripped them.

Crouched down behind him, Adele tugged on his arm. "Is it safe to come out? They're not fighting any more," she said.

"Maybe," Lou said. He watched Joe B. get to his feet and shamble over to the concrete drinking fountain in Shoreline Park. "But there's no risk if we stay put and see what happens next."

Joe B. bent over the fountain's chrome mouthpiece and gulped the cold water. He felt better right away. When he straightened he saw a line of men standing athwart the hotel driveway, just back from the gates.

He didn't know what was going on at the hotel, but he knew what these outsiders were there for – to keep him and people like him out of a place that was part of his home town.

*Son of a bitch,* he thought. He spat. The rage flared up all around the little circle that contained Joe B.'s consciousness. It roared at him from all directions, like a pride of snarling lions out in the darkness, pacing around a campfire's oasis of light. If he let them come in, he would ride their power.

A dangerous smile loosened his mouth. He flexed his hands, rolled his head easily on his shoulders, and went toward the line of mercenaries.

"Oh shit," said Lou Meecham. He saw the hotel verandah filling up with armed soldiers.

"What's wrong?" said Adele.

"We should get out of here, now!"

He took her hand, led her back down the side of the building. There was a lane running behind the block of woodframe stores and offices. They ducked around the corner, and found a pile of empty produce boxes stacked outside the back door of the grocery. Lou went to the pile and moved a few away from the wall, creating a small space.

"Get in there," he told Adele.

"Lou," she protested.

"I'm going to hide you here while I go and get us a car. Then we'll get the hell out of here, go hide in the bush until whatever DeVoin is doing is over."

He could see her reluctance, but Adele dutifully squatted down in the hidey hole. "I don't want you to go," she said.

"I won't be long," he said, piling boxes around her until he knew she would not be seen by anyone passing down the lane. "You'll be okay. Just stay still and quiet."

"Like a mouse," said her voice from within the boxes.

"Yeah, like a mouse." He turned to go, then stepped back and whispered, "I love you."

"Hurry," said the woman he loved.

# 11

Doc Macreedy had given up trying to restart his car. Now he shuffled along the sidewalk, checking the few parked cars – there were only two – for that sure sign that a vehicle's owner lives in a small town: a key in the ignition.

Jeff sat with Sharon on the curb outside Fung's grocery, his arm around her shoulders. He knew she was trying not to look at the blood that stained his shirt front. He knew he ought to feel something – guilt, sorrow – about what he'd done to Jerry Steves, but somehow whatever was working in his brain had blown out the "sorry" circuits.

He'd heard that cold-blooded killers were probably born with that short circuit permanently hard wired into them, so that they never felt remorse for what they did. Maybe that's what he'd turned into, he thought. Except there was nothing cold-blooded about how he felt. The rage was like a magnificent fire that would spread through his whole being, right now, if he just turned back to it and said *come on*.

Sharon bore the weight of her husband's arm across her shoulders but he could sense that she was not comforted. She kept wrinkling her nose and it came to him that she was repelled by the sickly sweet scent of blood. She was still pale but some of the hunted look had faded from her eyes.

Bob Preiss came to sit on the curb and lean sideways against the back bumper of the doctor's car. The gaze he laid on them showed the same lack of normal human contact that Jeff felt.

"How's it goin'?" he asked after a moment, as if it had just occurred to him that he ought to say something.

"Not so bad," said Jeff. "Hell of a day."

"You got that right," said Preiss.

Macreedy had had no luck with finding a car. Prescott Springs was no longer a town where people left the keys in the ignition overnight on Main Street. "Either of you know how to hot-wire a car?" he asked.

Preiss was looking across the road. "Hey," he said, "are those soldiers over at the hotel?"

Macreedy turned and looked, saw the uniforms, and let out a sigh of relief. He took a step toward the hotel, then stopped.

Sharon stood up. "They can help us," she said, and brushed past the doctor.

But he put a restraining hand on her arm. "No," he said. "I don't think they're here to help us. And I don't think it's any coincidence they're here at all."

Jeff looked up. "What do you mean, Doc?"

The doctor moved his hat back on his head. "You figure it out. Bunch of soldiers take over the hotel. Something gets put in the water." He ground his teeth. "Look at them – they're outfitted like a riot squad. Goddammit, this was no accident! They made us guinea pigs!"

"That doesn't make sense," said Sharon. "The government wouldn't do that."

"Who says they're the government?" said the tavern owner. "You ever hear that talk on the radio? The black helicopters? The Belgian troops in UN uniforms? Shit, it makes sense to me."

"I think we should get off the street," said Macreedy. "Get under cover someplace and think about what we're seeing."

"I'll get Frank and Joe B," said Preiss. He stood up. "Hey Frank! Get Joe! We're going!"

Frank was at the drinking fountain. He'd cupped his hands to collect the cold water and splashed it on his bruised face. He hadn't drunk any. He cleared the water from his eyes, waved at Bob Preiss and looked around for Joe B. He saw his friend standing at the hotel gates, hands on hips, head cocked to one side, regarding the men in combat fatigues and riot gear.

Frank called out, "Hey, Joe B.! What you doing?"

Joe B. didn't turn or make any answer. Frank looked beyond him at the men in the hotel grounds and saw what had made Lou Meecham want to get away from Prescott Avenue.

Beyond the rank of men with shields and batons, another group of about twenty soldiers was coming out of the hotel. These men carried assault rifles. They took up positions on the verandah and granite steps, slotting clips into their weapons and checking their actions.

Van Deming, the Belgian commanding the riot squad at the front gate, looked over his shoulder at the riflemen on the hotel's front porch and snorted. *Someone is overreacting*, he thought.

He looked back at the paunchy middle-aged man standing between the stone pillars of the hotel gate. He was not worried about what any of the townspeople might do. Sure, they were as crazy violent as the pre-mission briefing had said they'd be. But he'd watched the three-way fight with a professional's critical eye: they were fast – he'd give them that – but they were still amateurs. And even the fastest amateur would have a very short fight against real soldiers.

Van Deming was at one end of the line his squad formed across the driveway that led in from the gate. Now he took a step forward, and spoke to his men, his voice pitched just loud enough for the furthest man to hear him. "Ready now, boys."

He turned to face Joe B. "You want something?"

Joe B. spat. "Could be." His voice sounded strange, the words compressed almost into one syllable. But the Belgian understood the meaning.

He unholstered the Taser stun gun. "Well, why don't you come and get it?" he said.

The fresh dose of Paroxysm from the water fountain had by now permeated the lower regions of Joe B.'s brain. He felt anew the rushes of energy rippling along his spine, the hot trembling in his muscles, the belly-churning urge to close with an enemy, to do hurt and harm.

But it was different now. The first time, he'd had to watch impotently as the drug-induced rage hurled him at good friends. He'd stood on his own mental sidelines, distantly concerned, but unable to stop what his body was doing. Now he felt the beast raring to attack, and he held it in check only to savor the anticipation, so that the spasm of release would be that much more satisfying.

Then, when he saw the contempt in the soldier's face, in every line of the man's stance, that was the moment. He didn't even need to hear the slowed words the man spoke. It was time. He faded back to the edge and let the killer loose.

Joe B. went for the Belgian, crossing the distance between them so fast the man had no time to raise and fire his already drawn stun gun. Van Deming went down, with Joe B. on top of him. The riot squad reacted quickly – they'd trained for it – but they were not up to Joe B.'s speed. His blurring fists had landed eight times on his enemy's face, breaking the nose and knocking our four molars before the first lead-weighted hardwood club struck the back of his head and split the scalp.

Blood sprayed as a second, third and fourth blow rained down on Joe B.'s unprotected skull. He managed to hit his target three more times, with short chopping punches that broke Van Deming's front teeth and shredded his lips on the jagged fragments. Then the red rage faded to black and he slumped senseless on top of the battered Belgian squad leader.

"Get him off me!" Van Deming said through the ruin of his mouth. The squad rolled the unconscious man away, and the Belgian staggered to his feet. He shook his head, spraying his men with blood and spittle, and spat out fragments of broken teeth.

"*God verdomme! Bastard!*" he screamed. He left the stun gun where he had dropped it when Joe B. had borne him down. Instead he drew the small black automatic and slid a round into the chamber.

He pointed the gun at Joe B.'s gashed head. But the shot never came. Frank Tedesco's hand closed on Van Deming's wrist and yanked down, pulling the squad leader off balance so that he fell to his knees.

The Belgian looked up and Frank drove his knee into the man's face, pulping the already broken nose. Van Deming screamed as he flew backwards, landing flat out on the hotel driveway. Tedesco jumped and landed with both feet on the mercenary's chest. He heard the ribs crack like dry sticks.

Then the men with clubs moved in, swinging. Their target was tired and the initial energy of the drug was wearing off now, but the baton-wielding troops still moved like mimes doing slow motion. He stepped into their midst, kicked one in the knee, punched another in the throat, and head-butted the face of a third. He seized another's helmet by the rim and jerked it sharply to one side, snapping the man's neck.

The others swung their clubs. A grazing blow rang his head, another hit the back of his thigh and made the muscle spasm. He sank to one knee, but still managed to reach up and seize the shirt of a slow-moving attacker. He pulled the man down, and drove his fist up into the solar plexus. He hit the soldier so fast that his fist separated the abdominal muscles and shocked the heart into permanent stillness.

The dying man fell forward onto Tedesco. He threw the body clear and struggled to rise. The mercenaries hemmed him in. Clubs thudded onto his head and shoulders. Blood blinded him, but he reached out, hoping his dwindling speed would let him reach just one more of the bastards who had beaten his friend.

Then the blows stopped. There was light around him as the soldiers stepped back. He wiped the blood from his eyes and struggled to rise.

As he came to his feet, Macklin's first bullet took him in the chest, splintering his sternum, then glancing sideways and down to rip through the lower lobe of his left lung. The impact knocked Tedesco back, made him sit down hard on the driveway.

The agony was a fire inside his chest. But he put his hands flat on the asphalt to drive himself up. He saw the man with the pistol on the hotel steps, saw him take careful aim, saw the fire spurt from the muzzle.

His body wouldn't respond; things were broken in it now. But his brain was still almost as fast as when the first rush of Paroxysm had seized his senses. He saw the small dark shape emerge from the pistol's jet of flame. It grew rapidly until at the last instant it seemed as big as a softball.

Then Macklin's second bullet entered Frank Tedesco's forehead above the right eyebrow, drilled through his brain, and lodged in the occipital bone at the back of his skull.

Sandrini was horrified at what the screen showed. "General!" he shouted, his voice cracking.

DeVoin came to look over the balding man's shoulder. "What is it?"

"It's out of control is what it is!" Sandrini yelled.

"Lower your voice, mister," DeVoin hissed, at the same time digging his fingers into the rigid muscle that ran between the scientist's right shoulder and neck.

The pain shocked Sandrini. He flinched away.

"Now, what is it?" DeVoin asked.

With trembling hands, the scientist cued up and replayed the scene that had just transpired. "Look for yourself! Couple of small-town bubbas just took out a squad of the best money can buy, General. If Macklin hadn't shot that one, he could've got in here!"

DeVoin thought for a moment, then turned to Sergeant Major Leith. "Call in all the mobile OPs, except for Wexler at the bridge. Tell the men to draw rifles, then take up positions on the hotel grounds. Use a couple of the vans to block up the gateway."

"Yes, sir," said the Belfast man, reaching for his mike.

DeVoin patted the bruised place on Sandrini's shoulder. "Thank you for advising me of that development, Doctor," he said. "And now I'd like you to turn your attention to the matter of analyzing the sample Mr. Macklin will be bringing us."

When Joe B. had thrown himself at the Belgian mercenary and Frank had gone to help, the urge to join in had immediately overwhelmed Jeff Cameron. He flowed to his feet, reaching for his bloodied length of ash.

Sharon had shouted something, probably his name, but his attention was riveted on the scene unrolling on the hotel grounds. With Bob Preiss beside him, he had covered most of the distance between Fung's store and the hotel when the first shot rang out. He didn't stop.

Then he saw the gunman deliberately kill Tedesco. It made the rage seethe in him. He wanted that man's blood, wanted them all dead.

It was not like the first rush of Paroxysm, when his consciousness had been driven to the remotest corners of his brain, loosing the first, inchoate rage against people he loved. With a real enemy in front of him, he could integrate hot fury with coolest calculation. All that he had lost were mercy, moderation and compassion.

But letting the rage flow freely through him did not completely wash away a sense of self-preservation. Now he saw that the front of the hotel was thick with armed soldiers. They slowly formed a firing line at the base of the granite steps.

He stopped.

"Jesus," said Bob Preiss, beside him.

The man who had shot Frank was directing events. Jeff could hear his voice. He wondered if he could get through the riflemen and tear that man's flesh, snap his bones. *Why not?* he thought.

Then he heard another voice – Sharon's, right beside him. She put her hand on his arm. She was shaking her head, crying.

He looked back at the hotel. The rifles came up; to him they seemed slow, but he knew they meant business. He saw the black periods their muzzles made.

Even then, Jeff was not afraid. The stuff that flooded through his lower brain had shut off any feeling – like fear or pity – that might counter the impulse to violence. But now the separation between the rational man and the red beast was dissolving. They were becoming one entity, integrating into a new Jeff Cameron. He felt the process achieve completion, like a blurred double image suddenly resolving into three-dimensional focus.

He was calm and sure of purpose; at the same time, his being rippled with waves of delightful savagery. He had only to arrange the time and circumstances to feed his new appetite.

He turned and took Sharon by the arm, pushed her gently in the direction of Macreedy, who was already ducking around the corner of Fung's. "Run," he said.

Then he spun on his heel and ran in a blur to catch up with Bob Preiss, caught the tavern keeper by the shoulder. "This is not the time!" he said. "They're gonna kill us, we stay here."

Preiss looked back at him, his face an icon of rage. "They shot Frank!"

"They'll shoot us! Don't worry, we'll get 'em! But later! Come on!"

They turned and ran for the corner of Fung's.

Macklin watched them run. The speed was impressive. "Fire!" he ordered, his voice cracking a little with excitement. The headquarters squad opened up at full automatic, the roar of the rifles counterpointed by the tinkling of empty brass cartridges bouncing off the asphalt driveway.

Sharon and the doctor made it around the corner, safely out of the line of fire. Jeff Cameron and Bob Preiss sprinted for cover at superhuman speed, bullets striking the street like heavy rain, shattering the grocery store's front windows and thudding into the canned and packaged goods on the shelves. A round lightly creased Jeff's right shoulder, burning as if a hot wire had been laid on his flesh.

Another tore the heel off Preiss's boot; it felt like somebody had kicked him in the foot. A ricochet bounced back from the storefront and numbed the little finger of his left hand, then hummed off across the street; he scarcely noticed the injury. He and Jeff dove for cover behind the doctor's car, then snaked across the sidewalk on their bellies to join Macreedy and Sharon on the ground beside the store.

"Cease fire!" Macklin ordered and regarded the empty street with satisfaction. A career staff officer, he'd spent that career far from harm's way, and had never commanded on the firing line before. He liked it.

Now that the firing had stopped, Macklin could hear the moans that the Belgian with the broken ribs and nose was making. He looked around him. Tedesco had killed three of the riot-equipped mercenaries and injured two more besides Van Deming.

"Get these bodies out of the way and see to the wounded," he told the man commanding the HQ Squad, a German lieutenant named Schlimmer. "I'll take half your men across the street and make sure those people are not hanging around."

Schlimmer sketched a salute. He kneeled to check Joe B. "This one still lives," he commented.

Macklin pointed the pistol at the back of the unconscious man's head and fired. "No, he's dead," he said. "Get them out of here."

The lieutenant motioned to two of his men, and started to rise. He opened his mouth to say something to Macklin but whatever he was going to say was drowned out by the *crack* of a hunting rifle.

A small dark hole appeared in Schlimmer's forehead. At the same time, his eyes and tongue bulged out like something from a *Tom and Jerry* cartoon. Then the left rear quadrant of his skull blew out in an eruption of blood, bone and brains that spattered the men behind him.

The rifle cracked again, and Macklin found that he was hugging the ground with terror. Another of the mercenaries grunted and fell across the major's legs, where he began to squirm and shudder, screaming something over and over in a foreign language.

Macklin heard someone swiftly issuing orders – "That building! Second-story window! Return fire!" – then the comforting blast of the mercenaries' rifles shooting over his head.

Someone dragged the wounded man off his legs and hauled him away, the man's screams now fading to breathless sobbing.

"You wanna get up now, Major?" said the mercenary who had taken charge after Schlimmer went down. He was a bandy-legged little Texan named Bartlesby, with long-held opinions of staff officers that Macklin's cowering was doing nothing to change.

Bartlesby would have been closing out a thirty-year hitch in the marines as a gunnery sergeant, if he hadn't gotten drunk one night and run a humvee over his commander's piss-ant adjutant. Even so, the behavior might have been overlooked if he hadn't reversed and backed over the son of a bitch. He was about to give the screaming captain a third going over when the MPs yanked him away from the wheel.

He ordered the firing to stop, then helped Macklin to his feet. The major's hands were shaking.

"Kinda different when they's shootin' back," said the Texan. "Was you still anxious to lead some of the men over there, sir?"

Macklin peered across the street. The upper story of the grocery store was a mess: the stucco shattered, the window glassless, its frame splintered and smashed by high velocity impacts. Whoever had been shooting at him was either a lump of torn meat or running for cover like the others.

"Give me four men," he told the Texan.

Bartlesby pointed to the four nearest. "Escort the major across the street," he said. "And try to bring him back again."

Behind the curtains in his room on the hotel's fourth floor, Herb Trainor shook with fear. In the thrillers he liked to read, characters were sometimes described as shaking with terror. It was never the hero who was so affected; always it was some minor bit player in the main drama, whose loss of dignity contrasted nicely with the sang-froid of the star. It had never occurred to Herb Trainor, who identified closely with the protagonists of his favorite adventure series, that he could ever find his knees actually knocking together, and his hands vibrating on the window sill like Ginger Baker on an extended drum solo.

He closed the crack in the curtains through which he had just watched men die. The sight of Macklin coldly executing Joe B., and of the other soldier's head exploding right afterwards, had pasted itself onto the inner screen in

Herb's head. He kept seeing the red of the blood and the gray-pink splatter of brains.

Last night he had been too hungry to set aside any of his sandwiches for breakfast. Now he was glad; anything his stomach contained would be fighting its way up his throat. He stumbled to the bathroom and poured a glass of water. The mineral taste almost made him gag again, but he held it down.

After a minute, he had regained control of his breathing. He went back to the window and peeked out. The street was empty now, no one in sight, and the bodies had been removed from the hotel lawn. The quiet was reassuring. It allowed Trainor's brain to begin working again.

*I've got to get out of here,* he thought.

He finished dressing. He'd been just getting into his pants when the shouting had drawn him to the window. When he was clothed, he went to the door of the room and listened. He heard nothing, but it still took a long time before he could make his trembling hand turn the knob.

He pulled the door an inch toward him and put one eye to the crack. There was no one right outside. He let out a breath. After another eternity, he widened the crack and put his head into the hall.

It was empty.

*Okay, this is it,* he told himself. But still he had trouble moving. His legs kept wanting to bend and lower him to the floor. Finally, gripping the jamb with one hand, he pulled himself out into the corridor. The door to his room closed automatically.

Now that he was out and exposed, more of his system seemed to return to readiness. He fumbled his master key into the service door lock. His shaking hands made it rattle like all the alarm bells in the world chiming, "Here he is, come and get him!" But he managed to get the door to the staircase open, and stepped inside.

He sat on the top step for a while, and put his head as close to between his knees as his paunch would allow. After a while, his heart stopped trying to fight its way free of his chest, and he could breathe again. He stood up and began to descend the stairs.

He had planned to use service corridors and a few other nooks and crannies that long experience with the old building had made him familiar with. He had wanted to keep an eye on things, and then appear smoothly from the background precisely when he was needed.

But now all he wanted was to put distance between himself and the murderous men the new owner had brought in. *Downstairs to the tunnel and straight out,* he told himself, as he passed the door to the third floor. The shakiness in his legs had diminished. They were taking him nimbly down the stairs as if they had developed their very own instinct for self-preservation.

He went by the second-floor door and continued past the door to the kitchen without pausing. At the top of the flight that led down to the basement service corridor, he paused. Below was the open alcove which he would have to cross before he could make it down the last flight, open the locked door to the storage room, and get to the tunnel.

He listened. There were plenty of sounds from outside the hotel: shouts, running boots on asphalt. But the corridor seemed empty. Herb bit his lip and gingerly descended the next flight of stairs.

Halfway down, he could see something on the floor of the service corridor, just outside the opening of the alcove. He took another step, and the something resolved itself into a combat boot.

Herb froze and stared at the footgear. Someone was in the corridor! He had already begun to ease back up the stairs when he was struck by the oddness of the boot's position. It was instep-down, sole-up. Whoever had his foot in it must be lying prone on the floor corridor – and he wasn't moving.

The manager shifted his weight downward, then descended another step. He could see all of the boot now, and some of the khaki pants leg stuffed into its top. Still, there was no movement.

*It's a dead guy,* Herb thought. *It's okay.*

He listened and heard nothing, then came down the final few steps to the alcove. A body was sprawled face-down in the corridor. Herb peeked around the open doorway, and what he saw made his stomach lurch again.

The dead German lieutenant lay against the corridor wall, with a hole in the back of his head that a baseball would have fit into. Herb ducked back into the alcove and closed his eyes. It was only for a moment, but when he opened them he was looking into the upturned face of a soldier who had just backed in through the rear door of the hotel, bent over with the weight of the object he was dragging.

The object was Frank Tedesco's body. Herb looked from the startled soldier to the corpse's face. Its open eyes stared in different directions, and the bones of the head were distorted in odd ways.

The soldier reacted first. He let go of the shoulders of Frank's shirt. The lifeless head hit the concrete floor with a sickening *crack*. The mercenary unslung the rifle from his shoulder in one slick motion and pointed it at Herb Trainor's face.

The hotel man stopped breathing. The opening of the muzzle seemed enormous, a man-sized hole into which he was slowly, slowly tumbling. He was distantly aware of a wet warmth spreading down one leg of his pants.

The rifleman watched Herb Trainor wet his pants and faint. He poked the insensate man with the muzzle, found him inert.

"Corporal of the guard!" he shouted.

# 12

By the time the firing stopped, Jeff, Sharon, Macreedy and Preiss were in the alley behind Fung's grocery. Jeff scanned the deserted lane in both directions, and looked over fences into the back yards of the houses across from the back of the store. He saw no one.

The house that backed onto the lane directly behind the grocery was boarded up, its owners gone to live with their grown kids in Sacramento. The house fronted onto tree-lined Custer Avenue. Its back yard was empty.

"I think the soldiers'll be coming to see what they hit," Jeff said. "Let's cut through between the houses and put some distance between us."

"Until we can get ourselves some firepower," Preiss said.

"Right," said Jeff.

"Wait a minute," said the doctor. What are you talking about, firepower?"

"Don't have time right now, doc," said Preiss. He crossed the alley to a low cedar board fence and vaulted over. "Let's go," he called.

Jeff took Sharon's arm and said, "Come on."

Macreedy was going to say something more, but just then the rear door to the grocery store burst open. A man flung himself out through the portal, tucked and rolled swiftly across the gravel and came up in a kneeling stance that brought his rifle to his shoulder. The weapon was aimed at the doctor, then it swung to Jeff, then to Preiss, then back to Jeff.

Sharon gasped, stifling a scream. The gun flicked toward her then back to her husband.

Jeff did not move. The instincts that said *rush! attack!* were now completely under his control. He smiled at the man with the gun. "Arnie?" he said.

Arnie Fung held the rifle on him for another moment, then lowered it. "Sorry," he said. "Heard the voices, wasn't too sure."

He got smoothly to his feet, went to peek around the corner of the building. He held himself like an experienced hunter in a blind, waiting for the game to appear.

Jeff looked the storekeeper over. He was sure the man was hyped. The speed was there and the hard sharpness in the eye. But a coolness overlay the inner fire.

"Can I ask you something, Arnie?" he said.

Fung did not look around. "Sure."

"You feel any different today?"

Now the man looked back over his shoulder. "You know, I do, kind of. Funny thing, I felt like hell when I got up. Thinking about the cousins. But after I drank my tea, things started, I don't know, looking up."

"You felt kind of energized?"

"That's the word for it, Jeff. Scuse me."

A black van had turned into the far end of the alley. Jeff thought it was the one that had been parked at the end of his street. Arnie Fung stepped away from the corner of his store, snapped the rifle up, and put a round through the van's tinted windshield just below the roofline.

He fired a second shot before the van could reverse out of the line of fire. It hit an inch to the right of the first one, and now the dark glass looked to be home to two spiders. The van backed and turned out of sight, tires squealing and giving off wisps of black smoke. Then it shot across the mouth of the lane, heading for Prescott Avenue. They heard it racing along the main street heading for the hotel.

Arnie peered at the sights of his rifle. "No doubt about it. This thing shoots high."

Preiss said, "You guys, we gotta move."

"He's right," Jeff told Arnie. "The soldiers are probably gonna come here. Too many guns."

He helped Sharon over the fence. Arnie vaulted one handed, the rifle in the other, then took up a stance on the other side, looking for another target. "You coming, doc?" he said.

Macreedy had the look of a man who was having to take in too much in too short a time. "Wait a minute," he said, transferring the jar of water from one hand to another as he sought to order his thoughts. "This is nuts. You people are behaving like this is the psychotics' big day out or something. We've got to make some sense out of this."

Jeff found he could hold his impatience in check. He just wished it didn't take the old man forever to say his piece. "Couple of minutes," he said, speaking absurdly slowly, "the people who were just shooting at us are gonna be here. I think the only thing they're going to want to make out of this is some more corpses. What say we go somewhere a little quieter if you need to talk?"

Macreedy wanted to swear or maybe smash something. But Cameron was surely right. The doctor had seen soldiers in combat, back in Korea. The first rifleman to come into the alley would spray it with bullets, then look to see whether or not the people he had shot were in any way dangerous.

"Okay," he said, and let Jeff help him over the fence. Then they ran across the yard, along the side of the house, and out onto Custer Avenue. The house opposite was an old-fashioned, two-story woodframe with a big front porch. A body was stretched head-down on the steps. It had leaked a lot of blood. The bare foot of another protruded through the open front door.

"Come on," said Preiss, and led them across the street and up into the house. Sharon averted her eyes and went up the stairs two at a time. The doctor wanted to stop and examine the dead man on the steps, but Jeff lifted him by the armpit and pulled him into the house. An old woman was dead in the front doorway.

"It's Tom Peebles and his mother," Macreedy said.

"Yeah," said Arnie. "Looks like they went at each other over breakfast."

Macreedy looked. The old woman had been beaten to death with the splintered kitchen chair that lay beside her. But before she succumbed, she had managed to slash one of her son's arteries with a paring knife.

"Let's get away from the windows," he said. They moved into the kitchen. The Peebles' interrupted breakfast was on the table, scrambled eggs congealing on cold, soggy toast.

They sat on the remaining chairs. Sharon put her arms on the table and lowered her head onto them. Arnie swung his seat around so that he could look down the hall and out the front door, to see if anyone was following them.

Macreedy recognized that somebody had to bring some sanity to this situation before they all went completely off the map. But the instant he drew breath to speak he found Jeff Cameron's palm an inch from his face.

Macreedy wanted to say something, but Jeff beat him to it. It was easy: the doctor's slowness made it child's play to read his body language and facial expressions. Besides, right now Jeff was more interested in Arnie Fung.

"So, Arnie. You were saying about how things started looking up," he said.

The grocer kept his gaze fixed on the view out the front door. "Yeah," he said. "I started feeling all right, you know, and then I look out the window, and there's you and Bob and the guys. Damndest thing, I suddenly got this real urge to shoot you." He shrugged. "No offense."

"None taken," said Jeff.

"So, anyway, I go get my gun outta the attic, and I come back and see these military assholes shootin' up the street. It comes to me that they must be the bad guys, so I open up on them instead." He patted the stock of the rifle. "Dropped a couple of them, bing, bong. Then they all start shootin' back, I figure it's time to leave."

There was a drip coffee maker on the counter, its carafe half full. Jeff rose, got a clean cup from beside the sink, and poured some. It was still almost hot.

"Gotta tell you, Arnie," he said, "you're the first person I've seen today who isn't totally out of control."

"Yeah?" Fung thought about it. "Well, you remember I did a lot of martial arts stuff when I was a kid. My dad was into the heritage thing. I guess that training taught me how to get it on without going crazy."

Sharon lifted her head and looked at Arnie. "You don't think this is maybe just a little crazy?"

Arnie shrugged again. "Hell no. They started it."

She put her head back down again.

"Well we're gonna end it," said Bob Preiss. Tom Peebles' cup was still on the table, a half-inch of cold coffee in the bottom. Preiss threw the contents on the floor and reached for the carafe. He poured and drank.

The reaction was almost instantaneous, but the tavern keeper got a hold of it. "Man," he said. "It does kick."

Jeff took a gulp of his own, felt the renewed surge. "It does," he said.

Arnie looked questioningly from one to the other, then the light came on. "Ah," he said. "Something in the water."

"Yes," said the doctor, "and it has impaired your judgment. None of you is thinking straight." He tried to take Jeff's cup, but the young man effortlessly avoided the slow hand.

"We've got to get around town, find all the men we can and get them focused," Jeff said, taking another sip.

"We're gonna need more guns," Preiss said.

"Must be a hundred rifles and shotguns in this town," Arnie put in. He got up and found a cup, poured himself the last of the coffee.

"Hell," said the taverner, draining his cup, "this is Oregon. We're probably better armed than they are."

Jeff put the empty cup down. "First we'd better stash Sharon and the Doc somewhere safe."

"They're not like us, are they?" asked Arnie. He peered at the old man and the woman. "Didn't work?"

"Didn't drink," said Jeff.

They were talking at their own speed, but Jeff could see that Sharon was able to follow what they were saying. It must be like listening to a speeded up tape recording; after a while you got used to it. Now she sat up. "Not going to drink it. This stuff is making you guys crazy."

The three speeded up men exchanged a look. "So where should we stash 'em?" asked Preiss.

"Never mind that," Macreedy broke in. "It's time I examined all of you. The speed you're going can't be sustained. For all I know, your hearts are about to hit the wall at 90 miles an hour."

"We're kinda busy right now, Doc," said Jeff, slowly.

"Busy being nuts," said the doctor. "Let me take a look at you."

He moved closer so that he could look into Jeff's face, reaching for the eyelids to see if there was any pronounced pupil dilation or contraction. But Jeff batted the old man's hands away, so fast that the impact numbed both the doctor's wrists. Then, while the surprise was still slowly registering on Macreedy's face, Jeff reflexively closed his right fist and struck at the doctor's throat. He checked the blow barely in time, his clenched fingers just brushing the blue-veined skin above the knot of the old man's tie.

"Don't touch me, Doc," Jeff said.

The doctor stepped back, fear blossoming in his face. "Christ in a crino-line," he said, "will you look at yourselves? Your friends and neighbors have been killed! Each one of you is a flea's whisker away from running amok!"

He pulled off his hat and slapped the table with it. "We're not equipped to deal with this! I'm an old man, Sharon's in shock, and you're all hopped up to the limit! We've got to get the police in here!"

"What police?" said Fung. "The nearest cops are over in Evans, and what are they gonna do against military firepower?"

"Yeah," said Preiss. "We don't even know whose soldiers those are! That ain't US Army camouflage – maybe it's some kinda invasion!" He drank more coffee. "Time we find out for sure, we could all be dead."

"Bob's right, Doc," said Jeff. "Looks like we gotta handle this ourselves."

Sharon put her hand out to Jeff, and her voice trembled. "Will you listen to what you're saying? Handle what? Look, we don't know what's going on, but there are soldiers at the hotel, real soldiers with automatic weapons!"

Arnie smiled. "And we're gonna kick their sorry butts!"

Jeff patted his wife's hand. "Don't worry," he said, and he could see that his flippant tone made her want to scream. To the others he said, "Whattaya say we get together at the bottling plant, make that our home base. We get some more people and guns, then we figure out what to do next?"

He spoke slowly so Sharon and the doctor could understand. "In the meantime," he continued, "why don't you two take a drink and come up to speed? I guarantee you, you're gonna like it."

He went to the sink, filled a tumbler with water and offered it to Macreedy. The way the doctor backed off, it might have been a poisonous snake.

"Jeff," he said, "you've got to listen. You're not behaving normally. Whatever they put in the water, it wasn't for your own good. You're all doped out of your minds."

Jeff smiled, and continued to hold out the glass. "You're probably right, Doc, but so what? All I know is I feel better than I ever felt, the best day I ever had! I could run ten miles! I could tear down a building with my hands! For the first time in years, I feel like a winner again!

"Yeah, sure," said the old man. "So you're gonna get together with your buddies and fight a little war? That's being a winner?"

Jeff laughed, and took a drink from the glass. "What's going to make me feel like a winner is winning! You wanna know how I feel, Doc? I'm mad, crazy mad! I'm like the man in the movie, I'm mad as hell, I'm not takin' any more shit and it's fuckin' fantastic!"

He turned to Sharon, held out the glass. "Come on. Try some. It's like Christmas and your birthday and your first lay all rolled into one! I don't know how it's making me feel this good, but I know I don't ever want it to stop!" He put the glass into her hand, a little of the contents slopping over onto the table. "Here, babe, take a drink. Take it."

Sharon took the glass. She put it on the table in front of her.

"Don't," said Macreedy.

Sharon looked up at Jeff. She knew he was right about how he felt. He looked more alive than she'd seen him in a long time. Something had returned to his face that had gone missing in the past few years. He had won back the life force she used to see shining out of him when he'd come in off the pitcher's mound after striking out the best the other side could put up.

It was like seeing the young Jeff Cameron's face superimposed on the man he had become, like a trick photo. But the more she looked, the more she knew that it was not just a combination of old and new; there was a third face, the wolf face he had worn when he was strangling their son. It was under control now, but it was still there, and it frightened her.

She pushed the glass away. "No," she said.

"We're still pretty close to the hotel," Arnie said from the doorway. "We should move out."

They went through the kitchen door and across the Peebles' back yard. Jeff and Bob and Arnie sped across the neatly trimmed grass and eased over the fence like athletes on a training run. Sharon and the old man followed more slowly. The doctor still carried his jar full of water.

From the upstairs rear window of the Peebles' house, Lou Meecham watched them until they were out of sight. He listened to the house, ears open for the little creaks and whispers that would tell him if anyone had remained behind. After a couple of minutes, he was sure enough of its emptiness to go downstairs.

He'd been lucky. By the time the four men and the woman had come up the front stairs, he had already searched the downstairs and was exploring the upper rooms. He'd even found what he was looking for: a set of keys that ought to fit the old station wagon out front.

If he hadn't been so worried for Adele, if he'd just been out on his own, it might almost have been enjoyable to use the old skills once again; to slip silently from one hiding place to the next; to extend the senses to their limit, tuned for any sound that meant danger.

For a few moments, as he'd stood motionless in a bedroom that he now knew had belonged to a man named Peebles, following the conversation in the kitchen, he'd felt the old buzz. It was hearing what the red-haired guy from the hotel had said about feeling young again.

It would be good to feel like the Lou Meecham of all those years ago, the man he'd been before he met Macklin and DeVoin. That might be worth a little craziness.

He went down the stairs, paused to listen at the foot of the stairwell. The bodies were where they had lain. He listened again, heard nothing, and moved into the kitchen.

Sharon had left the glass of water untouched on the table. He picked it up, sniffed at it. Then he put it down. The temptation had been brief. He'd seen the speed and coordination with which the two beer bellies had taken on the mercenaries on the hotel driveway. But he'd also seen what the stuff had done for the Peebles.

He rooted around in the cupboards and fridge, finding some juice and chocolate covered cookies. He put them in a paper sack he found neatly folded under the sink and eased down the front hallway past the bodies.

He poked his head through the open doorway and checked the street. Nothing moved. He looked at his watch: it wasn't nine o'clock yet on a Saturday morning; probably half the town was still in bed.

He considered making a noise. Get a car and race up and down the street, blowing the horn and shouting out a warning to the people: *lock your doors and don't drink the water!*

It might even save a few lives. But his voice would call in every homicidal maniac loose in the town. He doubted he could take one of them, let alone a crowd.

And then who would rescue Adele, cowering right now in her fragile hideout? Who would get the woman he loved safely away from this place of blood and terror?

He went quickly and silently down the front stairs, stepping over the pool of blood at the bottom, and tried the door of the station wagon. It was unlocked.

Peebles had kept the car in good running order. The motor started on the first crank of the ignition, coming smoothly to life. Lou checked the gas gauge – half a tank – and revved the engine gently. it hummed a little louder then settled down to a purr.

The car was pointed toward Bridge Road. If he pulled out onto that thoroughfare, the mercenaries in front of the hotel might open up on him.

He u-turned on the narrow street and drove at a careful speed toward Rockwell. His eyes moved constantly, checking the houses' front porches, the ornamental bushes on the lawns, fences and corners, parked cars – anywhere that might conceal a man like Jeff Cameron, the nice kid who today felt good about getting together with the neighbors and dealing out some death.

He turned left on Rockwell, drove the hundred and fifty feet to the lane that paralleled Prescott Avenue, turned into the alley and stopped.

Macklin didn't like being off the hotel grounds. Even just going across the street to the tavern, with four armed professionals to guard him, he was sweating. He kept remembering how Schlimmer's eyes bulged just before his head blew open. He wondered if the man had felt anything, if he'd known he'd been hit. Or was it just *flash!* then sudden darkness? *Bang!* you're dead.

Macklin was no stranger to death. Frank Tedesco was only the latest in a long line of men and women Tag Macklin had seen die. Some of them he'd done himself, point blank, face to face, seeing the look in their eyes – could be rage, could be hate, could be numb despair – as he slowly tightened his grip on the little automatic, until it kicked back and spat its indisputable message right into their heads.

*You're mortal,* it said, *and here's the proof.* But in all the deaths he'd seen – by bullet, by chemicals that made the victims choke on their own fluids, at the end of a long plunge from a moving helicopter over the nighttime sea – in all of those, no one had been shooting at Macklin's own, unmarked flesh.

It had not been a pleasant experience when the sniper opened up on them. He'd barely been able to keep his sphincter closed. Now, as he scuttled to the other side of Prescott Avenue – two men already gone before him, two more crouched behind the hotel's low outer wall, waiting to follow up – his bowels wanted to let go again.

He made it across the asphalt and the sidewalk, flattened himself against the tavern wall, his breath coming in short puffs. He nodded to the two men crouched beneath the shattered window. They were the Canadian and the South Carolinian who had dumped Paroxysm into the lake. Now they stood up fast and each fired a burst into the saloon, then ducked to either side of the window.

Nothing came back at them.

"Inside," Macklin said. The men went through the door, blasting. Again, nothing.

The major signaled the two across the road to come over. They ran toward him, zig-zagging across the pavement, and crouched against the wall, rifles covering both directions.

"Keep your eyes open," Macklin said. Then, still expecting a bullet from anywhere, he crouched and ducked through the tavern door.

Bob's Tavern was a ruin. Most of the furniture was smashed. At every step, broken glass crunched underfoot. It looked to Macklin as if the Three Stooges had used the place for Olympic tryouts.

The first pair of mercenaries had passed through the main room. They'd checked the storeroom and the back door, found one empty and the other locked from the inside. They came back, shaking their heads.

"Find me something to get some water in, something with a lid," he said.

The Canadian went behind the bar, found a jar almost as big as his own head, half-filled with olives. "This do?" he said.

Macklin nodded. "Rinse it clean and fill it up. Then we'll get the hell out of here."

The mercenary opened the jar and threw the olives to the floor. There was a sink just back of the bar. He turned on the tap, then filled, emptied and refilled the jar a few times. Then he filled it a last time and sealed it.

"Done," he said.

Macklin took the jar, and tucked it inside his combat jacket. He stuck his head out the door. The two back-up mercenaries were alert.

"Anything?"

"Clear," said the senior man.

"Okay," said Macklin.

"Wait one," whispered the Canadian. He held a finger to his lips, then pointed to the back door.

Macklin froze, then he heard it: a car engine, quiet, outside in the alley.

The Canadian beckoned with a finger for the major to come away from the door. He stuck his head out front and hand-signaled the two on the sidewalk to watch for something to come out of the alley. Then he moved quietly toward the rear exit, the South Carolinian following.

Macklin drew his pistol. He didn't want the men to see how badly his hand was shaking, so he held it two-handed in a combat crouch and aimed at the back door. Even clutched in both hands, it still wavered.

But the two mercenaries had long since written the major off. The Canadian nodded to his buddy, then gently slid back the dead bolt on the back door. He inched the door open until he could look through the crack, ready to pull it wide and hose the alley if anything moved in his field of vision.

He saw nothing but the macadamized lane and the ramshackle fence directly behind the tavern. But the vehicle motor was louder now.

A car door slammed, close. The mercenary darted his upper body out the door for a quick look, then stepped through the opening, brought up his rifle and fired a burst.

132

Lou Meecham eased the station wagon down the lane, eyes moving. He had all the windows rolled down, the better to hear.

He was halfway to the place where he'd left Adele when he heard the short burst of automatic fire from the tavern. It sounded like two guns. Seconds later, he heard another burst.

*Not combat,* his old experience told him. *House to house stuff, sweeping a room before going in.*

That was good. That meant the soldiers were not yet positioned in the buildings. They were sniper-hunting, and they'd be cautious; they'd take time, check around each corner, set up before opening doors, look behind and under stuff – because the next turn might bring them into the sights of a crazy with a gun.

He knew what had happened on Prescott Avenue, even though he'd been a block away, looking for a car. He'd heard the *pop* of Macklin's pistol, then the fusillade of automatic fire as the mercenaries blasted the street.

Then he'd heard the sharper *crack* of a deer rifle, followed by an even longer and louder storm of automatic weapons, the shattering of glass.

*Sniper,* he'd told himself. That ought to slow them, keep their heads down.

So he figured there was just enough time to ease down the lane, recover Adele from beneath the pile of boxes, then back the car up the lane and out onto Rockwell. From there, he'd go east, look for a road leading into the hills, find someplace they could hide – even under a pile of leaves if they had to – until the madness was over.

He let the car roll gently to a stop behind Fung's. The pile of crates and cartons looked just as he'd left it. He got out, leaving the door open. He crouched low, looking around, watching for movements, shadows in windows, listening for the click or scrape that meant someone was near and dangerous.

Nothing. He could hear voices and engine sounds on Prescott Avenue, orders being given, boots running, vehicle doors slamming.

But nothing was coming this way. Doubled over, he moved around the back of the car and approached the pile of boxes near the front fender on the passenger side. He put his face close.

"Adele?" he whispered.

"I'm here," she said, and began to push her way out of the hiding place.

"Whoa! Easy!" he whispered. "There's men really close by. Shhh! Let me get you clear."

He quietly lifted the cartons away, setting them gently down. Adele was squatting on her heels, her back braced against the grocery store's wall. When she was uncovered, he took her hand and helped her rise.

She groaned softly. "I haven't moved since you left. Not even when they were shooting. God I was scared."

"We'll talk later," he said. "Now we gotta get in the car and go. Keep low."

She duckwalked to the passenger door and eased it open, while Lou went around the back and slid into the driver's seat. He was about to say, "Don't shut the door!" when she unthinkingly pulled it toward her. To Lou, the slam sounded like all the noise in the world.

He jammed the gearshift into reverse and floored the gas pedal. At the same time, a man in combat fatigues ducked his head out of the tavern's back door, then stepped out and let go a snap burst from his assault rifle.

"Down!" Lou shouted, one hand on the wheel, the other pressing Adele down onto the floorboards. He scrunched himself down as fast he could go, holding the wheel steady and hoping it would stay straight.

Bullets thrummed over his head. The windshield shattered, then the back window blew out. The driver's side mirror rang like a cheap gong as it was torn off.

The rifleman dropped to one knee, aimed and fired at the chromed grill. The steel jacketed military rounds poured into the engine compartment, ripped open the radiator and bent the fan out of shape. Then they cracked the block and the engine seized.

Lou Meecham knew what the sounds meant. He felt the car lurch. Before it could lose momentum, he shifted into neutral and cranked the wheel hard left.

The station wagon spun in a tight turn. It's back bumper burst through a picket fence. Inside, Lou threw himself at the passenger side door, away from the soft target his side of the car now offered to the man who was trying to kill them.

"Out! Out!" he screamed at Adele as he pushed her door open. He man-handled her up from her crouch in the passenger side footwell and bundled her out the door. Then he sprawled out of the car after her.

The Canadian loosed another burst that shattered the driver's side window and tore the armrest from the inside of the door. Then he paused and looked for movement, his eyes checking the windows of the buildings overlooking the lane, in case anybody was lining up for a shot at him.

The South Carolinian and the major came out of the tavern after him, then the back-up pair came into the alley from where it met Bridge Road. They got low and looked around.

The major saw the shot-up station wagon backed through the picket fence. "What was it?" he asked the Canadian.

"It's that guy, eh? The guy and his wife you put out front."

"Christ!" said Macklin. "Did you get 'em?"

"Not sure. Don't think so."

"You gotta get 'em! Both of you, go! Now!"

The Canadian and the South Carolinian exchanged looks. "How's that go, major?" said the Canadian.

"Those people, they know things. Names, histories. They can't be left alive."

"Then how come you didn't just pop 'em when you had the chance?" asked the South Carolinian.

"It didn't seem..." Macklin began, then recovered his dignity. "I'm not explaining this to you, soldier. I'm ordering you to go get those people. Now!"

Almost, Macklin brought up the automatic in his hand. It was his reflex. Whenever subordinates showed the slightest inclination to contest his will, he'd always dropped the hammer on them.

This time, almost, he was going for it as usual. But the look in the eyes of the two mercenaries stopped him. For the first time, he realized what it meant that there was no Uniform Code of Military Justice behind him. No Judge Advocate General. No military police. Just him and some armed men in an alley, hard men who'd kill him without taking time for a whole lot of mental debate. He relaxed his grip on the handgun.

Macklin didn't like the look on the Canadian's face, the smugness that said he was enjoying making the staff officer grasp the reality of his situation. "The thing is, Major," the man said. "We signed on for specific assignments, eh? Dump the shit in the lake. Security at the command post. Security on the way out. So we're not getting paid to play hunt-the-weasel in a town could be full of armed crazies. These folks already acting wa-a-ay different from your videos."

"Make your point," Macklin said.

"I think what the man's tryin' to say," said the South Carolinian, "is that goin' after them folks constitutes new terms of engagement, sir, for which additional compensation ought to be forthcomin'."

The major ground his teeth. "How much?"

The South Carolinian looked at the Canadian. "Five?" he asked.

The Canadian nodded. "Sounds right."

The South Carolinian turned to the major. "Five grand."

"Each," said his partner.

Macklin would have enjoyed skinning them both, slowly. But he said, "All right. Now, go get 'em."

The two mercenaries smiled at each other and moved up the lane. They skirted around the car, found it empty and passed through the broken fence. They were feeling good about the work: an extra five on top of the fifteen they were already making for the weekend. And rubbing the major's nose in his own shit.

"Chubby little guy and his chubby little wife," said the South Carolinian. "That's an easy five."

The Canadian nodded. "I'll go first. Watch my back, eh?" said the Canadian.

"Check, buddy."

They moved away from the lane. Macklin waved the other two men to follow him to the hotel, at the double. The jar of tap water sloshed in his jacket with each step that brought him closer to the safety of stone walls.

# 13

Lou and Adele had not gone far. Through the back yard and across Custer, as fast as they could, then ducked down behind a parked car. He got between Adele and the body of Tom Peebles a few doors down, but he knew she'd seen it: he'd heard her gasp.

Now his mind was racing through a dwindling number of options. They couldn't stay where they were. Whatever was supposed to have happened here, it obviously wasn't working. DeVoin and Macklin had put him and Adele out on the street as if it were a death sentence. But here they were, alive and chock full of information about who had done what to Prescott Springs. So somebody would be coming to make sure that what the Meechams knew would die with them.

He'd already checked the cars on this block. None of them had keys in the ignition or tucked in the sun-visor or snug in a magnetized box behind the bumper. He didn't know how to hotwire a modern car. And who knows? Try to pry up a locked hood, and he might even get a car alarm *wheep-wheeping* in his ears.

He didn't want to go into the houses. Behind any door might be a family of small-town Americans, real heartland cliches, sleeping in on a slow Saturday morning. Or there might be a speeded-up monster with a butcher knife, drenched in his loved ones' blood, just wishing someone new would wander in.

The Peebles place had already yielded up its only treasure. Besides, it might not be clear anymore. Somebody could've moved in by now.

The analysis left only one option; it wasn't too attractive, but it was thinkable. The waiter had talked about getting the townspeople together at the bottling plant. At least two of the people he'd eavesdropped on had not drunk the tainted water; maybe there would be others. Even the three men who had been under its influence had not been raging out of control.

"We've got to get to that old bottling plant on the bridge road," he said. "We'll be safer there."

He could see she was scared. He wished he could just hold her, keep her safe.

"Why don't we just try one of these houses? If we can get to a phone, we could call for help," she said.

"Tried it. Phones are out. Besides, there's no safety here. The general will send people after us, now he knows we're still alive."

"If you're sure," she said, and took his hand. Her fingers were cold.

He looked through the window of the car they were crouched behind. He could see through the sideyard of the house opposite, all the way to where he had crashed the station wagon through the picket fence. Two men with rifles were looking into the car's windows. "Come on," he said. "Stay low."

Crouching, they ran down the sideyard of the house they were in front of, cut diagonally across its back yard, climbed its rear fence and arrived in the service lane. Lou looked back the way they'd come and cursed under his breath.

The lawn had not been mowed for a while. There were no actual footprints, but a trained eye would see where two people had recently run through it. He swore again. He might as well be drawing chalk arrows to lead the pursuers on.

He squeezed Adele's hand. "We're gonna make it," he said. "Come on."

He led her down the lane toward Bridge Road. There were woods on the other side; they looked like parkland attached to the hotel. They might go all the way to the bottling plant, which he thought was not more than a quarter of a mile toward the bridge.

If he could get them across the road and into the trees, they'd have a better chance. *Less likelihood of crazies,* he thought. *And I know how to move and hide in the woods. At least I used to.*

He pulled Adele after him to the corner. There was a solid wood fence at the rear of the last house on Custer, the one next to the Peebles. He lay down on his side and put just the top half of his head around the corner. Chances were, anybody watching a block and a half away at the hotel would not see the movement.

There were no cars parked on Bridge Road. He had an unobstructed view of the Prescott Springs Hotel, but he could see no movement in the grounds. He lay still and watched for twenty seconds, holding his gaze steady on the front steps, letting his peripheral vision pick up any motion in his visual field.

*There, behind the pillar on the porch. And there, just poking up above the low wall around the parking lot.* DeVoin's men were probably right where they had been, but now they were keeping out of sight.

That was good. Fewer eyes watching, more time needed for them to get into firing position. He inched back out of sight and rose to a crouch.

"Listen," he told his wife. "I'll count, one, two, three, and on three we'll run across the road and into those woods. I want you to keep low and move as fast as you can."

She blinked and swallowed. "Are the soldiers there?"

"If we go fast, they won't have time to aim before we're across."

"Okay," she said. She was shaking but the grip that held his hand was strong.

"Ready? One... two... go!" He yanked her hand and they burst out of the lane. He could hear her feet slapping the pavement behind him, and her voice saying, "Ohgodohgodohgodohgod..." all the way across.

They were more than halfway when the first rounds hit the asphalt behind them and went whining off toward the bridge. Somebody *was* watching, Lou thought. The next burst was closer, the bullets closing in as the shooter swung his rifle in an arc to catch them.

But then they were off the pavement and onto grass, and he pulled Adele after him as he dove headlong into the underbrush between two big cedars whose ancient boles were thick enough to stop anything DeVoin could throw at them.

"Come on," he said. "Let's get out of sight of the road."

He snaked on his belly through the undergrowth, Adele right behind him. When they were thirty feet in from the road, he rose to a crouch and listened. He heard footsteps, then someone shouting.

"Let's go," he said. "There's a trail ahead."

They broke through a screen of bushes and found a graveled walking trail that ran south from the hotel. They turned left and ran.

The Canadian and the South Carolinian had crossed Custer and begun checking the back yards first. They came across the disturbed grass where Lou and Adele had run, and followed the trail. But they thought it better to shelter behind the fence for a look-see and listen before venturing into the lane.

"Guy's been out long enough to have found a gun, eh?" said the Canadian.

His partner agreed. "Small town, people been known to hang a 30-30 in their truck window. Not hard to get."

They listened for a minute, heard nothing. Then a rattle of rifle fire, and a second burst. The South Carolinian stood up, took a quick look toward Bridge Road. He was in time to see Lou and Adele disappear between the trees.

"And they're off," he said.

The two mercenaries went over the fence and ran to the corner, their bootheels thumping hard. They paused at the corner, and the Canadian put his hands to his mouth and called out, "Hey, the hotel! Two friendlies here! Hold your fire!"

He heard a Texan voice answer, "Slow and easy keeps you breathin'! Come on out where we can see you!"

The Canadian and his partner moved slowly out into view. Nobody fired. The South Carolinian sketched a salute and the two men crossed the road, pushed through the undergrowth and found the gravel walk. South of them, it climbed a small rise. They listened, heard a distant sound of running feet, and set off in pursuit.

Sandrini took the water sample from Macklin's hands and carried it over to the makeshift laboratory he had assembled in a corner of the ballroom. It stood on a table that was draped with a blue cloth that hung down to the floor.

DeVoin believed in planning comprehensively. The miscellaneous materiel for this mission included equipment that would allow Sandrini to conduct a detailed chemical analysis. The set-up was makeshift only in its temporary character – the equipment was state-of-the-analyst's-art: the latest Shimadzu gas chromatograph and a Waters mass spectrometer; a Varian nuclear magnetic resonance spectrometer; a Perkin Elmer inductive coupled plasma rig for combustion analysis.

The equipment was enough to support a decent private analytical lab – the kind that did employee drug testing for department stores or examines the urine of race horses that ran a little faster than their past form had indicated. In fact, that was what the suppliers of the gear thought it would be used for when they leased it to a balding chemist with impeccably forged references, who paid the first six months in advance, and who now intended to abandon it all in the next hour.

140

Sandrini was in a hurry. He decided to skip the ICP process: he already knew the carbon, hydrogen, nitrogen and oxygen contents of the sample, so a combustion analysis would be redundant. Instead, he mixed 250 milliliters of tap water from the tavern with a highly purified organic solvent, then drew off a few microliters of the resulting extract in a capillary tube.

He switched on the HP GC/MS and fed the extract into the tenax adsorption column. This was a length of fused silica tubing inside a temperature controlled oven. A flow of inert helium gas carried the sample along the tube, and the material coating its interior caused the organics to separate, so that they came out the other end at different times.

The mass spectrometer then analyzed the outcome, and fed the results into a computer that quickly compared them against known compounds, including Paroxysm. The scientist watched the list of identified substances come up, line by line, on the computer screen. And then the computer registered an unknown compound.

"There you are," said Sandrini. "Now, let's see if we can find out *what* you are." He turned to the NMR, which would sort out the fragment ions in the mass spectrum and analyze molecular atomic connectivity. The machine began to do its magic.

While he had been working, DeVoin had come to stand unnoticed behind him. That's why Sandrini jumped a little when the hard, flat voice spoke almost in his ear, "Where are we, Doctor?"

"Not there yet. I've isolated the new compound, and now I'm trying to nail down the details. We're probably not more than a few minutes from the answer."

"Let me know, soonest," said the general.

DeVoin went over to the communications post. The bank of video monitors now showed variations of the same scene. All the vans that had been dispersed around the town had come in. The men had picked up arms and ammunition, and most had been reassigned to perimeter security.

Two of the vans had been parked in the hotel's gateway effectively blocking that opening in the surrounding wall. Their cameras, equipped with telephoto lenses, now monitored the two approaches to the grounds along Bridge Road and Prescott Avenue.

DeVoin scanned the rows of screens, saw nothing moving on either thoroughfare. The absence of motion offered no comfort.

Although he could not afford to display any hint of concern, the fluidity of their situation worried him. He had expected to be at the center of an island of security amidst a sea of other people's troubles – a violent, maddened population, whose every member was intent on killing anyone who came within reach.

When he saw them using weapons, he'd been surprised, but not unduly alarmed. Out-of-control civilians flailing away with frying pans and garden implements were well within the handling capabilities of his hired force. Club, electroshock and a bullet or two where necessary could have handled things.

But then had come the fight on the front driveway. A couple of middle-aged losers had waded into his armed professionals and killed several of them. The second one would have killed more if Macklin hadn't shot him.

Then it got worse. Two rounds from a sniper and two men dead in as many seconds. That was something he had not counted on. They had brought only rifles, and no more than a hundred rounds per man. The planning had included the possibility of a quick slap-down of local law enforcement, if any cops had happened to be in town. They hadn't expected to need to lay down suppressive fire, so they had not brought even a squad machine gun, let alone mortars or rocket propelled grenades.

If Sandrini's worst fears were correct, if they had turned a town full of beer-bellied bubbas into hypercoordinated killing machines, then the first organized assault on the hotel could be the last.

DeVoin weighed his options then with characteristic speed he made his decision. He stepped out of the ballroom, crossed to the elevators and went upstairs. In the presidential suite was a small overnight bag; nestled among his shaving kit and toiletries was a compact mobile satellite telephone.

DeVoin should have returned the unit when he left the service. Somehow, he had neglected to do so. He flipped it open and punched in a number. The phone sent a signal directly to a military communications satellite in a geosynchronous orbit over the United States, and was redirected to its destination less than thirty miles from where DeVoin was standing.

At a small, private airfield on the other side of Evans, a similar phone vibrated silently in the pocket of a man seated in a folding lawn chair beneath the wing of a single-engined DeHavilland Beaver. The four-seater plane was fitted with floats as well as wheels, and could land on anything flat. It had been rented by the week.

The man fished the phone out of his jacket and answered it. He had piloted the general on several occasions. He flew where and when he was told to,

142

asked no questions other than *where to* and *when*, and kept his mouth firmly shut the rest of the time.

"She's warmed up and ready when you are, sir," the pilot said into the phone.

"You know where I am," said DeVoin. "I want you to put down at the far end of the lake and be ready to reach the pick-up point on the shortest notice."

"On the way," said the pilot, and closed the cover on the phone.

DeVoin put the phone into pocket of his combat jacket. He reached into the overnight bag, brought out a nine-millimeter automatic and checked to make sure its magazine was full and its chamber empty. He tucked the gun into the waistband of his loose-fitting fatigue pants and smoothed the jacket down over it. Then he went back to the ballroom.

"Anything to report?" he asked Sandrini.

"Not yet. Maybe half an hour."

The general moved over to communications. "Advise Blueberry that the schedule is changing. Bug-out time is now flexible. I want him ready to roll on my word."

"Yes, sir," said the noncom, and picked up his mike.

DeVoin turned to Macklin. "Major, there was a development while you were out getting that sample. We have a prisoner."

Macklin expressed surprise. DeVoin told him about Herb Trainor's overnight stay and his capture on the stairs.

"I think it's time we observed the effects of this agent at first hand," said DeVoin, "and Mr. Trainor should make a good subject."

Wexler was having a quiet morning at the bridge. He had turned back four vehicles during the night and two since sunrise, all inbound. No one had tried to leave town. There had been no more "flats" to fix.

He had heard the short bursts of automatic fire a little while ago, but they hadn't alarmed him. The shooting hadn't sounded like any kind of firefight, so even though the chance of gunplay had been minimized in Macklin's mission briefing, Wexler wasn't surprised.

It was an axiom of military science that no battle plan ever survived contact with the enemy. This mission, like every other mission he'd ever been on, was not going exactly according to plan. Only a full-weight asshole of a staff officer ever expected plans and timetables to turn into genuine four-dimensional reality. That's why the art of soldiering was so often the art of improvisation – especially the kind of soldiering Wexler did.

So when the word came that the carefully detailed schedule was now so much bum-wad, and that bug-out could be any time, Wexler took it in stride. But he prepared to improvise.

"Hagen, Medford," he called. "Get everything that's going with us into the truck."

The men moved to comply. Wexler thought for a moment. "Break out the M-16s, lock and load, and place them where they're handy."

"We got trouble?" asked Hagen.

"You'll get all the trouble you'll ever need, you don't do what I just told you."

He got a pair of field binoculars from the truck and took a good long look down Bridge Road toward the hotel. He could make out the vans parked around the entrance, but nobody was moving. He did see some movement near the bottling plant.

"I say jump," he told the men on the bridge, "be ready to jump."

Herb Trainor came to as he was being taped to a chair in his office. It was a sturdy piece of furniture, solid oak, that dated from the hotel's earliest days. He had found it in a storage room and had it refinished. Ordinarily, he liked sitting on it, with a brocade cushion to soften the ample seat. It made him feel as if he and the history of the hotel were somehow connected.

Now he was more connected to the place than he had ever wanted to be. The soldier who had pointed a gun at him was winding duct tape around his left arm, snugging it tightly to the chair. His right arm was already immobile, and so were his feet. A second soldier appeared from behind him, wrapping another band of gray adhesive around his chest.

"Oughta do it," said the first man, slicing off the end of the tape with a twin-bladed combat knife he pulled from a boot sheath. He cut the other man's tape for him, and they patted down the ends. Then they left, and neither of them looked at the captive.

There were few truly happy moments credited to the ledger of Herb Trainor's life. There had been many more on the debit side, including a handful of genuinely miserable times. But this was without doubt the worst.

A tear rolled down his cheek. He tried to wipe it on his shoulder, but could only erase the lowest part of its track. He contemplated his future from a window of despair: he had seen murder done, and he had read enough books to know that the killers would not leave any inconvenient witnesses to describe them to the authorities.

Eventually, someone would come into the room – his own office – and kill him. It might be the terrifying Macklin. Herb did not need to close his eyes to see him casually shooting Joe B. after his soldiers had just beaten him unconscious.

He would be found like this, trussed up like a Christmas turkey, his pants reeking of cold urine, his brains spattered on the wall. He guessed it would be on television, even down in the Florida retirement community where his mother had gone; she would see him, and cluck her tongue, and tell her blue-rinsed girlfriends that it was exactly how she'd expected him to end up.

Another tear followed the trail of the first. The manager tried again to cleanse his cheek. He heard a short burst of rifle fire in the distance, then nothing. Time went by, and he had nothing to focus on but his own misery and the complaisant ticking of the old clock.

Then he heard the lock turn on his office door. He looked to the opening door, and caught his breath. It was Macklin. Herb swallowed, and looked at the major's right hand. But instead of the neat black pistol, he saw a big pickle jar, mostly full of some clear liquid.

The incongruity made him blink.

Macklin put the jar on the desk. De Voin came in behind him and shut the door. The general looked almost apologetic. He sat on the edge of Herb's desk and poked through the little pile of keys, wallet and other impedimenta that the soldiers had taken from the manager's pockets when they searched him.

"Mr. Trainor," the general said, "you gave us quite a surprise. I thought I had made it absolutely clear that I wanted no one but my own men in the hotel this weekend."

"I just wanted to help," said Herb, hating the fearful quaver that made his voice sound despicable in his own ears.

"You have potentially compromised a matter of the gravest importance. National security, you understand."

Herb nodded. He did not understand, but the words "national security" often figured as an all justifying mantra in the thrillers he had read.

"I'm sorry," he said. "I haven't done anything, haven't seen anything really. Maybe I should just go home?"

Macklin snorted, but De Voin seemed to consider the matter seriously, before saying, "Well, the problem is, Mr. Trainor, that we're not totally sure of you now. Sneaking back into the hotel was an unusual move. By the way, how did you do that?"

Something told Herb that he should keep the tunnel a secret. But his fear of Macklin's pistol overrode that short-lived impulse toward bravery. He told them about the coal bins and the old rail route.

"I see," said DeVoin, when the tale had unfolded. "Well, you can be useful to us, Mr. Trainor. But first we need to know if you are one of *us*," he paused ominously, "or one of *them*."

"Them?" said Herb.

The general ignored him. He motioned toward a credenza behind the desk that supported a tray of glasses and an empty pitcher. "Pour Mr. Trainor a glass of that water will you, Major? And, Mr. Trainor, I want you to drink it all down."

The manager squirmed against his restraints. "Why? What's in it? What will it do to me?"

"Why, nothing," said the general. "That is, if you're not one of the people we came here to expose."

"I'm sorry?"

"I can't discuss it in any detail. I'll just say that there are certain people – agents of a foreign power – here in Prescott Springs. Never mind why. We are endeavoring to expose these agents, by means of a chemical marker we have placed in the water supply, which only they will react to. It has to do with an anti-toxin vaccine that they use."

Trainor couldn't have known that he was being lied to by a expert, nor that DeVoin prided himself on his ability to make the highly unlikely sound quite plausible. It had come in handy a number of times, when he had been required to testify before subcommittees that had the power to grant or withhold funds.

Macklin did not give the manager time to think about the nonsense he had just heard. He held the glass to the bound man's mouth and said, "Drink it."

"I don't want to," said Herb, straining to keep his clenched lips away.

Macklin withdrew the glass. He brought his pistol out and put the muzzle to a spot on the bridge of Trainor's nose, just between the eyes.

"Drink it or I'll kill you," he said.

Herb looked to DeVoin.

"It's the only way," said the general.

Macklin brought the glass back. Herb felt another tear brim in his eye, but he parted his lips and let the room temperature liquid fill his mouth and trickle down his throat.

Macklin and DeVoin watched him closely, the major moving back a little but keeping the gun trained on the hotel man's head.

They saw the effects begin within seconds. DeVoin made mental notes to himself: respiration up, rush of blood to redden the face, muscular tension.

"Mr. Trainor," he said. "Can you hear me? How do you feel?"

Herb Trainor was far away by then. He was a small boat being tossed about on a raging red flood. He was nothing; the flood was everything – it surged from one end of his being to another, howling its frustration inside his head, because *he could not move!*

His muscles alternately tensed and strained at the bonds that held him. His teeth ground together with a noise like snapping twigs. His eyes flashed from DeVoin to Macklin and back again, the pupils huge and black as cannon mouths. Then he opened his jaws and *roared* wordless hate and rage and violence into their faces.

Even Macklin, who had spent long hours in places where people did unspeakable things to their fellow human beings, who had seen and heard helpless fury and agony in all its myriad forms, even he moved back when Herb Trainor loosed a lifetime of withheld repression at him.

"Christ," he said.

DeVoin was more sanguine. "Mr. Trainor," he said, "tell me how you feel. Can you control the feeling? Tell me, Mr. Trainor. We need to know."

It was hard to swing the little boat around, to will it forward against the surge of the flood. It would have been easier if he could have first slaughtered the men in front of him. If he could just give the beast such a sop to its vast appetite, it would be less of a gargantuan effort to regain control of his voice, his body, his wide-open mind.

But, as the general steadily prodded for a response to his questions, Trainor found that he could somehow ride the frustration itself. It was like using a kind of mental jujitsu against his own overwhelming emotion, his small being becoming the center, the pivot around which all the wrath spun and churned.

He gripped the arms of the chair. He clamped his teeth until his jaw muscles bulged like knuckles under the skin. He focused on DeVoin's absurdly slow voice, and answered.

"I hear you. Let me loose."

"Speak slowly. I can't understand you," said the general.

Herb repeated himself. It was almost maddening to have to enunciate the words slowly enough that the two men could understand him.

"I don't think we can let you go just yet, Mr. Trainor. Wouldn't be wise." DeVoin examined him from several angles. "Tell me now, how's your memory? Can you remember the hotel phone number?"

The bound man roared again. The force drove the two officers back.

"Come now, Mr. Trainor," said the general. "The sooner you tell us what we need to know, the sooner we can release you."

But the part of Herb Trainor that needed to believe whatever superiors told him, the part that was drawn to toadyism as a natural counterpart to the petty tyrannies he exercised over his underlings, that part of Herb Trainor was drowned and lost beneath the flood.

They were not going to free him. He knew it. But if he could get them out of here, it might be possible for him to liberate himself. He grappled with the rage, turned it and set it spinning on a point of balance, kept it humming there while he replied to the hated interrogation.

"Memory's fine," he said, and rattled off the hotel number.

"How about perception?" asked the general. "How many fingers?"

"Two."

DeVoin pulled back a few feet and put a hand over his mouth. "Can you hear this?" he asked in a small voice.

It went on for what seemed to Trainor an agonizing eternity. He gave them only a fraction of his attention, concentrating instead on maintaining the balance, on not screaming at them.

Finally, DeVoin picked up the pickle jar and motioned Macklin to the door.

"Is it safe to leave him?" the major whispered, but Trainor's heightened senses heard every syllable. "What if he gets loose?"

The general shook his head, and whispered back. "If he was capable of it, he'd have done it when he so much wanted to kill us."

"I think we should..." Macklin gestured with the pistol.

"No. I want to see whether the effects decline over time. We'll check him again in a little while. Right now, we'll give this back to the doctor, then I think we should take a look at the tunnel. Bring his keys."

They went out.

A dynamo was spinning ever faster in the center of Herb Trainor, generating a howling power that electrified every nerve ending, every muscle fiber.

He fought the urge to scream. He sat very still, focusing the energy, keeping it under control. Then, steadily and rhythmically, he began to flex his arms and legs against the restraints.

# 14

Jeff, Sharon, Macreedy, Preiss and Fung had crossed from north to south through most of Prescott Springs. They'd gone the hard way, staying away from streets and open spaces, choosing instead to climb back fences and scuttle along behind bushes and down the narrow spaces between garages and the hedges people planted to mark their property lines.

The three hyped men had agreed that, to protect Sharon and the doctor, they'd keep to cover until the under-powered members of the group were safely hidden in the bottling plant.

But then they came to the bad street.

Garfield Avenue was the last east-west thoroughfare at the south end of town, three blocks of smaller frame homes. It was where the least affluent of Prescott Springs' citizens lived, the people who were last to be hired and first to be hired as the community's economic fortunes waxed and waned.

Jeff recalled that Zack Weaver lived on this street now. The bills from his wife's long illness had eventually cost them their home; Jeff believed they rented the shabby little bungalow on the southwest corner.

But it wasn't the poverty of the place that made Garfield Avenue a bad street. It was all the dead people.

"He started down there, I'll bet," said Jeff. "The brown house with the white trim." He could see the bloody mess on the porch. "When he finished there, he went from house to house."

They were in the sideyard of a house on the north side of Garfield. The doors to the four houses on the south side were open. Bloody footprints went from each house to the next, starting with the brown-and-white, and ending on the lawn of the last home on the street.

149

They could see the slippers that had made the gory tracks. They were on the feet of the corpse lying belly-down on the grass in front of the bungalow. The top of its head was missing. A blood-stained hatchet lay nearby.

"So, he got fired up and took out whoever that was on the front porch," said Arnie. "Then he went house to house, visiting the neighbors. Until he reached that place."

"Zack Weaver's," said Jeff.

"No shit. Well, it looks like Zack was ready for him."

"I'd say a shotgun did that," said Bob Preiss.

Jeff nodded. "Might still be around, too." He peered at the living room window and the open front door. There were shadows behind the plate glass, but he couldn't make out what they were.

"Look," he said, after a moment. "We shouldn't leave Zack, if it is Zack, all on his own."

"We could use him," said Preiss.

"Right," said Jeff. "So, Arnie, you got the rifle. You watch the windows and the door, keep his head down. Bob and me, we'll see if we can get in the back, try and turn him around."

"Okay," Arnie said, and wrapped the rifle's sling firmly around his left arm. He knelt beside the corner of the house they were sheltering behind, drew a bead on the open door of Weaver's home and said, "Ready. Be careful."

Jeff set himself for the dash across the open space. Sharon clutched at his arm.

"Jeff!" she cried.

The blood was pounding in his head again. He was ready to go. He looked at the woman, and for an instant his only thought was to shake her off.

"What?" he said.

She flinched from the anger in his face, but held on. "Don't do this! It's crazy! Let's get out of here!"

He shook his head, and gently but firmly removed her hand from his arm. To Preiss, he said, "Here we go."

He zig-zagged out onto the lawn, crouched low, then shoulder rolled to come up behind a tree. At the same time, the tavern-keeper went off on a tangent, and threw himself behind a parked car. They waited, but nothing came at them from the bungalow on the corner.

Jeff hissed at Preiss to get his attention, then looked back at Arnie. "On three," he stage whispered, counted down, then bolted from cover.

Jeff went left then right, then straight across the street. At the same time, Preiss came around the back of the parked car and ran for the opposite curb, where a pick-up with a flat tire was parked.

Halfway across the street, Jeff saw the movement in the doorway and launched himself down and forward. It was like sliding into home plate.

Arnie saw the movement, too. He fired, worked the bolt, and fired again. The bullets thudded into the bungalow's open door, and it was the combination of the two moving targets, the shots from the rifle and Jeff's headlong dive that made the charge of buckshot from Zack Weaver's shotgun hum over Jeff's head and blow a handful of cedar shingles from the wall of a house behind him.

Sharon screamed, and Macreedy put his arm around her. For the first time, she heard the doctor use an anatomical swearword.

Arnie snapped another shot through the open doorway, and Jeff jumped up and ran. The shotgun fired again, but too late this time. Jeff made it into the sideyard of the house next to Weaver's, and pressed himself against its stuccoed side. A second later, Preiss joined him.

The rest was easy. They cut behind the neighboring house and came out on Weaver's back lawn. There was a lightweight wooden door in the rear wall of the house, leading out onto a concrete patio. The two men held a brief discussion, then Preiss flattened himself against the wall beside the door, while Jeff went down the side of the house to the corner.

Now he was only three feet away from the open front door. He waited for Preiss's move. It came right away. The tavern-keeper banged hard on the back door, then immediately pulled back. A hole the size of a man's head appeared in the thin, veneer-over-hollow-space door as Zack Weaver turned away from the front of the house and fired at the point where his castle had come under a fresh assault.

As soon as he heard the blast, Jeff rounded the corner and was through the front doorway at full speed. Weaver was in a short hallway that led to the kitchen. The newly ventilated back door was directly in line with the hallway, and Weaver was on one knee, poised to send a second load of buckshot through the hole in the door, the moment he saw anything through it.

As Jeff's passage blocked the light from the front door, the catering manager swung the double barrels around. He was fast, the Paroxysm bubbling in his brain. But the younger man was faster, and he had momentum at his back.

Jeff threw himself at Weaver, knocked him backward, grabbed the shotgun's warm barrels. The gunman snarled, baring long, cigarette-yellowed teeth. He fought to free the weapon and club with its butt.

But Jeff fought only to hang on until the cavalry arrived. And in they now came: Arnie Fung charging through the open front door, and Bob Preiss kicking down the rear entrance. Arnie dropped the rifle, and both men joined Jeff in wresting away Weaver's shotgun.

They held him down and talked to him. It didn't take long. By the time Sharon and the doctor had run across the street, Weaver's face had cleared. He was back, and ready to listen.

The three men told him their tale: the invasion of the town, the spiked water, the plan.

"Let me up," Zack Weaver said. They let him stand. He swept back the long lock that crossed his bald spot from east to west. "I'm in," he said.

"All right," said Jeff, and gave him back the shotgun. "Let's go."

"Wait a minute," said Sharon, blocking the doorway. For a moment she thought they would sweep her out of the way, but Jeff held them back with an extended arm.

"What is it, Sharon?" he said.

But she spoke to Weaver. "Zack," she said. "where's your wife?"

He looked back at her with an expression she couldn't read. But something about the eyes chilled her. She didn't need to hear the words.

"She's in the bedroom," Weaver said.

"Let me see her," said Macreedy, and pressed past Sharon. June Weaver had been his patient for a long time – still was, even though he'd stopped charging when the bills Weaver got from the hospital overpowered his health insurance and cost him everything they had.

Weaver put out his hand and stopped the doctor. "There's nothing to see," he said, flatly. "I killed her."

There was a silence that began to stretch, until Sharon's voice climbed right through it. "That's all you're going to say? 'I killed her, it's Miller time, I'm going to Disneyland?' What the hell has to happen here before you people realize you're out of control?"

The four men on Paroxysm looked at each other, irritated. "Maybe we should let the doc and Sharon get on by themselves," said Preiss.

"Oh my god!" said Sharon. "I'm as bad as you are – worse, I'm not drugged up!"

"Now what?" snapped Jeff.

"Trevor! I forgot all about Trevor!" She leaned against the door jamb and put a hand over her heart. "I'm as bad as you," she said again, tears thickening her voice.

Macreedy said, "It's the shock, Sharon. It makes you concentrate only on the here and now.."

"Trev'll be okay," said Jeff. "Let's go."

It was too much. "Goddammit!" Sharon screamed. "He's not going to be okay! He's out there with the crazies, and if somebody's not doing *that* to him" – she gestured to the body on Weaver's lawn – "then *he's* doing it to some poor soul who didn't know it's kill-your-neighbor day!"

"That's enough," said her husband. He took her by the arm and led her out the door. The others followed. Only Macreedy looked at the dead man on the lawn.

Phillip Sandrini could always get lost in the science. Even now, when the thought of the danger swimming around this hotel put a cold trembling in his guts, the sheer elegance of scientific fact could draw him into its cool logic and make the bad things go away. It had been like that when he was a boy, staying late in the school chem lab until the thugs who hung around the exit doors had beaten enough tribute out of the wimps, and they'd head off to the pool hall or the arcade or wherever they went to enjoy the spoils of violence.

Science was his comfort, and ultimately it had been his strength. He knew he had killed more people than the collective body count of any street gang in any neighborhood in the land. The products of his mind, his intellectual power, had gone out into the world and they'd been *felt*.

That was something to keep in a corner of his mind now, a little knowledge to rub comfortably against when the fear started crowding in. He made things happen.

The nuclear magnetic resonator was doing its investigative job, feeding its findings directly into the computer in front of Sandrini. He watched the data build. *Not long now*, he thought. *Something is shaping up.*

Macklin's voice brought him back to mundane reality. "How much longer is this going to take?"

Sandrini heard the note of fear behind the major's snarl. He was attuned to all the manifestations of fear; they'd long been part of his own life.

*If he's afraid, I should be terrified*, he thought, but the prospect of rubbing a little gall into the arrogant son of a bitch's exposed nerves was too good to resist. He slowly spun his chair around and looked Macklin in the eye.

"It takes as long as it takes, Major," he said, lazily. "Why, you in a hurry?"

Macklin's hand dropped to his pistol.

Sandrini thought he managed a convincing chuckle. "I'd save the bullet. You might need it if the folks outside decide to come in here."

DeVoin's voice spoke from behind them. "That's enough, Doctor."

"Well, hell, general," the scientist said, "let's face it: the demonstration's a bust." He swung around to the two Yemenis. "You two gentlemen interested in an unknown psychoactive chemical that might just get us all killed?"

Hafiz lifted an eyebrow. "Doctor, forgive me, but for all your scientific genius, you seem to be somewhat lacking in practical intelligence."

"What's that supposed to mean?" Sandrini said.

"It means," said the Yemeni, "the mutated chemical agent may well be more useful to my organization than the original substance. We have many dedicated fighters, but too many are simple people." He shrugged. "They are motivated but they do not fight efficiently. However, if they could be given something before going into battle, something to stimulate them, then who knows?"

Sandrini laughed. "Of course. I see. Yes, I do see." He turned to DeVoin. "But, Jesus, General, we can do the analysis anywhere, anytime. Let's just take some samples and get down the road!"

The general shook his head. "No. The agent has shown itself to be unexpectedly dynamic. What we put into the water is not what came out of the taps, and it may still be changing. By the time we get set up somewhere else, it may have mutated further. We need to know what's working in those people's brains right now, and that means analyzing it right now."

Sandrini didn't know that there was another reason. Parker DeVoin had never yet entertained the notion that he could not reach into the world and seize whatever he wanted from it. No bunch of civilians – whatever might be lighting up their synapses – were going to deny the general his due.

"Work fast, Doctor," he said. "The moment you hand me a piece of paper with the formula for Paroxysm 2, we'll pull out."

The Prescott Springs Hotel had been built as a health spa in the days before becoming fit had anything to do with staying indoors and moving pieces of weight-laden machinery to simulate outdoor exercise. Its long-dead designers had favored tennis, golf and swimming and plenty of brisk walks in the fresh air. They had laid out the grounds to accommodate these aims, and – land then being cheap – had laid them out spaciously. Around the eighteen-hole golf course stretched a parkland of small hills and dells, crisscrossed by graveled paths. The lawns were broken up by little copses of evergreens and mixed forest.

In recent years, to save on maintenance, only a few holes of the former full-sized golf course had been kept up, and the undergrowth was left to grow wild in the roughs.

Lou and Adele Meecham ran through the rolling landscape, looking for cover. Lou kept them on the path until they reached the first of the overgrown roughs. Then he pulled Adele between a pair of low-hanging spruce. Inside the stand of trees it was dark, with the smell of wet ground. He crashed through brambles and blackberry creepers as thick as his thumb; thorns as big and sharp as wildcat claws tore at their clothes and scored their flesh with lines of red droplets.

"Come on, they're coming," he said. He saw her wince as thorns scored her legs. "You have to not mind the pain, tell yourself you'll deal with it later. Through here."

They came out the other side of the rough, and saw a path twenty feet away. The grass in-between was in the shade of the trees, thick and still wet with dew; he knew it would show their passage.

"Okay," he said. "Shuffle your feet in the grass so it makes a clear trail to the path."

"They'll follow us."

"Uh-uh." He took her hand and they plowed through the damp green blades to the path, then he stepped onto the gravel and made a couple of scuff marks.

"Now, back," he said, and they retraced their steps back to the edge of the rough. "This way," he said, "and try not to leave any traces."

They went another thirty feet or so along the edge of the trees, in the opposite direction from where the scuff marks would lead the pursuit, stepping on roots and stones where they could. He stopped and gently parted the screen of undergrowth, then insinuated himself into it. He crouched low and wriggled his way in a little, until he could reach back and hold the branches out of the way for Adele to follow.

In this part of the copse, there were thick bushes with small leaves and some kind of white berries on them, woven through with more blackberry creepers. He looked one of the bushes over and said, "Here."

He carefully lifted its lower branches. There was space there, and black earth. "Crawl in, lie on your stomach," he said, and she did. He crept in beside her, taking pains not to break a branch. When the bush closed over and behind them, they ought to be safe from anyone not actually ripping apart the foliage to find them.

"Lie still. We'll be okay," he said. She slid her hand over and took his. He could feel a pulse beating in her grip.

The Canadian and the South Carolinian topped the first rise in the parkland in time to see the Meechams enter the stand of trees. They followed at an easy jog, keeping their eyes open. The grounds seemed deserted – no early morning golfers were on this weekend's guest list – but so had Prescott Avenue until somebody started shooting mercenaries.

They came to the place where the quarry had entered the trees. The trail was not hard to follow; two middle-aged bodies moving at speed through thorns and brambles made for considerable disruption. Rifles at the high port, they pushed their way through the thicket and came to the other side.

No trouble with tracking here either, thought the South Carolinian. He followed the bent down grass to the path, saw a spot where a turning heel had dug through the gravel to the grit beneath, looked and saw another one a few feet on.

"This way," he said, and jogged in that direction, his partner on his heels.

But they didn't go far. After a hundred feet, the South Carolinian stopped and inspected a mark in the path, then walked forward, nose bent close to the ground, and looked at another. Then he straightened, and cast his eye slowly over the lawns that rolled down to either side of the path, ahead of and behind where they stood.

"Boy's smart," he said. "But not smart enough."

He turned and went back up the path to where the pursued had come out of the trees. The Canadian came after.

The South Carolinian retraced the trampled trail to the edge of the copse. He ran his eyes across the ground at the edge of the trees, first to one side of the Meechams' exit place, then to the other.

He got down on one knee and focused his experienced gaze on a small patch of moss. He studied it for several seconds, then reached down and lifted it with a finger. "Ho, ho," he said, softly, and to himself.

To the Canadian he said nothing, but indicated with combat hand-signs that the people they were hunting were back in the woods. He signed for his partner to follow.

Now that he was looking for them, the marks were neither hard to find nor to read. They had come this way, this far, gone in here. They might be looking at him right now, hunkered down with the cold sweats, needing to pee, afraid to breathe.

"Come on out, folks," he called. "Ain't gonna hurt you."

From not far away came two rifle shots, close on each other. Then the boom of a shotgun.

The two mercenaries dropped into a squat, eyes moving, but nothing came their way. Then came a second shotgun blast.

"Sounded like the same rifle, eh?" whispered the Canadian.

"Yeah. But he musta got somebody else to play with."

He turned back to the trees. "Now, folks, like I say, we just wanna talk a little. Ain't lookin' to spoil your day."

Trevor Cameron was having the best day of his life. He scarcely felt the bruises the fight with his father had inflicted, so intent was he on making the next kill. This one would be the best yet.

He slowly pushed aside a branch that obscured his vision. He was fiercely proud that, though the urge to burst from concealment burned like a hot wires through his muscles and the desire to kill bubbled in him like goofy laughter, he could hold himself perfectly still. He watched the two armed men come closer.

*I am the hunter,* he told himself. *I am death.*

His mind was clear. He was perfect. He was fully into the game, and it had never been this good before. It was wonderful to feel like this.

He'd played the game since he was a little kid, practically since he was old enough to be let out of the yard on his own. He could even remember the first time he'd come across the big road, all by himself with nobody to watch him, and entered the hotel grounds. He'd found a hole in the screen of bushes and worked his way through. When he saw the parkland spread out before him, the small rolling hills, the patches of dark woods, the little paths, it was as if he'd stumbled into another world, the kind that was in the books his mom used to read to him.

The hotel parkland was his play-world. He knew every bit of it: where the rabbits had their burrows, where the deer came to nibble the undergrowth, where to hide so that the groundskeepers wouldn't see him. Hiding from the hotel staff was a key part of the game; if they caught him they'd throw him out, and once his dad started working there, it made it even more of a danger.

So Trevor had learned how to be both the hunter and the hunted. The staff never knew he was there. He could snake silently through underbrush, putting the ball of the foot down before the heel. He knew how to go from point to point in the grounds unseen, skirting the edges of the woods and crossing open ground at the narrowest points.

157

The animals had been more of a challenge. But he had learned how to freeze and hold himself still, breathing quietly through his mouth. He had practiced moving slowly so as not to trigger the flight reflex of a deer. He had come within spitting distance of them, had hunkered down and sat by them until they tolerated him as if he was no more dangerous than the rabbits that foraged on the lawns.

Today the deer had found out that he was a lot more dangerous.

The moment he'd been free of the house, all he'd wanted to do was to play the game. The urge was overwhelming. Flashes of delight set his legs to trembling as he cut across town to the hotel grounds, and quickly worked his way across them. He came to his most secret place.

It was actually a little beyond the landscaped terrain that surrounded the hotel, in the second-growth forest that went back into the hills. He found a stick and went to a certain spot at the base of a dense mat of morning glory and blackberry brambles that grew among the spruce and pine. He pried up the lower edge of the thicket, reached beneath, and brought out a roll of canvas tarpaulin, bound with twine.

His fingers seemed to flicker, so fast did they undo the knots. He unrolled the tarp and revealed his most beloved possessions, the things he couldn't keep at home, because if his mother even knew they existed, she would forbid them.

One was a bone-handled hunting knife. It had a leather sheath with a pocket that held a small whetstone. To get it, he had traded two video games and had still had to throw in ten dollars saved from his allowance. But it was beautiful, the leather sheath lovingly oiled, and the knife's blade ground to as sharp an edge as its inferior steel would hold. It was already strung on an old belt.

The second of his treasures was a six-foot length of straight sapling, its bark scraped away and its knots smoothed down by a rasp. Into one end of the pole Trevor had carefully sawn a deep notch, and into that space he had slid a flat steel throwing knife, the kind a kid could get if he sent a twelve-dollar money order to a Pittsburgh company that advertised in the back pages of comic books. The trick was to have it delivered to General Delivery to the post office in Evans, then get a friend's big brother to pick it up – that cost another five bucks.

He had bound the knife into its space with wet rawhide thonging, then left it to dry and shrink. The result was a respectable lightweight spear, reasonably balanced, which the boy had learned to throw with considerable accuracy.

The last item in the cache was an old coonskin cap that his father had found in a second-hand store, and given it to him with some dumb dad-remark about Davy Crockett. Trevor had never worn it where other kids could see it, but somehow it had felt just right for the game.

He wore it now, pulled down low over his forehead, squatting in his camouflage pajamas, as he watched the men with rifles try to trick their quarry into revealing their position. Inside, where no one could hear it, the boy chuckled. The frightened man and woman weren't there anymore. As soon as they'd seen that their back-tracking hadn't fooled the soldiers, they'd snuck quietly out the other side of the copse and skedaddled south, toward the old factory where dad used to work.

Almost, he'd thought of going after them, but the soldiers looked to be more fun. Certainly they'd give him more enjoyment than the deer. That had been too easy. Not that he was complaining. All of it had felt good: moving up to where the animals browsed among the bushes; picking out the four-point buck; edging closer and closer – *silent, smooth and slow*, he'd kept repeating to himself, while the deer paid him scant heed; then cocking back his arm, the wooden shaft balanced perfectly on the ball of his thumb, all five fingers in a loose grip; finally, swinging the arm forward in one swift, tingling flood of energy.

The spear left his hand and flew straight to the deer. It entered the animal's body just where the hunter's guidebooks said it should, right behind the shoulder, a little low. The deer screamed – that was a surprise – and leapt forward in slow motion. But even as its forefeet came down, its front legs buckled and it fell over onto its side.

He rushed to it, pulled out the hunting knife to cut its throat and finish it. But the spear had pierced the animal's heart, and he saw the life go out of its eyes even as he drew the blade from its sheath.

He didn't know how to dress the kill, and wasn't much interested in doing it. But he cut open the belly and pulled out the liver – it looked a lot like the slices his mom cooked at home – and cut off a little chunk. It was warm and tasted like blood. He liked it.

The deer had given him a strip of bloody meat. The soldiers would give him guns.

"Now, come on, people," said the one with the mushy accent. "Y'all don't come out, we're gonna have to come in there. And then we ain't gonna be too pleased."

The other soldier hadn't said anything yet. He stood with the butt of his rifle resting on one hip, digging around in his nose with the forefinger of his free hand. Whatever he found, he wiped on his pants leg. He was close: if the boy extended his spear at maximum length, he could just about touch him.

Trevor saw how it would go now. The mushy voice would come into the trees. He'd poke around for the fat man and woman, while the nosepicker would stay outside and get them if they broke from cover. They boy knew what he would do when they made their move.

And now it came. The first man made a hand signal to the second and eased himself into the trees. The waiting man brought his rifle down and put his finger on the trigger. His eyes flicked back and forth over the undergrowth, the muzzle of his gun tracking from side to side as if it could find a target all by itself.

When the rifle swung away, the boy moved. At hyper speed, he launched himself from the bushes, the bloodstained spear held straight out in front of him as if he were making a bayonet charge.

The Canadian tried to bring his rifle to bear on the chunk of green that had suddenly separated from the underbrush and come at him. But the boy was already inside the arc of the weapon's swing before the soldier's brain had even registered the threat.

Trevor aimed for the man's middle. That's where you punched people to make them feel it; the spear ought to do real damage there. The double-bladed steel point had no real edge, but its tip was hard and sharp. The metal passed through the Canadian's solar plexus at an upward angle, and slightly from right to left. It was too low to hit the heart, and passed between both lungs, but it punctured his liver and kept going until it lodged in a rib, near the backbone.

The Canadian screamed, a high-pitched shriek that sounded to the boy's speeded-up senses more like a comically drawn out owl's hoot. The soldier dropped his rifle and grasped the wooden shaft protruding from his midriff. He tried to pull it free, but the point had wedged itself firmly in bone. Trevor also had both hands on the wood. He gave it a yank, but it was stuck solid.

The South Carolinian came crashing back out of the trees. He didn't wait for a clear target but fired toward the sound of the screaming as he broke though to the open ground. The rounds went high, hitting his partner in the right shoulder and the side of his head. The brain case burst and the top of the Canadian's head flew away in dripping fragments. The dead man was still falling when the mercenary brought the rifle down, without letting up his pressure on the trigger, to hose the kid who was trying to yank the spear out of the body.

Trevor saw the muzzle swing toward him, saw the slow-motion belch of smoke and flame and the small dark shapes coming out like angry hornets. He flung himself to his left, away from the bullets – but the shooter was too close. The next few rounds would catch him.

160

The South Carolinian pulled the M-16 down and to the right. The bullets smacked into the ground, chasing the kid as he dove to get away. *Fast,* the South Carolinian thought, *very fast. But not fast enough.*

Then the rifle's bolt clicked on an empty chamber. He hadn't put in a fresh magazine since he'd come across Prescott Avenue with the major – hadn't thought he'd need to be loaded for bear to chase mom and pop over a few back fences. And now the kid in the camouflage pajamas was looking up at him from where he was sprawled on the ground, with the damndest idiot grin on his face.

The South Carolinian dropped the rifle and reached for the K-bar knife on his belt. He had once been an instructor in close combat with the 101 Airborne at Fort Campbell. There were not too many things he had to be afraid of, if he had a knife in his hand.

But one of those things turned out to be the twelve-year-old who came up off the ground and at him so fast the motion seemed to blur like trick photography. The boy knew nothing about knife fighting; he just stuck his dime-store hunting knife into the mercenary's belly – once, twice, three times in less than a second. He ripped through the man's small bowel and spleen, punctured one kidney and half severed the renal artery.

The South Carolinian felt only a slight stinging. It was like taking three quick, light blows to the stomach. He saw the boy step back to watch him intently, as if he'd just set up an experiment in school and was now watching to see how it went.

"Okay, kid," the man said. He meant to do it quickly: throw a fast feint at the eyes – that always made an amateur flinch – then lay open the throat with a down-and-sideways slash.

But it didn't happen. The boy easily dodged the feint and was just not there for the killing stroke. The slash pulled the South Carolinian off-balance; something seemed to have gone wrong with his coordination. A sticky warmth was spreading across his belly, He looked down. His pants were soaked with blood.

He began to feel a dull ache in the middle of his stomach. *Got to do this and get some help,* he thought. He set himself to go after the boy again.

The kid had been watching, weighing him up, it seemed. But then the boy nodded, very fast, as if telling himself that he had just got the solution to his problem. As the mercenary raised his K-bar, the boy came in again, so very fast. The cheap knife flicked out at the South Carolinian's eyes. The man didn't even have time to blink before the point was sinking into the left side of his neck, tearing open the jugular vein and nicking the windpipe.

Dark blood welled out of the cut. The South Carolinian made a sound like an old man's dry cough. His eyes turned back in his head, and he dropped like an empty sack.

Trevor stood back and watched the mercenary slowly sink to the grass. Clearly the throat was better than the belly, although the spear had done a good job in the solar plexus. But the man had known what he was doing, and he had gone for the throat first thing. Trevor would remember the lesson.

Quickly, he stripped the two dead men of their weapons. One of the rifles was empty, so he hunted through the second man's pockets and found a full magazine. After only a little experimentation he got the empty one out and the full one in. He knew you had to pull back the bolt to cock the weapon. They were always doing that on tv.

He found two more clips on the first man, in pouches on a web belt. This he slung over his shoulder, along with the spare rifle. He also took the K-bar knife, first removing its sheath from the dead man's belt and threading his own through it. He strapped it around his waist and buckled it tight.

He gave one more tug on the spear that stuck up from the first man's middle like the mast of a ship. But it wouldn't budge. He decided to leave it. Much as he'd liked the weapon he'd made, an assault rifle was better.

He pushed through the trees and saw the trail that the running man and woman had left in the grass. He cantered after them.

# 15

Lou stumbled haphazardly through the woods, Adele's hand tight in his grasp. He could heard her gasps for breath over his own labored breathing, and once she cried out in pain, but he pulled her after him. The armed mercenaries might be right behind them; if they were, to stop now would be to stop forever.

He made no attempt to disguise their passage. He'd watched as one of their pursuers had easily seen through his backtrail ruse. Their only hope now was to reach the bottling plant where the waiter and his companions had said they would gather. There they might find safety.

He knew it was a slim hope. Whatever DeVoin had dumped in the water had turned these small-town folks into ruthless killers. If they could sit calmly around a kitchen table while its former owners – their own neighbors – lay torn and dead only a few feet away, they'd have no qualms about blowing away a couple of strangers who came blundering into their midst.

Ahead lay a substantial risk of death. But behind was a dead certainty. Lou tightened his grip on Adele's hand and battered his way through the undergrowth.

A thin, high sound came from back in the hotel grounds. He stopped, panting, to listen. Lou had heard something like it once before, on a supposed-to-be-quiet day in a Honduran training camp for Contras. He'd been sitting beneath a tree, digesting lunch and thinking about the afternoon's drill when a mis-aimed mortar shell had arced in from over the trees and exploded just outside the communications tent.

A piece of shrapnel had opened up the back of a radioman who had just stepped out to stretch. One of the medics later told Lou the wounded man's ribs were laid bare, and he could see the lung expand every time the guy sucked in a breath to scream again. The shrieks had sounded like what he was hearing from back in the hotel grounds.

The distant keen was abruptly cut off by the rattle of an M-16. He listened, and heard nothing more, not even the sound of pursuit through the woods. *Maybe they ran into some kind of surprise,* he hoped. *Something to delay them.*

"Come on," he told Adele. "I don't think it's far now."

She had no breath to answer, but she nodded. Her face was red with exertion and she breathed through her open mouth like a fish plucked from its environment. Lou wanted to put his arms around her and shelter from this world of violence and rage, but there was no safety in his arms. They had to keep moving.

He'd been leading them south. He was fairly sure they were heading in the right direction; he'd kept track of the angle of sunlight in the upper branches. If he was on course, the bottling plant ought to be just over the next rise or the one beyond.

They scrambled up a slope, slipping on old leaf mold and pulling themselves up by grasping tree roots and the branches of scrubby bushes. Then they crested the hill, and Lou saw a tarred roof with a weatherworn brick wall beneath it.

"That's it," he gasped. "Almost there."

They slid and side-stepped down the incline, weaving between the trees, and came out at a weed-choked ditch. Beyond it was a chain-link fence, eight feet high, then a paved sideyard, then the blank side of the building.

To their left, some fifty yards away, was Bridge Road, where the front gate led through the fence. Lou didn't want to be out on that road – there was a clear line-of-sight from there to the hotel entrance. If anyone was looking for them with field glasses, they'd be spotted. There might be other armed men looking for them, besides the two from the parkland.

He turned right and led Adele along the edge of the ditch, keeping his eye on the base of the chain link fence. A few yards distant, near the back corner of the enclosure, he found what he was looking for: somebody, probably kids, had snipped the loops that bound the mesh to the bottom wire.

Lou held the fence up for Adele to scrabble under it, then she returned the favor. They were in the back parking lot of the bottling plant. Green things were growing through cracks in the asphalt. Dead leaves lay on the raised concrete apron above two empty loading bays. A dilapidated tanker truck rested on old railroad ties and cinder blocks in the far back corner of the lot.

"Let's find a back door," Lou said.

They climbed the concrete steps that led to the loading bays. The big steel shutters were closed solid, but there was a smaller wooden door beside them.

Lou put his ear to it and listened. He heard nothing from within. He tried the doorknob; it was locked, but it rattled loosely.

"Doesn't seem to be a deadbolt," he said. "Look around for something that could pry it open."

At one end of the loading area he found some short lengths of steel pipe. They were of different diameters, and one was thin enough to force into the space between the door and the jamb.

Lou put his weight onto the improvised crow bar. "Help me," he said.

Adele leaned with him. The doorframe splintered a little, and the loosely hung door moved sideways toward the hinges. Then it popped open, swinging outward with almost no sound.

"Come on," Lou said. They went in, and he closed the door after them.

The interior of the building was dimly lit from far above by skylights whose opaque glass was smeared by dust and rain. There was a cubicle where the shipping clerk had sat, and a short stack of cardboard cartons piled near the metal doors. They were printed with the label "Chester Springs Natural Mineral Water." Out of the shadowy belly of the building came a long, ball-bearing conveyor, on which were some cartons that proved to contain plastic bottles full of water from the hotel spring.

Lou opened one and passed it to Adele. "Drink it. It'll be safe."

He opened another for himself, tilted his head back and took several gulps. As he brought the bottle down, he heard a sound from the shadows.

He turned. His brain had only time to register that something was coming at him, too fast for his eyes even to focus on it. It was only when a shoulder connected with his midriff and drove the air from his lungs that he could be sure it was a man.

The water bottle flew from his hand. He saw an arc of droplets, frozen like a bead necklace in the air above him, as he was borne backwards by the impact. He heard Adele scream.

His shoulders hit the floor, then the back of his head smacked hard against concrete. Stars flashed in his vision. He couldn't get a breath.

His attacker moved with incredible speed. One moment he was sitting on Lou's chest; the next, he had eased up his weight, grabbed the shoulder of Lou's shirt and a side pocket of his pants and rolled him over onto his stomach.

Instantly, Lou's arms were pulled together, so fast there was no time to pull against the pressure. Then his wrists were tightly bound with what felt like wire.

"This one's clear," the man said. Lou recognized the rapid-fire manner of speech, the burst of syllables compressed into each other.

"So's this one," said another voice. "Let's get 'em up."

Lou was jerked roughly to his feet. He looked for Adele. She was unhurt, but shaken, her hands bound like his. Two men stood beside her. He recognized one from the Peebles' place – the Asian guy who'd had the rifle. The other one was familiar from the hotel; it was the restaurant manager who hadn't wanted to seat them for lunch.

He couldn't see the one who stood behind him. But he knew the man who now came out of the shadows.

"You remember us," Lou said. "You brought us lunch yesterday. I don't know your name."

"Jeff Cameron. You're not powered up, are you?"

"We didn't drink any of the water," Adele said.

The one behind Lou jerked on his bound wrists. "How'd you know about the water? You with those bastards that killed Frank and Joe B.?"

"Christ, no!" said Lou. "But we know what happened. Now they're trying to kill us!"

"I think we need to have a talk," said Jeff. "Let's go back to the office."

The one behind Lou pushed him forward. "Wait!" Lou said. "There's two of those mercs chasing us. They might be right outside now. They've got automatic weapons."

"So they're mercs," said the Chinese-looking one. "So what the hell's going on? Who're they working for?"

"Look, I can tell you what I know, but we've got to get somewhere safe. Those two come in here after us, they'll kill us all on sight."

"Let us worry about them," said Jeff. "Bob, you want to take these people to the office and sit 'em down with Sharon and the doc. Me and Arnie and Zack will go see about these assholes." He spoke to Lou, "Which way they coming, through the woods?"

Lou nodded. "Yeah, but you don't want to tackle these guys. They're killers."

Arnie said, "We've seen their work. Don't worry about it."

He went to the back door, Jeff and Zack following. They had the deer rifle and a shotgun between them. They looked outside for a moment, then went through the door at full speed. To Lou, it was as if they had simply disappeared.

"Let's go," said the one Jeff had called Bob. He pushed Lou's shoulder and head-motioned Adele to follow.

The Meechams followed the conveyor line into the gloom of the old plant's interior. In the dimness, the vats and piping and bottling machines had the threatening stillness of a mad scientist's evil creations, lying dormant until a lightning strike could bring them to malevolent life.

The plant manager's office was set in one corner at the building's front, behind painted walls of wooden siding broken by a few small windows and a door with a sign that read *Manager – Knock Before Entering*.

They went into a secretary's area that had a connecting door leading to the manager's sanctum. The outer walls of both the now long-gone secretary's and manager's offices were partly formed of glass bricks that let a diffuse light wash across the scarred desk and the few chairs scattered around the office.

Seated on the desk was the old man they'd called Doc. He was slumped over, his hands in his lap. He looked up and Lou saw in the old man's eyes an expression he'd only ever seen on the faces of kids after they'd spent some time in combat – kids who'd had to deal with too much, too fast.

The woman who had been at the Peebles' house sat in the manager's chair. She kept twisting her hands together. She had bitten her lower lip raw. Lou could see that she was distraught, but he couldn't tell whether she'd overcome it soon, or flip out altogether.

"Who are these people, Bob?" the doctor asked their escort.

"Don't know," said Bob. "But they got something to do with what's happening at the hotel."

"No, we don't," said Adele. "We're just tourists."

"We should get out of here," Lou said. "It's dangerous. There are armed men chasing us."

Sharon looked up, alarmed. The doctor put a hand on her shoulder.

"Jeff and Arnie and Zack went to deal with it," said Bob. "But this guy knew there was something in the water."

Macreedy tipped back his hat and looked the two prisoners over carefully. "How'd you know that?"

"I know who's behind it, that's all," said Lou. "He was in chemical warfare when I was training contras in Central America."

"Then I think we'd better hear about it," said Macreedy. "Bob, you can untie these people."

"No way."

"Bob, they've obviously not had any of this" – he picked up the jar of water that was on the desk and shook it – "so you could take both of them, and Sharon and me too, if we decided to join in."

Bob curled his lip. But just about everybody in Prescott Springs was used to taking instructions from the town doctor. Habit won out. He unwound the wire from the Meechams' wrists.

"Good," said Macreedy. "Now how about we sit down, introduce ourselves, and do a little talking?"

They did. Lou told them what he knew of DeVoin and Macklin and about what they'd done in the Sandinista war. He related how he had bumped into Macklin by accident, and how they had been held at gunpoint and kept overnight.

"You never told me about what you did in the army," said Adele, when her husband paused. "I thought you were just a supply clerk."

Lou couldn't look at her. He fixed his eyes on the dusty floor. "I didn't want to talk about it, didn't want it to be part of what we were making. And I couldn't face what I didn't do that day."

He wiped his eyes. "You know, I saved some soldiers' lives, kept 'em from doing stuff that would've got them killed. But I didn't stop DeVoin that day, and I should have. I had a sidearm. I could've shot the son of a bitch, and Macklin too. Instead, I just followed orders. I fired the mortar for those bastards, and killed a bunch of poor farmers and their families."

Adele took his hand and wiped the moisture from its back. Lou still couldn't look at her.

Bob spoke, his voice so fast, the others had to ask him to repeat the words more slowly, "Forget that shit. Tell us about now," he enunciated. "What are they doing here?"

Lou shook his head. "I don't know. My guess is DeVoin's gone freelance. Those aren't government soldiers; they're hired mercenaries. Some of them are foreigners."

"But why are they doing this to us?" asked Sharon.

Lou looked up. It was the victim's age-old question, the same one the little Miskito girl would have asked, if she'd had the breath.

"Who knows?" he said. "Best I can figure, it might be some kind of product demonstration for a prospective customer. It's costing somebody a lot of money, somebody who wanted to see what the product would do."

"It makes people crazy mad," said Macreedy. He looked at Bob. "That's what it does – homicidal psychotics on tap."

"Yeah, but I'm thinking this operation has gone wrong, badly wrong," Lou said. "DeVoin kicked us out onto the street like he didn't think we'd live very long. And I'm sure they didn't expect their troops to work up a sweat handling any trouble from you people.

"I figure you were all supposed to drink your morning coffee, go nuts and start killing each other. You weren't supposed to get a handle on the problem and start shooting DeVoin's men. So the thing is blowing up in the general's face. By now he probably realizes it's a screw-up, and he'll be running for cover. We just have to stay out of sight."

"Nice plan," said Sharon. There was a crack in her voice that made Lou look up. "But it's not going to happen."

"Why not?" asked Lou.

"Because my husband and his buddies don't want to stay out of sight. They want to raise an army. Just a little army. But more than a little crazy. That's how they like it, though. And they're going to have themselves a war."

She pushed back her hair with shaking hands, then gripped them together again. "Meantime, my kid's out there somewhere, and I don't know what's happening to him."

She started to cry. Adele went to her, put her arms around the weeping woman, and made soothing noises. Sharon clung tightly and let the tears come.

There was a clatter of noise from beyond the partition walls. Bob looked out the door. "Well, speak of the devil," he said.

Jeff, Arnie and Zack entered from the secretary's office. Jeff had two assault rifles and a belt with a combat knife slung over his shoulder. His free hand held the arm of his son.

The first thing Sharon saw was the blood on Trevor's pajamas. "Oh my god," she said, and rushed to him. The boy reacted instantly, as if he was under attack. But Jeff pulled him back, while Arnie stepped between Trevor and his mother.

"He's all right," said Arnie. "But he's kinda pissed off we wouldn't let him keep the rifles."

"Listen," Jeff said to the boy, "you can have the knife back if you don't make any more commotion. But the guns are for men."

Trevor glared at him.

"Now you got to clamp down on that feeling," said his father. "If you can't control this thing, we're gonna have to tie you up. Then you'll miss out on all the fun."

The boy made an effort. They could all see the struggle inside him, but in a moment more he had it under control.

"Good," said Jeff. "Now let your mom see you're okay, and I'll give you back the knife."

Sharon put her hands to his face. "Are you okay, honey?" she said. "I was so scared."

"I'm fine. Let me alone," the boy said.

She looked at the patches of dried and sticky blood on his shirt front, and the smear of red on his chin. "Oh god, what have you been doing?" she said.

169

He smiled. "I was hunting. I got a deer and two soldiers." The smile faded. "Dad won't let me keep their guns." His nose was running, and he wiped it on his sleeve.

Sharon sat down. Tears poured down her cheeks. "What have they done to my kid?" she sobbed.

"Can I have the knife now?" Trevor asked his father. Jeff gave him the belt that held the K-bar, and the boy buckled it on.

Lou was staring at the boy. He figured the kid couldn't be more than twelve or thirteen, yet he'd apparently killed two armed professionals and taken their weapons.

"Son," he said, "did you really kill those men?"

The kid held his head proudly. "I got one with my spear – he screamed. Then I got the other one with a knife. I was coming to get you when dad caught me."

Lou looked into the boy's hard eyes. He'd known men who had that same flat stare, men who'd endured things that no man should have to face. But he'd never seen it in the face of a kid who plainly couldn't wait to do and see more horror.

Lou wanted to be somewhere else. He wanted to take his wife and go somewhere where children didn't become stone-faced killers in blood-stained pajamas.

Jeff put a hand on his shoulder. "Now," he said, "I want to know what you know."

Lou told them what he had told the others. When he was finished, Jeff said, "A sales demonstration makes sense. Now we'll give them a little demonstration of our own."

"No," said Lou. "That's nuts. Let them go."

"You think we can't take them?" said Arnie. "Between us, we already killed four. Joe B. and Frank, they must've taken out three or four. How many more they got, couple dozen?" He snorted.

"Sure," said Lou. "You sniped at a couple from cover. I don't know what the boy here did. For all I know, the two he got thought he was a harmless kid. But going up against the kind of men DeVoin has, now that they're warned and ready, it's suicide."

They plainly didn't believe him.

"Look," said Lou. "How many of you have actually been in combat?"

"I was on NATO exercise in Germany in the seventies," said Bob. The others said nothing.

"Well I was a combat soldier," said Lou. "A recon specialist. I've been in everything from squad-sized ambushes to company-strength firefights. You know why they say the ratio of shots fired to enemy targets hit in combat is more than a hundred to one?"

"You got a point?" said Jeff. He was examining the Canadian's assault rifle. The South Carolinian's he had given to Bob Preiss.

"I got a point. The reason troops fire off a hundred rounds or more for each bullet that hits an enemy is 'cause the majority of men in combat don't fire their weapons at the enemy. That's a fact: they either aim high or they don't fire at all."

"I aim to kill," said Arnie.

"Me too," said the boy.

"So do those men at the hotel," said Lou. "Most soldiers in most armies are conscripts or poor kids who signed up to learn a trade and get the benefits. Even after combat training, they don't want to kill anybody. But every one of DeVoin's men is a cold-blooded professional. Now that they know there's danger, they'll be careful and they'll be absolutely ruthless. You won't get any more free shots. They'll make damn sure anyone comes near them gets dead."

"I don't think so," said Jeff.

"They're safe behind stone walls. They know about overlapping fields of fire, eliminating dead zones, concentrating fire on avenues of approach. You go after them, you'll just end up getting more of your friends and neighbors killed. We're safe here. Why not just wait for them to leave?"

"We'll do just that," said Jeff. "They'll try and go out over the bridge. Won't be any stone walls or overlapping whatever out on the road. We'll trap 'em, and we'll kill 'em all."

Lou could see that the plan was already forming in Jeff's mind. The young man thought he knew how it would go, and the pictures in his head were exciting him. Lou had seen kids like this before, the ones who came out of boot camp like they were going to play in the big game, all full of gung-ho adventure. Most of them he'd managed to turn around. Those he hadn't been able to reach usually ended up going home in black plastic bags. And now he wasn't reaching this one.

"In the meantime," Jeff was saying. "We need some more people, so we'll go out and find some."

"Don't take Trevor away!" Sharon was on her feet again.

"I'm coming too!" said the boy.

"Tell you what," said Jeff. "You stay here and guard these folks till I get back, and you can be in on the ambush when we hit the bad guys."

"No!"

"And I'll see you get a rifle."

The exchange was spoken so quickly that those operating at normal speed missed most of it. It was enough for Sharon that her son acquiesced and would stay with her. She put a hand out to him, but he turned his back.

The four speeded-up men put their heads together and made a plan. Then they were gone.

Sandrini moused the cursor from pixel to pixel on the screen, clicked on a couple of icons, engaged the imaging program. *Here it comes*, he thought.

The NMR scan had done its work and dumped its findings into the computer. Now, on the monitor's screen, the computer was building a three-dimensional model of a molecule – the traditional balls and connecting rods – based on the data flowing from the NMR. The different elements whose atoms made up the compound were color-coded: blue for oxygen, black for carbon, white for phosphorous, and so on.

Then came stuff that hadn't been in the original Paroxysm compound: a dose of chlorine from the water treatment plant; a dash of fluorine – *must have been a natural occurring mineral in the lake water*, he thought, *rural Oregonians ain't never gonna stand for no fluoridation*; and a pinch of calcium.

He moved the mouse and rotated the model in front of him. *That's elegant*, he thought. Then he looked closer. *No, by god, it's perfect!*

He made the computer flip the long molecule end for end. Its component elements meshed and balanced each other as if they had been designed for harmony, as if this nameless new compound had been a chemical jigsaw puzzle, its pieces left lying around since the formation of the world, just waiting for somebody to come along and fit them together.

"It'll be rock-solid stable," he said aloud.

DeVoin heard. "What's that, doctor?" He came across the room and peered at the model. DeVoin knew enough chemistry to grasp the basics of what he was seeing. "Jesus," he said.

"Damn right," said Sandrini, the excitement lighting up his nondescript features. "Look how it coheres, how it dovetails! This sucker's gotta be cheap to make, and no way it's gonna breakdown. Hell, we're talking shelf life that just won't quit, General!"

"Well done, Doctor," said DeVoin. "I'd like a print-out of the formula, please, as soon as you can arrange it."

"You got it!" Sandrini switched on the printer and moved the mouse. The printer began to whir.

The general turned to Sergeant Major Leith. "I want the hard drive out of that computer and in my pocket in five minutes."

"Sorr!" said Leith.

DeVoin spun on his heel. "Major Macklin, you will alert the men. We're bugging out. Get all the equipment loaded and the troops back in civilian clothes. Oh, and make sure somebody picks up any brass left lying around from the firing. I want this command ready to roll in twenty minutes."

Macklin saluted and turned his back before he let the relief show on his face. They were going. In twenty minutes there would be no more crazies with guns shooting at him. Nobody would ever shoot at him again.

He marched out of the ballroom.

Hafiz had crossed the floor to look at the model on Sandrini's screen. The colored rods and spheres looked to him like a child's toy. He knew no chemistry, but he did know men. He knew that these men now owned something that was far more valuable than what they had stolen from the American government.

"General," he said, in a tone that bespoke polite inquiry, "we still have an agreement, do we not?"

"We do indeed," said DeVoin, beaming. "Although I believe we may have to adjust some of its terms."

"Which terms would those be?" said the Yemeni.

"Why, the price, Dr. Hafiz," said the general. "The price has just gone up."

Hafiz did not let his expression change. Whatever the price, it would be worth it to control this weapon.

Jeff Cameron's recruiting force did not have far to go before they came across their first volunteer. As soon as they had dashed across Bridge Road from the bottling plant to the straggle of comfortable houses surrounded by spacious lots on the other side, they were charged by a man wearing pajamas and wielding a baseball bat.

Both the weapon and the man's face were smeared with blood and what looked like brains. It wasn't until they had subdued him and got him back in

173

control that Jeff even recognized the features beneath the gore. It was Ignatz Morens, the hotel chef. Jeff remembered that he lived somewhere down this way.

Rapidly, they explained to Morens what had happened to the town and what they planned to do about it. The chef wanted in. "Bastards made me beat my dog to death," he said.

"You got a gun, don't you, Ignatz?" Zack Weaver asked.

"I got a rifle. Used to get my own venison."

"Let's get it," said Jeff.

Mitch Wallace and Terry Stowe, Herb Trainor's assistants, were still in bed when the posse arrived. They'd decided that the unexpected Saturday off was an opportunity to sleep in, then drive over to Evans for a leisurely brunch, a little shopping, and a movie.

They hadn't even heard a creak on the stairs. They were talking about their plans for the day, heads together on the pillow, when the bedroom door burst open. The intruders moved so fast, Mitch and Terry couldn't keep them in focus until the motion stopped and they suddenly found themselves pinned immobile by the weight of four men kneeling on the covers.

Then they recognized faces. Mitch was first to recover a shred of his normal aplomb. "What the hell do you..." he began, but was cut off by a rapid-fire burst of syllables from Zack Weaver.

Jeff Cameron was the one standing by the bathroom door. Mitch saw him listen to Weaver, then do a speeded-up pantomime of a man in deep thought. That finished, he ducked into the bathroom, there came the sound of water running, and he was back with Terry's toothbrush glass, filled from the tap.

He leaned over the bed and said something too fast for either of the assistant managers to comprehend. It sounded like, "You're being drafted." Then he slowed it down. "Drink," he said.

The two men fought to get up, but to no avail. A hand held Mitch's nose, two more stopped him from turning his head. His mouth was forced open and the cold liquid slopped in. He had to swallow or choke.

Almost instantly, it hit him. While Terry looked on, terrified now, his partner thrashed and kicked at the restraining covers, while the men talked to him in their rapid-fire gibberish.

After a few more seconds of struggle, Mitch suddenly quietened. He turned to Terry a face his lover had never seen before, and said, "Drink it."

174

Terry was scared, but he did as he was told. Three minutes later, he and Mitch were dressed and heading out the door with the others. They'd had no weapons in the house, but the kitchen knives were of the finest quality and well tended.

They stood at the bottom of the front steps. "We should split up now," Jeff said. "Someone needs to keep an eye on the road out of town, in case they make a break for it early. Hold 'em up until the rest of us get there."

"I'll do that," said Arnie.

"Me, too," said Bob.

"Good stuff," said Jeff. "We'll get some more people."

# 16

Wexler lowered the field glasses and picked up the radio mike. "Homestead, Blueberry. Copy?"

DeVoin's voice came back over the static. "What do you have, Blueberry?"

"Not sure, sir. See some activity on the road by the bottling plant. Could be a concentration of forces. I'd like to check it out."

There was a pause. "Roger that, Blueberry. Leave four men to guard the bridge. You and a driver take your vehicle and scout toward the hotel. If you come under fire, do not – repeat, do not – attempt to engage. Just identify where it's coming from and get clear."

"Copy Homestead. In and out. Blueberry out."

He turned to his command. "Hagen, Medford, Alvarez and Weisskopf, draw weapons and a spare radio, and stay here. Nobody in or out. Shoot if necessary. Medford, that decision's yours. Chaffey, you drive. Let's move."

Wexler climbed into the shotgun seat of the highways department vehicle. Chaffey, a wire-thin brown man with a shaven head, looked to him for orders.

"Straight down the road to the bottling plant," the lieutenant said. "Moderate speed so I can see what's what. If nothing happens, go one block past the place and we'll head back. If we get shot at, floor it and clear the killing zone. Understood?"

Chaffey nodded.

"Then let's go."

The boy couldn't stand waiting around the office, so he went out to explore the rest of the plant. Ordinarily, most kids in Prescott Springs would have jumped at a chance to poke around the old machinery, to clatter down the rollers on the big conveyor, or hammer their fists against the sides of the enormous settling vats and make small thunder.

But Trevor had known bigger game. There was a great, enticing hunt going on outside, while he was stuck here in the smell of dust and decay, with people who spoke in absurdly slow voices about stupid things. He drew the K-bar knife and scratched its edge against his thumb; he wanted to try it on flesh.

Sharon followed the boy. She stood in the office doorway and watched him prowl the old plant, afraid now to let him out of her sight. The speed and rage that she saw in his every movement frightened her, and fed a sick anger that was growing in the lowest part of her stomach – that anyone should do this to her child.

Almost, she envied her husband and son their insulation from normal human emotion. The drug had taken away their fear and hesitancy, had stripped them of whatever instinct it was that connected one human being to another. It had turned them into monsters, but they were happy monsters, untroubled by the sickening sense of abandonment that possessed her.

She looked back at Macreedy's jar on the manager's desk. It would be easy enough to rip the lid off, take a big long swig and join the party.

The doctor seemed to recognize the urge that was building in her. He put the jar of water down on the floor, out of sight behind the desk, then got up and came to her, put his thin old arm around her shoulder.

"Sharon," he said, "I keep telling myself this will be all right. This will pass. Whatever they poisoned our town with, it will wear off, and things will be normal again. We've just got to get through it – could be a day, maybe just a couple of more hours – then we go back to how it was."

She watched her son circle the plant, in his hand a killing knife that shone through the gloom. "You think so," she said. Then she shook herself.

"You're right, I know," she said. "That's not my kid who wants to kill people. That's not my Jeff out prowling the streets." She sighed. "It's just the stuff in their brains, and when the stuff is gone, they'll be mine again. Only..."

"Only what?" said the doctor.

"Only, just for a moment, I wanted to be part of what they've become. I wanted to hurt the people who are hurting us."

The Meechams had been listening from where they sat in a corner of the office. Now Adele spoke. "Don't give in to that, dear. It can't help. I've always believed good people ought never to be afraid to do what's right. But you don't stand up for yourself by sinking to the lowest level."

She touched her husband's hand. "Lou, whatever happened in that war, I know you never did less than your best. I've seen what kind of man that general is. He's evil. But you didn't make him that way, and it's not your fault that that evil man got power over you for a while. What counts is who you are inside. And you're a good man. I'll always be proud of you."

"Oh, babe," Lou said, covering her hand with his own. "You're more than I deserve."

She kissed his cheek. "Well, that's true, but you can spend the next thirty or forty years making up for it."

Macreedy said to Sharon, "Let's leave them alone." She followed him out into the main area of the plant.

The highways department carry-all crept down Bridge Road. Chaffey held the speed down to twenty miles an hour in second gear, and straddled the center line. He kept his eyes moving, but the road was deserted.

Wexler had equipped himself with a MAC-10 machine pistol, its two magazines taped together in an L-shape. As they approached the bottling plant, his gaze flicked from point to point along the sides of the road ahead, checking every bush and tree and post, assessing the potential of each to provide cover for an ambush.

Because he was looking for it, Wexler saw the man with the assault rifle as soon as he slid the weapon around a utility pole on the right side of the street, and aimed at the truck. The lieutenant saw the second man almost at the same instant, coming up out of the ditch with a deer rifle.

There was no time to do anything more than see the threat, however. The ambushers moved too fast. The first man's automatic fire shredded the left front tire, then crept up across the grill and began to rip into the engine. Even as Chaffey floored the gas pedal, the man in the ditch had put two bullets through the safety glass and into the driver. The first shattered his left collarbone, was deflected down toward the shoulder bone, and rebounded from there up into the trapezius muscle. It broke through the skin again with enough residual momentum to destroy the hinge on the left side of Chaffey's jawbone. The arm attached to the injured parts spasmed, yanking the steering wheel down into a sharp left turn.

The second shot was a clean miss. It passed through the air where Chaffey's skull would have been if the impact of the first bullet hadn't thrown his head back and to the right. But the first had been enough. The driver was screaming, his muscles gone rigid from pain and shock. His right foot held the pedal to the floor as the truck's engine roared in low gear. Steam poured from the perforated radiator.

As the vehicle swung left, Wexler saw the man with the M-16 step clear of the utility pole and raise the weapon for another burst. He was faster than any human being had a right to be, but Wexler had brought his machine pistol up the moment he had seen the target.

Even as the vehicle swerved, the effects of years of practical experience came into play. The MAC-10 spat a cone of steel-jacketed bullets at the ambusher, Wexler's arm swinging counter to the truck's arc to keep the weapon's fire on its target.

Bob Preiss stepped out for another try and saw too late the eruption of flame from the machine pistol's muzzle. His speeded-up senses identified the streaks of light rocketing toward him as bullets, but even his Paroxysm-enhanced reflexes could only dodge one or two. Most of the burst struck his upper chest, his throat and the bottom half of his face, ripping away bone, cartilage and muscle, and nearly severing his head from the ruin of his neck.

Wexler tried to bring the MAC-10 to bear on the second ambusher, but the carry-all now struck the curb outside the bottling plant. It bounced over the sidewalk and crashed through the chain-link fence at the front of the building, still accelerating.

Wexler grabbed for the wheel, but Chaffey's grip was unbreakable. He hammered at the driver's wrists with the butt of the machine pistol. The man moaned but his hands remained clenched. At the last moment, Wexler hurled himself into the passenger-side footwell, then the truck smashed into the glass bricks at the front of the bottling plant.

The impact loosened Chaffey's grip and flung him over the steering wheel, through the shattered windshield and into the wall of thick glass. The collision flattened his forehead and upper cranium from his eyebrows to the crown of his head, like a cartoon character hit by a frying pan. But Chaffey's head would not spring back to normal. He was dead.

Down in the footwell, Wexler had turned his back to the direction of travel, and had suffered no more than a heavy bruising impact against his shoulders.

The vehicle's roaring engine had died, and in the sudden silence he levered himself up and over the twisted passenger seat to look out.

The carry-all had broken clean through the semi-transparent wall, and now poked its front end into some kind of office. Wexler kicked at the warped passenger door once, then once more, and it fell open. He slid over the seat and out of the truck, wincing at a sharp pain in his neck, and feeling for a steady foothold on the loose glass bricks that lay piled around the front wheels of the vehicle.

He saw dust and broken furniture and a wooden wall with a door in it. He stumbled toward the door, and his peripheral vision picked up a motion in a corner of the room. Without thinking, he sprayed that direction with the MAC-10. He heard a moan, looked, saw no more movement. He stumbled over the bricks to where the floor was clear, and flattened himself against the wall beside the door.

He peeked around the jamb, then went out into the adjacent secretary's work space, and repeated the maneuver at the door to the main plant. An old man and a woman stared at him from the middle of the open space. He brought up the machine pistol fast, but his practiced eye had already told him they were unarmed. He weighed up the situation fast – at least one shooter outside, two controllable hostages in his hands.

"You two! Over here!" he ordered.

They stared at him in shock.

"Or you're dead!" he said.

They moved toward him slowly. The woman kept her eyes on the machine pistol. The old man looked like he wanted to say something, but was holding it back.

"Button it, grampa," said Wexler. "I probably only need one of you. Now move your ass!"

He didn't have time to waste. The rifleman outside might be coming in from any direction at any moment. Wexler stepped out of the office, started to cross the floor to the prisoners.

He saw the woman's eyes flick to her right, saw her mouth open to say something. The mercenary didn't think, just spun to his left and fired.

But, this time, reflexes and training would not be enough. The kid was crouched low, so the first burst passed over his head. There was no time for a second.

The boy came in so fast, his legs and feet were a blur. But the focus of Wexler's attention was the eight inches of shining, needle-pointed steel in the kid's outstretched hand.

The knife crossed the twenty feet of concrete floor faster than if it had been hurled. With that speed and with all of the kid's weight behind it, it entered Wexler's belly as easily as if the flesh had been water. It ripped up, in a diagonal slash from near the groin until the blade bit into a lower rib, and his bowels fell out.

The woman screamed now. To Wexler's dying brain, it sounded like "Never!" But he would never get to know what she had said. He made a small sound of surprise, then his legs buckled. He slumped to his knees, and fell forward into a mess of his own fluids.

"Trevor!" Sharon screamed again.

The boy ignored her. He'd stood back like a child who had just busted open a pinata, fascinated to see what happened to the man he'd ripped with the K-bar. But now he dashed forward and seized the machine pistol.

Arnie Fung came out of the office, rifle at the ready. He had climbed through the truck's back doors and out its front. He took in the scene at a glance.

"You do that?" he said.

"Yeah," said Trevor. He walked over to the dead man, wiped his knife clean on the back of Wexler's shirt his other hand tight on the grip of the machine pistol. He looked like any little leaguer who had just hit a home run but he wasn't letting go of the MAC-10.

"Cool," said Arnie.

Sharon looked at the horror her son had made of the soldier. She fought back the urge to vomit, and turned away.

"Help me," a voice said, and she turned back. Lou Meecham stood in the office doorway, his face and arms smeared with blood.

"It's Adele," he said.

When they'd heard the rifle fire from outside, the Meechams had been holding hands and sitting on chairs where the bottling plant's supervisors used to sit whenever the manager called a meeting to discuss production schedules.

A second later, when the shadow of the truck loomed beyond the glass wall, they were already moving toward the door. But it was too late. They were both hurled off their feet by the crash, and Adele was thrown on top of Lou.

A flying glass brick glanced off the side of her head, cutting open her scalp and momentarily stunning her.

Lou saw the blood seeping from the wound and reached to press it. At his touch, Adele moaned. Instantly, the room shook with the thunder of automatic fire. His wife's body jerked as the bullets slammed into her back, making her move against him in an obscene parody of lovemaking.

He saw the agony crest in her eyes then die. She opened her mouth, as if to speak, but all that came to him was her last breath as her lungs emptied.

Her head fell onto his chest. She smelled of blood and her favorite shampoo. Lou's eyes filled with tears, and a deep, low moan rose out of him to lose itself in her hair. He struggled out from under her, softly calling her name, while a voice kept repeating in his mind, *she's dead, she's dead, she's dead, she's dead*.

He heard a woman's scream from outside the office, but paid it no heed. Somebody climbed through the truck and went into the plant. Lou ignored him.

He laid Adele on the office floor, kicking aside loose bricks to clear a space. He folded her arms across her abdomen and closed her eyes. *That's what you do with dead people. Then you get a body bag.*

He looked around for something to cover her with and saw the driver's body dangling head down through the missing windshield. The corpse's knees and ankles were entangled in the steering wheel. *I have to get her away from here*, he thought. *I don't want this son of a bitch near her.*

He stumbled to the office door and called for help. Sharon came, and the doctor. They lifted Adele and took her into the secretary's office, where they laid her gently on the old linoleum. The old man examined her briefly and shook his head. "I'll get something to cover her," he said.

He went out and came back with some sheets of cardboard, cartons that he had pulled apart where they were joined. He laid them over the body. Then he looked at Lou.

"You hurt?" he asked.

Lou shook his head.

"Sit down," Macreedy said. He looked into the smashed manager's office. "My bag's in there somewhere. I can give you something that will help."

Lou sat on the edge of the secretary's desk. He looked down. One of Adele's feet protruded from under the cardboard. Her shoe was missing, and he could see a snag in her stocking.

He looked away, and his eye fell on the jar of water Macreedy had put down beside the manager's desk. Somehow it had survived the devastation in the other room and had rolled safely into the secretary's area, coming to rest not three feet from where he sat.

Lou stared at the jar, at its clear liquid contents. Once it had held jam or peanut butter. Now it held the stuff that Adele had died for. Slowly, deliberately, he eased his weight off the desk. He stooped and picked up the jar.

Then, methodically, he unscrewed the lid.

Macreedy came back from the manager's office, his medical bag open and one hand digging around in its internal compartments. "This'll help calm you..." he said, then he saw what was in Lou's hand.

The doctor dropped the bag and grabbed for the jar. "No!" he said. "That won't do you any good!"

But Lou held him off with one arm, and with the other he raised the jar to his lips.

"For god's sake, man," Macreedy pleaded, "you heard what your poor wife said. "Don't let them bring you down."

Lou lowered the jar an inch. He turned on the doctor a face that every medical practitioner sees at some time: the look of a terminal patient who has come to terms with dying, who has done all that life requires, and is absolved from further involvement with the living.

"If I'd done what was right all those years ago, she'd still be alive. None of this would have happened if I'd had the balls to kill those bastards when I had the chance. Everything that's happened here today, I could have stopped it. Well, now I've got nothing better to do with the rest of my life."

He drained the jar and closed his eyes.

Macreedy watched the effect. For thirty seconds, the man stood, trembling, the empty jar still raised. Then his eyes snapped open, and he returned Macreedy's stare. The moribund Lou Meecham was gone, and in his place was the same blood-loving beast that had looked out of Jeff Cameron's eyes, and the boy's and all the others.

But this one was worse. The others had been pressed into the service of death without a choice. This one had wanted nothing else than to be a killing thing.

Lou Meecham dismissed the doctor from his mind. He stepped back into the destroyed room where Adele had died and stepped into the smashed carry-all. Chaffey's M-16 was jammed down between the two front seats. A canvas pouch with two full clips lay on the floor.

Lou picked up the weapon and the ammunition. He popped the clip and checked that it was full, then reinserted it and worked the bolt. *Lock and load,* the words came back to him.

There was a portable radio clipped to the dashboard, a sturdy piece of equipment that had survived the collision. As Lou backed out of the vehicle, the radio hissed and crackled.

"Blueberry, Homestead. Copy?" said a voice. Then repeated the call.

Lou reached for the set. It spoke again in his hand. "Homestead, this is Medford on the bridge. The lieutenant drove into that old building. We heard firing. Now we don't hear nothin', can't see nothin'."

"Wait one," said the first voice. Five seconds later there came a voice Lou Meecham recognized. "Medford, this is Macklin. Just hold it. We're taking another look."

In the command center, Wexler's scouting expedition had been played out under the long-distance surveillance of a video camera mounted on a van outside the hotel gates. The screens had shown the highways department vehicle looming out of the rippling haze that resulted when warming air rose off blacktop through a telephoto lens's field of view.

No one had seen the two ambushers until they made their moves. A replay of the tape had confirmed that Chaffey and one of the townspeople had both been hit when the carry-all veered out of shot. Wexler had still been alive and shooting. His target had gone down and stayed down. The other shooter was no longer visible either.

The directional mike on the surveillance van had picked up the crash. There followed one more burst from the lieutenant's machine pistol, muffled as if he were firing within a building. Then all had gone quiet.

It was possible that Wexler had survived the ambush, Macklin thought, killing one man on the road then getting the second as he came after the truck. If so the mercenary would probably be holed up in the old factory, maybe wounded, maybe just making sure there were no more surprises before he checked in on the radio. Or his radio might have been put out of commission in the fighting.

Macklin didn't care one way or another. What he wanted to know was whether or not the road to the bridge was open. If there were lurkers in the bushes with automatic weapons and scope-mounted deer rifles, he wanted to know about them – so he could send someone to clear the way. That straight stretch of road was the only route out of town.

He waited a few seconds more, then keyed the transmitter button on the mike. "Wexler? Wexler, are you receiving? If you can receive but not transmit, fire two shots now. We'll send some people to secure your position."

The major listened to the hum from the speaker. Sweat trickled down his temple and he wiped it away with his cuff. Then there was an electronic pop as someone depressed the send button on Wexler's portable.

"Wexler? This is Macklin. Copy?"

The radio popped again. A voice said something, too clipped and rapid to understand.

"Wexler? Say again," Macklin said. "Did not copy."

The voice spoke again, still fast but recognizable. "Macklin," it said. "Wexler can't talk to you. He's got no stomach for it any more." There was a kind of laugh. Suddenly, Macklin's skin felt cold.

"Who the fuck is this?" he screamed. "Get off the air."

"I'm coming for you, Macklin," said the radio. "Shoulda done it years back. But I'll do it now."

The voice sent a chill prickle up Macklin's neck. "Who is this?" he whispered.

"Meecham," was the reply. "Wait one, Macklin. Won't be long."

The radio clicked and went silent. Macklin stared at the mike in his hand then let it drop. There was a sheen of sweat on his palms. He rubbed them on his pants legs.

"Sir," he said to the general, "I recommend that we withdraw."

When Jeff Cameron and his posse started entering houses, they found that Paroxysm had done a more effective job than was evident from the quiet that prevailed on most streets.

There were a lot of dead, especially in larger households. Usually, one person had been the first to be affected. Often it was a pre-teen kid who got up to watch Saturday morning cartoons, drank something and then killed the others in their beds. None of them had bothered to seek out a gun, if there was one in the house; the weapons were whatever came to hand – knives, furniture, toys – or fists, feet and teeth.

Some of the children responded well to the adults' efforts to refocus them. Others were too far gone: they either ran away from superior force, or fought until they had to be killed.

The Paroxysm-high adults were easier to work with. Most were poorly armed. Once restrained, they could usually be talked down in less than a minute. The few with guns took a little longer. Two of them would not come around, and were shot. But all the surviving new recruits were eager to arm themselves and take on the soldiers who had invaded their town, once the enemy had been identified.

People, young or old, who had not yet drunk any water were easiest of all. The posse entered their houses while they were still in bed, overpowered them and forced Paroxysm down their throats.

Only one such recruitment failed: a man named Royston. He was a hard-core drunk and a brawler; the only thing he liked more than having his fist around a drink was putting it into somebody's face. He was sleeping off Friday night, when Jeff and a few others broke in, dosed him with Paroxysm-laced water, and tried to get him focused.

It couldn't be done. Royston broke one of Zack Weaver's fingers, and closed Mitch Wallace's left eye. Even after they sat on him and talked to him for several minutes, he was unaffected. Finally, Jeff set his heel on the man's throat, put his weight onto it, and stayed there until the choking noises stopped.

Afterward, as he came downstairs in Royston's house, Jeff felt a sudden, slight dizziness. The stairs led down to the kitchen, and he stopped at the bottom to lean against the wall.

"You okay?" asked Mitch.

Jeff shook the odd feeling from his head. "I guess so. Just felt a little funny for a moment there."

His mouth was dry, and there was a spreading weakness in his arms and legs. The ripples of delight that had made a lattice-work of power in his muscles only a few minutes ago were now fading. His mind felt spongy, not sharp and focused the way it had been all morning.

He went to the sink and ran some water. Royston had nothing clean to put a drink in. The sink was jammed with greasy plates and pans. Jeff let the water fill his cupped hands and drank from them.

In a moment he felt a little better. He drank more, and the lights began to come back on all along the network of nerves and muscles.

"That's better," he said. "Guess I was just thirsty." He drank another double handful and felt renewed. "Let's go get some more troops."

As the posse grew, it divided into smaller units, the more quickly to cover the town. They moved fast. Within twenty minutes of leaving the bottling plant, the recruiters had visited every home in the main core of Prescott Springs and several of the outlying houses.

The night before, their town had had a population of one hundred and seventy-four, including invalids and small children. By nine o'clock that morning, there were forty-eight survivors, including Sharon Cameron and the doctor: all were able bodied; none was under twelve years of age; the great majority were male.

The gathered at the bottling plant, arriving in twos and threes after ducking quickly across Bridge Road. But they drew no fire from either the hotel or the soldiers on the bridge.

"Looks like they don't have a lot of ammunition," Lou Meecham told the crowd that filled the plant's open space. He jumped onto the canvas conveyor belt which had once carried bottles to the spigots that filled them with Prescott Springs mineral water, and held up the ammunition pouch he had taken off Chaffey's corpse. "Only a few rounds per man, not enough for a sustained firefight."

"Who the hell are you?" said a man in the front of the crowd. He was small, and his close-set eyes and low hairline gave him the look of a mean-tempered ferret.

"He's one of us," said Jeff, climbing up beside Lou. "And he knows the people we're up against. I want to hear what he's got to say."

"I've been thinking this through," said Lou. "They only got a few men at the bridge. At the hotel, there's more of them, but not as many as us. They're gonna want to get out soon, and they'll have to go out the way they came in."

"So?" said the ferret face.

"So we take the bridge, and that bottles them up. Then we hit the hotel and roll 'em up fast."

Dr. Macreedy made his way to the front of the crowd. "Stop this!" he cried. He struggled up onto the conveyor belt. "How many more dead people do you need to see before it dawns on you what you're doing?"

"Somebody shut the old fart up!" said a voice from the crowd.

"He needs a drink!" called another.

Jeff held up his hands for calm. "What are you saying, Doc?"

The doctor took off his hat, slapped it against his leg. "I'm saying, if they want to get out of town let them get out of town!"

"And what do we do?" said the ferret. "Wave bye-bye?" A few people sniggered.

"Nothing!" Macreedy answered him. "That's what we do. We sit tight and wait for the authorities. Look, the phone's are down. That alone draws attention. Pretty soon, if not already, somebody on the outside's got to figure that something screwy is happening in Prescott Springs. The cops could be heading here from Evans right now!"

"Who gives a shit?" said a voice from the crowd. Others joined in, jeering at the doctor.

The old man swore. "Listen to me!" he shouted. "None of you is thinking straight! You're all doped up! Look around, there's maybe fifty people here, out of the whole town! Most of your neighbors are dead, and most of *you* did the killing!"

Lou Meecham cut him off. "We're not waiting for any cops! I know the man who did this to us. I know his kind. They can buy cops. They can buy judges and any damn thing they want, any damn time they want!"

The ferret wanted in on the debate. "If the system was worth a pinch of rat shit, men like that would be in cages! Instead, they're running the goddamn zoo!"

But Macreedy was not an easy man to intimidate. "Don't give me that crap about the system! You're not out to make a better world, none of you! You're going to go after those men in the hotel the way you went after your neighbors and your own families! Because you got that stuff in your veins, stuff that's let you loose on the world! No rules, no regrets, and you just love it! Anything that's been eating at you – your wife doesn't understand you, you hate your boss – now you can vomit it out in one big violent spasm! Those men at the hotel are evil, sure, but you're no better!"

He turned his back on them and stiffly got down from the conveyor belt, on the other side from the crowd. He walked into the shadows that lay around the plant's disused equipment. Sharon was there. She took his hand.

"It's no good," she said. "They're not going to listen to you or me or anybody. All I can do is hope that Jeff and Trevor live through it, until that poison is out of them."

"We should get away from these people," Macreedy said. "They're dangerous."

She looked at the mob gathered around her husband and Lou Meecham. Trevor was at the front, holding his MAC-10. His eyes were as bright and feral as those of the man with the ferret face.

"There's a catwalk up above the settling vats," the doctor said. "We'll be out of sight and out of mind."

They walked to the back wall of the plant. Steel steps rose into the darkness. Macreedy led the way up.

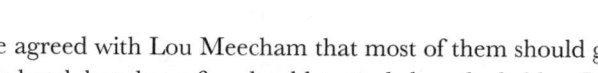

The townspeople agreed with Lou Meecham that most of them should go after the men at the hotel, but that a few should go and clear the bridge. Jeff led his son and five others south through the woods west of Bridge Road. It was less than a quarter mile to the river.

The rest of the group comprised Arnie Fung, Zack Weaver, Mitch and Terry, and a woman who used to keep parakeets and cockatiels. They stopped at the edge of the trees a hundred and fifty yards from the span. No one had thought to bring binoculars, but Trevor's eyesight was twenty-twenty.

He peered through the branches. There was nothing to see. "I think they're gone," he said.

# 17

The soldier named Lester Medford had heard Lou Meecham promise the major he'd be coming for him. He had made the call on Wexler's radio, and that meant Wexler was dead. So was Chaffey.

Medford was thirty-seven years old, lanky and long-fingered, with pale eyes and a blotchy red face. He was the product of an Oklahoma town that had never been much and would be even less once the oil ran out. He'd enlisted in the U.S. Army two days after he got out of high school by the expedient of knocking his gym teacher cold. He'd found himself a home in a Ranger battalion and earned a couple of stripes. He might have made a career of it if he hadn't got drunk and broken a captain's jaw in two places.

He left the stockade with his discharge papers and nowhere to go. He drifted, spent some time as a driver and knee-capper for a loan shark in Baltimore, until he chanced to see an ad in a men's magazine. Three weeks later, he was on a plane for Honduras to spend a few years helping to turn peasants into contras and providing security services for a man who called himself Capitan Aguilar.

Since then, life had been a succession of short-term engagements wherever there was a market for a man who coupled solid military skills with a complete disregard for the lives and dignity of whomever his various employers sicced him onto. He'd become a known name in the relatively small international community of mercenaries.

When one of his contacts, an ex-Green Beret named Wexler, offered him a lucrative short-term contract, he'd taken it. He'd found it agreeable to work with Wexler before; the man was a professional.

But now this strange little engagement had turned into the kind of horror show that got professionals like Wexler suddenly dead, and made staff officers like Macklin scream in panic at unknown voices on the radio.

The moment he heard the radio exchange between Macklin and the man who called himself Meecham, Medford began to reassess his situation. He used Wexler's field glasses to keep an eye on the hotel and on the road in front of the bottling plant. He saw plenty of activity at the hotel – trucks and the bus being loaded – but he also saw several groups of townspeople cross the road to the old factory. Most of them had firearms.

That meant that the main force at the hotel would encounter resistance when it tried to leave Prescott Springs by the only road out. Medford was no master tactician, but he knew how the commander would use the four men on the bridge. He'd order them to bust up the ambush by attacking from the townsfolk's rear. Medford could make a pretty good assessment of his chances of surviving that noble action.

But the initiative might not be the general's to take. If whoever was in charge of the armed mob forming between him and the hotel had any combat experience, he'd be sending a force up the road any minute now, to remove Medford and the others before they became a problem.

Their position on the bridge was indefensible. They had only a couple of clips each, no heavy weapons, not even grenades. If anything came down the road at them, they'd last long enough to use up their ammunition. Then they'd be overrun. And Medford doubted anybody would be taking prisoners and making sure the Geneva Convention was punctiliously observed.

Medford had a rule for this kind of situation, garnered from long years of mercenary work: when it all turns to shit, the guys who run for the trees are the guys who get to keep their balls.

So it was time to go. There was only one way out – upstream and into the hills. He didn't see any sense in trying to join up immediately with the main force at the hotel. Even if they made it, the general would not be glad to see them. And then they'd be trapped.

Neither did he contemplate taking the road south toward Evans. They were on foot. Whoever came down the road after them would be moving a lot faster. If it was the crazy townsfolk, they'd be caught and killed. If the main force broke through the expected ambush and caught up to them, their employer would kill them for deserting their post.

He put the field glasses to his eyes and focused on the Land Rover that had belonged to the man Wexler had garroted. It was parked at the side of the road, just this side of the bottling plant, only thirty yards from the spot where the lieutenant had been ambushed. He resisted the temptation to send Hagen down to get it.

He rotated to scan the river to the west and then to the east. To the west, he knew from the briefing maps, the river ran into the lake, not too far from the hotel – a bad direction. Eastward, the river came down from the hills where there was only forest, scattered farms and hunters' cabins – a good place to hide or find a vehicle.

He put the glasses down and turned to the other three mercenaries. "Listen up," he said. "Wexler and Chaffey are dead. Any minute now, a lot of pissed-off people with guns are probably gonna be shooting at us from the woods. The operation's a bust, and the general's gonna throw us away to save his own ass."

He paused and looked at each one in turn, then said, "So I'm going up-river. Anybody wants to come with me, let's go."

Hagen spoke first. "That's desertion, man."

Medford felt his mouth drop open. He was prepared to do a little arguing with Weisskopf or Alvarez – they were pros and might not want to bug out until they had seen the caliber of the opposition. But Hagen was just some dumb kid from Akron, with fuck-up written all over him.

"This ain't a movie," Medford said. "This is real life. We are outnumbered and outgunned. We can't defend this position."

"We should ask the general for orders."

"He'll just invite us to get our asses killed for him."

Hagen shrugged. "Maybe, but he's the guy paying us."

"Fuck that noise," said Medford. "I'm outta here."

"No!" said Hagen, and pointed his rifle at Medford's mid-section. "We stay."

Medford looked to Weisskopf and Alvarez. They were partners who had served together in a dozen different theaters, and people sometimes wondered whether they had swapped names. Weisskopf was of small stature, with dark hair and brown eyes; Alvarez was tall and fair. Both hailed from Argentina.

"What about you guys?" Medford said.

The two partners exchanged looks. "We're with Hagen," said Weisskopf. And while the kid was still smiling at his sudden victory, Alvarez raised his rifle and shot Hagen through the heart.

"Get his ammo," said Medford. They divided Hagen's magazines among them, then they dragged his body down the bridge embankment and threw him into the water. Then they set off east along the riverbank.

They were already out of earshot when the radio they had left at the bridge squawked and Macklin's voice said, "Blueberry, Homestead." When there was no answer, the call was repeated. By the fifth repetition, the major's voice was starting to crack.

DeVoin's technicians had cleared almost all of the equipment from the command post. They had then changed into civilian clothes, drawn weapons and gone to augment the perimeter defenses. Only one monitor remained connected to the video control board.

Macklin ordered the van with the telephoto lens to focus on the bridge. The image zoomed toward him as if he were flying along Bridge Road at superhuman speed, then stopped at its maximum magnification. He saw the highways department barriers still in place; he even saw what must have been a portable radio transceiver on the railing of the bridge. But of the four men who should have been guarding the only route out of town, there was no sign.

DeVoin was across the room, talking quietly with the Yemenis. Sandrini hovered nearby, anxious to be gone. Ashen faced, Macklin crossed the empty dance floor, his boots echoing on the undersprung wood, and reported to the general.

DeVoin glanced at the screen and confirmed his aide's assessment. "Regrettable," he said, "but do try to keep things in perspective, Major. A gaggle of civilians, no matter what may be circulating in their bloodstreams, will not stop a fast moving convoy that is shooting back. The best part of the gear is now stowed, and we can leave. I remind you that we will be traveling in an armored limousine. Unless the people of Prescott Springs have found themselves some artillery, I fail to see how they can pose us much threat."

The general's calm cut through Macklin's burgeoning fear. He was embarrassed. Having had, for the first time, a few shots fired in his direction, he'd panicked. He drew himself to attention. "Yes, sir," he said.

"That's better," said DeVoin. "Now, we can forget about what's left here," – he indicated the video equipment and Sandrini's gutted computer – "so let's mount up."

"What about the prisoner?"

DeVoin dismissed the question with a wave of the hand. He had visited Herb Trainor three times since the first interrogation; there had been no change. The effect of the new Paroxysm appeared to be long-lasting.

"Forget him," said the general. "The moment we pull out of here, they'll lose the common enemy that's holding them together. They'll go back to killing each other. Order the men onto the buses, then I'd like you and Dr. Sandrini to wait for me in the limousine. I want to discuss something with the Yemenis."

"Yes, sir," said Macklin. He motioned to Sandrini. "Saddle up, Einstein. We're leaving."

The scientist did not even bridle at the discourtesy. He was getting out; that was enough.

DeVoin watched them go. He did not expect to see them again.

When the room was empty but for him and the two Yemenis, the general said, "Dr. Hafiz, I am in fact less sanguine about the chances of our safely driving out of here. I have therefore taken the precaution of providing another means of escape."

"I am glad to hear it, General," said the Yemeni.

DeVoin brought the satellite phone out of his jacket pocket and punched in a number. The pilot who answered might have been in the next room, instead of at the end of a signal bounced down from orbit.

"Now," said the general.

"Five minutes," was the answer.

The ballroom windows offered a panoramic view of the lake. DeVoin pointed to the east. "He'll come from that direction," he said. "When we see him, we'll go out to the dock."

"Excellent," said Hafiz.

Jeff's group skirted the edge of the trees beside the river, moving toward the bridge. Almost all of them had guns; Trevor particularly wanted a chance to try out the MAC-10 machine pistol.

They reached the point where the woods met the west side of Bridge Road. From here they had a clear view of the deserted span. Moments later, they were on it. They found Hagen's abandoned M-16, and a man who had only an ax seized it.

A trail of blood led from the concrete bridge deck down the grass embankment. Trevor followed it; the time he had spent following deer sign around the hotel grounds and the adjacent woods was now repaid. He saw where a group of men had carried a body down to the river and thrown it in. He saw the corpse itself, hung up on one of the pilings that had once supported a railroad bridge just west of the road, but it did not interest him. He was following the sign of the living.

194

He followed the trail a few yards. Here was a heelprint, there a broken branch. They must have been going fast, not bothering to disguise their passage.

He called to the people on the bridge, "They went this way!"

Their heads all swung toward him, like a pack of wild dogs when one of its members has found the scent of prey. Trevor turned and began to follow the trail. The others started after him, but were scarcely clear of the bridge before the sound of gunfire from the hotel brought them up short.

The mercenary force DeVoin and Macklin brought to Prescott Springs had numbered forty-eight on Friday evening. By eight-thirty on Saturday morning, it totaled thirty-three effectives.

Ten of the casualties were dead. Two men had been killed at the bottling plant, and another two in the parkland. Arnie Fung had fatally shot two more, after Frank Tedesco had killed three with his bare hands. Hagen rounded out the list of those killed in action.

Van Deming and one of his riot-equipped squad had been so badly injured while subduing Frank and Joe B. that they were no longer fit for duty. And Medford, Weisskopf and Alvarez had gone over the hill.

The losses represented almost a third of the force, and would have had a demoralizing effect on those remaining, if anyone had told them the whole situation. But the men who waited behind the waist-high wall that surrounded the hotel's front yard and parking lot knew nothing of the bridge crew's premature bug-out. And for all they knew, the two men who had gone haring off after the Meechams were no more than missing, could even be goofing off, to come bouncing back at any moment.

Still, they were all aware that this operation had definitely not gone according to plan. The briefing had said that any opposition would come from crazed civilians, unarmed and uncoordinated. The reality of contact with the enemy had shown them to be highly coordinated, as adept as any professional in the use of small arms, and dismayingly focused on the business of killing mercenaries.

The original force had included two men of nominal officer's rank, Wexler and Schlimmer. Both were now dead. That left three non-coms: the Texan Bartlesby, Leith from Belfast, and Van Deming, and the Belgian was stretched out on the back seat of the bus, moaning softly through a fog of painkillers.

Bartlesby and Leith had divided up the tasks of maintaining security while preparing for the pull-out. They had assigned half of the men to stowing the operation's surveillance and other equipment back into the luggage compartments of the bus. As the work progressed, they had steadily drawn men away from the carrying crews, and put them behind the walls.

The Texan had taken charge of the section facing west into the parkland and south onto the intersection where Bridge Road met Prescott Avenue. Some of Leith's men were also on the south wall, with the bulk of them facing east into the lake-side park that ran along the top of Prescott Avenue.

The non-coms' orders had been succinct. "Shoot anybody who comes within range," Leith told them. "I don't care if it's your own sainted mother coming to kiss you good-night. Knock them down and make sure they stay down."

"And for those of you didn't see what happened on the driveway there," the Texan added, "these folks move mucho fast. If you're trying to hit them running, make sure you lead 'em plenty."

The men took up their positions behind the wall. The bus was almost loaded; they were only waiting for the order to get on board and move out. Drivers were bringing the leased surveillance vans, now stripped of their audiovisual gear, into the hotel parking lot, where they would be abandoned.

Crouched down behind the wall, Bartlesby scanned the view down Bridge Road through field glasses. It was empty. There was activity of some kind at the bridge, but no gunfire – and no sign of any opposition moving into ambush position between the hotel and the bridge.

He looked west, into the parkland. Here the view was obscured in places by clumps of trees, and there were areas of dead ground hidden by rises in the rolling terrain. But as far as the Texan could see, nothing bad was coming his way.

He waved to catch Leith's attention, then hand-signaled the absence of threat. The Belfast non-com confirmed the same for his sector, then indicated that it was time to get the troops onto the bus.

Bartlesby signed his assent, then told the nearest soldier to pass the word: every third man to get on the bus. The designated men began leaving the wall, staying low and heading for the bus's open door. Leith's section was doing the same. The vehicle's diesel engine throbbed into action.

The last of the first dozen men had boarded the vehicle when a look-out at the front gate shouted, "Enemy in front!"

Bartlesby trained the glasses back down Bridge Road, and there they were, a stream of people coming out of the bottling plant and running toward him down the straightaway. *Trust civilians to act like fuckin' civilians,* he thought, and, *Christ, they're movin' fast!* Then he yelled, "Don't wait for 'em – fire!"

All along the front of the hotel, the men behind the south wall opened up at full automatic on the crowd.

Lou Meecham's plan had been simple. It had to be simple: most of Prescott Springs' people had had no military training, except for a handful of older men who'd been drafted in the seventies – none had seen any combat.

So they'd sent Jeff Cameron and a few others to remove any threat to their rear from the men on the bridge, and they'd put a young man with good eyesight out on Bridge Road to watch the hotel until the first group got back.

Then they'd hung around the bottling plant, the individual members of the mob milling and circling in the open space like zoo wolves confined to too small a cage. Nobody stood still for more than a moment. Nobody talked. Nobody formed groups.

They were like so many star athletes waiting for the dressing room door to open, eager to run down the tunnel and out onto the field, to get their hands on something tangible – a ball, a bat, somebody's flesh – and *get busy!*

Lou Meecham was no different. He paced and circled with the rest, his hands squeezing the handguard and pistol grip of Chaffey's M-16. He wandered to the door of the former secretary's office, looked in, his eyes constantly moving. His gaze passed over the gap the townsfolk had made in the glass wall, widening the hole where the van had broken through. He wanted to go out through that hole, down the road and to wherever the men he wanted to kill where lurking. He ached for it.

Adele's foot protruded from beneath the cardboard Macreedy had covered her with. He registered the object without reaction. All the parts of him that should have felt something at the sight of his dead wife were packed away now. The Lou Meecham who had loved that woman and feared for her, whose heart had broken at her death, that Lou was stranded somewhere far off, on the other side of a roiling red sea called Paroxysm.

All that was left on this side was a desire to kill Tag Macklin and Parker DeVoin. The urge to go and do it now ate at the small piece of him that was still rational. There was no fear – he didn't care if he died, didn't even contemplate the possibility. It was only the thought that, on his own, he might not be able to get to them, that kept him from racing immediately down to the hotel, tearing aside anyone who stood in his way.

He made a noise in the back of his throat and turned away from the office door. A man was turning over the corpse of the soldier who had been disemboweled, and now came up with an automatic pistol. The man bared his teeth – it couldn't have been called a smile – and sprang to his feet, brandishing the gun.

"Let's go-o-o-o-o!" he cried, the last word elongating into a howl. The call energized the others. They turned toward the man with the pistol, made grunts and guttural sounds that might have been words. They moved toward the office doorway – the exit.

Lou felt the will of the crowd tugging at his resolve. There was something moving in him, something below the level of individuality, a left-over from the earliest days of the human species. When the pack went, he wanted to go with it.

He fought the urge. "No!" he cried. "We stay until the others come back! Then we attack together!" He put himself in the doorway.

"Come on!" said the man with the pistol. "Let's get the bastards!" He came forward, the mob falling in behind him.

"No!" Lou shouted into the man's face. "Wait for the others!"

The man snarled. Lou saw that he was ready to use the gun to clear the doorway. Lou swung the M-16 around.

"The bus!" yelled a voice from outside. It started high and rose steeply in pitch. "They firing up the bus!"

The teenager they had sent out to watch the hotel was fairly dancing on the other side of the glass wall. "They're getting on it! We're gonna miss 'em!" he squeaked.

With that news delivered, Lou could not hold the crowd, nor did he want to. The thought that Macklin and DeVoin might get away created an urgency that was more than he could withstand. *To hell with the ambush!* He was one of the first through the hole in the wall and out onto the road.

The others scrambled with him through the hole in the wall, the younger, faster ones soon leaving him behind. They ran for the hotel. There was no thought for strategy, no consideration of a plan of attack. The mob howled and shrieked its way down the road, the fastest moving at speeds that would not have disgraced an Olympic sprinter.

They had covered half the distance between the plant and the wall surrounding the hotel when the mercenaries opened fire. The leading elements of the charge went down in a heap, but those behind leapt over them and kept coming.

The troops continued to pour fire into the mob. More bodies fell. In the middle of the pack, Lou saw them tumbling across the asphalt in front of him. A voice rang in his head, the reflex trained into him all those years ago: *Cover! Cover! Cover!*

Lou fought down the compulsion to close with the enemy at any cost. "Take cover!" he shouted at the man to his left, pushing him toward the bushes that screened the hotel's parkland from the road. He grabbed another by the arm and swung him around, as bullets *zizzed* past them.

Others heard his words and repeated them. More than a dozen veered left and threw themselves into the undergrowth. But a handful were too far gone, lost in the glorious rage of the charge.

They ran straight into the soldiers' fire, the bullets ripping their flesh, smashing their bones, shattering their bared teeth. They stumbled and jerked with the impacts, sliding and rolling on the blacktop.

The troops continued to spray the corpses in the road and the bushes beside it, long after nothing moved. Many of them emptied their magazines, popped in a fresh clip and fired another burst at the dead.

"Cease fire! Cease fire!" Bartlesby was yelling. "Save your ammunition, goddammit!"

He scanned the road, counting the dead – nine, he reckoned. One of them had been an old woman waving a frying pan and wearing a bloodstained nightgown. But most of the mob had got away into the parkland. He weighed it up and made up his mind.

"You on the bus – get over to the west wall!" The men on the bus dismounted and ran to where he indicated. The Texan went down the line of men crouched behind the wall facing south and slapped each on the shoulder. "West wall," he said, and they went.

The man who doubled as the general's driver was nearby. The Texan detailed him to find the general and tell him what was happening. Then he scooted over to where to the other non-com squatted behind the east wall and hunkered down for a talk.

"Anything?"

"Not a whisper," said Leith.

"They don't seem too experienced, you know what I mean," said Bartlesby. "I figure they'll try another rush on the west side. If we got enough firepower there, we'll finish 'em and get the hell out of here."

The Belfast man nodded. "You'll be wanting some of my lads."

"Yeah."

"I'll keep three here, on the off chance," said Leith. "You take the rest."

"Good," said the Texan. A minute later, he had twenty-four men waiting behind the wall that faced into the hotel parkland. One man had been left on the south wall, to give warning if any more of the townspeople came down Bridge Road or appeared along Prescott Avenue.

"They'll be coming soon now," he told the men on the west wall. "A few minutes work and we knock off for the day. Just don't waste any shots."

Jeff Cameron came up from the river bank and out onto Bridge Road just as the soldiers at the hotel were cutting down the last few charging townsfolk who had not had the presence of mind to get out of the way. The killing zone was little more than half a mile down the straight road; stray rounds from the fusillade thrummed past him.

"Into the trees!" he yelled and broke right. The men who were with him followed, crashing through bracken and brambles into the second-growth timber on the east side of the road. Not far into the green there was a trail worn into the forest floor. It meandered from the end of Carson Street to the river bank east of the bridge, and had been made by generations of kids, fishing poles over their shoulders and bait cans in their hands. Now Jeff's small force carried guns and knives and anything they had found that could kill.

They left the woods at the end of Carson and headed toward Prescott, dashing between the two rows of houses – some of them empty and boarded up, others with their doors wide open and corpses sprawled open-eyed in their rooms. As they ran, Jeff was thinking. Without an enemy directly in front of him, it was easier to concentrate.

*The others went right at the soldiers and got shot up,* he thought. *The soldiers were ready for them.*

They were nearing the corner of Prescott and Carson. If they ran out onto the main street, they'd be in full view of any troops watching the eastern approaches to the hotel. Speed might not be enough.

Jeff slowed. "This way!" he yelled, and swung into the lane that ran between Custer and Prescott. The others followed, and a few seconds later, they came out on Rockwell across from the baseball diamond. They ran across the infield, the stores along Prescott blocking any view of them from the hotel, then across Greeley and into the trees beyond.

Twenty feet into the woods, Jeff stopped them. "Listen," he said, "you saw what happened out in front of the hotel. We can't just charge in there. We gotta sneak up on these bastards, blindside 'em and whack 'em hard."

He laid out the plan he'd been working on as he'd led them back from the bridge. They would cut through the woods to the shore of the lake, then skirt along the low retaining wall that separated the grass of the shoreline park from the stony beach of Prescott Lake. Nobody along the hotel's east side would see them until they came up the concrete steps that led down to the water – they'd be almost in spitting distance.

They would wait at the bottom of the steps until they heard shooting from the main force, wherever they now were. Then they'd break from cover and hit the soldiers from an unexpected direction.

"Ah, fuck it," said Weaver, cradling his shotgun. "Why don't we just rush 'em now?"

They all wanted to. Just hearing it said was enough to start Jeff moving. He hadn't even fired his rifle yet.

But he fought down the aching urge to jump into it. He was like a kid playing hide-and-seek in the park on one of those long, magical summer nights, when you wanted to burst from hiding and run for home base, but you had to wait *forever* until whoever was "it" would get far enough away that you could make that sweet, golden rush to triumph.

"No," he told them. "We go too soon, we might not get them. We gotta wait. We gotta hold it, till we get in close."

"He's right," said Arnie Fung. When Mitch, and his partner Terry backed him up, Weaver subsided.

"Yeah, okay," he said.

Jeff looked at each member of the group. The woman who had killed all her pet birds held up the garden fork she carried and said, "Just so we don't have to wait too long."

"Hey," Jeff said, noticing for the first time that someone was missing, "where's my kid?"

"He stayed at the river," said Weaver. "I think he was tracking the ones that run away."

A tiny murmur of concern sounded in the back of Jeff Cameron's head. But there was no longer anyone there to hear it. "Let's get down to the beach," he said.

# 18

"When I open fire, those with guns start shooting," said Lou. "Those without guns rush the wall."

They were in a line of trees that topped a gentle rise above a lawn that sloped down about sixty yards to the west wall of the hotel. Of the thirty-seven townsfolk who had charged down Bridge Road with him to attack the hotel, nine had died on the road, and two more had been hit after they sought cover in the bushes. Twenty-seven were left. Of those, seventeen had guns of some kind; they ranged from his M-16 to a single-shot .22 target pistol. The other ten had knives, axes, garden tools – anything that had come to hand.

"The moment someone is over the wall, the rest of us charge." He looked into their eager faces. Some of them had been wounded, though none seriously. Pain meant nothing. They couldn't wait to get started.

He spread them out along the top of the rise, concealed by the trees and the long grass that grew between the trunks. They positioned themselves quickly, and without much effort to be quiet about it. There would be no element of surprise, Lou knew – just shock and speed.

He crawled forward to the edge of the trees, and parted the grass a little to get a clear view of the hotel's west side. The gray stone wall was about four feet high, broken by a closed cast-iron gate that led onto a gravel path that meandered away into the parkland.

He couldn't see any of the mercenaries, but he knew they'd be crouched behind the wall, waiting for their targets to appear. Beyond the stone barrier, in the hotel's side parking area, the big highway bus stood with its diesel engine idling. Behind it was the limousine in which DeVoin and Macklin had no doubt traveled.

Back in Lou Meecham's soldiering days, the moments just before the shooting began were always the toughest. Once things started, he was fine. But during the waiting, his mind would resist thinking about what he was going to do, would drift instead to memories of home and friends and girls he had known. He would have to force himself to concentrate on the here and now.

Paroxysm had relieved him of that difficulty. Any part of him that might want to dwell in soft memories was shrunk to the dimensions of a gnat's anus. Lou Meecham wanted to kill Macklin and DeVoin. He didn't even think of his dead wife.

He inched the M-16 forward until its muzzle cleared the grass, set its selector switch to fire three-round bursts, and looked for a target. He saw what might have been hair – just a patch of brown – appear above the rim of the wall, as one of the mercenaries shifted position; then it disappeared.

Impatient, he scanned the length of the wall. If he had to, he'd fire at nothing just to get the assault moving. Then his peripheral vision caught a vague motion and his eyes instantly sought for it. For a second, two, there was nothing, then it registered: a shifting of shadows behind the darkened windows of the limousine. *There's somebody in there!*

He pressed the rifle stock to his shoulder, put the sights on the rear passenger window of the long black car, and squeezed the trigger. At once, three tightly grouped holes radiated cracks through the smoky glass. A fraction of a second later, every gun along the top of the rise spat fire toward the stone wall.

As the bullets broke chips of stone from the top and outside of the wall, the gunless townsfolk raced from the trees. A long, wavering howl came up from the throats of the ten who charged.

No, it was eleven, Lou saw. The man who had found the disemboweled soldier's pistol was also running forward, emptying its magazine at the mercenaries, who now raised themselves up and poured fire into the attack. The pistolman shot one through the head and managed to aim at another before he was hit by fire from several rifles that cut him almost in two.

As soon as the soldiers' heads and shoulders popped into view, Lou forgot about the limo and laid his sights down on the clear targets. Still firing bursts of three, he started at the south end of the wall and worked his way along, like knocking down floating ducks in a carnival shooting gallery.

Lou Meecham had been in more than a few firefights, most of them quick jungle ambushes. The only sizable actions he'd even been involved in had been the couple of times he'd helped defend forward base positions against company-strength attacks by VC or NVA regulars.

He had never staged a frontal assault, but he'd seen them from the other side of the wire, and knew the procedure. That's why he'd sent the gunless townsfolk on the suicide charge: to draw the fire of the defenders so that those townspeople who had guns would have targets to use them on.

And the tactic was working. He figured the defenders must have lost a dozen men within ten seconds of their standing up to shoot the ax- and knife-wielding first wave. Now, as the last of the gunless attackers went down, none of them having made it to the wall, the mercenaries were shifting their aim to the top of the rise.

A bullet spun over Lou's head and thwacked into a tree behind him. *Single shots,* he noted. *They're short on ammo.*

He could just make out the top of a blond head behind the wall, a rifle muzzle appearing over the stones close beside. Lou noted the angle and the motion of the barrel. *He's reloading,* he thought. *And now up he comes.*

As the man stood up to fire his reloaded rifle, Lou's three-round burst tore away his face and hurled him backwards.

He heard a roar of rage from a few feet away. One of the Prescott Springs people had been hit. The shot had grazed the man's head, ripping loose a patch of scalp, and the impact had maddened him. He got to his knees, drawing more fire. He held a pump-action shotgun, his left hand blurring with speed as he emptied it at the men behind the wall. But now half the mercenaries still capable of firing a rifle put their weapons on him and ripped him apart.

Over the firing, Lou heard a distant voice. "Fall back!" it said. "Into the hotel!"

The mercenaries were dropping back from the wall in twos and threes, giving each other covering fire as they went, making for the solid protection of the stone building. It looked to Lou as if they were down to little more than a dozen men.

He got up. "Come on!" he yelled, and went forward, firing from the shoulder. Out of the trees at the top of the rise came a dozen of the townspeople. One of them was the ferret-faced man from the bottling plant. A bullet had shattered his left arm, but he had clamped a double-barreled shotgun under the armpit, so that he could break its breech and put two more shells in. Before he could snap it close, a slug opened his throat and he went down choking.

"Come on!" Lou yelled again, and ran for the wall. Bullets hummed around him, but he felt a surge of energy rush like blue lightning along his backbone and into his limbs. He sprinted forward, leaping over the dead strewn on the slope, as light-footed as a colt.

He was smiling.

Macklin took comfort from the solid sound of the limousine's door as it swung closed. Sandrini was nervous, wriggling around in the seat beside him, but the major was beginning to feel that glow of self-satisfaction that always followed a successful operation.

Through the darkened windows, he watched the troops reposition themselves. He supposed he ought to be outside directing preparations for the defense. But DeVoin hadn't ordered him to do so, and things seemed to be going fine under the barked commands of Sergeant Bartlesby. Besides, he much preferred having armor plate and bullet-proof glass between him and people who would kill him if they got him in their sights.

Macklin let the bandy-legged Texan take command – along with the risk of being outside where death would arrive unannounced at better than two thousand feet per second. He settled back into the car's plush rear seat and contemplated the future. Though the Prescott Springs operation had gone hinky, it was coming out all right in the end. The new version of Paroxysm looked to be worth much more than the original. The world was full of states that wanted to give somebody – their neighbors or their own civilian populations – a damn good pummeling. Now they could issue their cheapjack conscript armies a breakfast of champions, transforming them instantly into crack troops.

Osama's jihadists would be only the first customers. He could think of a number of places around the globe where a weapon like the one they had discovered this weekend would alter the local geopolitical situation overnight.

Macklin craned to look past Sandrini and through the car's window on the side facing the hotel service door, to see if the general was coming. As he moved, his ears rang with a sound like the *crack* of a giant whip. He swung around; three neatly grouped holes the thickness of his little finger had appeared in the glass of the window facing west. Three corresponding holes had been punched through the rear window.

Macklin threw himself onto the floor of the limo as a sudden roar of riflery engulfed his part of the world. With a squeak, Sandrini dove on top of him.

Dull thuds like hammer blows banged on the side of the car. An arm rest abruptly tore loose from the rear door and flew across the back seat, tumbling to rest on the floor where Macklin's pressed his face into the carpet. A twisted soft-nosed slug was buried in the velvet-covered plastic.

*The goddamn thing's not armored!* was the first clear thought to make it through the major's panicked mind. Another round hit the west-side window and shattered it, showering the cowering men with tiny rectangular jewels of smoky glass.

Macklin thrust his hand at the door handle and slapped it down. The heavy door opened, and Sandrini crawled over him to get clear of the car. Cursing, Macklin followed.

As ricochets whined and bullets gouged flakes from the stone wall of the hotel, the two men scrambled on hands and knees for the hotel service door. They pushed through it and flung themselves onto the floor as a round hit the half open door and keened away down the corridor.

Lieutenant Schlimmer's corpse lay belly down beside Macklin, the dead face turned toward the major. Nobody had bothered to close the dead man's eyes, and he seemed to stare at Macklin with an air of bland unconcern.

"Shit!" said the major. He crawled over the corpse's booted feet into the alcove that led to the service stairs. Sandrini, gibbering, came after him.

Macklin wanted time to think. Something bad was happening here. DeVoin had sent him and the scientist to wait in the car, told him it was armored. The general was not a man to make a mistake about such a thing. His mind clicked through the facts: the general had the formula; the formula was everything; he no longer needed Sandrini; did he also no longer need Tag Macklin?

The major had perpetrated enough double-crosses to recognize one from the receiving end. DeVoin wanted him and Sandrini out of the profit-sharing plan, and so he had quietly put them in harm's way. That must mean the general had another route out of Prescott Springs.

He thought about the tunnel. After Herb Trainor blurted out his secret, DeVoin and Macklin had quietly explored the underground passage. But then they had locked each set of doors, and the keys were still in Macklin's pocket.

There had to be another way. *By boat across the lake?* he wondered. And then he heard the drone of the plane. He drew his pistol and used it to prod Sandrini. "Upstairs," he said.

As a soldier, Parker DeVoin was fundamentally an administrator. Family connections had enabled him to attend West Point, and had been sufficient to put him in the right commands at the right times. His considerable organizational talents, combined with the persistent ruthlessness of the born sociopath, had moved him steadily up to the rank of brigadier without ever taking him into combat. He wore the Combat Infantry Badge, without which few rise higher than Lieutenant Colonel, but the closest he had actually come to hearing shots fired in anger had been while conducting the kind of field trials that had ruined the life of Lou Meecham.

He was used to giving orders, and he was used to having them carried out smoothly and efficiently. He was not accustomed to having his will frustrated by the random, chaotic disruptiveness that is endemic to the battlefield.

When his driver had come to report Sergeant Bartlesby's disposition of the men, DeVoin had received the information, then instructed the man to advise the Texan that a small plane would be inbound to the dock out back of the hotel in the next few minutes. The plane was to be treated as friendly.

The driver saluted and went to deliver the message. But as he exited the hotel's service door, the townsfolk opened fire. The man was scuttling across the parking lot toward Bartlesby when a slug from a 30-30 deer rifle smashed the top of his shoulder and sat him heavily down on the asphalt. Dazed, he struggled to rise and was hit by a second round in the chest. The bullet missed his heart, but the concussion from the impact was so powerful that its shock stopped the organ.

So when the general's pilot brought the Beaver in from the east, low over the water and angling in toward the little jetty that ran out from the hotel's elevated rear patio, it was just another target to the men of DeVoin's command.

Sergeant Major Leith and the three mercenaries squatted behind the east wall, listening to the firefight that had broken out on the far side of the hotel. Peering over the top of the stone barrier, they worriedly scanned what they could see of the park and beach to the east. All of them were uncomfortably aware of the long stretch of dead ground behind the retaining wall – enough hidden terrain to hide a company.

The approach of the plane was welcome: at least it was something on which to focus their anxieties. They waited until the aircraft was so close they could make out the pink blob of the pilot's face behind the windshield. Then they opened fire.

Even at full automatic, it is not easy to shoot down airplanes with small arms fire. A plane coming in to land often appears to be moving more slowly than it is, and shifts its position constantly through three dimensions. The DeHavilland Beaver that was coming for the general's party was a particularly sturdy craft, designed and built for service in the rugged wilderness of northern Canada.

Most of the rounds fired at it missed, and those few that did hit the plane failed to damage any components whose loss would have disabled it. The pilot gunned the throttle, banked hard, and slid away to the north.

One of Leith's men fired after it, rising to his feet. The moment his torso rose above the low wall, a rifle bullet struck him just below the right armpit, tore across the tops of both lungs and broke through the ribs on his left side. The man had not hit the ground before Leith and the two remaining mercenaries had turned to fire at the small group rushing them from a concrete stairwell that cut through the raised terrace of the shoreline park and connected with the beach.

Jeff heard the plane first, far off toward the east end of the long lake. He and the rest of his group were clustered at the foot of the beach stairs, waiting for the fighting to start. When the low buzz of the Beaver's single engine came murmuring across the water, they turned and saw the morning sunlight glimmering on its propeller.

Arnie raised his rifle and sighted on the distant mote of light bouncing against the dark green of the hills. Jeff touched him on the shoulder.

"Wait," he said. "It comes in, it could be a distraction – give us a chance to rush 'em."

Arnie lowered the gun.

The plane first headed for the southern edge of the lake well to the east of the hotel, then angled to come in parallel to the shoreline. It was less than a mile from the hotel's jetty, with the pilot clearly intending to put his floats down on the water, when the firefight broke out to the west.

At the sound of screams and gunfire, Zack Weaver growled and moved toward the stairs. Jeff grabbed his belt and hauled back, and the catering manager turned with a snarl.

"Ten seconds!" said Jeff. "Just till the plane comes in!"

Weaver's face writhed from the struggle taking place within him. He ground his teeth, but finally nodded.

They watched the aircraft float slowly toward their position, saw the pilot's face looking curiously at them, then his shock as the mercenaries behind the east wall suddenly opened fire.

"Now!" said Jeff. The six of them boiled up the steps from the beach and onto the grass of the park. The hotel wall was less than fifty feet away. They could see the tops of the mercenaries' heads. The soldiers' rifles were turned away, blasting at the now departing Beaver.

One of the mercenaries stood up to fire. Arnie paused at the tops of the steps and dropped the man with a single shot. He waited for another clear target while the others rushed by him.

Weaver charged forward, screaming. He leveled his shotgun and let fly with both barrels. The pellets passed harmlessly over the crouching men. Weaver didn't bother to reload but reversed the weapon and rushed the wall.

Jeff was behind him and to one side. A great wave of savage delight swept through him as he came up the steps and saw the enemy. He let the red beast have its roaring head and followed it.

He sprayed the wall with the M-16, saw the bullets strike too low. He raised his aim just as the mercenaries turned – so slowly – and brought their weapons to bear on the charging townsfolk.

The soldiers were fast and accurate. One loosed a long burst that brought down Zack Weaver in mid-stride then tracked toward Jeff. Jeff shot him, saw him fall, and brought his weapon around to take out the next man.

But that soldier's bullets were already reaching out for Jeff Cameron, and the distance was too close for even his Paroxysm-spiked neurons to take him out of the way in time.

An impact in his chest spun him around and knocked the air from his lungs. Something twisted and tore in his left knee, shooting a sharp rip of agony up his inner thigh. He fell onto his back, his head toward the wall. Gasping, he saw Arnie Fung standing at the head of the steps, calmly taking aim and firing.

A long streamer of red suddenly appeared beside Arnie's head. To Jeff, it looked like a colored ribbon, the kind that Sharon used to tie up her hair with when she was a school girl.

A look of surprise came over his old catcher's face. Arnie dropped his deer rifle and fell backwards down the stairs. Jeff realized that the ribbon was Arnie's blood, spewing from a severed artery in his neck. He'd been shot. A distant part of Jeff's mind knew he should have been horrified, but he pushed that fragment far, far away. And then it was gone for good.

The rifle fire stopped. Jeff heard brief screaming, and a sound like heavy cloth tearing. He thought it might be knives cutting into flesh. He tried to stand up, but his knee refused to bear the weight.

The rage still seethed in him, overpowering the ache in his chest and the howling protest from his knee. He forced himself to roll over onto his belly, then pressed himself to his hands and his good knee. He looked toward the wall.

Zack Weaver lay nearby, riddled. Not far beyond him was the bird woman, her garden fork beneath her. Of the four mercenaries who had been behind the wall there was no sign.

Jeff pushed himself higher, until he was upright on one knee. Beyond the wall he could see Mitch and Terry heading for the hotel, knives gleaming in their hands. Terry was falling behind, limping on one leg, and Mitch came back to help him. Together, Terry's arm over Mitch's shoulder, they reached the bottom of the front steps.

A burst of fire from the front door ripped into them. They fell onto the steps and lay still.

Now Jeff wanted nothing more than to get to the hotel and kill whoever had fired those shots. He found his rifle, but it was smashed. He realized what had happened when the mercenary had fired at him: a bullet had struck the rifle of Jeff's M-16 and slammed back it into his chest. The impact must have bruised a rib, maybe cracked it.

The pain in his chest had crested and now began to subside. He could breathe almost freely. He stood up on his right leg and hobbled to the wall.

On the other side, four mercenaries lay dead. Three had been shot. The fourth, a big bullet-headed man, had been cut several times, parts of his face sliced away and his throat opened so far that Jeff could see the gleam of gray-ish bone at the bottom of the wound.

He heard an odd noise, very near. When it was repeated, he realized it was the sound of bullets narrowly missing him. Someone was shooting at him from the hotel.

He ducked down, so that the wall hid him from view. He pressed his cheek against the grass and tried to think. His weapon was destroyed; he needed another.

There were rifles on the other side of the wall, but if he crawled over to get them in his present state, he'd be shot. He thought about the chances, and decided he didn't want to die; he wanted to kill.

He remembered Arnie's deer rifle, how it had gone down the steps with Arnie. He crawled to the steps and looked down. His friend's body was sprawled head down on the concrete stairs. The rifle lay on the stones at the bottom.

Jeff slid down the steps on his belly. He did not look at Arnie's face as he passed. At the base of the stairs, he swung his legs around and rested his back against the retaining wall.

He picked up the rifle and examined it. It was undamaged, but when he worked the bolt and opened the breech he saw that its five-round magazine was empty. He crawled up the steps, searched his friend's pockets for more ammunition, found nothing.

The plane was coming back, the distant noise of its engine growing steadily louder. Jeff descended to the stony beach and looked to the east. The plane was making the same approach as before, coming in low along the south shore of the lake. It would pass right by him.

He looked to the jetty behind the hotel. Three men stood at its end. Two of them were waving to the plane; the third was talking on a portable phone.

Now two more men came through the french windows that connected the ballroom with the hotel patio. One of them held a pistol.

Macklin pushed Sandrini through the french windows and followed him out onto the patio. The open space was on a stone platform built about ten feet above the beach. At its farthest edge, three steps descended to a stone jetty with a wooden deck that ran out over the water. Another flight of steps, set at a right angle to the jetty, led down to the sand. The patio was crowded with white-painted cast-iron tables and chairs, some of them shaded by large umbrellas. But the major could see well enough what was happening.

In less than a minute, a float plane would pull up to the end of the dock, and DeVoin would be gone, the formula for Paroxysm 2 snug in his pocket. The general and the Yemeni clients were bugging out, leaving Tag Macklin to die.

He pushed Sandrini again, this time toward the dock. DeVoin saw them coming and said something to Hafiz, who glanced Macklin's way then spoke to his aide.

The younger Yemeni did not hesitate. He drew a gun from a shoulder holster and sank to one knee. He brought the gun up two-handed, and fired.

It was only as the gun came up that Sandrini realized he was Macklin's walking shield. He screamed as the Yemeni's first shot hit him in the side. The slug passed cleanly through the excess flesh that spilled over his waistband, but its impact spun him around and threw him down onto the concrete.

He tried to rise, but pain thrust through his body like a red hot iron. He looked down at his side, saw a spreading stain of blood on his shirt, and fainted.

Macklin fired wildly, emptying his pistol as he backed up toward the french windows. The Yemeni was cooler. Although he flinched as the major's bullets gouged splinters from the wooden deck on either side of him, he methodically squeezed off shot and after shot.

A bullet tore through Macklin's outer thigh. It ripped the muscle and knocked him down, but missed the femur and the femoral artery. He scrambled for the french windows, and the Yemeni's last shot burrowed into his right buttock and struck his hipbone. The blow was like an elephant's kick, and drove him forward into the ballroom.

The Yemeni did not pursue him. The plane was coming in.

211

Jeff watched the gunfight, saw the two men go down. He didn't know how he knew it, but there was no doubt in his mind that the men on the jetty were the instigators of what had happened to Prescott Springs. He didn't know why, and was in no state to care, but he was certain that these were people who had meant him no good, who had done him all the harm they could.

And now they were planning to get on a plane and fly away. The red tiger in him growled. The thought of those men rising above the town and sailing through the air to some place of comfort and safety fanned his anger into a bright blaze. He wanted them dead.

Again, he looked about for a weapon. There was only the stony beach where he had played as a kid, where the teenage Jeff Cameron had come down after the last inning on a hot summer day to swim in the clear, clean water.

He bent and picked up a black, water-smoothed rock, about the size and shape of a regulation baseball. He walked to the water's edge, the lump of basalt clumping against his thigh.

The plane came droning in from the east, the disc of its propeller spinning like a majorette's baton in a Fourth of July parade. Its left wing dipped a little and it slipped slightly closer to the shoreline, growing steadily larger in Jeff's vision. In a moment, he could make out the struts supporting the wings; then the painted trim on the engine cowling; then the pilot's face looking at him from the side window.

He drew back his arm, the rock heavy as destiny in his fist. And now it came over him again, the lucid timelessness he had known so often as a boy, the oneness of being and action held in a moment of perfect completion.

The stone flew from his hand to reach a precise point in space at an exact instant in time. It was there, it had always been there, *had* to be there. The vast universe that surrounded it, the eternity that stretched before and after it, were illusion. There was only this. There was only now.

The rock entered the open window of the plane, crushed the pilot's left temple and rendered him unconscious. Splinters of bone entered his brain and tore through delicate blood vessels, initiating a build-up of pressure in the cranium which would eventually be fatal, if he lived long enough to die of that cause.

But only seconds remained to the dying aviator. His hands fell from the control column and his feet came off the rudder pedals, while the plane rumbled on.

The plane's floats had been barely above the water. Now, without the pilot's skill to correct its attitude, the Beaver's left wing dipped ever lower, pulling the plane around in that direction. Thirty yards short of the dock, the wingtip touched the water and dug in.

The aircraft cartwheeled across the intervening space and smashed against the huge broken rocks that supported the wooden deck of the jetty, not far from the end that extended over the water. The impact tore a gash in the starboard fuel tank and splattered the dock with aviation gas.

A shower of sparks from the grating of twisted metal against the jetty's granite foundation ignited the fuel. A fireball billowed skyward with a noise like a giant's cough, then dissipated to leave a pillar of oily black smoke rising from crackling flames.

Jeff had seen the men on the jetty running back toward the hotel as the plane came toward them. When the aircraft struck, it sprayed burning fuel across the wooden deck. He heard one of them scream.

He saw the man stumble and fall, making squeaking sounds as he rolled on the planks, his jacket on fire. One of the other two stopped to help beat out the flames and pull the burning garment away. The last of the three kept running.

Jeff picked up an armful of rocks and walked toward the gate in the chain-link fence that ran from the hotel's east wall into the lake, separating public from private beach.

# 19

Bartlesby got his men through the heavy metal service door at the side of the hotel and slammed it shut. The strong lock on the inside ought to hold it.

He counted heads. Of the twenty-four men who'd waited behind the west wall for the townsfolk' attack, fifteen had made it into the hotel. Three were walking wounded. The wounded who couldn't run, including Van Deming and his man on the bus, had been left to the citizens of Prescott Springs.

"Come on," he said, and led the survivors down the service corridor to the main stairs. A few seconds later, they were in the lobby, piling the old-fashioned plush furniture into barricades across the big front doors. They heaped more tables and chairs across the two hallways that fed into the lobby, one from the restaurant, the other from the ballroom.

Bartlesby looked out the windows that flanked the stained glass doors. The man he had left to watch Bridge Road from behind the south wall was sprawled on the grass.

He looked to where Leith's and his three men should be, and saw them lying inert beneath the wall. Two men with knives in their hands were coming toward him across the east lawn. One had a limp, and the other slowed to help him.

The Texan broke the window with his rifle butt, reversed the weapon and shot the two men down. He saw another one behind the distant wall and snapped off two rounds. The man disappeared, but the Texan didn't know if he'd been hit.

He looked around at the small force left to him. None of them looked ready to crack; he figured most of them had been in worse situations. He had been himself.

"Okay," he told the men, "they're fast, but they're just a buncha goddamn civilians. There's only a few left. So we'll let 'em come in, we'll kill 'em, and then we'll fuck off outta here."

He had them set their fire selector switches to single-shot, then told them to shoot anything that moved. He was going to the command center to find the general.

He climbed over the barricade that blocked the corridor that led to the ballroom. As he approached the big double doors, he heard the approaching rumble of an aircraft engine, and the distinctive sound of handguns being fired.

He'd heard the plane's first approach, while the townies were attacking his men at the west wall, but he had been too occupied to give it much attention. Now, as he reached the ballroom door, the rattle of pistol shots ceased.

Carefully, his rifle at the ready, the Texan eased open the ballroom door and looked in. The first thing he saw was the useless staff officer trying to crawl across the floor, his right leg soaked in blood. Beyond, through the french windows, he saw the fat scientist apparently lifeless on the patio.

Beyond that, he had a clear view of the general and the two Arabs at the end of the jetty. The plane engine grew steadily louder. Bartlesby sized up the situation in a second.

The sergeant had been in tight situations before. Once, when he'd been "advising" some Honduran-based contras who periodically went over the Nicaraguan border to fight Sandinistas, they'd been caught in a well laid ambush.

Three Sandinistas had opened up with AK-47s from behind a barrier of logs they had built across a dirt road that ran along the bottom of a wooded hill. It was only when Bartlesby led a flanking force upslope that the main ambush was sprung.

A whole platoon was dug in a few dozen yards back from the road. They let fly with rocket propelled grenades and machine guns, and the contras started dying faster than turkeys at Thanksgiving.

They needed heavy weapons to reply. Bartlesby called for the two fifty-caliber machine guns mounted on jeeps that traveled at the rear of the contra column. But the vehicles also carried the former Somocista police colonel and his aides who nominally commanded the unit.

Even before the main Sandinista force revealed themselves, El Puerco and his sycophants had spun the jeeps around and run back down the road to Honduras.

The Nicaraguan militiamen hunted Bartlesby and the few others who survived the massacre through miles of stinking bad jungle. While the Texan ran and hid, the colonel and his party were back at base camp, soothing their rattled nerves with good scotch. Then they'd called their CIA contact in Tegucigalpa and told them to round up some more recruits.

When he saw DeVoin and the Yemenis out on the jetty, waiting for the plane to take them out of the trouble they had organized, Bartlesby nodded. *When the officers abandon the men, it's* sauve qui peut, *as the froggies say,* he told himself. *Let every man save his own ass.*

A moment later, through the french window on the northeast corner of the ballroom, he saw the plane appear. It was already pinwheeling across the water, and the men on the dock were running.

Bartlesby watched the aircraft hit the jetty and explode. One of the Yemenis got burned, and the other one stopped to help him. DeVoin was running back to the hotel.

In the ballroom, the major had stopped crawling. He had rolled over onto his left side and was gazing out a french window at the scene outside, as his practiced hands ejected the pistol's spent magazine and inserted a full clip.

*Sauve qui peut,* thought the Texan, and returned to the men in the lobby. The staff officers could save their own asses.

The soldiers outside the hotel were all dead. The townspeople Lou had led in the attack on the west wall had made sure of that, beating the wounded to death with gleeful ferocity. Then they'd found the two on the bus.

The mercenaries who had escaped into the building had not had time to recover their dead comrades' weapons. Now every surviving member of the Prescott Springs population – there were eight of them besides Lou – had an M-16 rifle and at least a couple of dozen rounds of ammunition.

But they'd wasted time killing the wounded, getting their arms and trying the door the enemy had disappeared through, before they came around to the front of the hotel. Lou stopped at the bottom of the stairs when he saw the barricades behind the big glass doors.

"Hold it!" he yelled, and grabbed at a couple of men who were trying to run past him. He managed to take hold of one and swung him around, but the second one was small and got past him.

Lou called after him, but the little man ran up the stairs. He ducked his head as if trying to see more clearly through the glass, then fired at whatever he saw. Instantly, several guns barked from inside the lobby, and the small man crumpled like a wet paper doll.

Lou pushed and pulled the others away from the stairs, herding them back to the side of the building. "Listen," he said, "that's what they want us to do, come busting in. We don't have enough people for that."

The bus's engine had never been switched off. It continued to idle. Stray rounds had taken out some of the vehicle's glass in the firefight, but it remained in running order.

"Anybody ever drive one of these?" he asked.

A thin man with blood on his shirt sleeves held up his hand. "Drove truck. Same thing," he said.

"Let's get on board," Lou said.

The floor of the bus was sticky with gore from the two corpses in the rear, but none of the townsfolk minded lying down in it, at Lou's instruction. He knew that everybody, even professionals, tended to shoot high.

The thin man got into the driver's seat, and Lou told him what to do. The man engaged the gears and pointed the big vehicle toward Bridge Road.

The big bus easily pushed the two vans out of the gate. The driver went down Bridge Road to Custer, made a left, then went down the block and made another one onto Jackson. The next left turn brought him back onto Bridge Road facing the hotel.

"Now," said Lou, kneeling behind the driver's seat, "punch it!"

DeVoin ignored Sandrini. With the formula in his pocket, it didn't matter whether the scientist was alive or dead. As he came up onto the elevated patio from the jetty, the general saw the trail of Macklin's blood leading into the ballroom.

He paused outside the french windows, drew the service automatic from the waistband of his fatigue pants and quietly slid a round into the chamber. Holding the pistol straight down beside his leg, he put his head into the dimness of the unlit room, and said, "Major Macklin, are you all right?"

Macklin was sitting with his back against one leg of the heavy, cloth-draped table that had held Sandrini's analytical equipment. He held his little Czech automatic in both hands, just like the Yemeni had, pointed straight at the place where he had expected DeVoin to come through the opening.

He lowered the pistol an inch, adjusting for the general's stooped posture as the target peered around the jamb of the french window, and fired. The round passed through DeVoin's right cheek, ruining the expensive bridge-work that taxpayers had paid for. It sliced through his tongue, almost severing it, then was deflected straight up by its collision with the left jawbone. The bullet exited through DeVoin's left eye socket in an eruption of blood, bone chips and jelly.

The impact snapped the general's head sharply up and to the left, so that Macklin's second shot entered just behind the temple and made porridge of DeVoin's brain, by bouncing around inside the cranium before it finally came to rest.

"I'm feeling a whole lot better now, thank you, sir," said Macklin. He dragged his wounded leg over to the general's corpse, and quickly rifled the pockets for the formula and the hard drive on which it had been written.

He looked out through the french window and saw Hafiz, sitting on top step of the short flight that rose to the patio, his back toward the hotel. The Yemeni's hair had been scorched away on the left side of his head, and the ear below it was blackened. The younger one kneeled beside him, his head swiveling back and forth from his uncle to Macklin.

The major thought about shooting the man who had shot him, but decided he had other priorities now. He put the paper and the disc drive in a jacket pocket and buttoned it closed. Then he waved away the young Yemeni in a motion that said, *forget it.*

The other stared back at him with expressionless dark eyes, then redoubled his efforts at urging Hafiz to rise, but the senior man shook his head as if dazed and remained seated. The deck of the jetty continued to throw up gouts of black smoke.

The keys to the tunnel jangled in Macklin's pocket as he struggled to stand up. The pain in his hip was as bad as any he'd ever felt, the tear in his thigh less so. If he gritted his teeth, he could limp at a fair speed.

He set off across the ballroom.

Hafiz looked at the burning jetty and wished the explosion had killed him. It would have been quick and a less humiliating death than the one that awaited him if he were captured.

First would come the long incarceration at Guantanamo Bay. There would be torture, of that he was sure. There would be some kind of military tribunal. Finally, there would be a firing squad.

His nephew continued to squeak at him, urging him to get up, to run from here.

Hafiz made a derisory sound deep in his throat. "Say 'God is great,' then put your pistol in your mouth and pull the trigger," he advised. "There is nothing more to be done."

The pain in Jeff's chest was fading. He used a rock to break open the lock on the gate in the fence separating the public park from the hotel's private beach. Stepping through, he passed from stones to clean white sand, brought in by the truckload from a quarry on the coast.

The twisted knee slowed him down. It wasn't the pain – he could override that – but the leg just didn't want to work properly. He stumped along, mechanically, like a movie character created by special effects. In his arms he cradled a clutch of fist-sized rocks.

He reached the bottom of the steps that connected the jetty to the sand, and began to ascend. He had to climb like a toddler: left foot onto the step, right foot beside it; left foot onto the next step, and so on.

His head rose above the level of the patio deck, and he saw the two men on the top of the steps leading from the jetty to the patio. They looked like Arabs. The younger one was bent over the elder, ineffectually pleading in a foreign tongue and trying to draw him to his feet, while gesturing toward the hotel. An automatic pistol lay on the top step.

When he saw Jeff, the young one went for the pistol. Jeff had to come up another step before he had room to fling a rock. Climbing was a slow process; it gave the young Arab time to bring up the gun and fire one round, before the stone left Jeff's hand.

The rock struck the man in the exact center of his face, smashing his prominent nose and driving the nasal bone up and into his brain. Death was almost instantaneous.

The pistol dropped into the lap of the second man. Jeff saw that the man was breaking out of the shock that must have enveloped him when burning aviation fuel had set fire to his head. The Arab's hands closed about the weapon in what looked like a practiced grip, and he brought it up fast. Jeff thought, *He has done this before.*

But Jeff had already selected another rock from the pile cradled in his left arm. Before the man could squeeze the trigger, the missile was in the air.

Hafiz had come halfway around the world for a sophisticated modern weapon; he died as the most primitive element in mankind's vast arsenal, a hurled lump of basalt, crushed the frontal bones of his skull and turned his brain to pulp.

Jeff stumped up the remaining steps to the two bodies and picked up the pistol. He looked toward the hotel, saw a corpse in combat gear and with its head shattered lying just outside the french windows, and another sprawled and leaking blood onto the patio.

Another pistol lay beside the dead soldier. Jeff limped over and picked it up. He glanced at the bleeding body of a fat and balding man in civilian clothes. It made a sound, a small moan.

*Still alive,* Jeff thought, and pointed the Arab's pistol. But before he could fire, he was rocked by a noise from within the hotel. It sounded to Jeff like Godzilla kicking in the front door, followed by a sustained roar of rifle fire in a confined space.

He forgot about the bleeding man and went to the sound of the guns.

Macklin limped down the hallway that connected the ballroom to the lobby. There he would turn right and descend the service stairs to the corridor at whose end was the steps leading to the tunnel. Once into the storage rooms, with the doors locked behind him, he would be safe.

At the end of the corridor, where the faded elegance of the lobby should have led to the big stained glass doors, rose a barricade of plush furniture and marble topped tables. From behind the barrier, a mercenary dispassionately watched the major make his painful way toward him.

Macklin heard a distant rumble – an engine of some kind, rapidly coming nearer. He thought for a moment that a second plane was coming in.

He heard rifle fire. Then someone shouted an order. Macklin couldn't make out the words over the roar of the big diesel. The sentry on the inner barricade looked over his shoulder as the order was repeated, the voice frantic now. Then the light filtering through the stained glass doors suddenly dimmed to complete darkness.

Macklin had an impression of something enormous filling the doorway. Then there was a tremendous metallic *bang!* and a rain of shattered glass. The frame of the door, the colored glass in its panels and all the furniture piled across the front entrance were bulldozed across the lobby by a fast-moving wall of stainless steel and glass. It shoved the first barricade into the second, trapping and mangling the soldier who had been looking at Macklin, then drove the whole tidal wave of debris straight at the major.

He had only time to register the screaming face of the crushed soldier sweeping toward him amidst the wreckage before he was struck in the chest by an overstuffed loveseat and flung backwards down the hallway. The back of his head cracked against the marble floor and he lost consciousness.

When Sergeant Bartlesby saw the bus turn onto Bridge Road and surge toward the hotel gates, he told the men at the windows to wait until they had a clear shot at the driver. But that moment never came.

As the vehicle hurtled through the gates and accelerated up the driveway toward the front steps, he saw no driver. The man must have ducked down below the level of the window.

The men at the windows opened fire on their own initiative, but Bartlesby knew it was too late. "Behind the desk!" he shouted, waving at the barrier of solid oak decorated with floral carvings that stretched along the east side of the lobby.

A couple of the men began to move. The others just looked at him – they hadn't made out the words over the roar of the bus and the gunfire.

"Behind the desk!" he shouted once more, flinging himself toward the carved wood. As he dove across its polished surface, the lobby abruptly darkened. A split second later, the bus hammered into the front doors, shattering them into shards and splinters.

The vehicle filled the doorway, driving itself tightly into the opening, its steel sides screaming and sparking against the stone that had held the door frame. Even as it bulled its way across the lobby, men with rifles appeared in the windows and opened fire on Bartlesby's startled troops.

It was all over in seconds. The mercenaries scarcely had time to return fire before they were cut down.

The Texan didn't bother. He stayed down behind the oak desk, and scuttled along its length to the door at the other end, the one with a brass plaque that said, *Manager – Private*. The strap of his rifle got hung up on something, and he left it.

His ears full of the blast of rifle fire and the grunts and screams of dying men, Bartlesby pushed open the door and wriggled through. He would go out a window and run like hell.

It had been the most terrible, most wonderful morning of Herb Trainor's life.

The soldiers had bound him well, and all his stretching and flexing against the tape that held him to the oak chair had availed him nothing. DeVoin's periodic visits to ask him stupid questions drove him to a place beyond frustration, until Trainor became a little hard point of light at the center of a great rolling galaxy of black rage.

At some point, twisting and pulling, he had fallen over backward. Then he had lain staring at the sculpted plaster of the ceiling, tears of impotent rage running from the corners of his eyes, until by rocking he managed to tip himself onto his right side.

The frustration had been beyond anything he had ever had to bear. And yet, lying with his face against the worn Persian rug, with the old-fashioned mantelpiece clock on the credenza ticking away the minutes and seconds, he had forced himself to master the agony of his helplessness.

He fought down the coruscating rage and focused his vast anger on one single objective: to get free. And it was when he broke through to that clarity of purpose that he realized that he was already free of one lifelong constraint – for the first time ever, Herb Trainor was not afraid.

He moved his eyes over as much as he could see of the room from carpet level. From this angle, it all looked different. He made himself examine everything he could see – the twin pedestals of the big old desk, the molding along the baseboards, a wall socket set into the paneling – searching for something that could help free him.

He saw nothing that met the need. Next he mentally inventoried the parts of the room he couldn't see from his present position. He thought of the tray with its pitcher and glasses on the credenza: could he knock them over, break the glass and cut himself loose?

He found that he could just touch the floor with the outer edge of his right foot, though it was firmly bound to the leg of the chair. If he pushed with the foot and simultaneously thrust his body upwards in the chair, he moved a fraction of an inch.

He practiced the move, until it seemed almost natural to slide by infinitesimal degrees around the floor of his office. He took it as a great victory. Nothing he had ever done had ever given him as profound a sense of accomplishment.

But when he had swung himself around to a point where he could see the credenza, he realized that the glasses would remain out of reach. The vast solidity of the manager's desk lay in his way, and nothing would move it.

But as that hope dimmed, another flared. His eyes fell upon a small improvement that ancient Mr. Gladhew had made during his latter years in the office, a concession to the aging former manager's thin blood. In addition to the steam-heat radiator on the outer wall of the office, the old man had had an electric baseboard heater installed below the window.

It was of thin steel, coated in dull gray paint, about six feet long. Trainor laboriously scooted the chair over to it, until he could run the fingers of his right hand over its surface. He was feeling for a sharp edge, but the rim of every surface he touched was rounded and smoothed by paint.

He chugged the chair along the entire length of the baseboard. There was nothing. It would be as useless to rub the tape against the harmless metal as it had been to attempt to stretch his bonds.

And then his questing fingers found the end of the unit. Here, the top panel curved over, and at the very corner of the sheet that had been shaped to form the heater's upper surface, there was a point – not a sharp point, but a point that was perhaps sharp enough.

After fifteen minutes of trying, Herb had to accept that the curve of the oaken chair's arm made it impossible to apply the tape that bound his right arm to the sharpness. But, after another ten minutes of experimental motion, he found that he could snag the edge of the tape that secured his right leg onto the corner of the heater.

He pulled – and was rewarded by the tiniest sound of fibers parting. He repositioned himself, and pulled again. Then again. Then once more.

Each time, it took several seconds to bring the fraying band of tape against the sharp corner. But, as the seconds moved into minutes, and the minutes piled together, Herb Trainor loosened the constriction that bound his right leg to the chair.

When the last fibers parted and his leg came free, it was the most glorious achievement of his life. He wanted to howl with glee. Instead, he used his free limb to flip the chair over. Then he brought the tape on his left leg into contact with the tool of his deliverance, and went back to work.

Throughout all the time he labored to cut his lower limbs free, no one came into the office. From outside, Trainor heard muffled voices, occasional shouts and gunshots. By the time he had almost freed his left leg, the action had intensified – he heard sustained rifle fire, screams and curses, then the clump of heavy boots in the lobby.

Men were moving furniture about to the orders of a Texan accent that combined staccato commands and inventive profanity. He heard an airplane engine, then a blast from somewhere in the rear of the hotel, followed by more gunfire. The sounds scarcely impinged on Herb's consciousness – he was fully engaged in setting himself free. He did not even contemplate what use he would make of his freedom – he was completely absorbed in the here and now.

It was wonderful to be alive and unafraid and cutting through the last strands that bound his left leg to the chair. It would be only seconds before that victory would be his.

The next sounds the manager heard could not be ignored: an engine, shouts and rifle shots, and a grinding crash as something smashed into the front of the hotel with enough force to shake the floor beneath him.

He redoubled his efforts and tore through the last threads that bound his left leg to the chair. It came free! Trainor gave an animal grunt of satisfaction and rolled onto his knees, the chair tied to his arms and back like the shell of a turtle.

Now he was almost ecstatic. He could move! Now there was only one thing he wanted to do. He looked up in delight as the office door opened and a man crawled through on his belly. Here was exactly what he'd been waiting for.

Bartlesby rose to his feet as he cleared the door to see a little man kneeling on the other side of the room, his arms strapped to a chair, an odd expression on his pudgy face.

"Jest passin' through," the Texan said, and made for the window.

He was halfway across the room before the meaning of the look on the other man's face registered. It was an expression of unalloyed pleasure.

224

*The man's overjoyed to see me,* was the Texan's last thought. Then Herb Trainor came up off his knees, chair and all, and threw himself headfirst into the mercenary's chest.

The impact broke three ribs and separated the sergeant's breastbone at its lower end. It drove all the air from Bartlesby's lungs, and the concussion alone was almost enough to kill him.

Trainor's momentum carried both of them through the door into the devastated lobby. Bartlesby's back struck the edge of the big front desk. The sound of his spine snapping was no louder than a pencil breaking. It couldn't be heard over the sound of Herb Trainor's ecstatic laughter.

The Texan slid to the floor. He was already dead when the hotel manager began to stomp on his chest and face.

Jeff Cameron got to the lobby in time to shoot the last surviving mercenary. The man was wedged between a wall and a broken sofa. He had already taken a burst of fire from an M-16 wielded by one of the townsfolk who had ridden the bus through the hotel doors, but he still had enough life left in him to whisper a word over and over.

"Was that 'hellfire' he kept saying?" Jeff asked Lou Meecham, after he had shot the wounded mercenary through the heart. He liked the way the general's pistol jumped in his hand like something alive when he squeezed the trigger.

"Nah. It was *hilfe*. It means 'help' in German," Lou said.

"I think we'd better cut Herb loose," Jeff said. The hotel manager was still behind the big front desk, kicking at the man he had killed. The other townsfolk had spread out through the hotel, looking for any other survivors.

"Hey, Herb," Jeff offered, "you want us to cut you free of that chair?"

Trainor looked at him across the desk, his eyes dancing with merriment. "That'd be great, Jeff."

"Well, if you could stop stomping on the dead guy, I'll come on over there," Jeff said. He pulled a combat knife from the boot sheath of a dead soldier and climbed over the big oak counter. A second later, Trainor was free.

The manager stretched and laughed. "This is just excellent," he said. "I never felt so good my whole life long."

Jeff's knee still pained him, but he had to agree.

225

Lou had been checking each of the bodies in the lobby, climbing over the debris of broken furnishings. "Either of you guys see Macklin? He was one of the officers."

Jeff said, "There's an officer in the ballroom got his head blown half off."

Lou went to see, but came back shaking his head. "That was DeVoin."

"What about the bald guy on the patio?"

Lou shook his head. "There's no bald guy on the patio," he said. "Just two dead Arabs."

Herb Trainor would really have liked to find another target for his emotions. "I want to go see," he said.

He had to squeeze through the narrow space where the front of the bus had nosed into the corridor that led to the ballroom. The floor of the hallway was half buried in debris. When he crawled over an upturned armchair, a moan came from beneath it.

"Hey," he called to the others.

Lou Meecham came, saw what Trainor had found, and said, "This one's mine."

Macklin was only half conscious when they lifted the chair off him. His compact Czech automatic was still in his hand. Lou removed it, then slapped the major firmly until he came around.

He waited until the man's eyes focused on him, then he said, "Well."

Macklin flinched. His eyes moved from side to side, and he licked his lips. Lou popped the magazine out of the little black pistol and counted the rounds in it – eight, and one more in the chamber.

He slipped the clip back into the grip and stood up.

"Meecham," Macklin said, "listen to me. I can give you anything you want. It's right here" – he patted his jacket pocket proprietorially – "money, power, anything you want, you name it."

Twice before in his life, Lou Meecham thought about killing this man. Each time, something had prevented him – fear, mainly, but also his own refusal to get down in the filth with the likes of Macklin.

Now that restraint was gone. Lou feared nothing, desired nothing. Dignity, love, compassion, all the qualities that had separated men like him from the brutes in human guise he had encountered, were all gone, all buried with the unfeeling dead.

But there were some emotions left, Lou found. He let one of them fill him now. It was hot and black.

"There is something I want," he told Macklin.

226

The major swallowed. He tried to get up, but Lou pushed him back down with his foot. "Name it," Macklin said.

Lou smiled. "I want satisfaction," he said.

Then, slowly and methodically, taking careful aim, he emptied the Czech pistol into Major Tag Macklin, being careful not to place any but the last round into a vital organ.

When the last shot ended the screaming, Lou looked up. His face wore a smile of almost beatific satisfaction, the aspect of the holy warrior. Jeff Cameron and Herb Trainor nodded approvingly. A few of the other men had come back at the sound of gunfire and they voiced their approbation.

"So," said Trainor, "what's next?" He had acquired an M-16 and was fiddling with its movable parts.

Nobody had an answer. Then Jeff had a thought. "I'm gonna see about the bald guy."

They made their way to the ballroom. DeVoin's body was where Macklin had left it, the two Yemenis still sprawled on the steps, their faces distorted out of any human cast by the violence Jeff had done to them.

Jeff pointed to the small pool of blood near the french windows. "Here's where he was," he said.

"Is that him?" said Herb, pointing with his rifle up the beach. A balding man in a blood stained shirt stood at the water's edge, trembling and gazing out over the lake.

The hotel manager let loose a shot, but he was still excited and his aim was poor. The bullet tossed up a spire of water a few feet out from shore.

The bald man turned and looked at them. Trainor loosed a second shot. The man by the water dodged it.

"Hey, he's one of us," said Lou Meecham. He pushed the rifle down.

"I don't recognize him," said Jeff.

"But he's powered up like us," Lou said and beckoned to the man on the shore. "Hey, buddy, come on up."

227

# 20

Phillip Sandrini had come to on the patio, with the side of his shirt soaked in blood. When he lifted his head, the first thing he saw was the body of Parker DeVoin. He looked around, and saw Hafiz and his aide with their faces broken.

*This is not a good place to be,* he told himself. He got to his feet. He could hear moans and screams from the front of the hotel; then they were cut off by bursts of rifle fire.

*Along the beach and into the woods,* he thought. But the pain in his side was bad, and his head was dizzy. There was no way he could make it to a hiding place before the hyperkinetic killers of Prescott Springs would find him.

A tear rolled down the scientist's cheek. It was all DeVoin's fault. He went over and kicked the general's corpse. *You should have set the demonstration up in some third-world shithole.*

But the Yemenis had wanted to see the effects of Paroxysm on Americans. *Guess why?* Sandrini thought. And now somebody was going to come and shoot him or hack at him until he was dead.

Did the general have a weapon? It might help. He gingerly patted the body, but there was nothing. He could hear voices now from the corridor leading to the lobby, fast-talking, gobbledygook voices.

*This is it,* he told himself. He wiped away another tear.

Then he saw the pickle jar. It stood on the blue cloth draped table where his analytical equipment had been. There was maybe a cup of liquid in it.

He forgot about the pain in his side and went to the jar, grabbed it and hugged it to his soft chest. *I'm not going to die,* he thought.

Then he heard footsteps from the corridor on the far side of the ballroom. Panicked, he threw himself under the covered table and crouched there, knees drawn up, the liquid in the pickle jar sloshing slightly as he clasped it tightly.

A man walked rapidly across the ballroom, stopped briefly at DeVoin's body then went out onto the patio. Seconds later, he came back inside and left by the inner doors.

Sandrini released the breath he had been holding. He quietly unscrewed the lid of the pickle jar and raised it to his lips. The water was room temperature, tasting slightly of chlorine. He sipped it, then gulped it down.

And, suddenly, Dr. Phillip Sandrini's world was a much better place.

He had a good idea what the drug would do to him. Neural pharmacology was his area of expertise. He'd supervised field trials and interviewed voluntary and involuntary experimental subjects who'd been dosed with the original Paroxysm, and he could make a highly educated guess as to what the new version would feel like. So the physical rush, the heightened ability to focus, these were expected.

But it wasn't the new sensations that astonished and delighted him; it was the instant absence of an old and constant companion, of an emotion that had been part of his psyche for so long, that had filled him so pervasively, that he had been no more consciously aware of it than a fish is aware of the liquid medium in which it passes its whole life – until suddenly it is taken away.

For the first time in all of the life he could remember, Sandrini was not even the tiniest bit afraid.

Sitting in the dimness under the blue-shrouded table, the scientist sorted through the new sensations coursing through his being. He was angry, full of rage, in fact. When he thought of different people who had abused or harmed him at some time in his life – DeVoin and Macklin had been only the latest in a long succession – an amazing surge of fury flooded through him. It was so powerful, it threatened to dislodge his consciousness and send it spinning away into the dark at the edge of his mind.

But he fought it down and held it under control, because Paroxysm 2 had brought him the more astounding perception of a world without fear.

He pushed aside the table cloth and crawled out from under the table. He stood up. His side pained him, but he dismissed the discomfort. He looked around the empty ballroom. He'd spent most of the past twelve hours here, but now it was as if he was seeing for the first time, as if it was altogether a different place.

It had been an oppressive room – too full of hard faced people, too full of demands, too full of pressures. now it was full of calm and clarity. The air seemed somehow to have grown more transparent, as if it had always been slightly clouded before.

Sandrini stepped over DeVoin's body and went outside. The sun danced on the ripples that the wind fanned across the lake. The deck of the jetty crackled

229

with yellow and orange flames under an exclamation point of black smoke. The dead Yemenis stared at the clear blue sky.

*This is how the world looks when you're not afraid,* the scientist realized. *This is how it looks to the people who own it, who control their own lives.*

He went past the bodies on the steps and descended to the beach on the west side of the jetty. He picked up a handful of sand, saw the grains of silicon glistening like jewels. He walked a little way along the water's edge and stopped to stare into the wavelets that lapped the shore.

He let the sensations of calm, fearless power wash through him. *I love this,* he thought. *I fucking* love *it.*

A spout of water leaped out of the lake in front of him, followed almost instantly by the sound of a rifle shot. He turned around.

A group of men were on the patio. One of them aimed a gun at him and fired again. Sandrini saw the bullet leave the muzzle and grow in size as it sped toward him. There was enough time to move his head to the side, and he let the round go by.

One of the others, a soft-looking man like himself, pushed the rifle barrel down and called to him. Right away, the scientist knew he had to talk to these men. He had something important to tell them.

Sharon and the doctor heard the men coming back to the bottling plant. The looked out the high window at the rear of the building and saw the hotel's pick-up arrive. There were several townspeople sitting on the sides of the truck bed, their feet resting on big sacks and sealed plastic pails.

The truck stopped at the loading bays. The men got out and began hauling the cargo into the plant. They seemed animated and happy, going about the work with the same energy and purpose they had lately applied to killing each other.

Macreedy peered down at the sacks they were bringing in: they were organophosphate pesticides and some kind of fertilizer, the kind that the hotel used to keep the grounds free of weeds and pests. The buckets contained chlorine dioxide taken from the little filtration unit built over the intake for the town's water supply.

"Let's go down," he said to Sharon. They descended the steel staircase, the woman's eyes casting about for a sight of her husband and son. Of the men and women who had gone out to fight the soldiers, so few had returned.

230

She found Jeff at the place where the water pipes from the hotel's spring entered the bottling plant. He and another man were busily diverting the feed from the mineral springs that used to empty into the bottling plant's big vats, reconnecting the pipes to the town's water main, so that the vast containers could now be filled with water from the lake.

Jeff and the other man – she realized it was Ignatz Morens, the hotel's chef – were smiling as they worked. She couldn't remember when she had last seen her husband so cheerful; she didn't think she'd ever seen a smile come near Morens's face.

She stopped a few feet away. Their speed and energy frightened her. "Jeff?" she called.

He turned. It was that strangely melded face again – the young one she had fallen in love with, but darkened from behind by the killer who had risen up from deep within.

He smiled at her, then turned back and kept working.

"Honey," she said, "where's Trevor?"

"He went off up the river," her husband said, not pausing from his work.

"Is he all right?"

"Sure." He glanced over his shoulder at her, then went right back to work. "Can't talk. Got to get this done."

"Is it all over?" she asked.

"Fighting's over," he said.

"Thank God," she said, and put a hand on his arm. "We have to go look for Trevor, try to get things back to normal."

He turned and looked at her then. "Why don't you have a drink, see how you feel?"

"But it's over, you said. You don't need that stuff now," she said.

He didn't say anything, but returned his attention to the water pipes.

Macreedy approached the group who were gathered around one of the smaller sampling vats. A balding man he didn't recognize was using a one-quart scoop to transfer chemicals into the vat from the supplies that had come on the truck.

The man looked up. "Are we ready with the water yet?" he called. His voice was a rapid nasal gabble.

"Almost," Jeff called.

"What are you doing?" Macreedy asked the man.

The man looked up. "Saving you," he said. He cocked his head to one side and examined the doctor. "You're not... with us, are you?" he said.

Macreedy shook his head.

"It shows," said the man and went back to his mixing. "Well, we'll have a nice fresh batch in not too long."

"You're making more of that filth they put in our water?" Macreedy put his hand on the man's arm. It was thrown off with a violent flick.

"It's called Paroxysm 2," the man said, "and it will set you free."

"I'm already free," said the doctor.

"No, you just think you are." He motioned with his head to one of the others. "Give him a drink," he said.

Macreedy fought, but he was an old man and they were all stronger and much faster. They got water from the town mains. Somebody found a styrofoam cup and filled it. One of them held his nose and another poured it down his throat.

Even then, as the drug leached through his brain, he fought it. He tried to hold down the rage that boiled up inside him. But the only choice Paroxysm 2 gave him was to ride the whirlwind or be swept into oblivion.

Finally, in a mix of joy and despair, he grabbed at the roaring beast and held on. He embraced its delightful savagery. The others saw the change come upon him. They let him up.

"You see how it is, Doc," said a man Macreedy had treated for thirty years. "We can't go back now. We know what we've done. We killed a lot of people, and once we stop being crazy mad, we're gonna have to deal with it. And we can't do that. So it's this or nothing."

"I understand," said the doctor. He shivered and drew in a long delicious breath. "The trouble with righteous anger has always been that it feels so good. It's a tiger ride – a hell of a trip, but only one way."

"It's more than that," said the scientist. "It's a new way of life. No more fear. No more... complexity. The world gives us so much to be mad about, and now we can be as mad as we always wanted to be. You a doctor?"

"Yeah. Macreedy."

"Sandrini. How's your chemistry?" asked the scientist.

"It'll do."

Sandrini indicated a stoppered erlenmeyer flask on the floor near the pesticide sacks. "Then pour me about fifty cc's of that solvent."

Macreedy reached for the flask.

Jeff Cameron hauled up on the big wrench, making the last connection tight. "Water's on tap," he told Sandrini.

He looked around for Sharon. It was time she joined the rest of them.

She wasn't there. He looked for her outside, ran down the side of the building to Bridge Road. He reached the road just as she wheeled the Land Rover that had been parked there in a u-turn, and drove away toward the bridge, tires squealing and smoking.

He shook his head. They'd catch up with her later.

By the time the mixture was ready, Jeff and the other men had got the old tanker truck down off its blocks and brought it over to the big standpipe at the rear of the building.

They emptied the vat into the tank, then they put the truck on the road. Jeff drove, his hands on the wheel and gearshift that his father had held. He'd taken another long drink; the pain in his chest and knee was distant now. Sandrini and the doctor rode with him. The rest of the men followed behind in the pick-up.

They left Prescott Springs to its dead. Well before noon, they turned off the two-lane blacktop and followed a narrow road that led to the reservoir above Evans. The big tanker went easily through the chain-link gate.

A man with a badge but no gun came out of a small shed and asked them what they were doing. They enlisted him.

They pumped half of the load of concentrated Paroxysm 2 into the water, then backed out. The security guard said there were two smaller reservoirs further south. They'd do those, then go back and refill the tanker.

It would be a busy day, but they had lots of energy.

Sharon drove the Land Rover at high speed to Evans, and slid to a halt, blowing its horn, outside the new aluminum and glass police headquarters.

A police officer coming down the front steps told her she couldn't park there, but she brushed by him and ran into the building. The cop looked into the jeep and saw a plastic tarpaulin with a hand sticking out from under it.

Three minutes later, Sharon Cameron was in a holding cell. Despite all her protestations, nobody was prepared to deal with her until they had removed

Tresider's body, identified the deceased and done a preliminary examination of the Land Rover.

Eventually, they questioned her. It was a long time before they even thought about taking her seriously – too long.

By then, the 911 center was already jammed with calls.

Trevor caught up with the three mercenaries about nine. They had found a tumbledown log cabin and were checking it out, peeking in the windows and trying the door.

He knew he had to act before they could take shelter inside, so he opened fire with the MAC-10 as soon as he saw them. The big blond one and the little brown one went down fast, but the third man was shielded by their falling bodies. He threw himself through the doorway and kicked it closed after him.

Trevor put himself on the ground under a bush and began to work his way around the building. There was a windowless wall at one end. He could lie there, very still and perfectly quiet, until the man thought he had gone away. Then he would get him as he came out.

But Medford had fought in jungles. He watched the bushes for movement, and read the signs that betrayed the passage of even the most careful boy. The mercenary fired his rifle through the glass in the window, and the bullets stitched Trevor Cameron to the earth forever.

The soldier listened closely. The forest was silent for a while after the shooting, then its normal noises resumed.

Lewis Medford lowered the M-16. He relaxed. Then he realized that, over the reek of gunsmoke, there was a strong odor of blood and some musty animal smell in the dark cabin.

He turned. Right behind him was an old woman who had draped her head and shoulders with the horns and fleece of a ram. She regarded him with delight, the way his grandmother used to look when he handed her a crayon drawing he'd made for her.

Then she brought up the wicked hook of her blood-smeared gelding knife. She moved so fast, so decisively, so joyously.

Medford never had a chance.

234

# About the Author

The name I answer to is Matt Hughes. I write fantasy and suspense fiction. To keep the two genres separate, I now use my full name, Matthew Hughes, for fantasy, and the shorter form for the crime stuff. I also write media tie-ins as Hugh Matthews.

I've won the Crime Writers of Canada's Arthur Ellis Award, and have been shortlisted for the Aurora, Nebula, Philip K. Dick, and Derringer Awards.

I was born in 1949 in Liverpool, England, but my family moved to Canada when I was five. I've made my living as a writer all of my adult life, first as a journalist, then as a staff speechwriter to the Canadian Ministers of Justice and Environment, and -- from 1979 until a few years back-- as a freelance corporate and political speechwriter in British Columbia. I am a former director of the Federation of British Columbia Writers and I used to belong to Mensa Canada, but these days I'm conserving my energies to write fiction.

I'm a university drop-out from a working poor background. Before getting into newspapers, I worked in a factory that made school desks, drove a grocery delivery truck, was night janitor in a GM dealership, and did a short stint as an orderly in a private mental hospital. As a teenager, I served a year as a volunteer with the Company of Young Canadians (something like VISTA in the US). I've been married to a very patient woman since the late 1960s, and I have three grown sons.

In late 2007, I took up a secondary occupation -- that of an unpaid housesitter -- so that I can afford to keep on writing fiction yet still eat every day. Any snail-mail address of mine must be considered temporary; but you can send me an e-mail through my web site. I'm always interested to hear from people who've read my work.

You can find me at:
http://www.matthewhughes.org

# Also by Matt Hughes

*Fools Errant* (as Matthew Hughes)
*Downshift*
*Fool Me Twice* (as Matthew Hughes)
*Gullible's Travels* (omnibus edition of Fools Errant and Fool Me Twice)
*Black Brillion* (as Matthew Hughes)
*The Gist Hunter and Other Stories* (as Matthew Hughes)
*Majestrum, A Tale of Henghis Hapthorn* (as Matthew Hughes)
*Wolverine: Lifeblood* (as Hugh Matthews)
*The Spiral Labyrinth, A Tale of Henghis Hapthorn* (as Matthew Hughes)
*The Commons* (as Matthew Hughes)
*Template* (as Matthew Hughes)
*Hespira, A Tale of Henghis Hapthorn* (as Matthew Hughes)
*The Other* (as Matthew Hughes)
*To Hell and Back: The Damned Busters* (as Matthew Hughes)
*Song of the Serpent* (as Hugh Matthews)
*To Hell and Back: Costume Not Included* (as Matthew Hughes)
*Old Growth* (as Matt Hughes)
*To Hell and Back: Hell To Pay* (as Matthew Hughes)
*Nine Tales of Henghis Hapthorn* (as Matthew Hughes)
*The Meaning of Luff and Other Stories* (as Matthew Hughes)
*Paroxysm*